REXODUS™

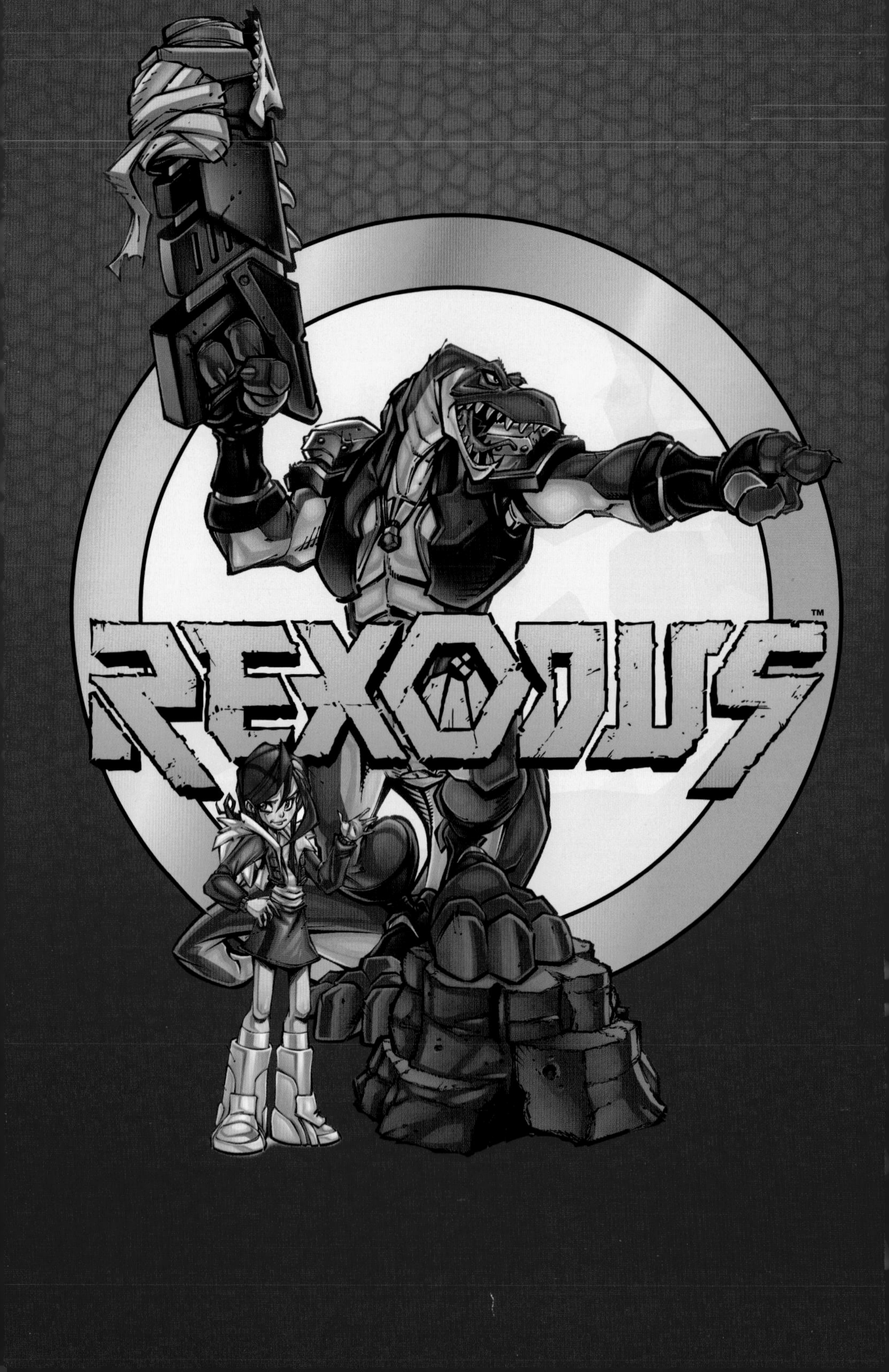
REXODUS™

Based on an original concept by
ERIC LEE and **PAUL WIZIKOWSKI**

Story
KEVIN ANDERSON
JAMES FARR   ERIC LEE
MARK STEELE
PAUL WIZIKOWSKI

Script
JAMES FARR

Pencils
JON SOMMARIVA

Inks
SERGE LAPOINTE
KEVIN PATAG   SEAN PARSONS

Colors
CAMILA FORTUNA
DUSTIN EVANS   JOHN RAUCH

Letters
ANNA FILM and **JASON YANG**

Cover and Chapter Break Art by Jon Sommariva
with Serge LaPointe, Sean Parsons, and Eric Lee

Dark Horse Books

Character Designs by Sean Galloway
Additional Concept Art by Eric Lee

Produced by Kevin Anderson and Mark Steele

Designer: Justin Couch, Collection Editors: Shantel LaRocque and Sierra Hahn
President and Publisher: Mike Richardson

Special thanks to Chris Tongue

Neil Hankerson, Executive Vice President · Tom Weddle, Chief Financial Officer · Randy
Stradley, Vice President of Publishing · Michael Martens, Vice President of Book Trade Sales
· Scott Allie, Editor in Chief · Matt Parkinson, Vice President of Marketing · David Scroggy,
Vice President of Product Development · Dale LaFountain, Vice President of Information
Technology · Darlene Vogel, Senior Director of Print, Design, and Production · Ken Lizzi,
General Counsel · Davey Estrada, Editorial Director · Chris Warner, Senior Books Editor · Diana
Schutz, Executive Editor · Cary Grazzini, Director of Print and Development · Lia Ribacchi, Art
Director · Cara Niece, Director of Scheduling · Mark Bernardi, Director of Digital Publishing

DARK HORSE BOOKS
A division of Dark Horse Comics, Inc.
10956 SE Main Street
Milwaukie, OR 97222

DarkHorse.com

First edition: June 2015
ISBN 978-1-61655-448-4

1 3 5 7 9 10 8 6 4 2
Printed in China

International Licensing: (503) 905-2377
Comic Shop Locator Service: (888) 266-4226

CHAPTER
1

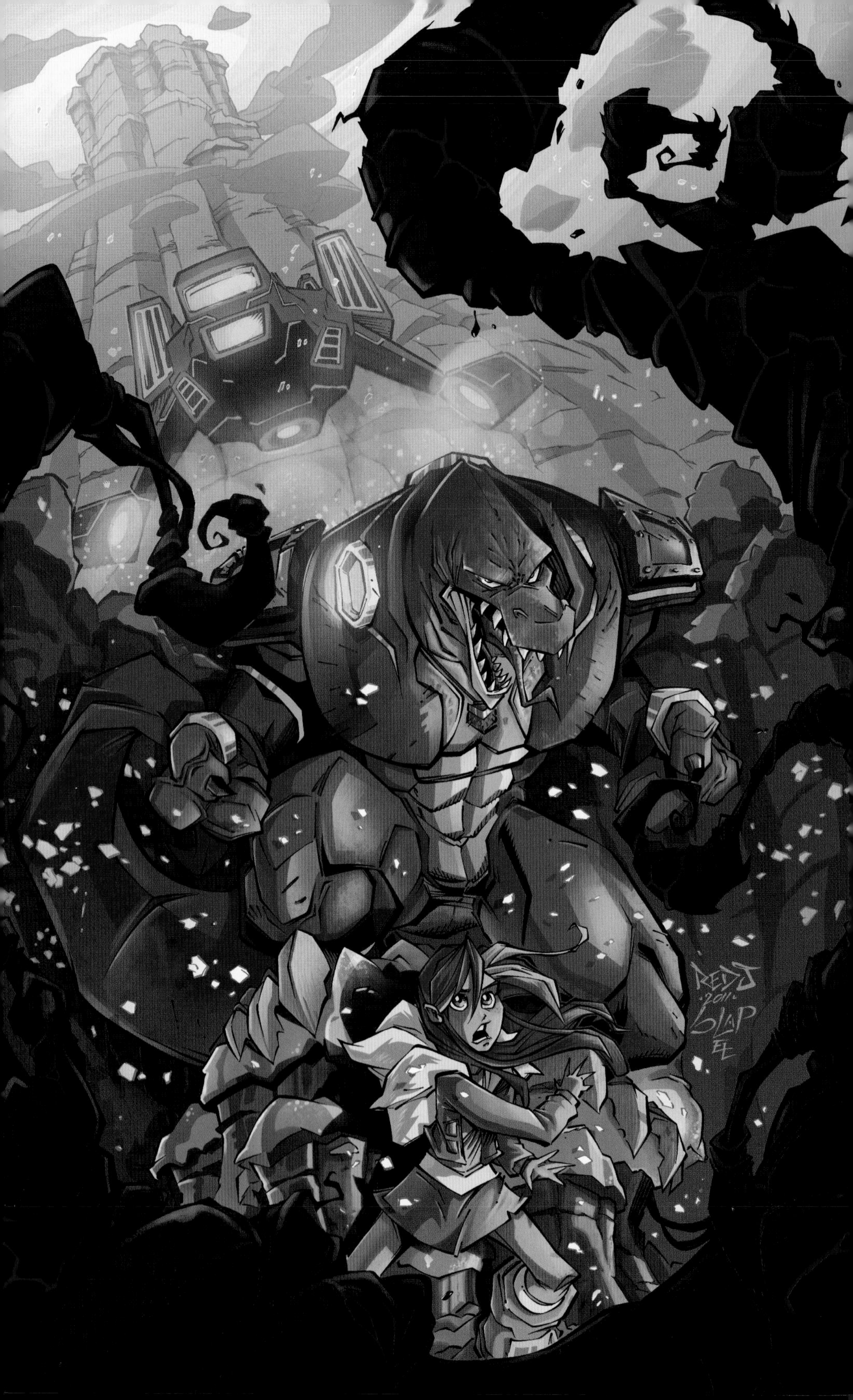

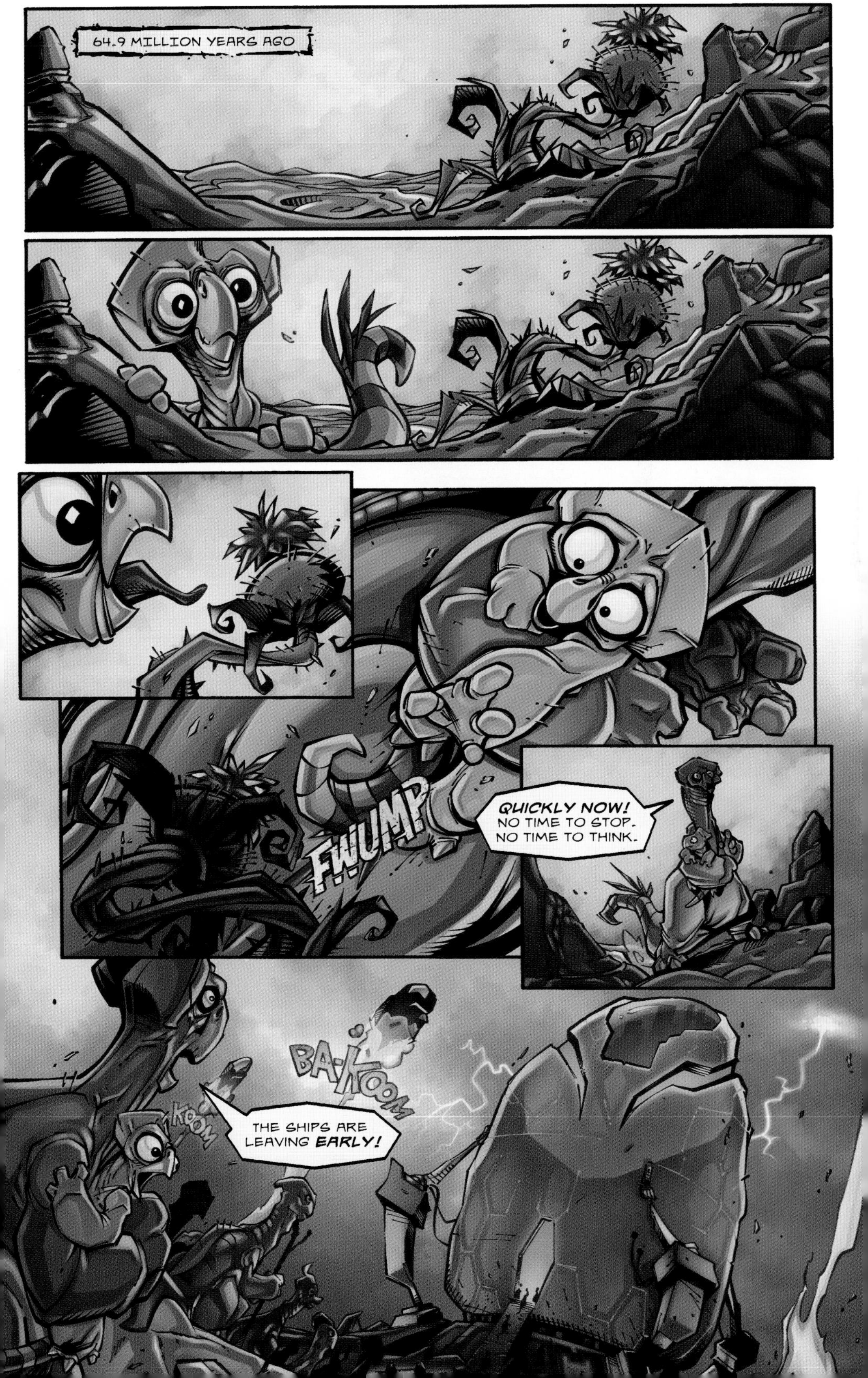

64.9 MILLION YEARS AGO
FWUMP
QUICKLY NOW! NO TIME TO STOP. NO TIME TO THINK.
BA-KOOM
KOOM
THE SHIPS ARE LEAVING EARLY!

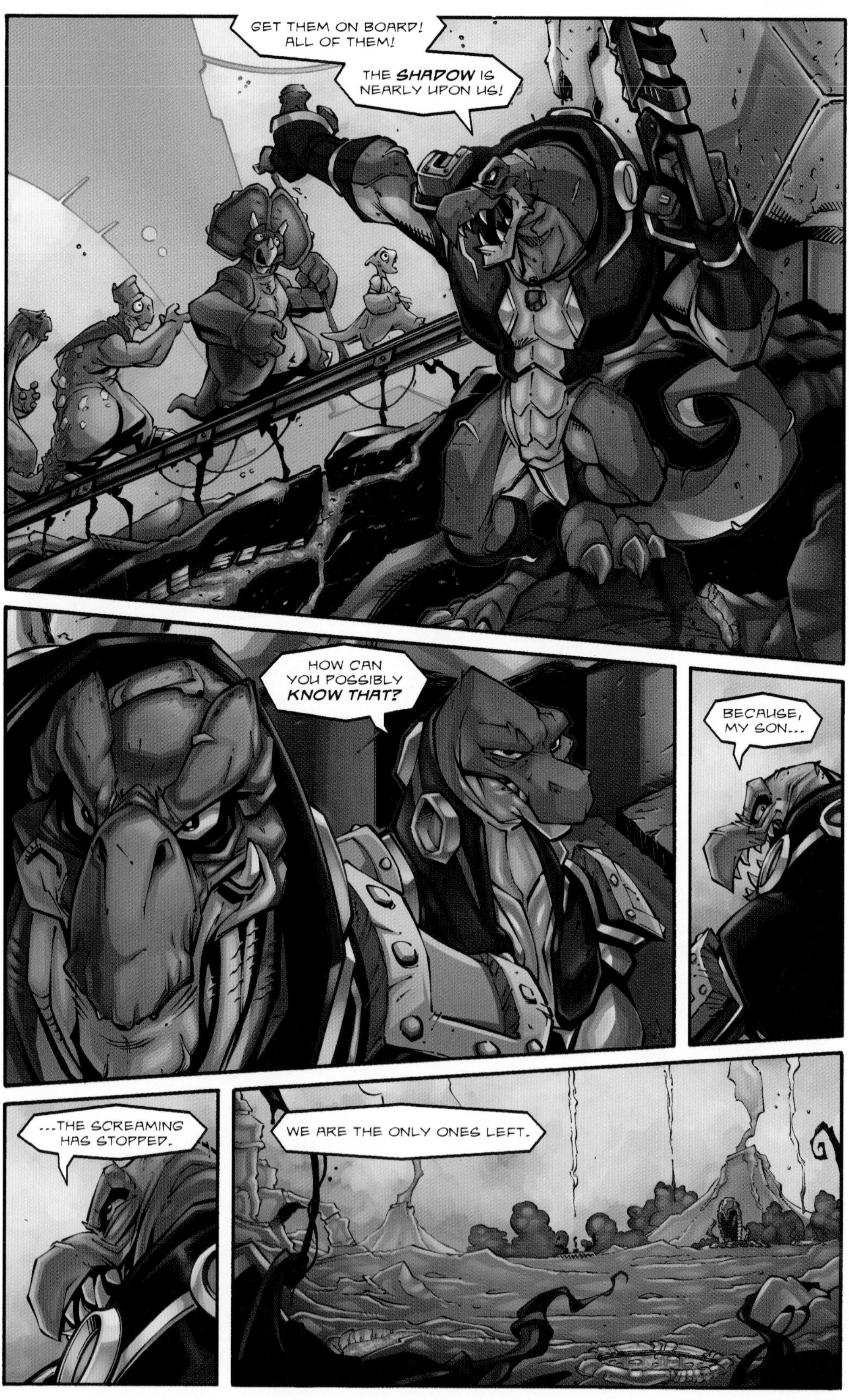
GET THEM ON BOARD! ALL OF THEM!
THE SHADOW IS NEARLY UPON US!
HOW CAN YOU POSSIBLY KNOW THAT?
BECAUSE, MY SON...
...THE SCREAMING HAS STOPPED.
WE ARE THE ONLY ONES LEFT.

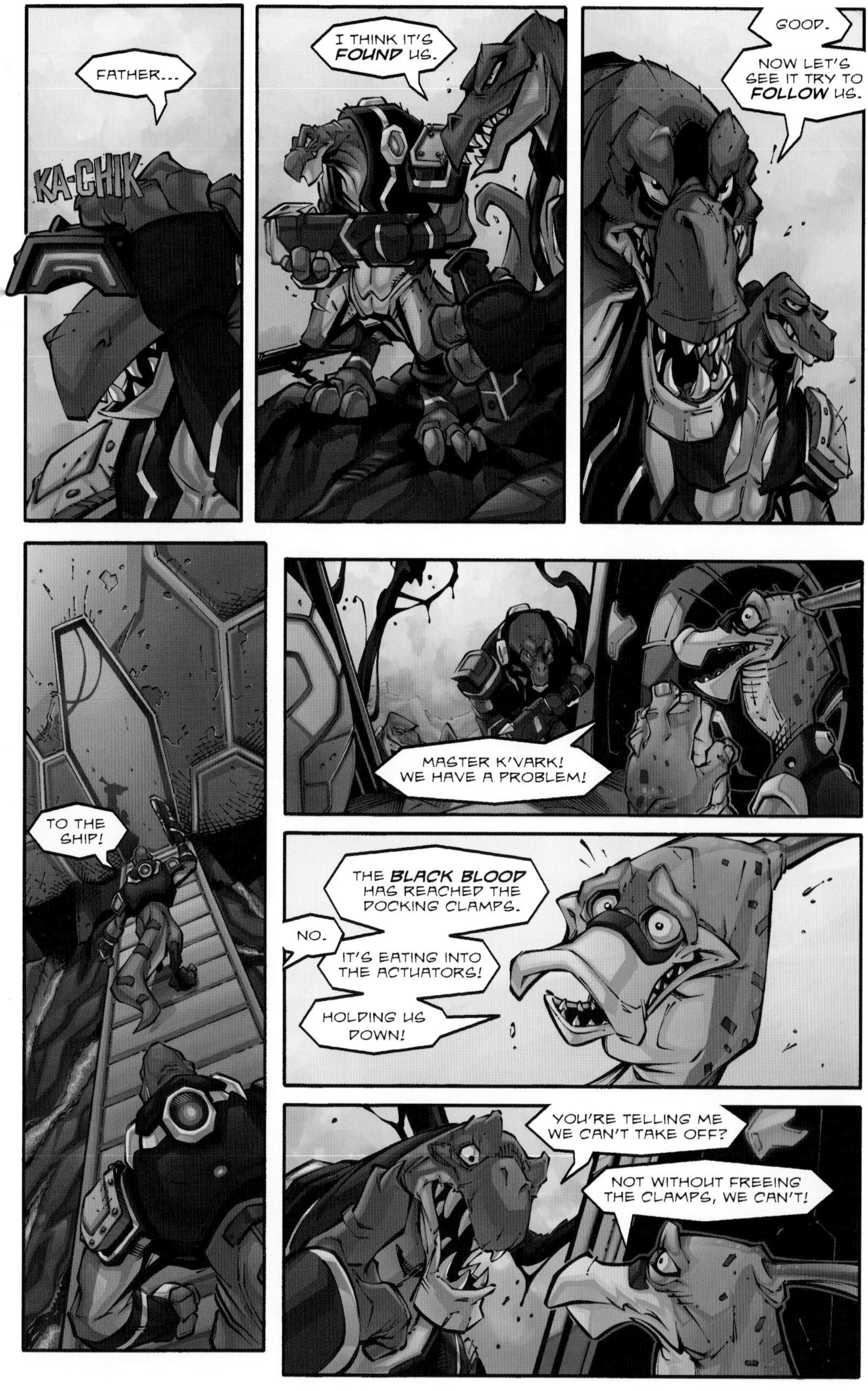
FATHER...
KA-CHIK
I THINK IT'S FOUND US.
GOOD.
NOW LET'S SEE IT TRY TO FOLLOW US.
TO THE SHIP!
MASTER K'VARK! WE HAVE A PROBLEM!
THE BLACK BLOOD HAS REACHED THE DOCKING CLAMPS.
NO.
IT'S EATING INTO THE ACTUATORS!
HOLDING US DOWN!
YOU'RE TELLING ME WE CAN'T TAKE OFF?
NOT WITHOUT FREEING THE CLAMPS, WE CAN'T!

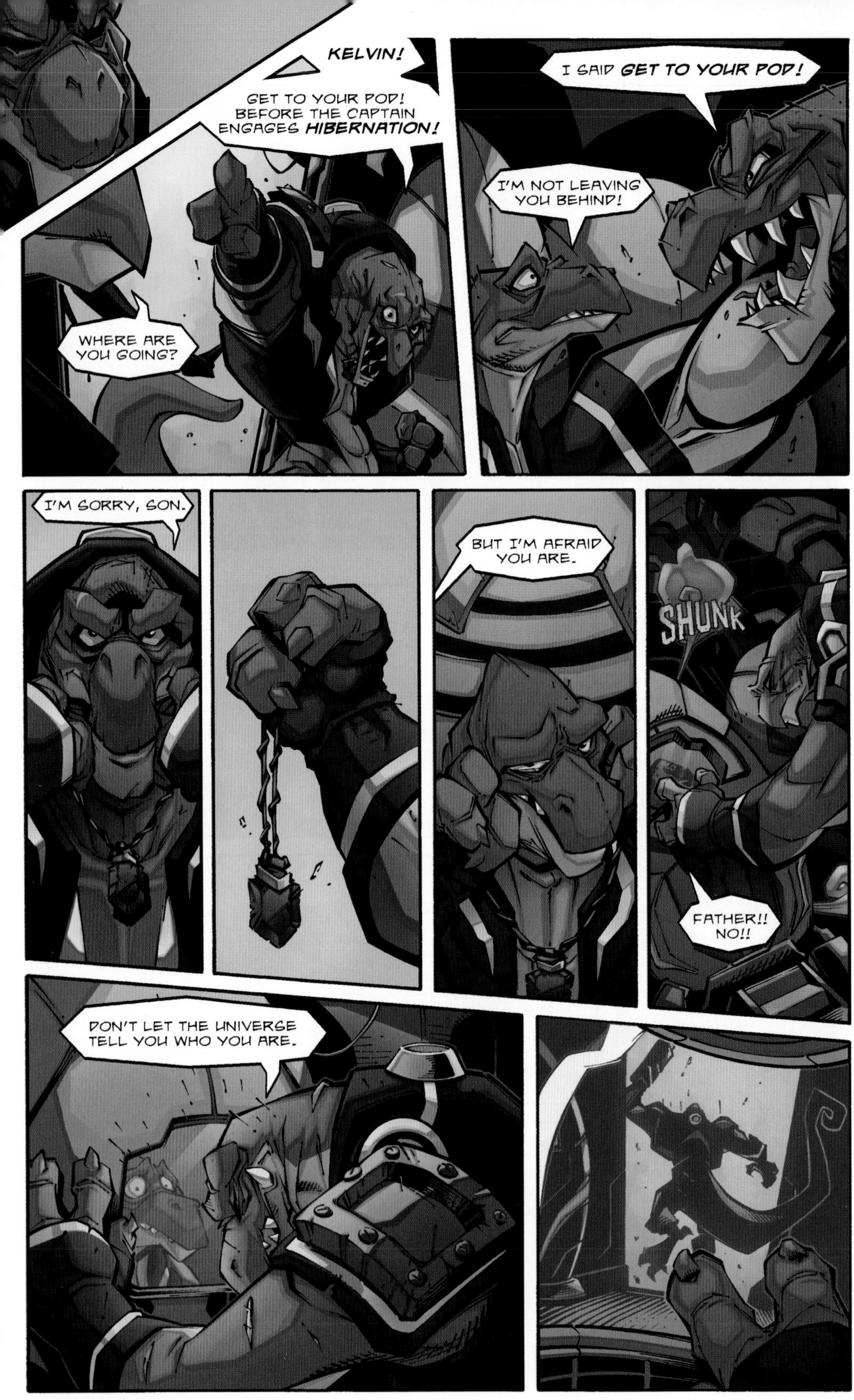
KELVIN!
GET TO YOUR POD! BEFORE THE CAPTAIN ENGAGES HIBERNATION!
WHERE ARE YOU GOING?
I SAID GET TO YOUR POD!
I'M NOT LEAVING YOU BEHIND!
I'M SORRY, SON.
BUT I'M AFRAID YOU ARE.
SHUNK
FATHER!! NO!!
DON'T LET THE UNIVERSE TELL YOU WHO YOU ARE.

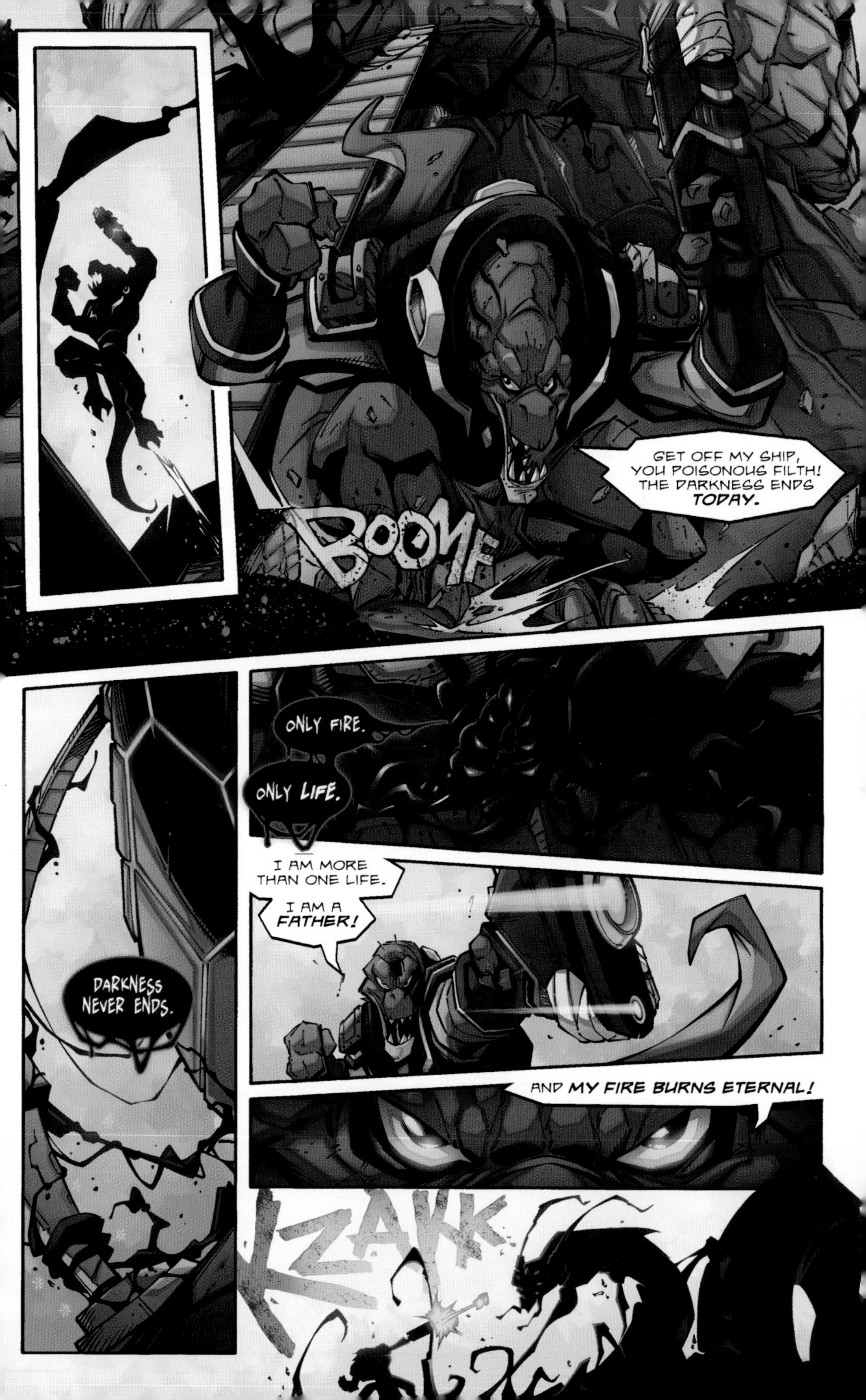

GET OFF MY SHIP, YOU POISONOUS FILTH! THE DARKNESS ENDS **TODAY.**
BOOM
ONLY FIRE.
ONLY **LIFE.**
DARKNESS NEVER ENDS.
I AM MORE THAN ONE LIFE.
I AM A **FATHER!**
AND **MY FIRE BURNS ETERNAL!**
ZAKK

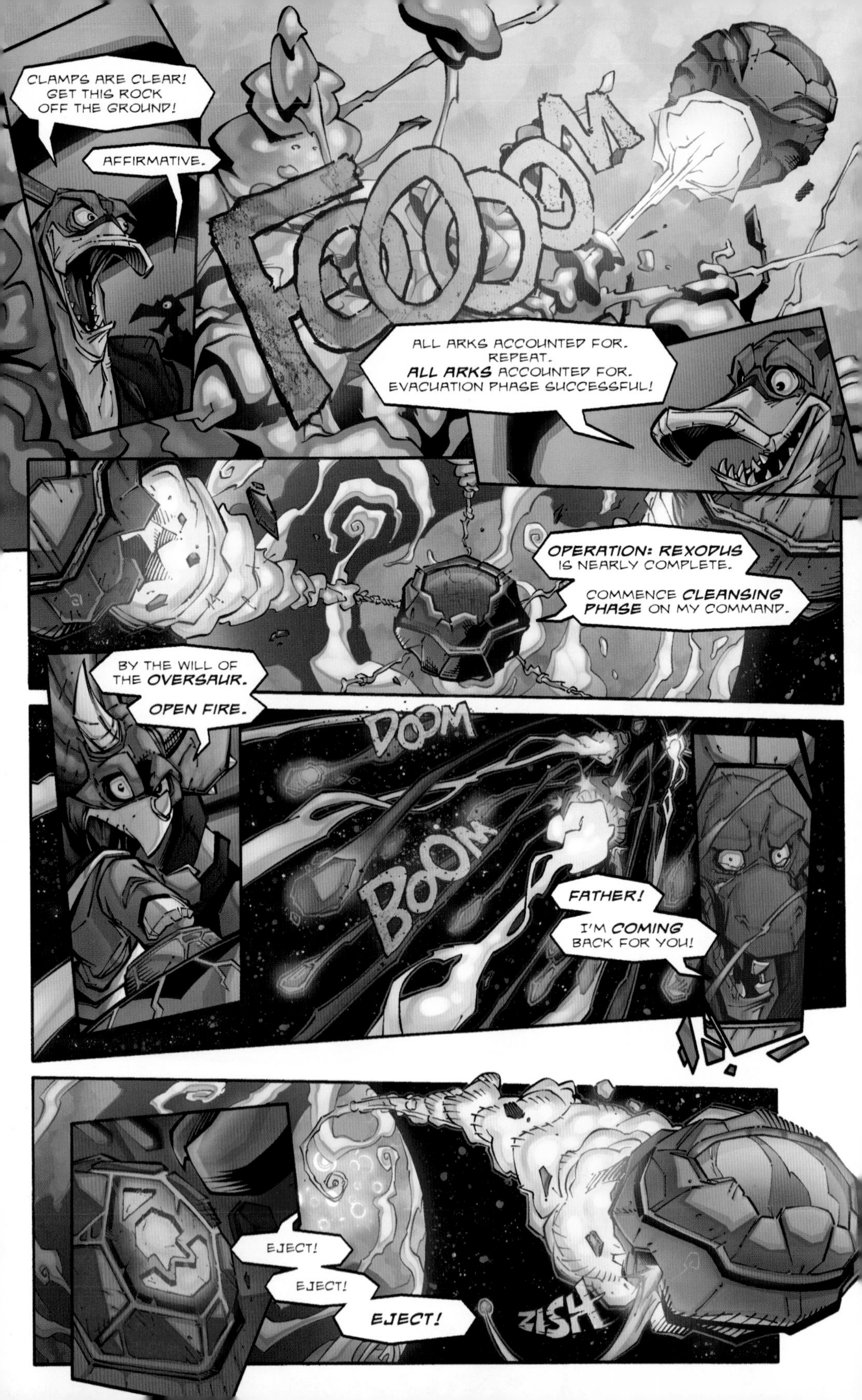
CLAMPS ARE CLEAR! GET THIS ROCK OFF THE GROUND!
AFFIRMATIVE.
FOOOOOM
ALL ARKS ACCOUNTED FOR. REPEAT. ALL ARKS ACCOUNTED FOR. EVACUATION PHASE SUCCESSFUL!
OPERATION: REXODUS IS NEARLY COMPLETE.
COMMENCE CLEANSING PHASE ON MY COMMAND.
BY THE WILL OF THE OVERSAUR.
OPEN FIRE.
DOOM
BOOM
FATHER!
I'M COMING BACK FOR YOU!
EJECT!
EJECT!
EJECT!
ZISH

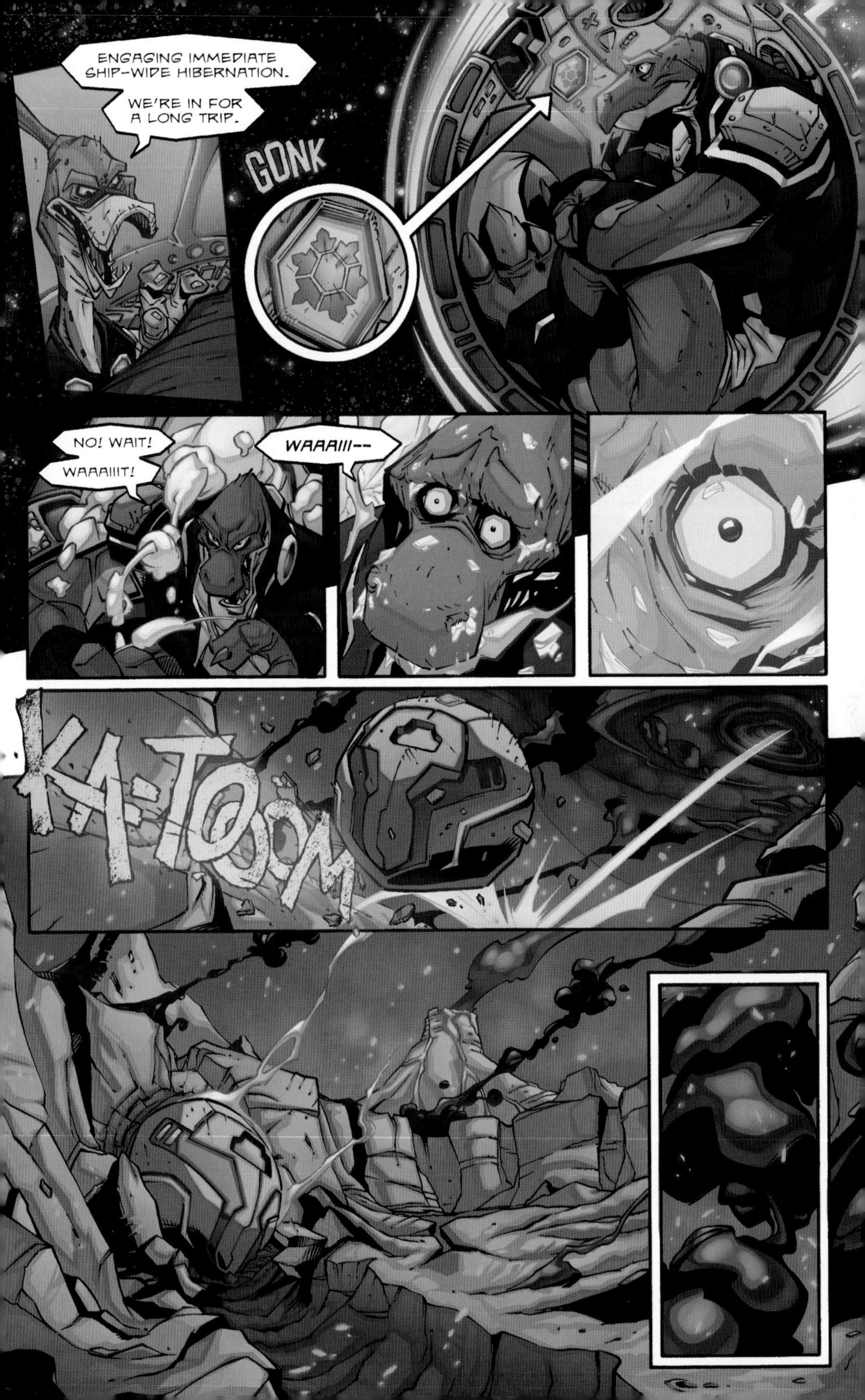
ENGAGING IMMEDIATE SHIP-WIDE HIBERNATION.
WE'RE IN FOR A LONG TRIP.
GONK
NO! WAIT!
WAAAAIIIT!
WAAAAIII--
KA-TOOOM

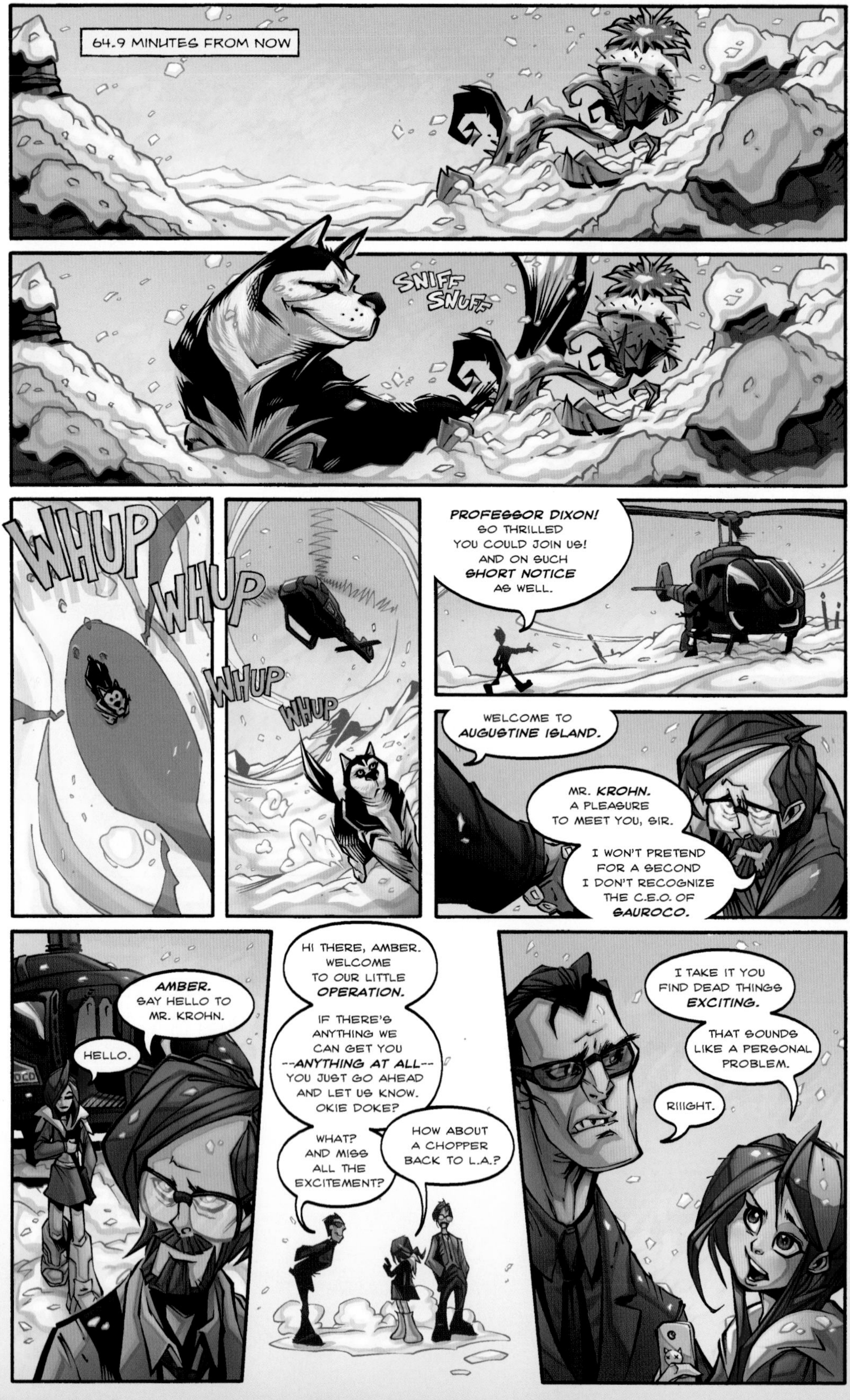
64.9 MINUTES FROM NOW
SNIFF SNUFF
WHUP WHUP WHUP WHUP
PROFESSOR DIXON! SO THRILLED YOU COULD JOIN US! AND ON SUCH SHORT NOTICE AS WELL.
WELCOME TO AUGUSTINE ISLAND.
MR. KROHN. A PLEASURE TO MEET YOU, SIR.
I WON'T PRETEND FOR A SECOND I DON'T RECOGNIZE THE C.E.O. OF SAUROCO.
AMBER. SAY HELLO TO MR. KROHN.
HELLO.
HI THERE, AMBER. WELCOME TO OUR LITTLE OPERATION.
IF THERE'S ANYTHING WE CAN GET YOU --ANYTHING AT ALL-- YOU JUST GO AHEAD AND LET US KNOW. OKIE DOKE?
HOW ABOUT A CHOPPER BACK TO L.A.?
WHAT? AND MISS ALL THE EXCITEMENT?
I TAKE IT YOU FIND DEAD THINGS EXCITING.
THAT SOUNDS LIKE A PERSONAL PROBLEM.
RIIIGHT.

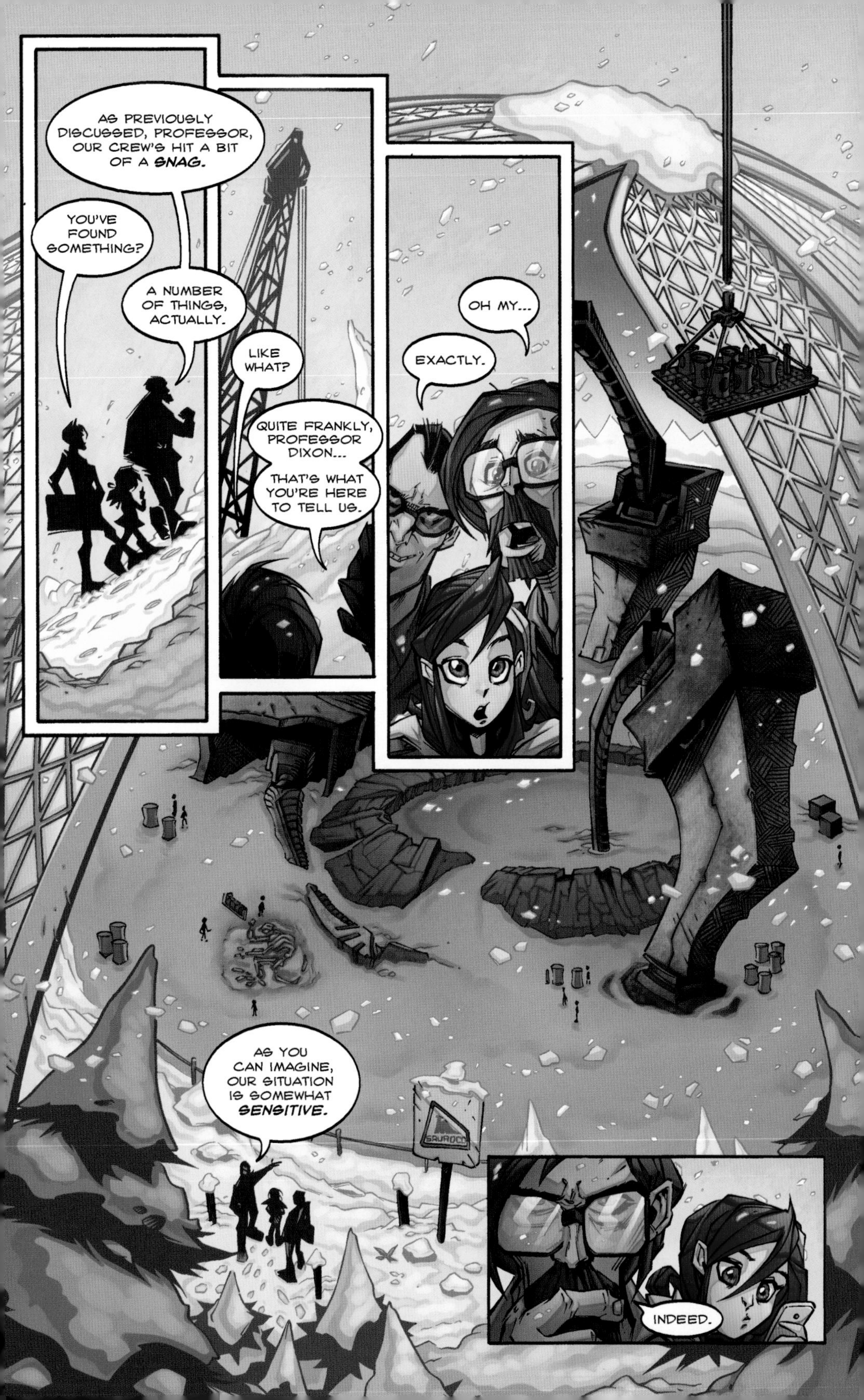
AS PREVIOUSLY DISCUSSED, PROFESSOR, OUR CREW'S HIT A BIT OF A SNAG.
YOU'VE FOUND SOMETHING?
A NUMBER OF THINGS, ACTUALLY.
LIKE WHAT?
QUITE FRANKLY, PROFESSOR DIXON...
THAT'S WHAT YOU'RE HERE TO TELL US.
OH MY...
EXACTLY.
AS YOU CAN IMAGINE, OUR SITUATION IS SOMEWHAT SENSITIVE.
SAUROCO
INDEED.

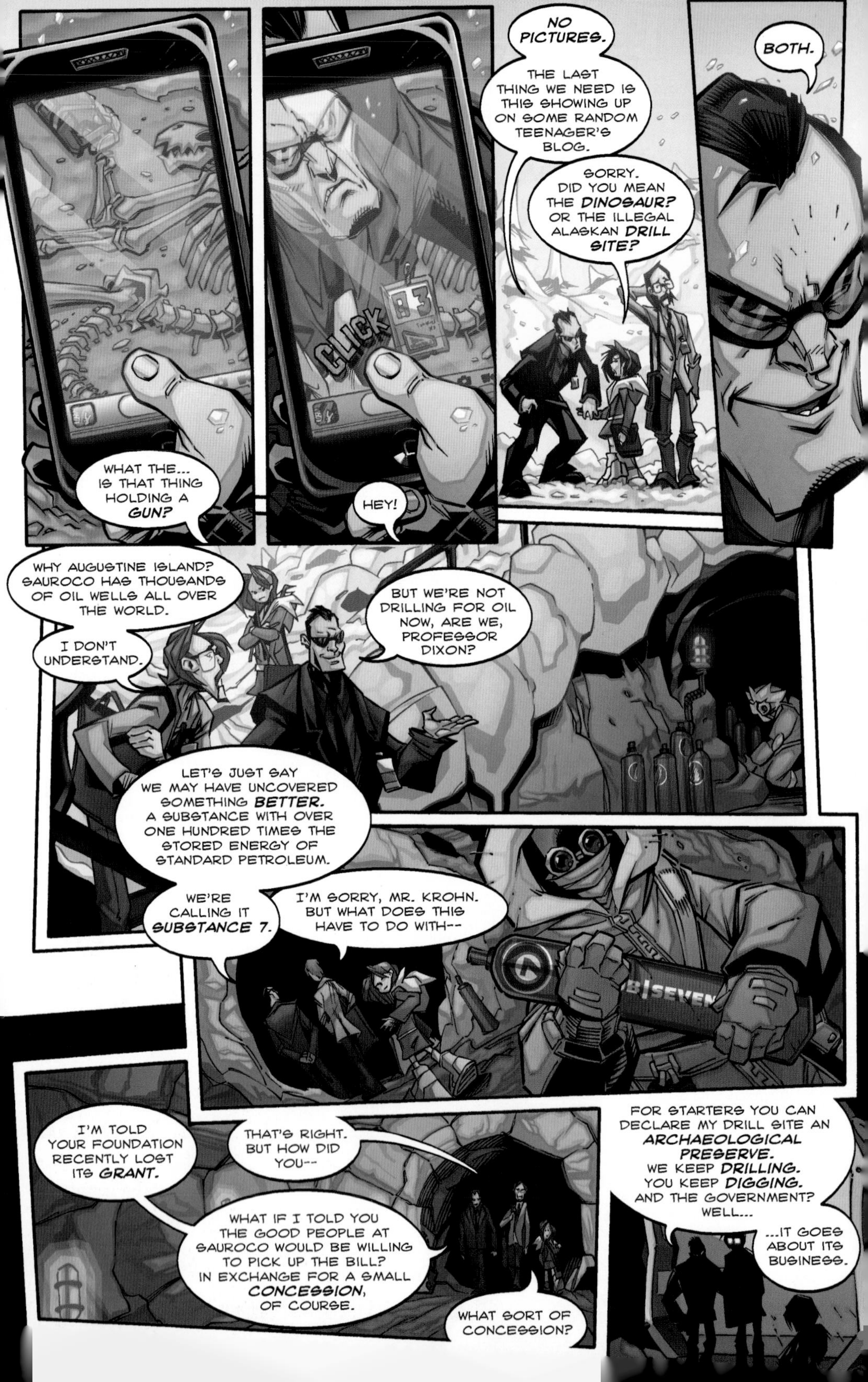
CLICK
WHAT THE... IS THAT THING HOLDING A GUN?
HEY!
NO PICTURES.
THE LAST THING WE NEED IS THIS SHOWING UP ON SOME RANDOM TEENAGER'S BLOG.
SORRY. DID YOU MEAN THE DINOSAUR? OR THE ILLEGAL ALASKAN DRILL SITE?
BOTH.
WHY AUGUSTINE ISLAND? SAUROCO HAS THOUSANDS OF OIL WELLS ALL OVER THE WORLD.
I DON'T UNDERSTAND.
BUT WE'RE NOT DRILLING FOR OIL NOW, ARE WE, PROFESSOR DIXON?
LET'S JUST SAY WE MAY HAVE UNCOVERED SOMETHING BETTER. A SUBSTANCE WITH OVER ONE HUNDRED TIMES THE STORED ENERGY OF STANDARD PETROLEUM.
WE'RE CALLING IT SUBSTANCE 7.
I'M SORRY, MR. KROHN. BUT WHAT DOES THIS HAVE TO DO WITH--
I'M TOLD YOUR FOUNDATION RECENTLY LOST ITS GRANT.
THAT'S RIGHT. BUT HOW DID YOU--
WHAT IF I TOLD YOU THE GOOD PEOPLE AT SAUROCO WOULD BE WILLING TO PICK UP THE BILL? IN EXCHANGE FOR A SMALL CONCESSION, OF COURSE.
WHAT SORT OF CONCESSION?
FOR STARTERS YOU CAN DECLARE MY DRILL SITE AN ARCHAEOLOGICAL PRESERVE. WE KEEP DRILLING. YOU KEEP DIGGING. AND THE GOVERNMENT? WELL...
...IT GOES ABOUT ITS BUSINESS.

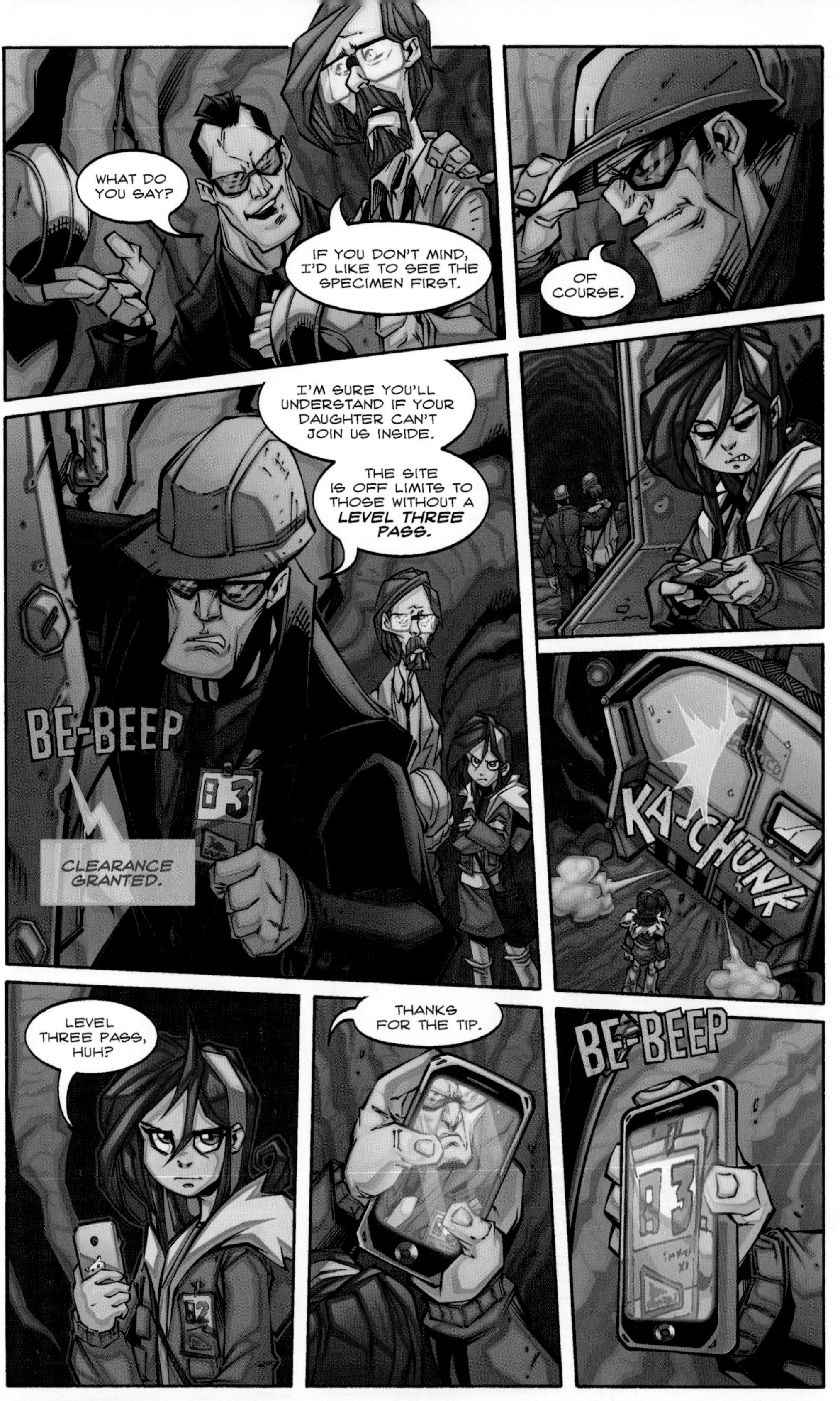
WHAT DO YOU SAY?
IF YOU DON'T MIND, I'D LIKE TO SEE THE SPECIMEN FIRST.
OF COURSE.
I'M SURE YOU'LL UNDERSTAND IF YOUR DAUGHTER CAN'T JOIN US INSIDE.
THE SITE IS OFF LIMITS TO THOSE WITHOUT A LEVEL THREE PASS.
BE-BEEP
B3
CLEARANCE GRANTED.
KA-CHUNK
LEVEL THREE PASS, HUH?
B2
THANKS FOR THE TIP.
BE-BEEP
B3

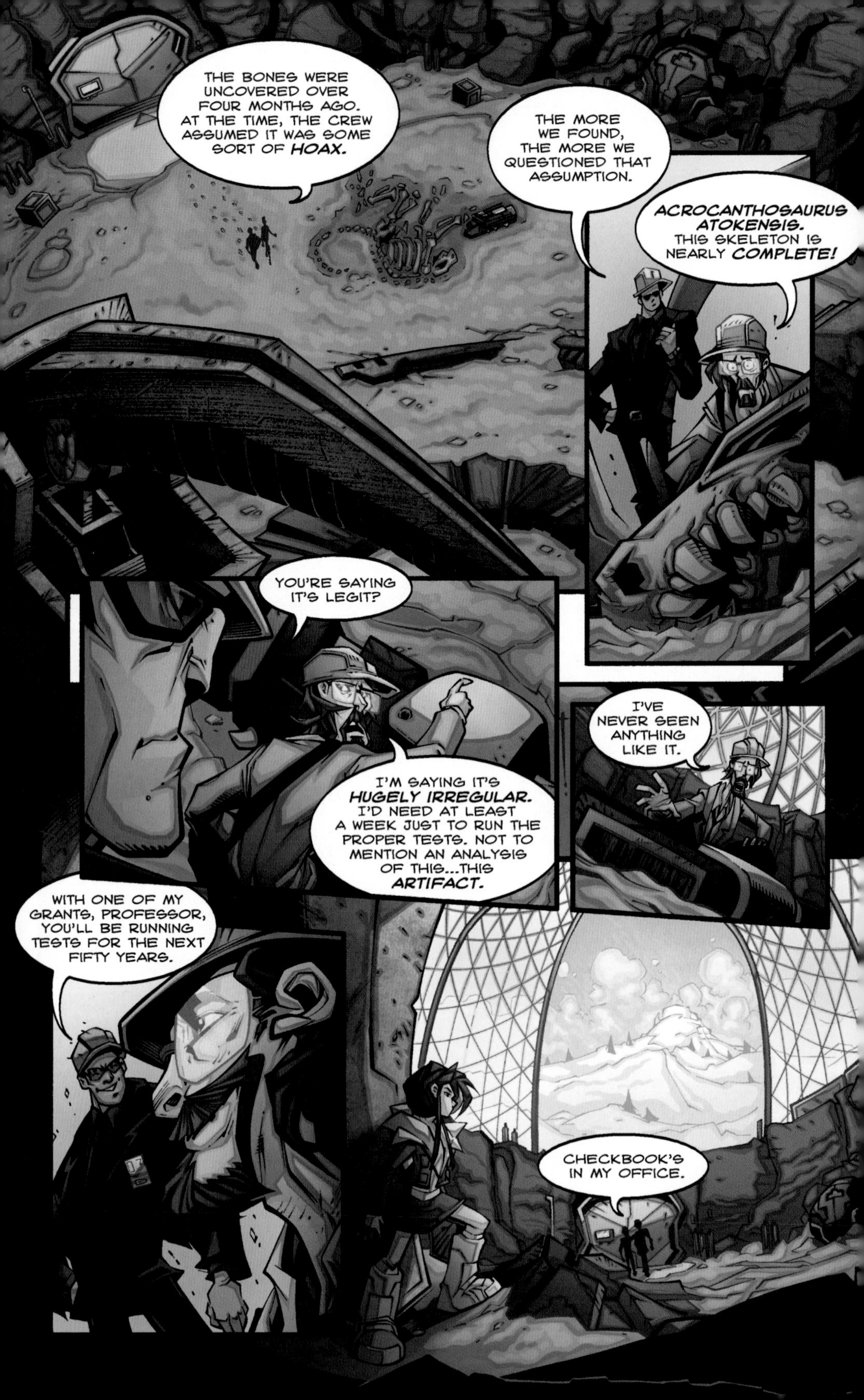
THE BONES WERE UNCOVERED OVER FOUR MONTHS AGO. AT THE TIME, THE CREW ASSUMED IT WAS SOME SORT OF HOAX.
THE MORE WE FOUND, THE MORE WE QUESTIONED THAT ASSUMPTION.
ACROCANTHOSAURUS ATOKENSIS. THIS SKELETON IS NEARLY COMPLETE!
YOU'RE SAYING IT'S LEGIT?
I'M SAYING IT'S HUGELY IRREGULAR. I'D NEED AT LEAST A WEEK JUST TO RUN THE PROPER TESTS. NOT TO MENTION AN ANALYSIS OF THIS...THIS ARTIFACT.
I'VE NEVER SEEN ANYTHING LIKE IT.
WITH ONE OF MY GRANTS, PROFESSOR, YOU'LL BE RUNNING TESTS FOR THE NEXT FIFTY YEARS.
CHECKBOOK'S IN MY OFFICE.

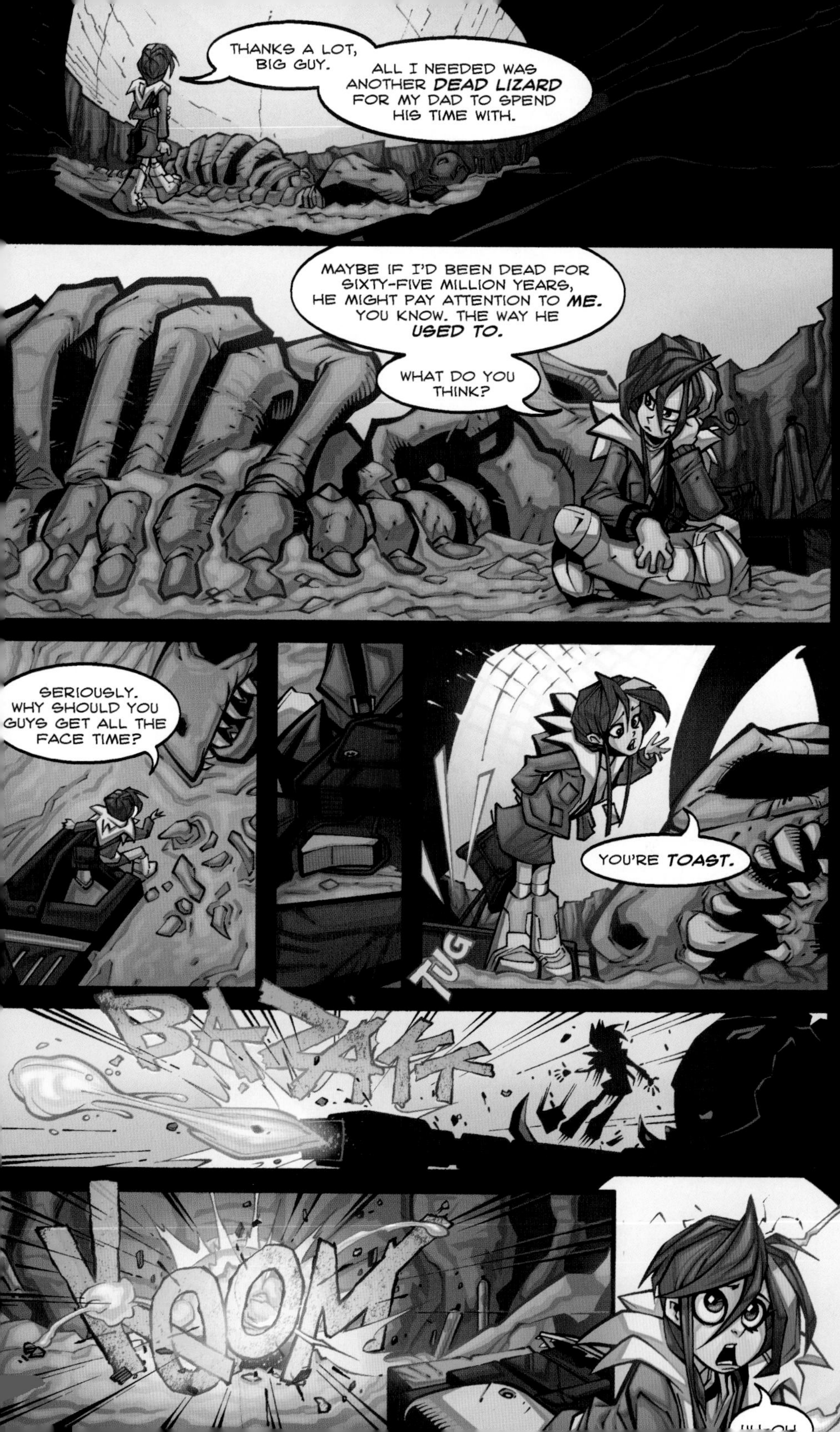
THANKS A LOT, BIG GUY.
ALL I NEEDED WAS ANOTHER **DEAD LIZARD** FOR MY DAD TO SPEND HIS TIME WITH.
MAYBE IF I'D BEEN DEAD FOR SIXTY-FIVE MILLION YEARS, HE MIGHT PAY ATTENTION TO **ME.** YOU KNOW. THE WAY HE **USED TO.**
WHAT DO YOU THINK?
SERIOUSLY. WHY SHOULD YOU GUYS GET ALL THE FACE TIME?
YOU'RE **TOAST.**
TUG
BAZAKK
VOOM

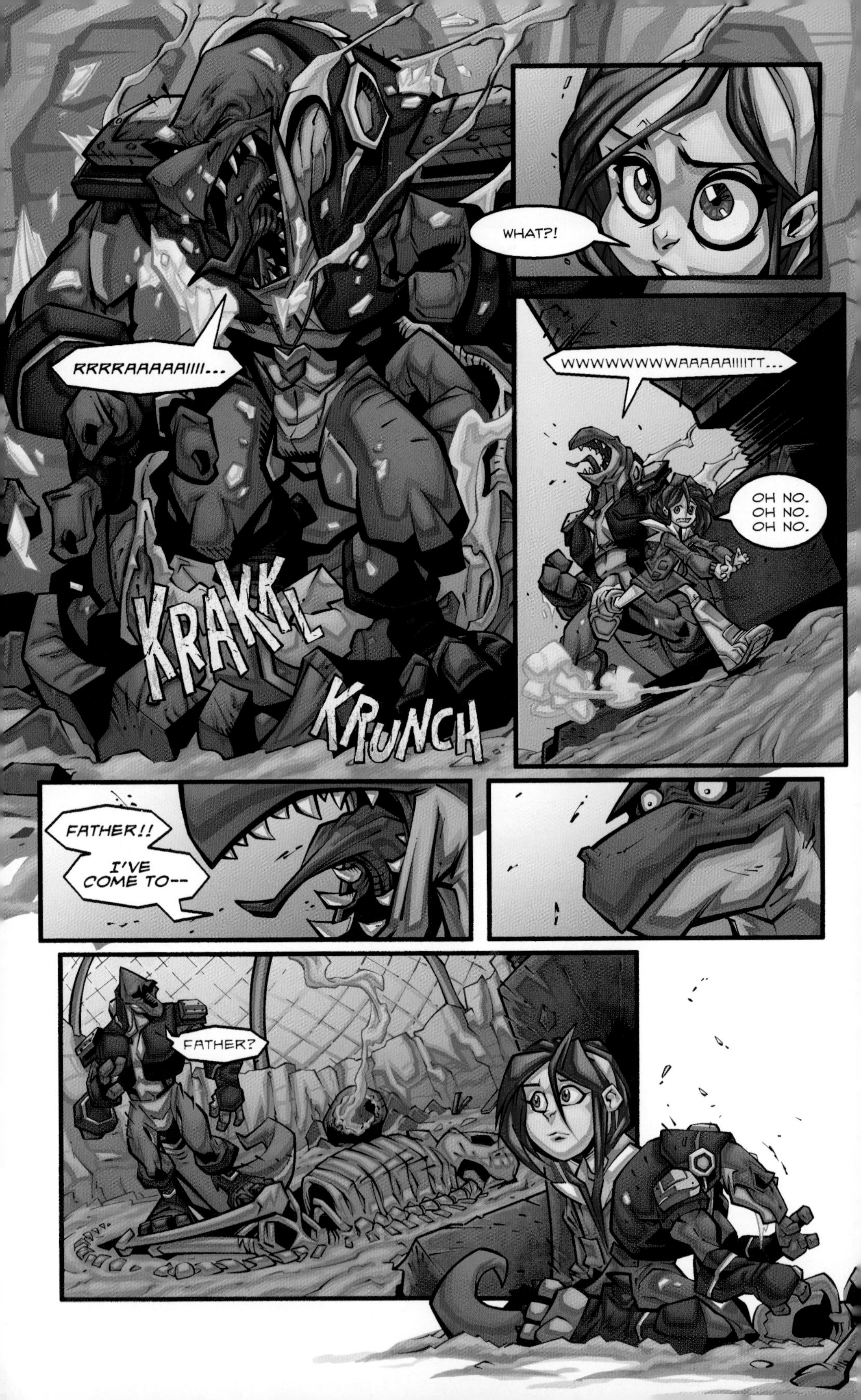
WHAT?!
RRRRAAAAAAIIII...
KRAKKIL
KRUNCH
WWWWWWWWAAAAAAIIIITT...
OH NO. OH NO. OH NO.
FATHER!!
I'VE COME TO--
FATHER?

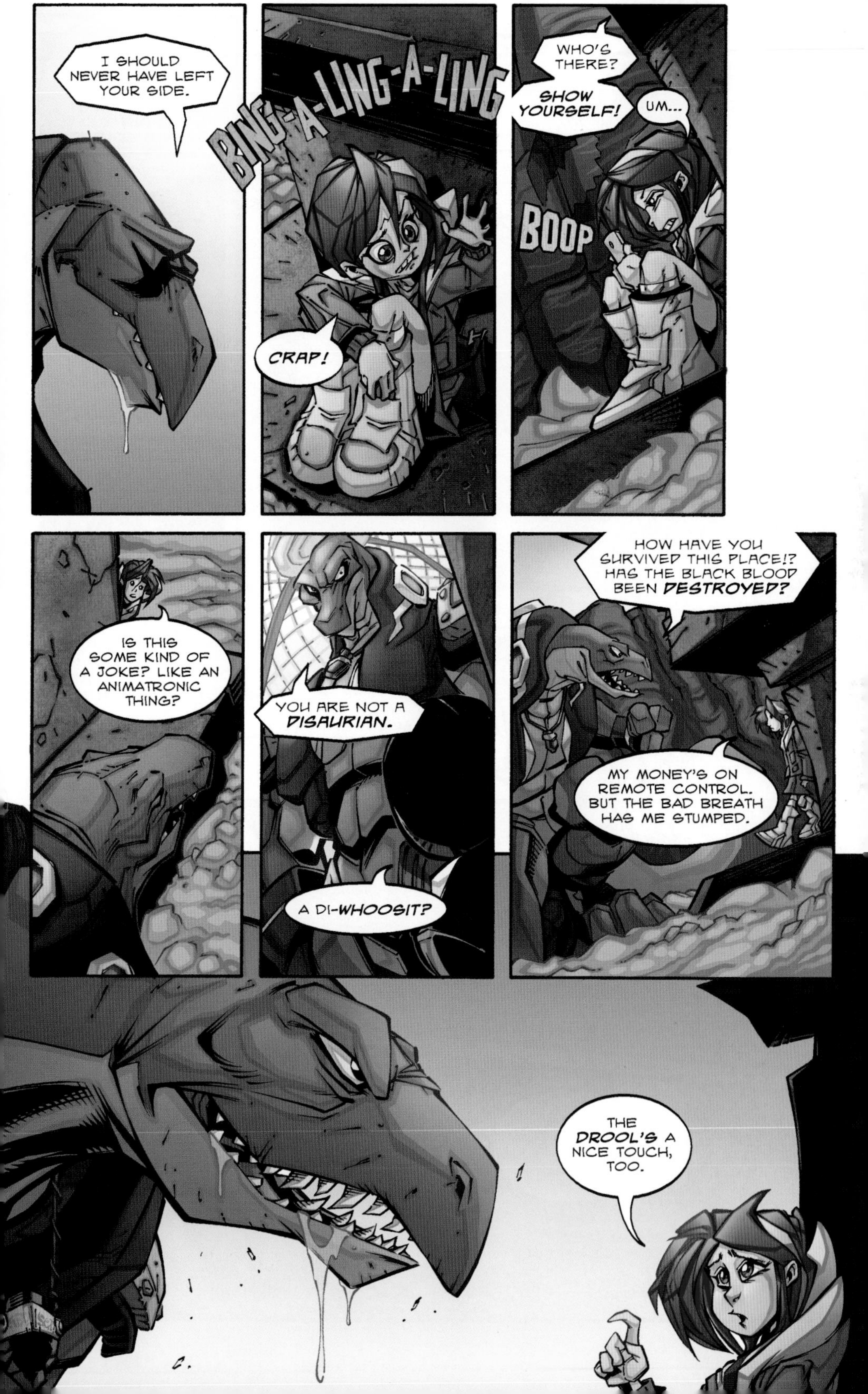
I SHOULD NEVER HAVE LEFT YOUR SIDE.
BING-A-LING-A-LING
CRAP!
WHO'S THERE?
SHOW YOURSELF!
UM...
BOOP
IS THIS SOME KIND OF A JOKE? LIKE AN ANIMATRONIC THING?
YOU ARE NOT A DISAURIAN.
A DI-WHOOSIT?
HOW HAVE YOU SURVIVED THIS PLACE!? HAS THE BLACK BLOOD BEEN DESTROYED?
MY MONEY'S ON REMOTE CONTROL. BUT THE BAD BREATH HAS ME STUMPED.
THE DROOL'S A NICE TOUCH, TOO.

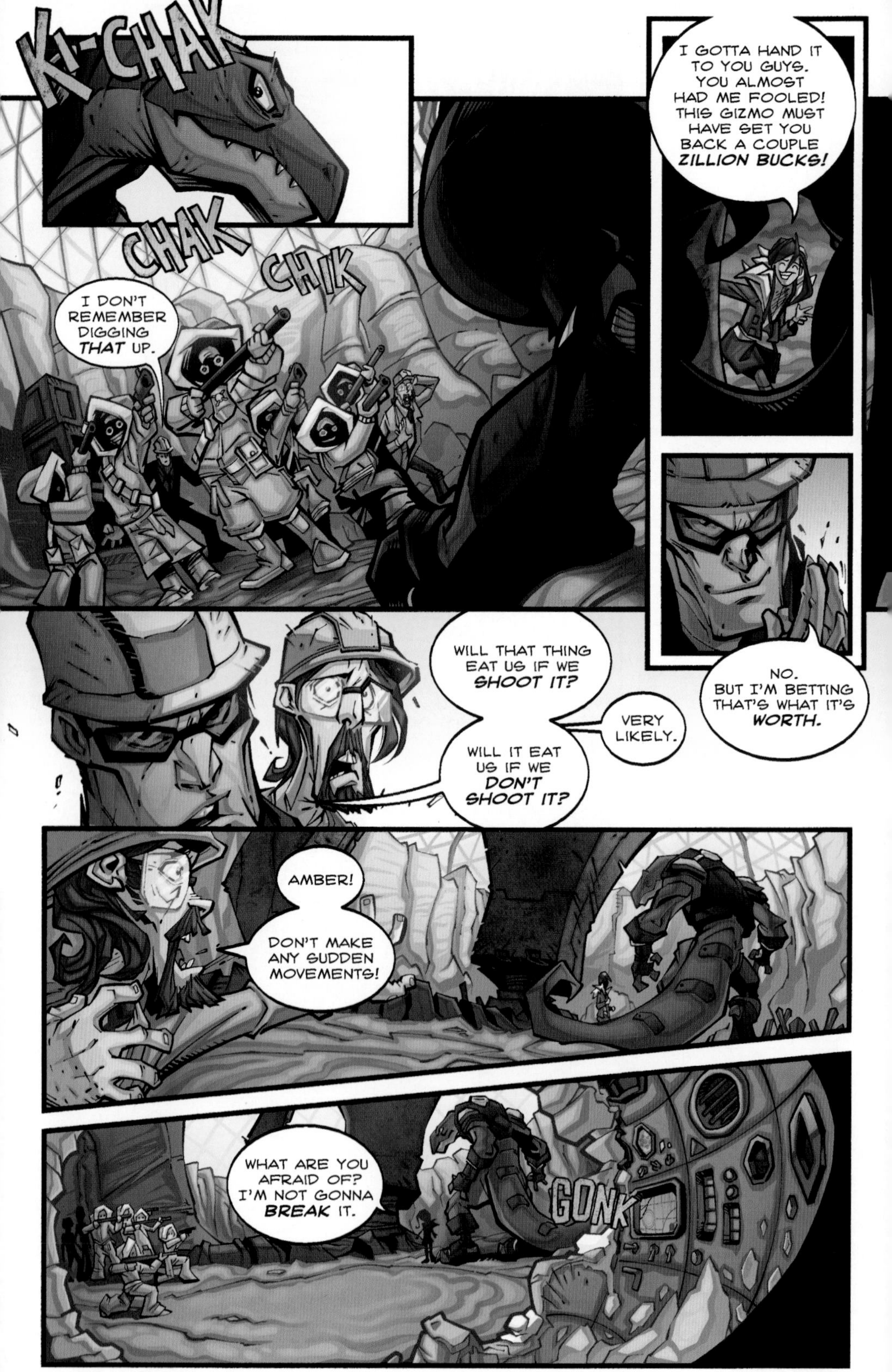
KI-CHAK
CHAK
CHIK
I DON'T REMEMBER DIGGING THAT UP.
I GOTTA HAND IT TO YOU GUYS. YOU ALMOST HAD ME FOOLED! THIS GIZMO MUST HAVE SET YOU BACK A COUPLE ZILLION BUCKS!
WILL THAT THING EAT US IF WE SHOOT IT?
WILL IT EAT US IF WE DON'T SHOOT IT?
VERY LIKELY.
NO. BUT I'M BETTING THAT'S WHAT IT'S WORTH.
AMBER!
DON'T MAKE ANY SUDDEN MOVEMENTS!
WHAT ARE YOU AFRAID OF? I'M NOT GONNA BREAK IT.
GONK

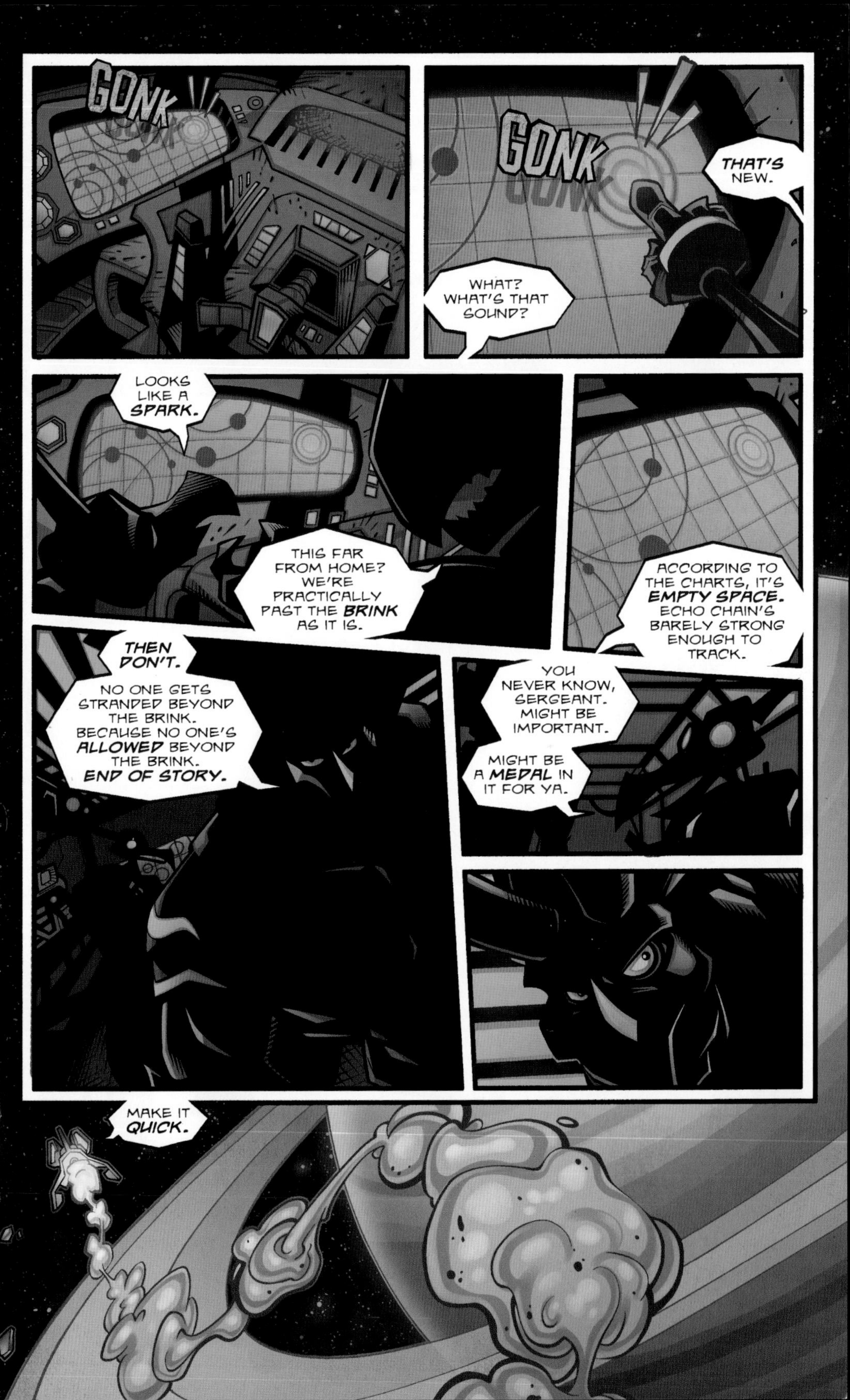
GONK
GONK
THAT'S NEW.
WHAT? WHAT'S THAT SOUND?
LOOKS LIKE A SPARK.
THIS FAR FROM HOME? WE'RE PRACTICALLY PAST THE BRINK AS IT IS.
ACCORDING TO THE CHARTS, IT'S EMPTY SPACE. ECHO CHAIN'S BARELY STRONG ENOUGH TO TRACK.
THEN DON'T.
NO ONE GETS STRANDED BEYOND THE BRINK. BECAUSE NO ONE'S ALLOWED BEYOND THE BRINK. END OF STORY.
YOU NEVER KNOW, SERGEANT. MIGHT BE IMPORTANT.
MIGHT BE A MEDAL IN IT FOR YA.
MAKE IT QUICK.

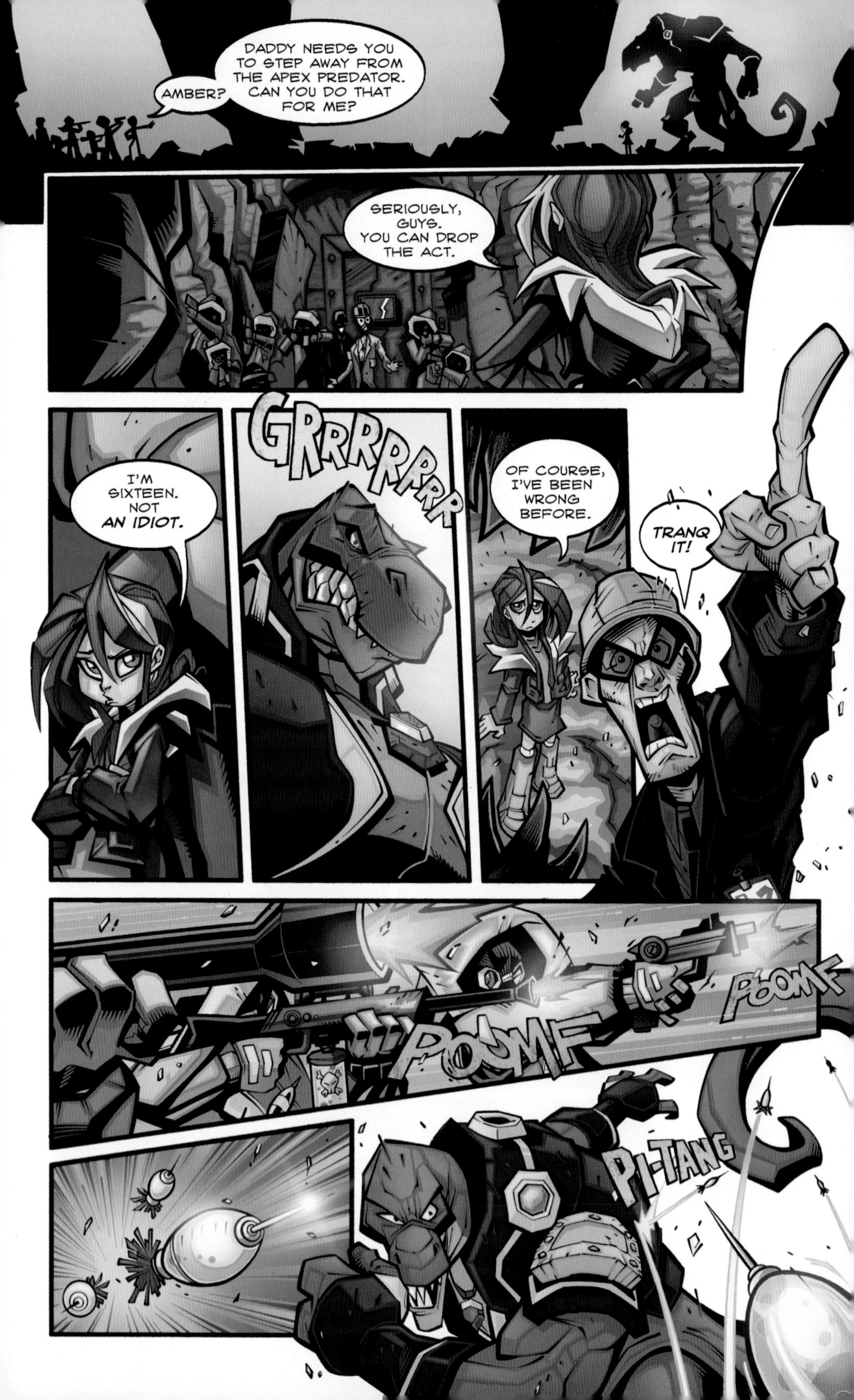
AMBER?
DADDY NEEDS YOU TO STEP AWAY FROM THE APEX PREDATOR. CAN YOU DO THAT FOR ME?
SERIOUSLY, GUYS. YOU CAN DROP THE ACT.
I'M SIXTEEN. NOT AN IDIOT.
GRRRRRRR
OF COURSE, I'VE BEEN WRONG BEFORE.
TRANQ IT!
POOMF
POOMF
PI-TANG

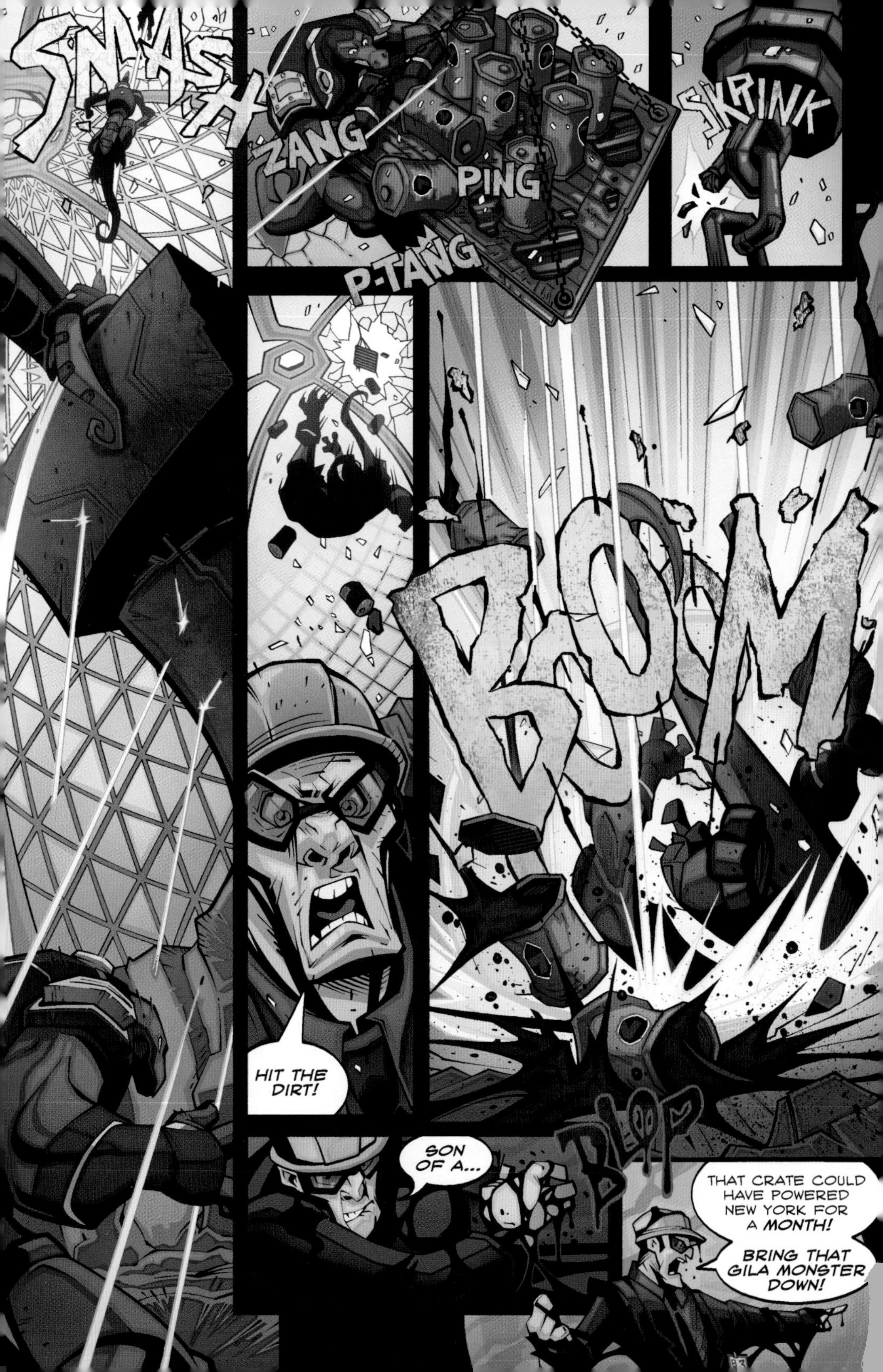
SMASH
ZANG
PING
P-TANG
SKRINK
HIT THE DIRT!
BOOM
SON OF A...
THAT CRATE COULD HAVE POWERED NEW YORK FOR A *MONTH!*
BRING THAT GILA MONSTER DOWN!

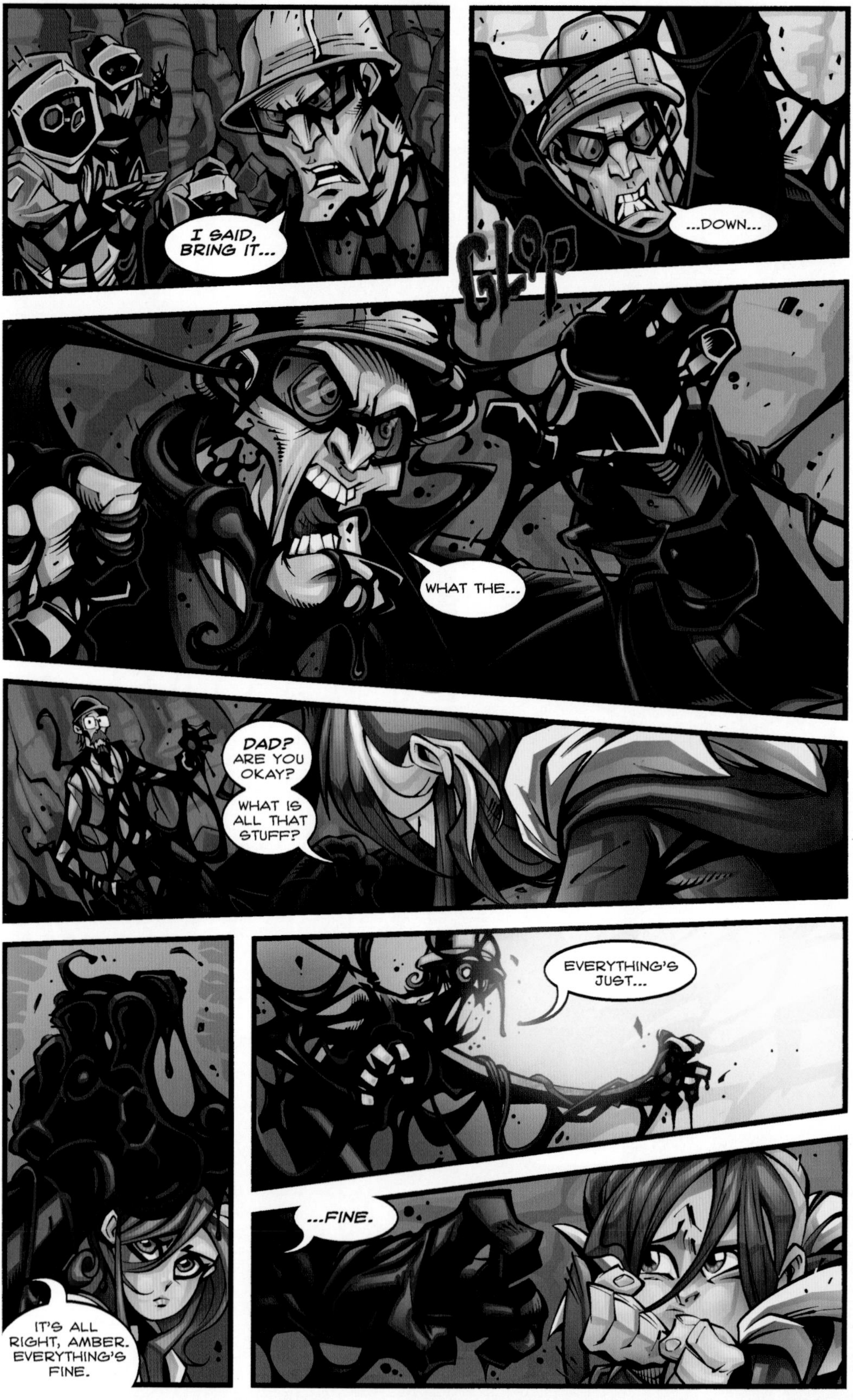
I SAID, BRING IT...
...DOWN...
GLOP
WHAT THE...
DAD? ARE YOU OKAY?
WHAT IS ALL THAT STUFF?
IT'S ALL RIGHT, AMBER. EVERYTHING'S FINE.
EVERYTHING'S JUST...
...FINE.

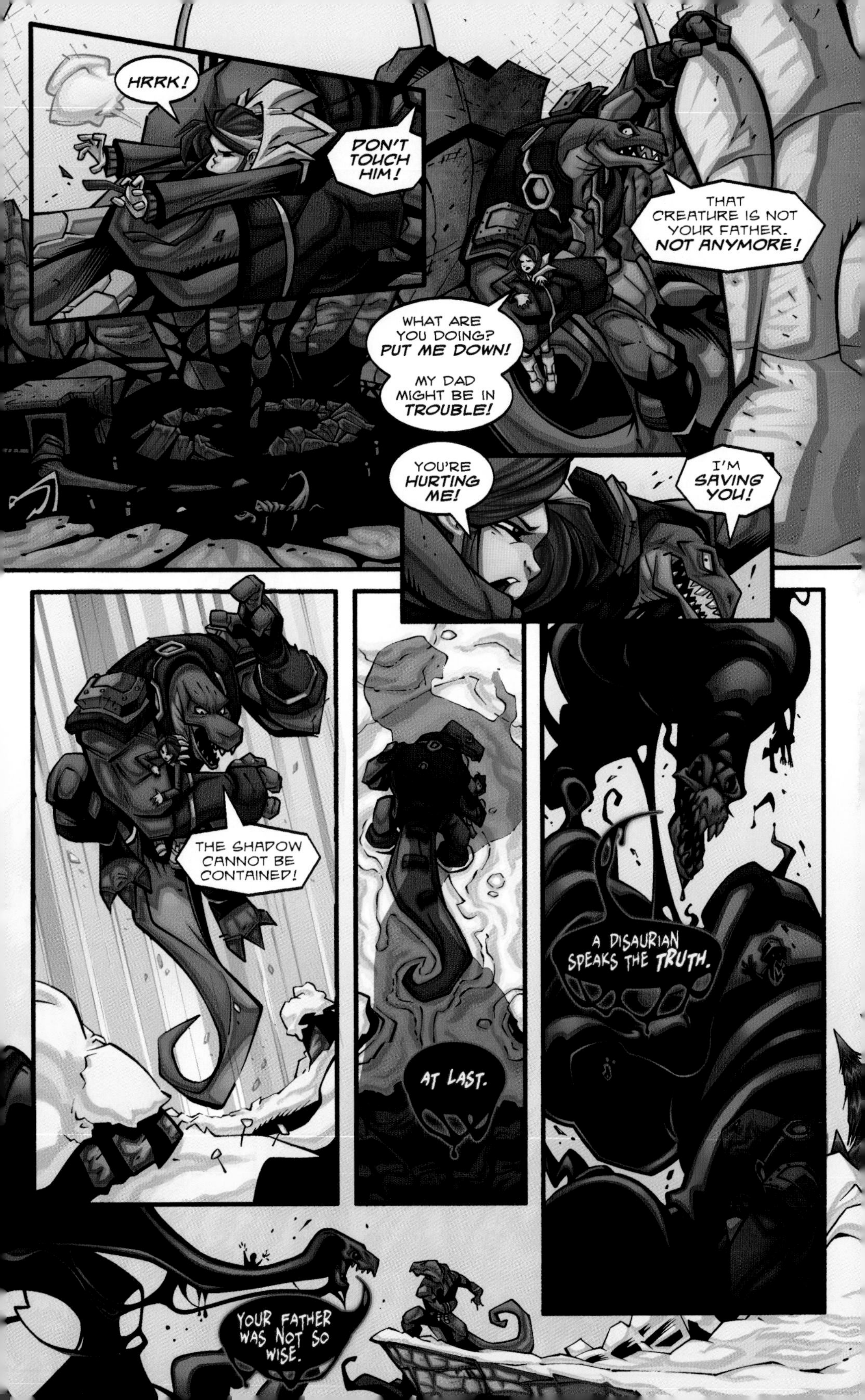
HRRK!
DON'T TOUCH HIM!
THAT CREATURE IS NOT YOUR FATHER. NOT ANYMORE!
WHAT ARE YOU DOING? PUT ME DOWN!
MY DAD MIGHT BE IN TROUBLE!
YOU'RE HURTING ME!
I'M SAVING YOU!
THE SHADOW CANNOT BE CONTAINED!
AT LAST.
A DISAURIAN SPEAKS THE TRUTH.
YOUR FATHER WAS NOT SO WISE.

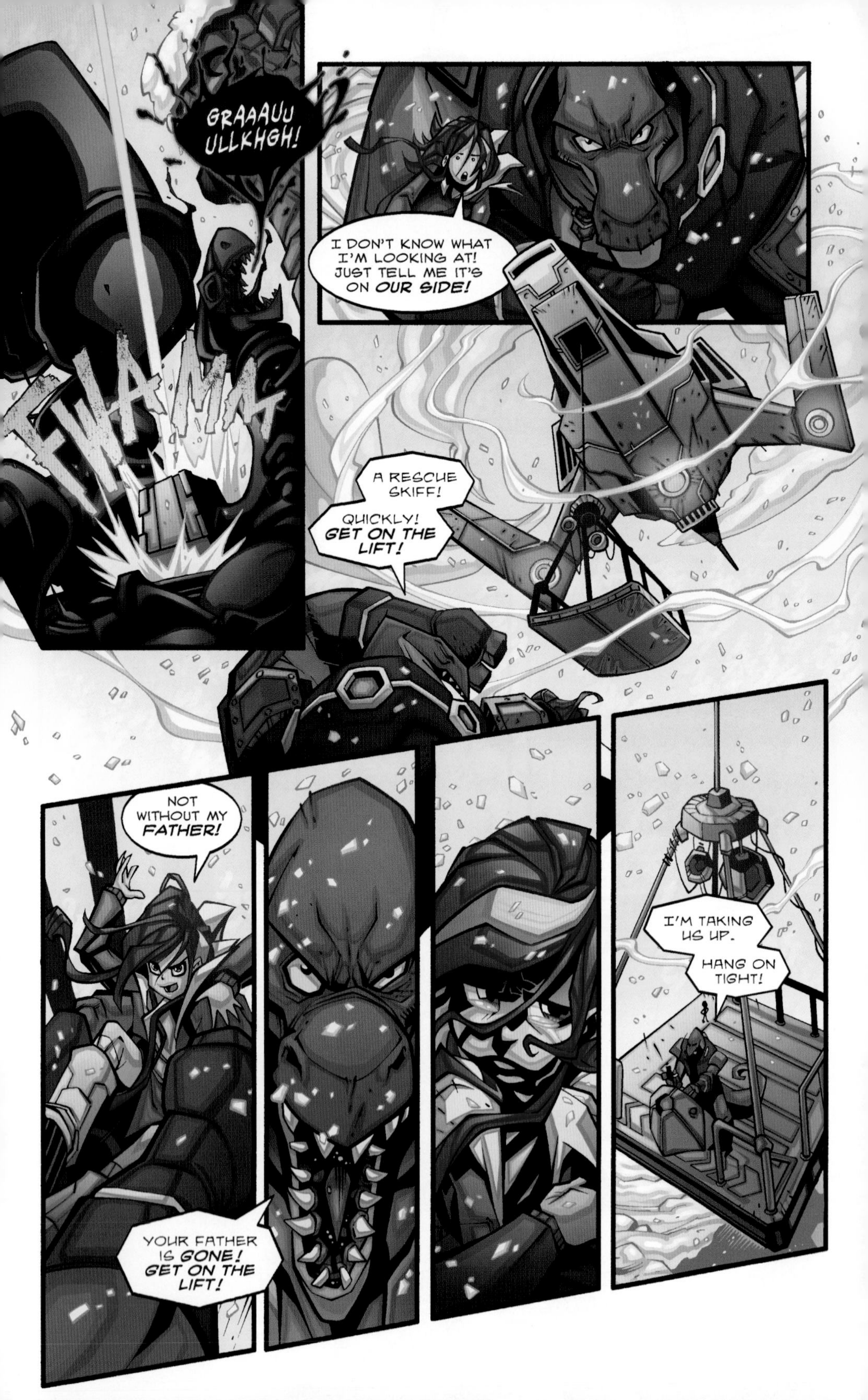
GRAAAUU ULLKHGH!
FWAMS
I DON'T KNOW WHAT I'M LOOKING AT! JUST TELL ME IT'S ON OUR SIDE!
A RESCUE SKIFF!
QUICKLY! GET ON THE LIFT!
NOT WITHOUT MY FATHER!
YOUR FATHER IS GONE! GET ON THE LIFT!
I'M TAKING US UP.
HANG ON TIGHT!

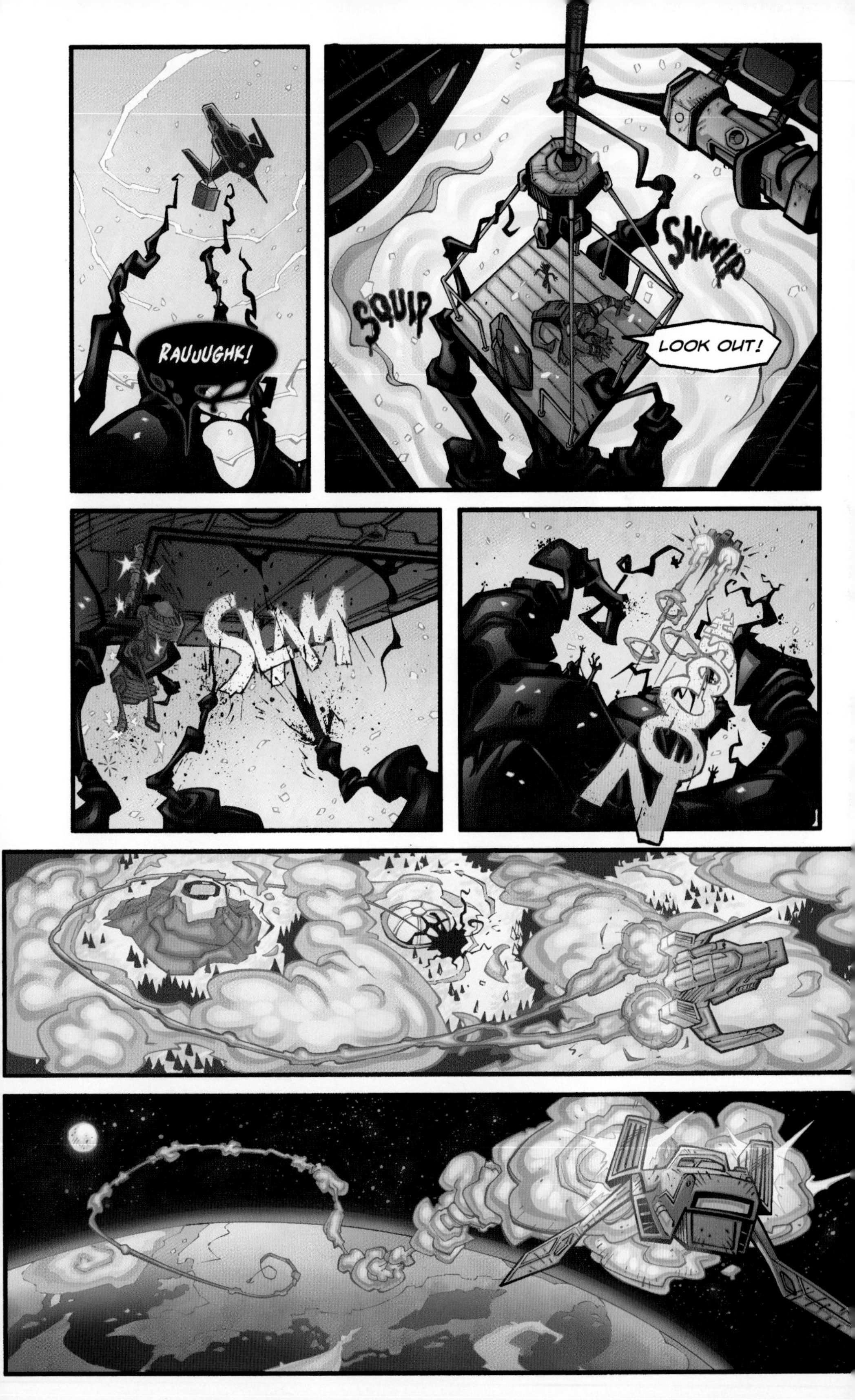
RAUUUGHK!
SQUIP
SHWIP
LOOK OUT!
SLAM

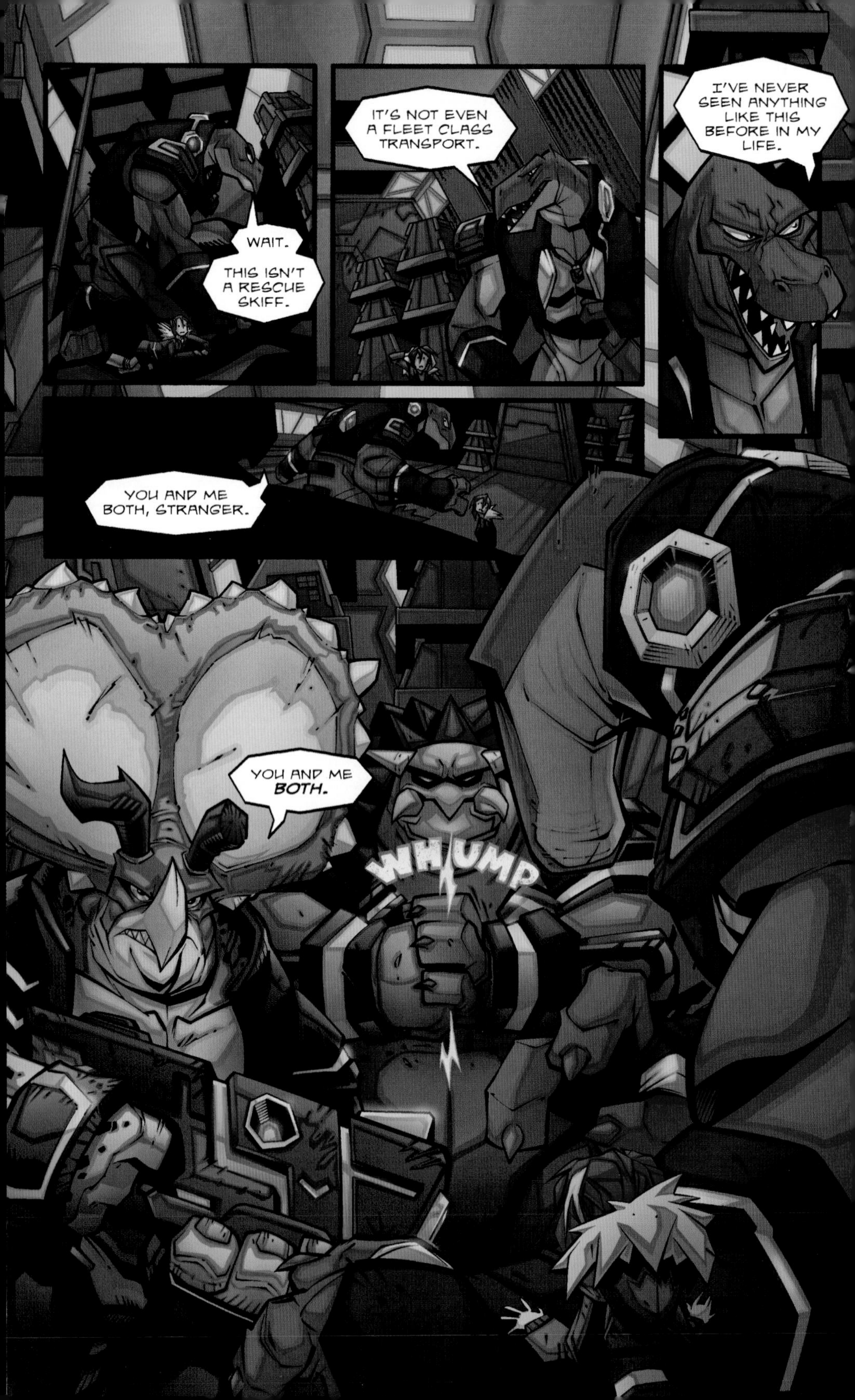
WAIT.
THIS ISN'T A RESCUE SKIFF.
IT'S NOT EVEN A FLEET CLASS TRANSPORT.
I'VE NEVER SEEN ANYTHING LIKE THIS BEFORE IN MY LIFE.
YOU AND ME BOTH, STRANGER.
YOU AND ME *BOTH.*
WHUMP

CHAPTER
2

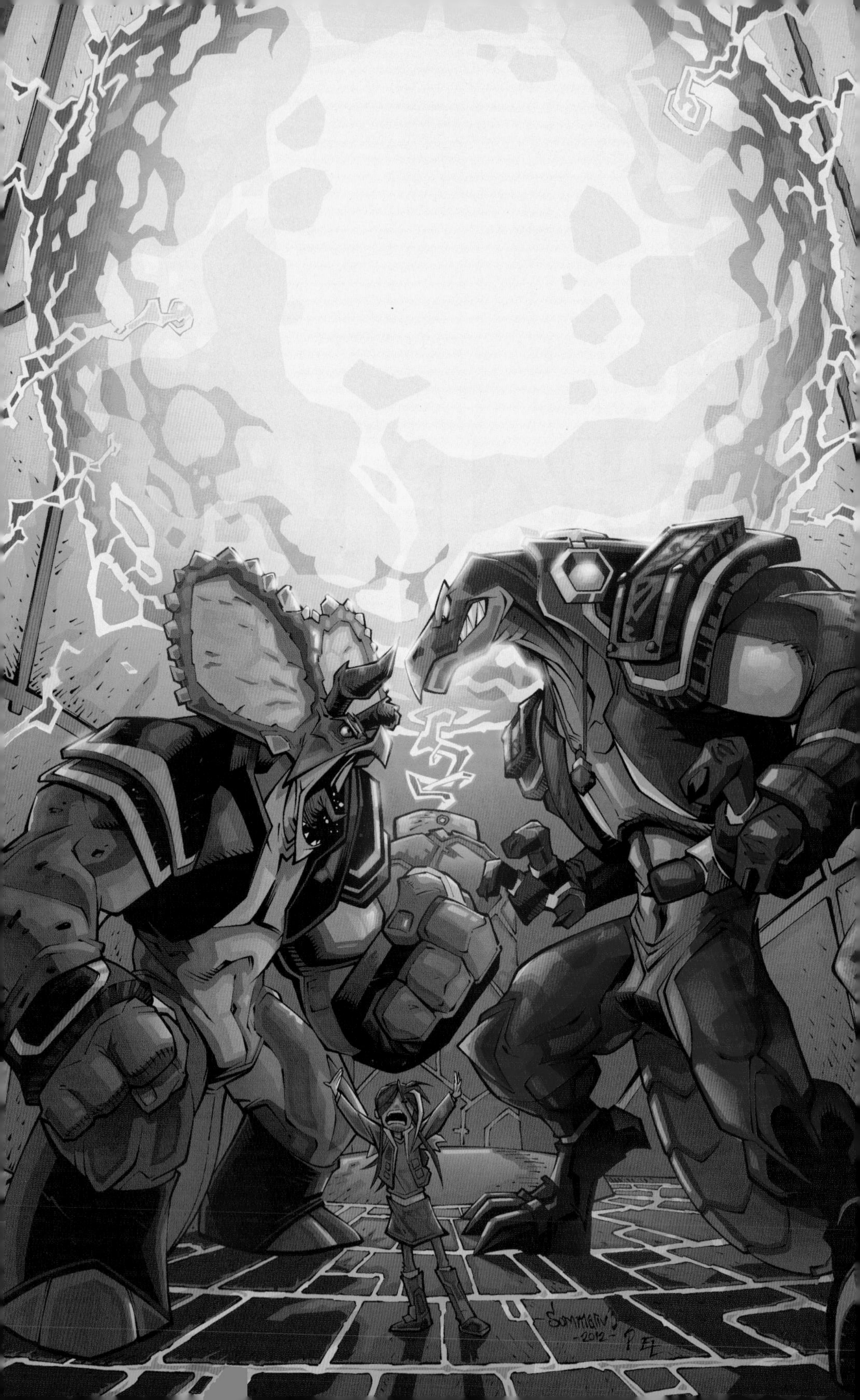

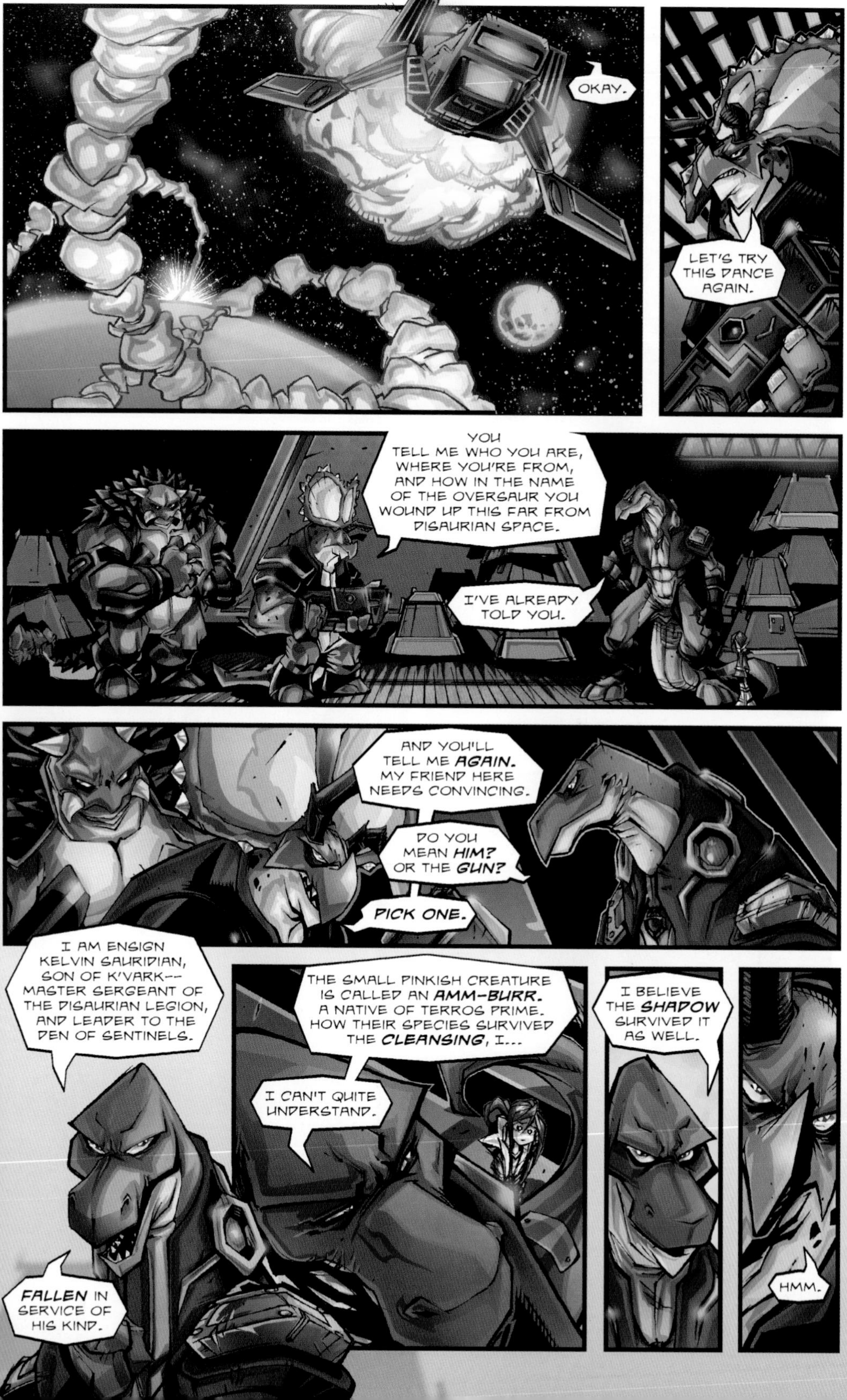
OKAY.
LET'S TRY THIS DANCE AGAIN.
YOU TELL ME WHO YOU ARE, WHERE YOU'RE FROM, AND HOW IN THE NAME OF THE OVERSAUR YOU WOUND UP THIS FAR FROM DISAURIAN SPACE.
I'VE ALREADY TOLD YOU.
AND YOU'LL TELL ME **AGAIN.** MY FRIEND HERE NEEDS CONVINCING.
DO YOU MEAN **HIM?** OR THE **GUN?**
PICK ONE.
I AM ENSIGN KELVIN SAURIDIAN, SON OF K'VARK-- MASTER SERGEANT OF THE DISAURIAN LEGION, AND LEADER TO THE DEN OF SENTINELS.
FALLEN IN SERVICE OF HIS KIND.
THE SMALL PINKISH CREATURE IS CALLED AN **AMM-BURR.** A NATIVE OF TERROS PRIME. HOW THEIR SPECIES SURVIVED THE **CLEANSING**, I...
I CAN'T QUITE UNDERSTAND.
I BELIEVE THE **SHADOW** SURVIVED IT AS WELL.
HMM.

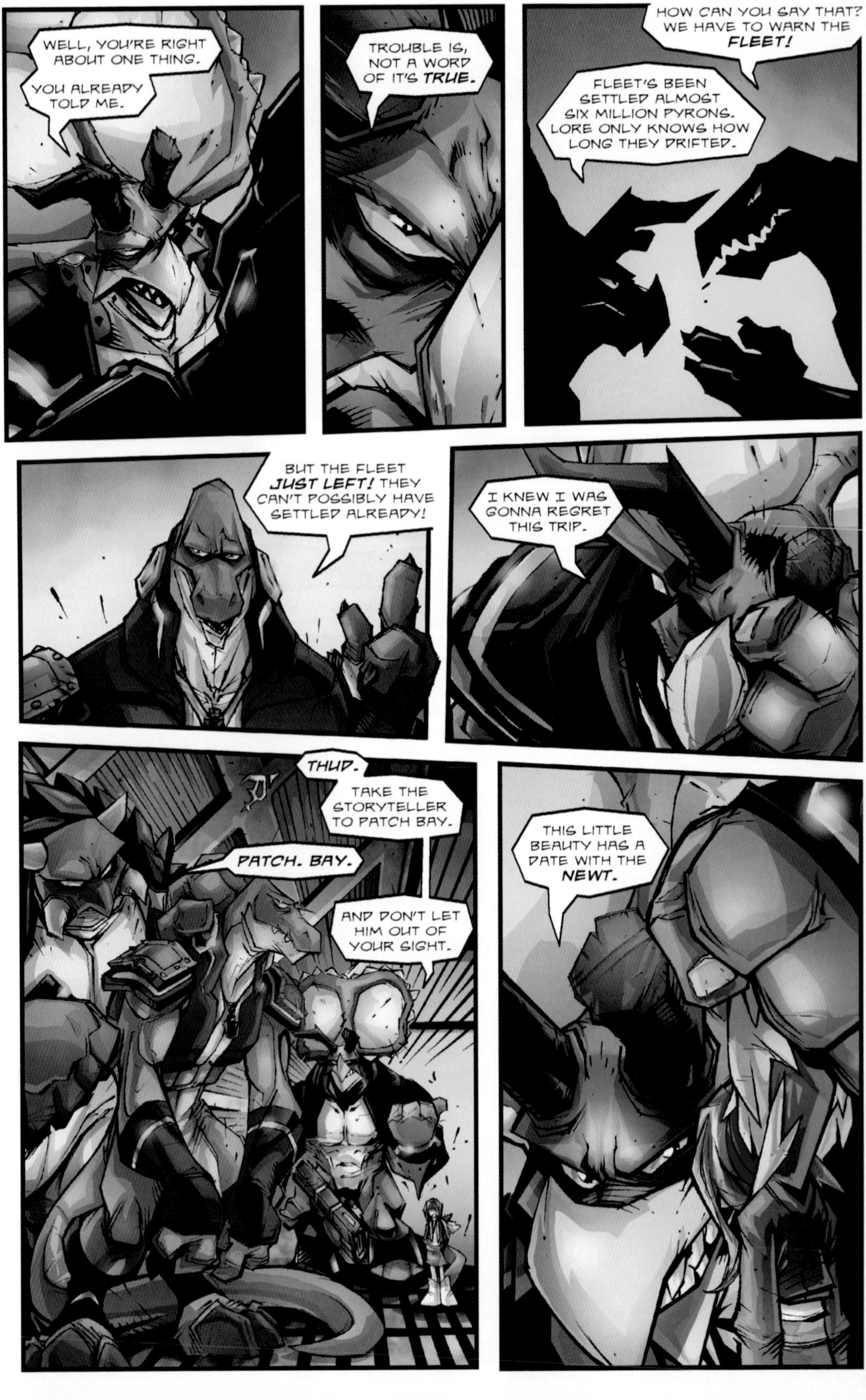
WELL, YOU'RE RIGHT ABOUT ONE THING.
YOU ALREADY TOLD ME.
TROUBLE IS, NOT A WORD OF IT'S TRUE.
HOW CAN YOU SAY THAT? WE HAVE TO WARN THE FLEET!
FLEET'S BEEN SETTLED ALMOST SIX MILLION PYRONS. LORE ONLY KNOWS HOW LONG THEY DRIFTED.
BUT THE FLEET JUST LEFT! THEY CAN'T POSSIBLY HAVE SETTLED ALREADY!
I KNEW I WAS GONNA REGRET THIS TRIP.
THUD.
TAKE THE STORYTELLER TO PATCH BAY.
PATCH. BAY.
AND DON'T LET HIM OUT OF YOUR SIGHT.
THIS LITTLE BEAUTY HAS A DATE WITH THE NEWT.

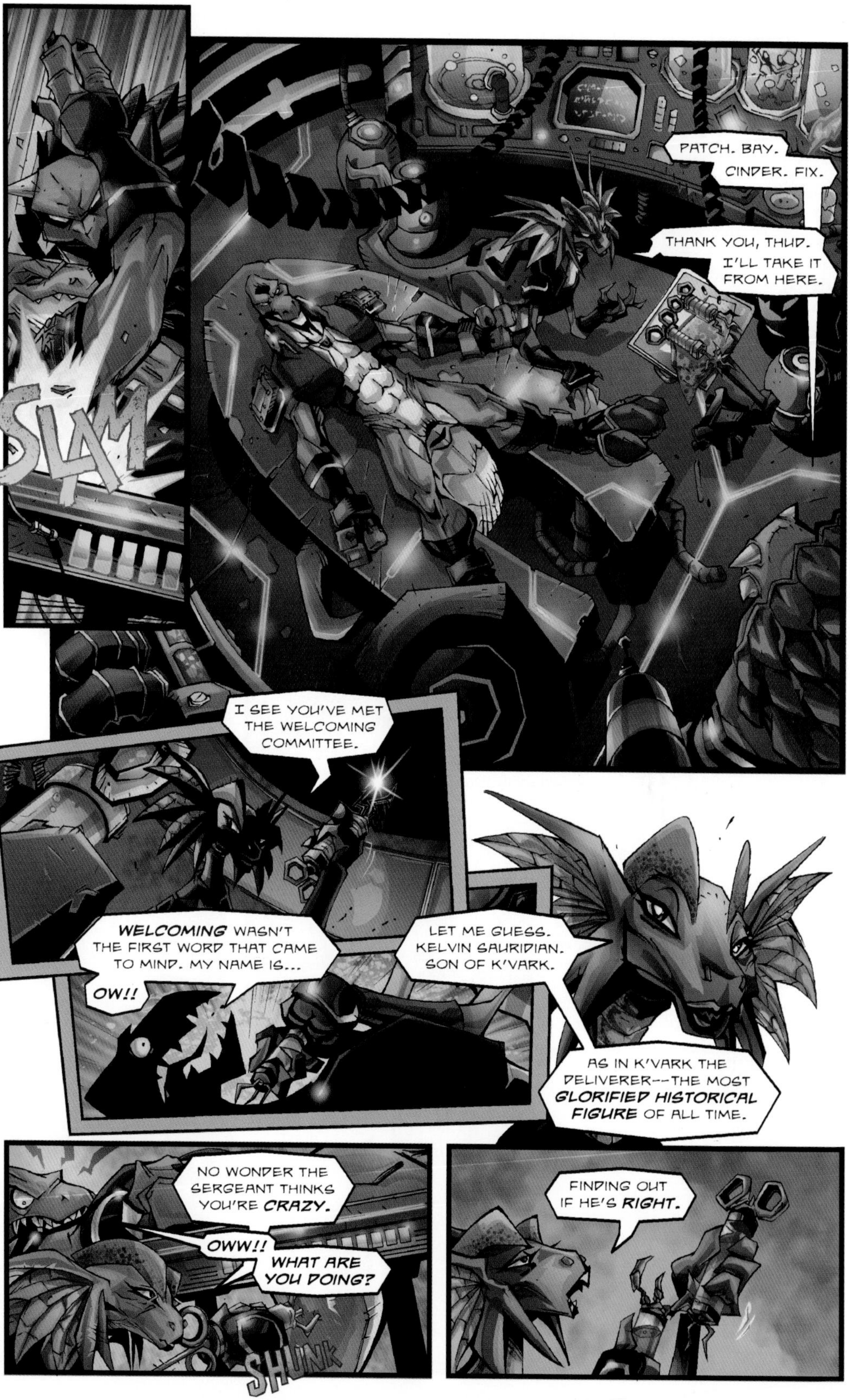
SLAM
PATCH. BAY.
CINDER. FIX.
THANK YOU, THUD.
I'LL TAKE IT FROM HERE.
I SEE YOU'VE MET THE WELCOMING COMMITTEE.
WELCOMING WASN'T THE FIRST WORD THAT CAME TO MIND. MY NAME IS...
OW!!
LET ME GUESS. KELVIN SAURIDIAN. SON OF K'VARK.
AS IN K'VARK THE DELIVERER--THE MOST GLORIFIED HISTORICAL FIGURE OF ALL TIME.
NO WONDER THE SERGEANT THINKS YOU'RE CRAZY.
OWW!!
WHAT ARE YOU DOING?
SHUNK
FINDING OUT IF HE'S RIGHT.

IT'S ALL YOURS, NEWT.

OOF!

PLUNK

ENJOY.

TESTS. TESTS. SO MANY TESTS!

PERHAPS A SPORE? A MUTANT MICROBE?

A STRAIN OF SEMI-GELATINOUS BIPEDAL PATHOGEN?

NO, NO! WAIT! PLEASE!

I'M NOT A SPORE! I'M A PERSON!

A HUMAN PERSON FROM THE PLANET EARTH.

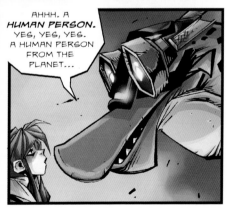

AHHH. A HUMAN PERSON. YES, YES, YES. A HUMAN PERSON FROM THE PLANET...

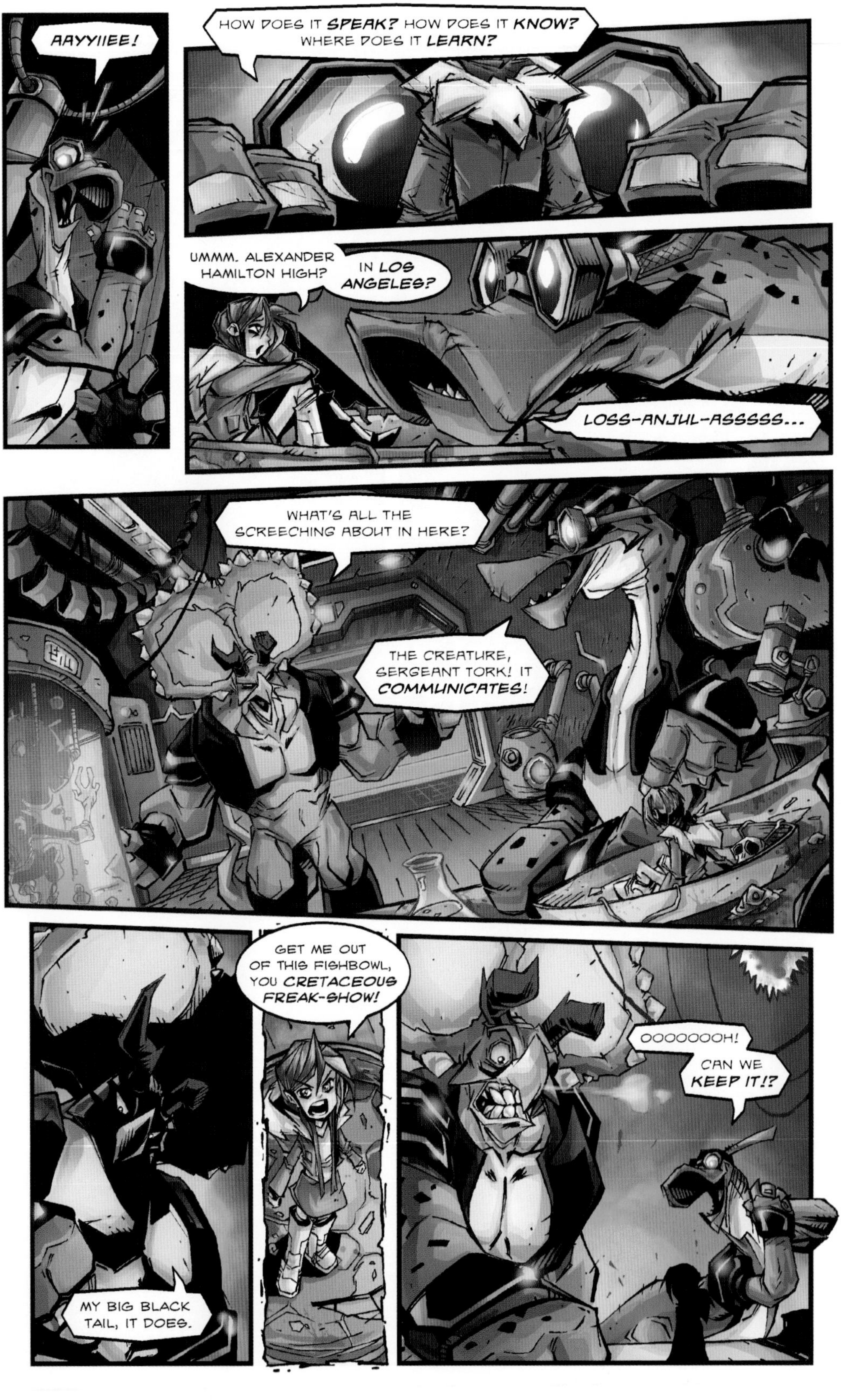
AAYYIIEE!
HOW DOES IT SPEAK? HOW DOES IT KNOW? WHERE DOES IT LEARN?
UMMM. ALEXANDER HAMILTON HIGH?
IN LOS ANGELES?
LOSS-ANJUL-ASSSSS...
WHAT'S ALL THE SCREECHING ABOUT IN HERE?
THE CREATURE, SERGEANT TORK! IT COMMUNICATES!
MY BIG BLACK TAIL, IT DOES.
GET ME OUT OF THIS FISHBOWL, YOU CRETACEOUS FREAK-SHOW!
OOOOOOOH!
CAN WE KEEP IT!?

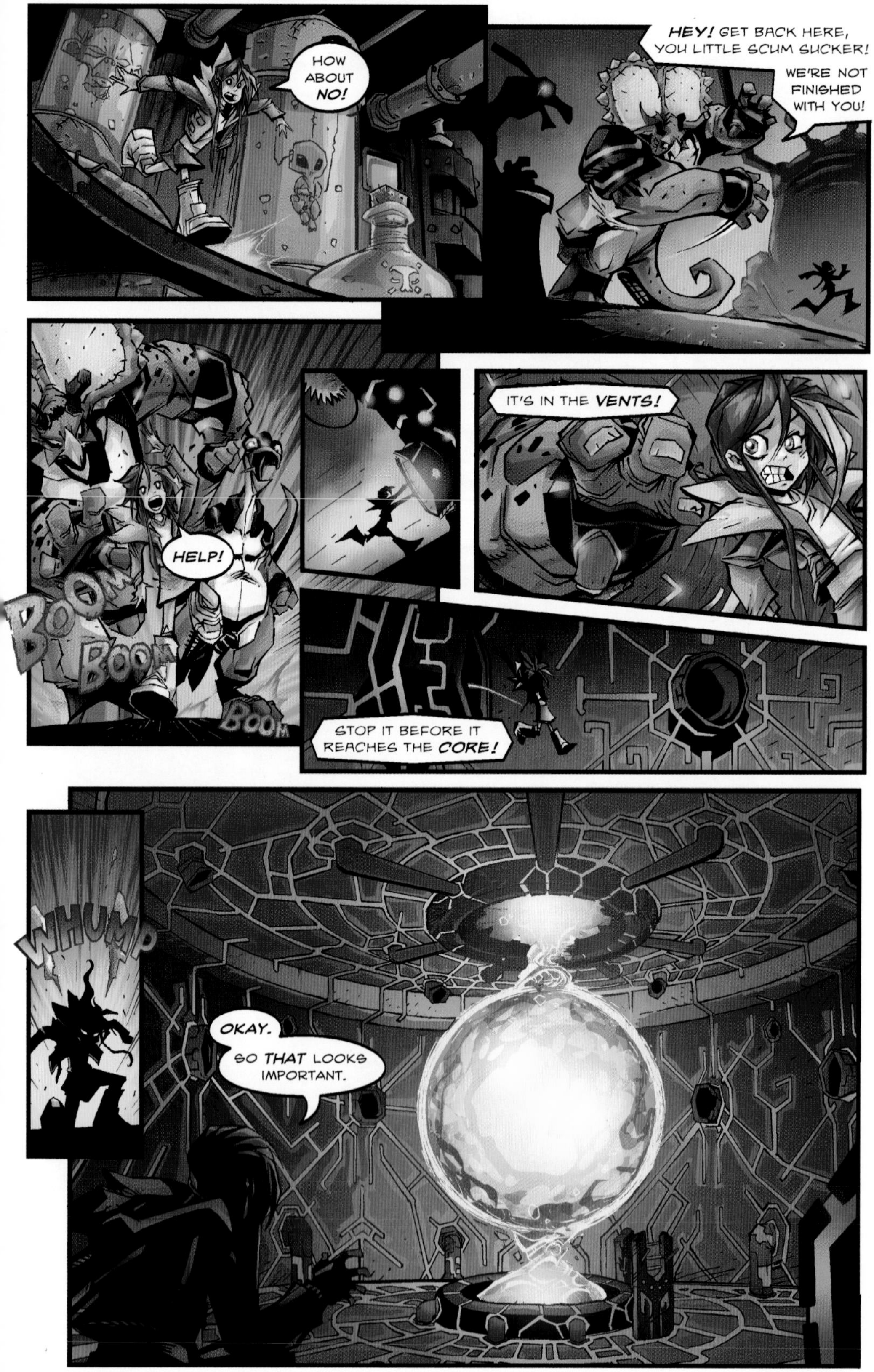
HOW ABOUT NO!
HEY! GET BACK HERE, YOU LITTLE SCUM SUCKER!
WE'RE NOT FINISHED WITH YOU!
HELP!
BOOM
BOOM
BOOM
IT'S IN THE VENTS!
STOP IT BEFORE IT REACHES THE CORE!
WHUMP
OKAY.
SO THAT LOOKS IMPORTANT.

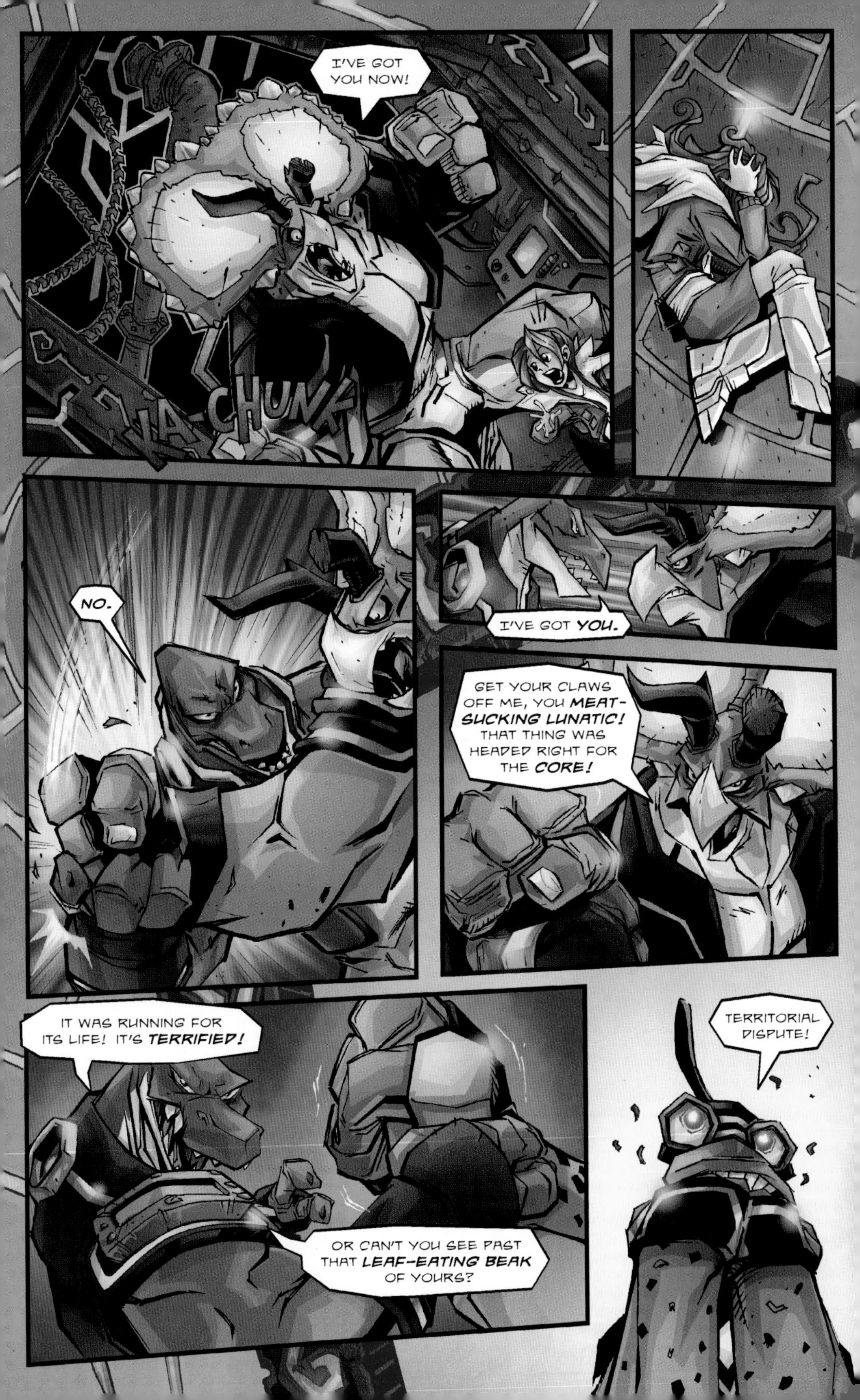
I'VE GOT YOU NOW!
KA-CHUNK
NO.
I'VE GOT YOU.
GET YOUR CLAWS OFF ME, YOU MEAT-SUCKING LUNATIC! THAT THING WAS HEADED RIGHT FOR THE CORE!
IT WAS RUNNING FOR ITS LIFE! IT'S TERRIFIED!
OR CAN'T YOU SEE PAST THAT LEAF-EATING BEAK OF YOURS?
TERRITORIAL DISPUTE!

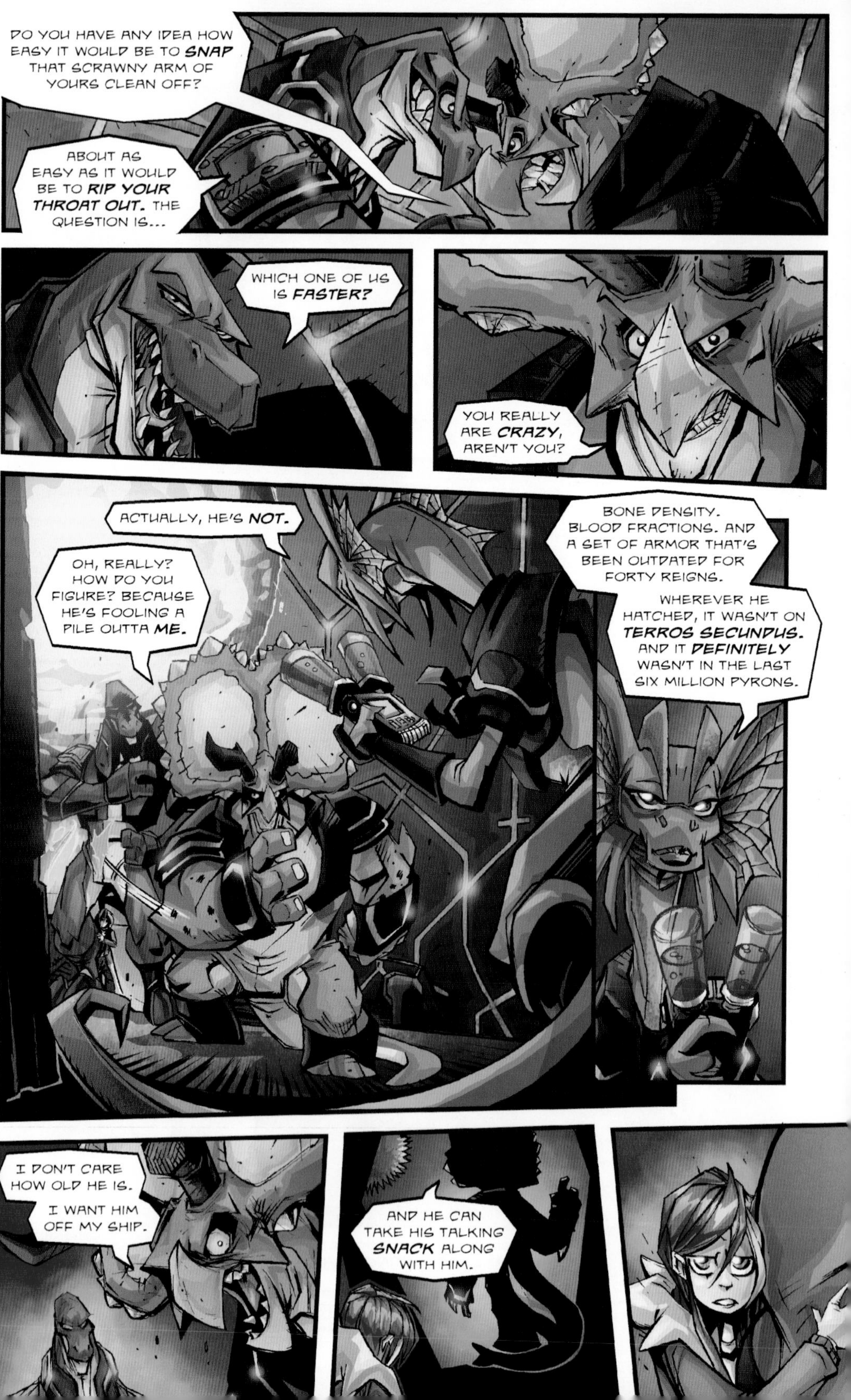

DO YOU HAVE ANY IDEA HOW EASY IT WOULD BE TO **SNAP** THAT SCRAWNY ARM OF YOURS CLEAN OFF?
ABOUT AS EASY AS IT WOULD BE TO **RIP YOUR THROAT OUT.** THE QUESTION IS...
WHICH ONE OF US IS **FASTER?**
YOU REALLY ARE **CRAZY**, AREN'T YOU?
ACTUALLY, HE'S **NOT.**
OH, REALLY? HOW DO YOU FIGURE? BECAUSE HE'S FOOLING A PILE OUTTA **ME.**
BONE DENSITY. BLOOD FRACTIONS. AND A SET OF ARMOR THAT'S BEEN OUTDATED FOR FORTY REIGNS.
WHEREVER HE HATCHED, IT WASN'T ON **TERROS SECUNDUS.** AND IT **DEFINITELY** WASN'T IN THE LAST SIX MILLION PYRONS.
I DON'T CARE HOW OLD HE IS.
I WANT HIM OFF MY SHIP.
AND HE CAN TAKE HIS TALKING **SNACK** ALONG WITH HIM.

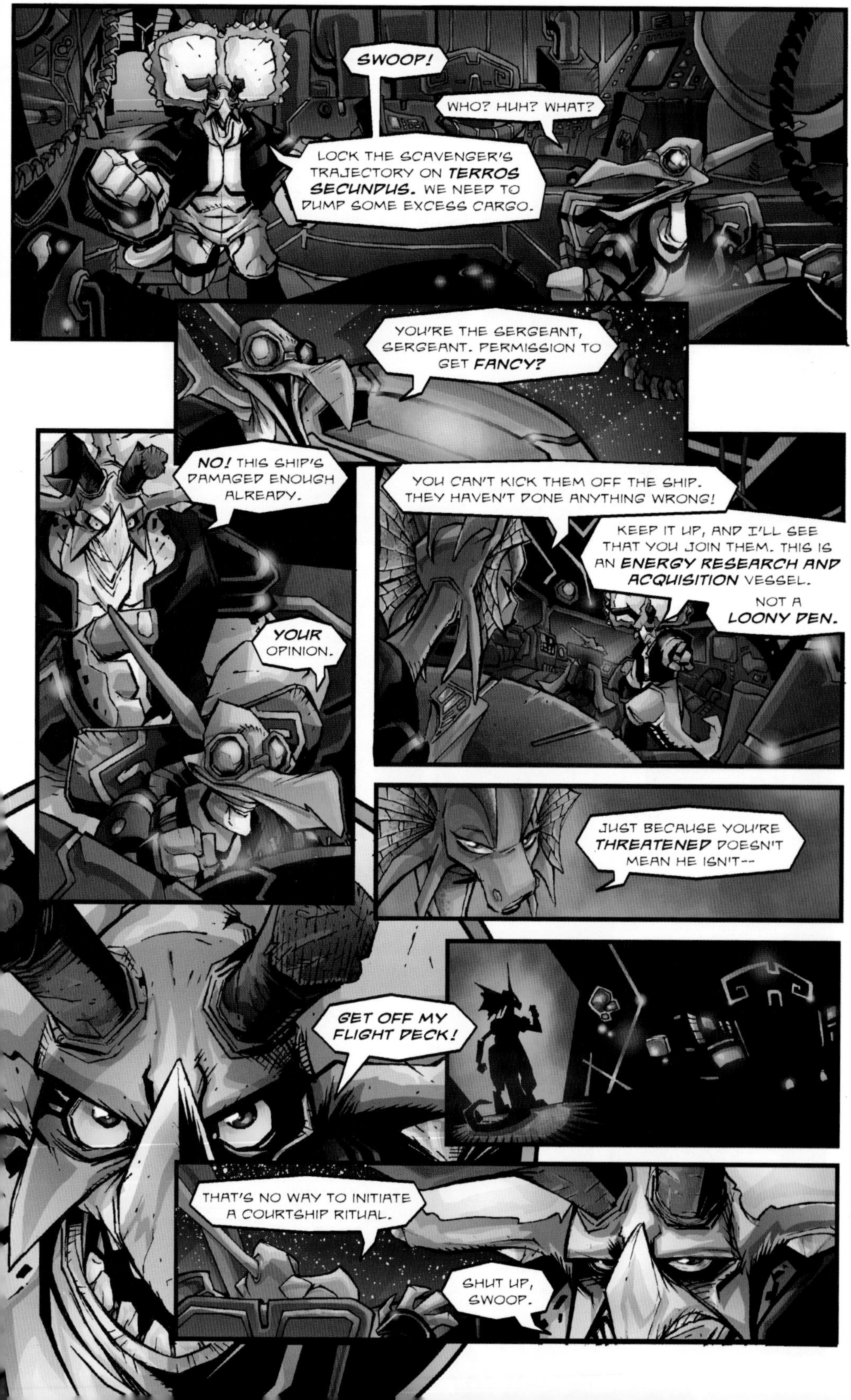
SWOOP!
WHO? HUH? WHAT?
LOCK THE SCAVENGER'S TRAJECTORY ON TERROS SECUNDUS. WE NEED TO DUMP SOME EXCESS CARGO.
YOU'RE THE SERGEANT, SERGEANT. PERMISSION TO GET FANCY?
NO! THIS SHIP'S DAMAGED ENOUGH ALREADY.
YOUR OPINION.
YOU CAN'T KICK THEM OFF THE SHIP. THEY HAVEN'T DONE ANYTHING WRONG!
KEEP IT UP, AND I'LL SEE THAT YOU JOIN THEM. THIS IS AN ENERGY RESEARCH AND ACQUISITION VESSEL.
NOT A LOONY DEN.
JUST BECAUSE YOU'RE THREATENED DOESN'T MEAN HE ISN'T--
GET OFF MY FLIGHT DECK!
THAT'S NO WAY TO INITIATE A COURTSHIP RITUAL.
SHUT UP, SWOOP.

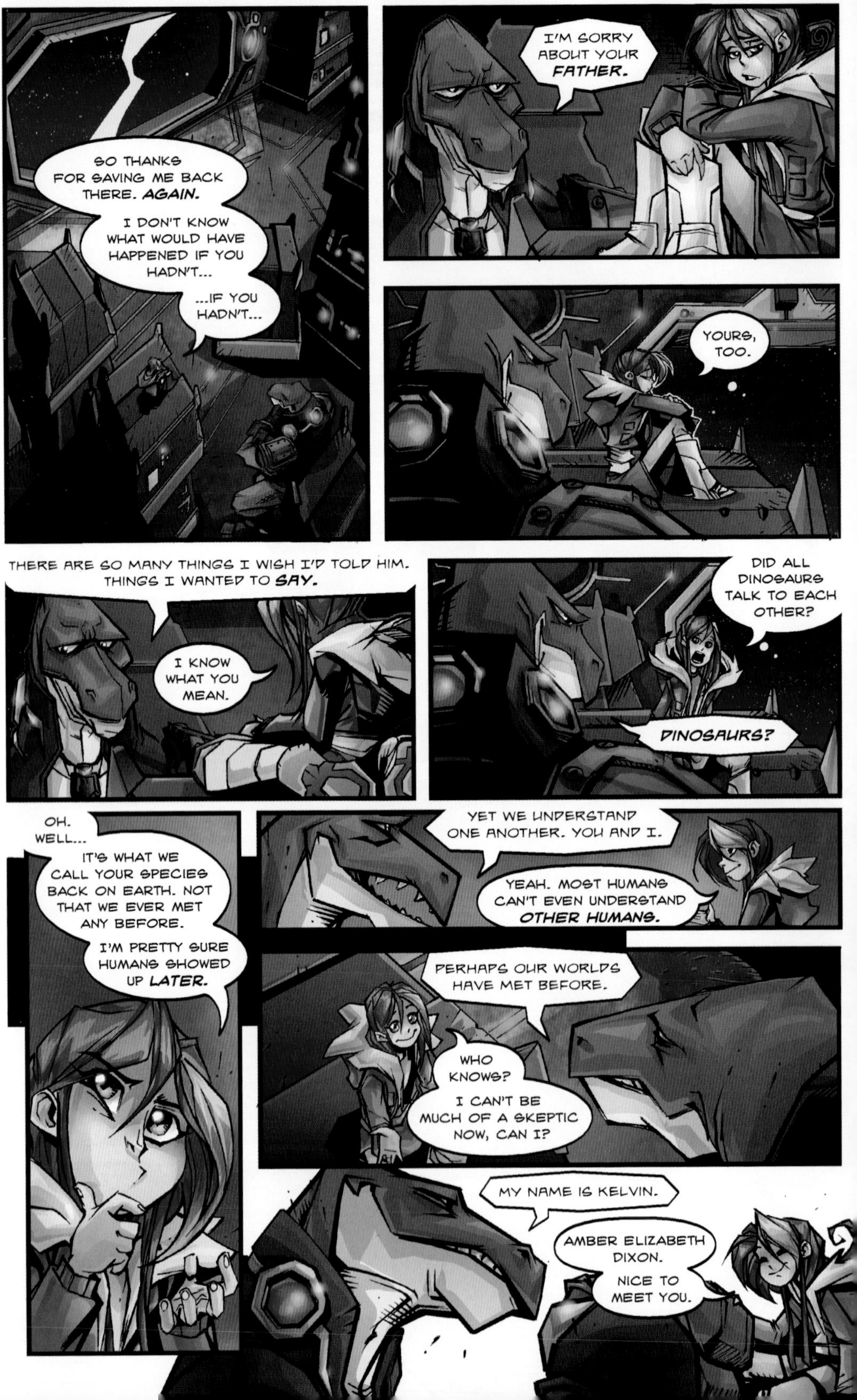
SO THANKS FOR SAVING ME BACK THERE. AGAIN.
I DON'T KNOW WHAT WOULD HAVE HAPPENED IF YOU HADN'T...
...IF YOU HADN'T...
I'M SORRY ABOUT YOUR FATHER.
YOURS, TOO.
THERE ARE SO MANY THINGS I WISH I'D TOLD HIM. THINGS I WANTED TO SAY.
I KNOW WHAT YOU MEAN.
DID ALL DINOSAURS TALK TO EACH OTHER?
DINOSAURS?
OH. WELL...
IT'S WHAT WE CALL YOUR SPECIES BACK ON EARTH. NOT THAT WE EVER MET ANY BEFORE.
I'M PRETTY SURE HUMANS SHOWED UP LATER.
YET WE UNDERSTAND ONE ANOTHER. YOU AND I.
YEAH. MOST HUMANS CAN'T EVEN UNDERSTAND OTHER HUMANS.
PERHAPS OUR WORLDS HAVE MET BEFORE.
WHO KNOWS?
I CAN'T BE MUCH OF A SKEPTIC NOW, CAN I?
MY NAME IS KELVIN.
AMBER ELIZABETH DIXON.
NICE TO MEET YOU.

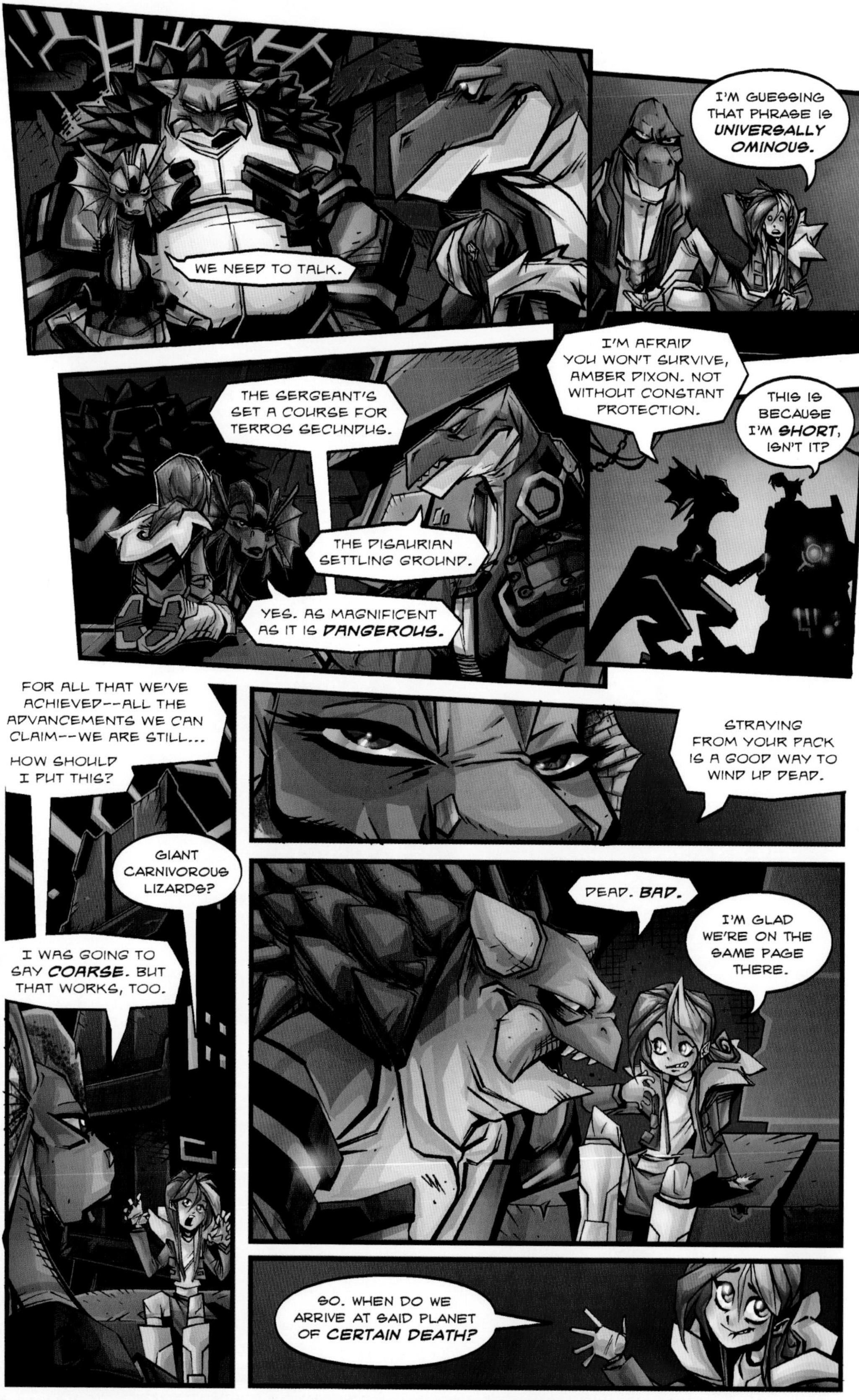

WE NEED TO TALK.
I'M GUESSING THAT PHRASE IS UNIVERSALLY OMINOUS.
THE SERGEANT'S SET A COURSE FOR TERROS SECUNDUS.
THE DISAURIAN SETTLING GROUND.
YES. AS MAGNIFICENT AS IT IS DANGEROUS.
I'M AFRAID YOU WON'T SURVIVE, AMBER DIXON. NOT WITHOUT CONSTANT PROTECTION.
THIS IS BECAUSE I'M SHORT, ISN'T IT?
FOR ALL THAT WE'VE ACHIEVED--ALL THE ADVANCEMENTS WE CAN CLAIM--WE ARE STILL...
HOW SHOULD I PUT THIS?
GIANT CARNIVOROUS LIZARDS?
I WAS GOING TO SAY COARSE. BUT THAT WORKS, TOO.
STRAYING FROM YOUR PACK IS A GOOD WAY TO WIND UP DEAD.
DEAD. BAD.
I'M GLAD WE'RE ON THE SAME PAGE THERE.
SO. WHEN DO WE ARRIVE AT SAID PLANET OF CERTAIN DEATH?

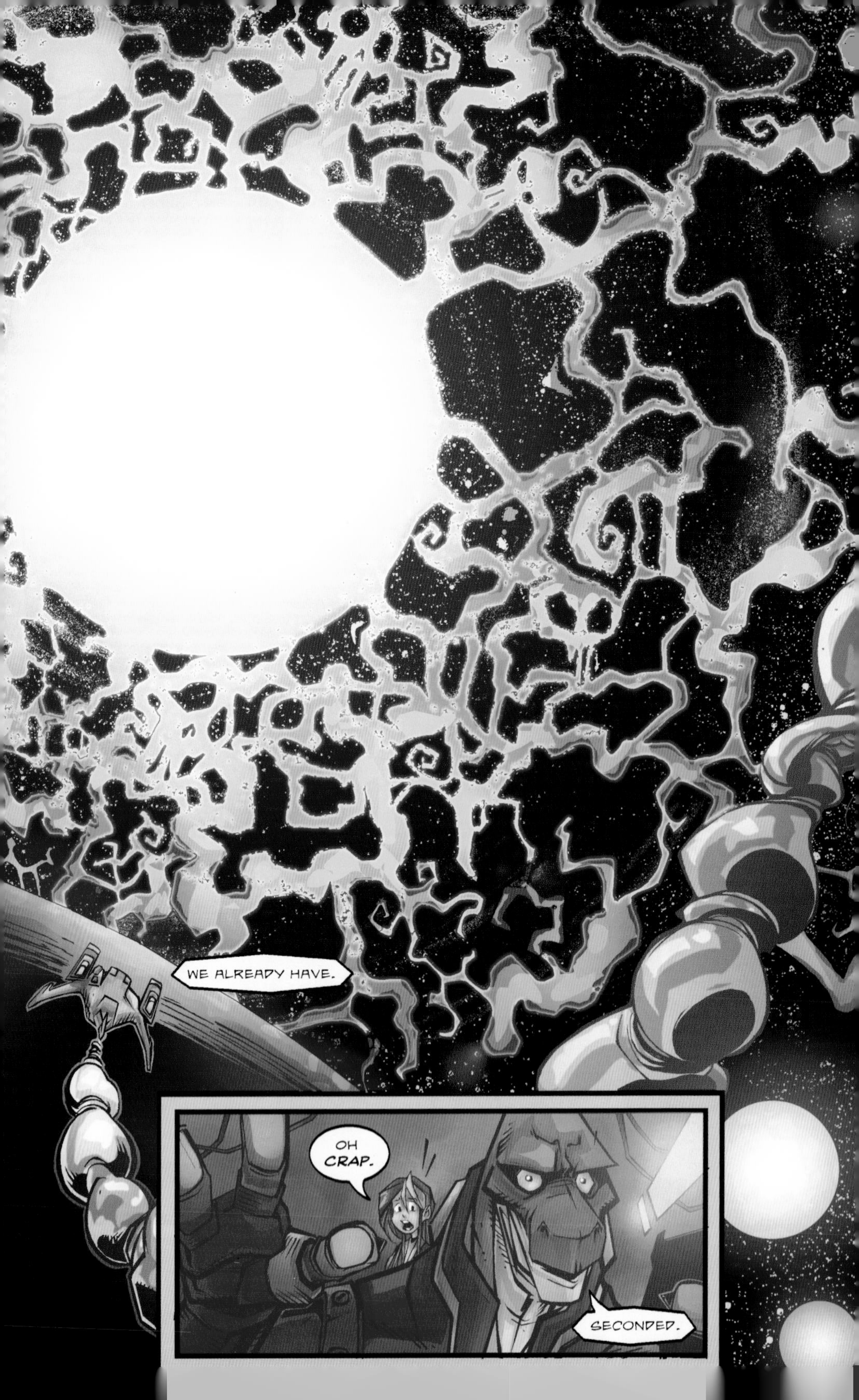
WE ALREADY HAVE.
OH CRAP.
SECONDED.

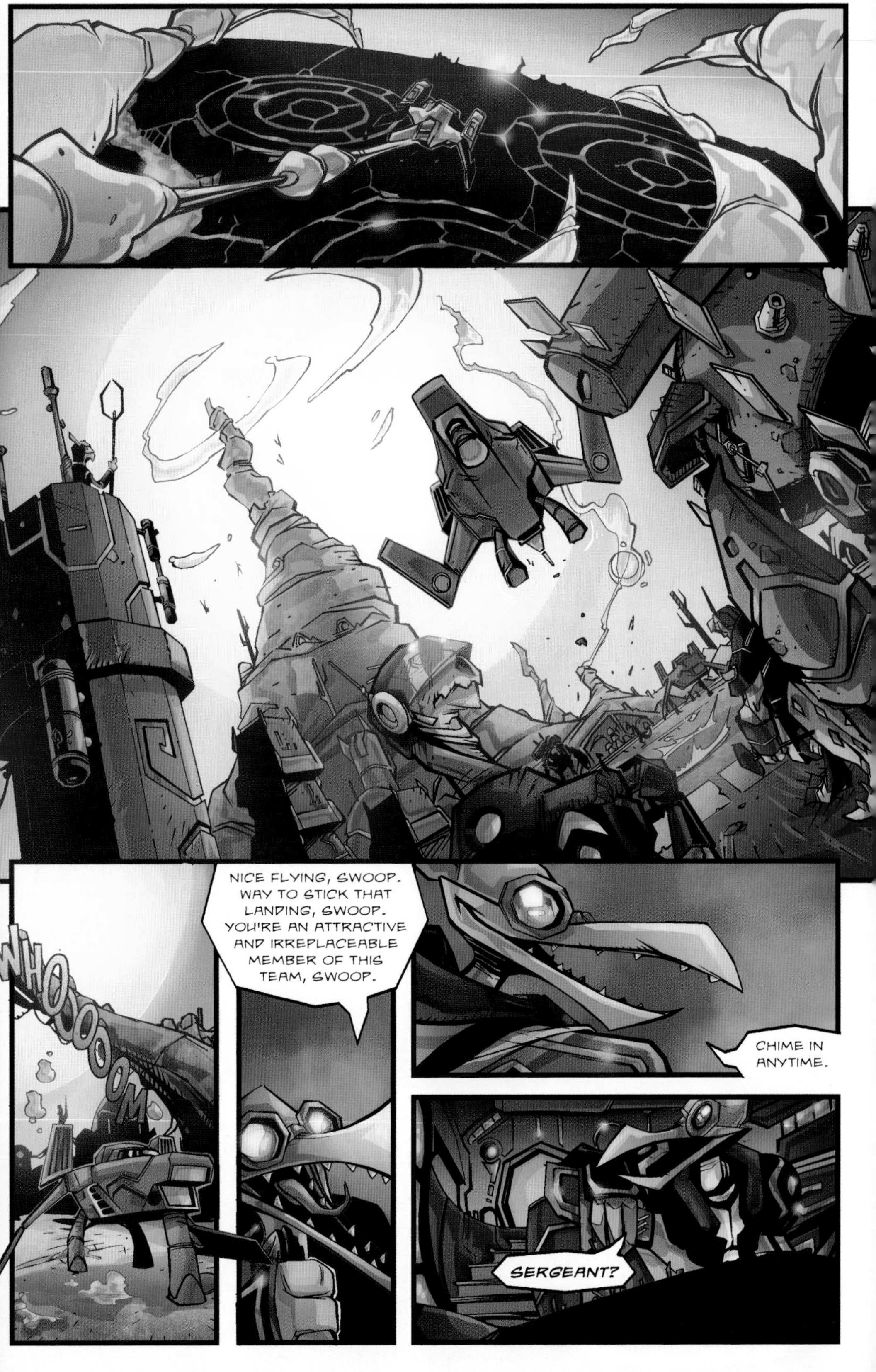
WHOOOOOOM
NICE FLYING, SWOOP. WAY TO STICK THAT LANDING, SWOOP. YOU'RE AN ATTRACTIVE AND IRREPLACEABLE MEMBER OF THIS TEAM, SWOOP.
CHIME IN ANYTIME.
SERGEANT?

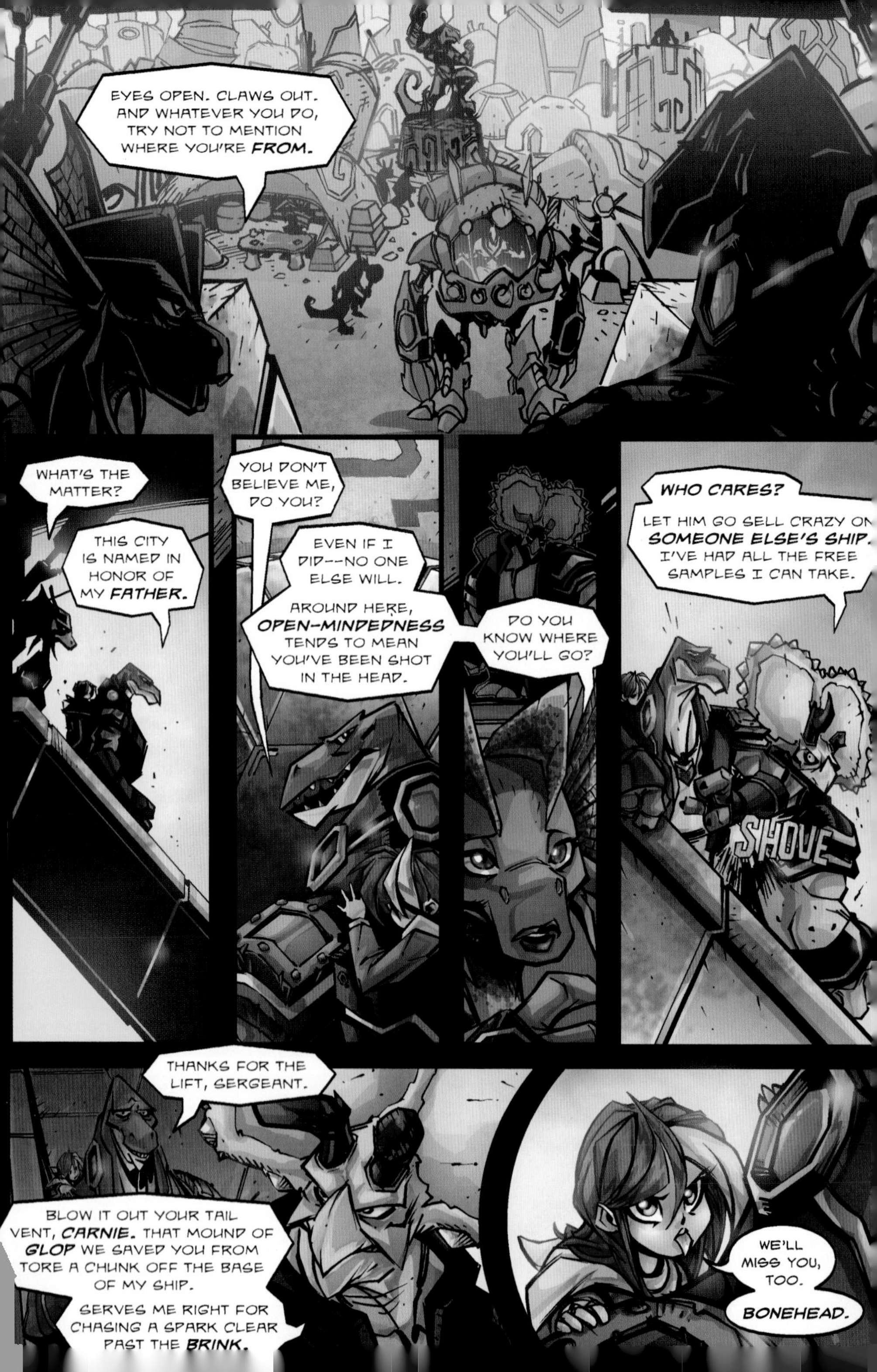
EYES OPEN. CLAWS OUT. AND WHATEVER YOU DO, TRY NOT TO MENTION WHERE YOU'RE FROM.
WHAT'S THE MATTER?
THIS CITY IS NAMED IN HONOR OF MY FATHER.
YOU DON'T BELIEVE ME, DO YOU?
EVEN IF I DID--NO ONE ELSE WILL.
AROUND HERE, OPEN-MINDEDNESS TENDS TO MEAN YOU'VE BEEN SHOT IN THE HEAD.
DO YOU KNOW WHERE YOU'LL GO?
WHO CARES?
LET HIM GO SELL CRAZY ON SOMEONE ELSE'S SHIP. I'VE HAD ALL THE FREE SAMPLES I CAN TAKE.
SHOVE
THANKS FOR THE LIFT, SERGEANT.
BLOW IT OUT YOUR TAIL VENT, CARNIE. THAT MOUND OF GLOP WE SAVED YOU FROM TORE A CHUNK OFF THE BASE OF MY SHIP.
SERVES ME RIGHT FOR CHASING A SPARK CLEAR PAST THE BRINK.
WE'LL MISS YOU, TOO.
BONEHEAD.

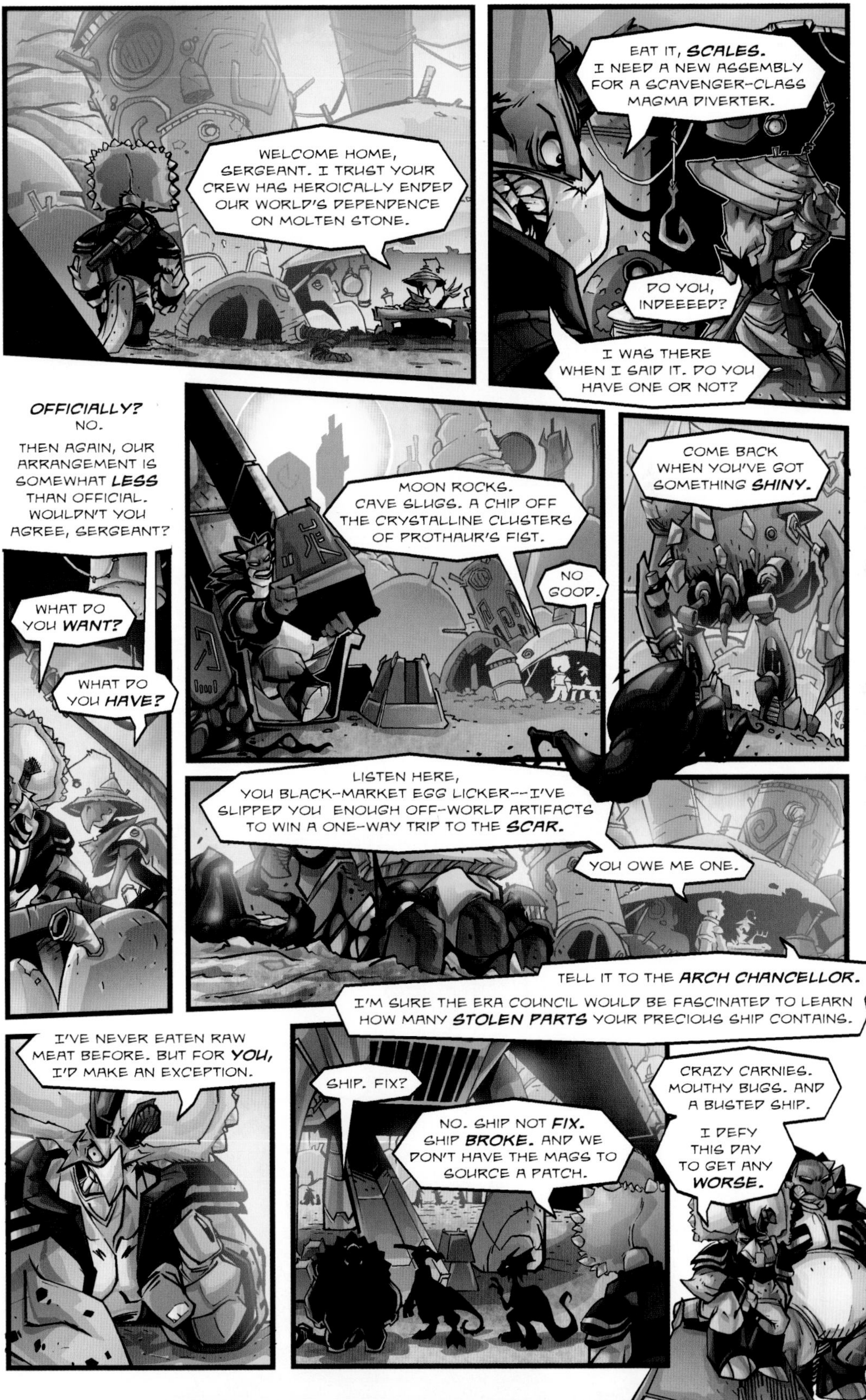
WELCOME HOME, SERGEANT. I TRUST YOUR CREW HAS HEROICALLY ENDED OUR WORLD'S DEPENDENCE ON MOLTEN STONE.
EAT IT, **SCALES.** I NEED A NEW ASSEMBLY FOR A SCAVENGER-CLASS MAGMA DIVERTER.
DO YOU, INDEEEEED?
I WAS THERE WHEN I SAID IT. DO YOU HAVE ONE OR NOT?
OFFICIALLY? NO.
THEN AGAIN, OUR ARRANGEMENT IS SOMEWHAT ***LESS*** THAN OFFICIAL. WOULDN'T YOU AGREE, SERGEANT?
WHAT DO YOU ***WANT?***
WHAT DO YOU ***HAVE?***
MOON ROCKS. CAVE SLUGS. A CHIP OFF THE CRYSTALLINE CLUSTERS OF PROTHAUR'S FIST.
NO GOOD.
COME BACK WHEN YOU'VE GOT SOMETHING ***SHINY.***
LISTEN HERE, YOU BLACK-MARKET EGG LICKER--I'VE SLIPPED YOU ENOUGH OFF-WORLD ARTIFACTS TO WIN A ONE-WAY TRIP TO THE ***SCAR.***
YOU OWE ME ONE.
TELL IT TO THE ***ARCH CHANCELLOR.***
I'M SURE THE ERA COUNCIL WOULD BE FASCINATED TO LEARN HOW MANY ***STOLEN PARTS*** YOUR PRECIOUS SHIP CONTAINS.
I'VE NEVER EATEN RAW MEAT BEFORE. BUT FOR ***YOU,*** I'D MAKE AN EXCEPTION.
SHIP. FIX?
NO. SHIP NOT ***FIX.*** SHIP ***BROKE.*** AND WE DON'T HAVE THE MAGS TO SOURCE A PATCH.
CRAZY CARNIES. MOUTHY BUGS. AND A BUSTED SHIP.
I DEFY THIS DAY TO GET ANY ***WORSE.***

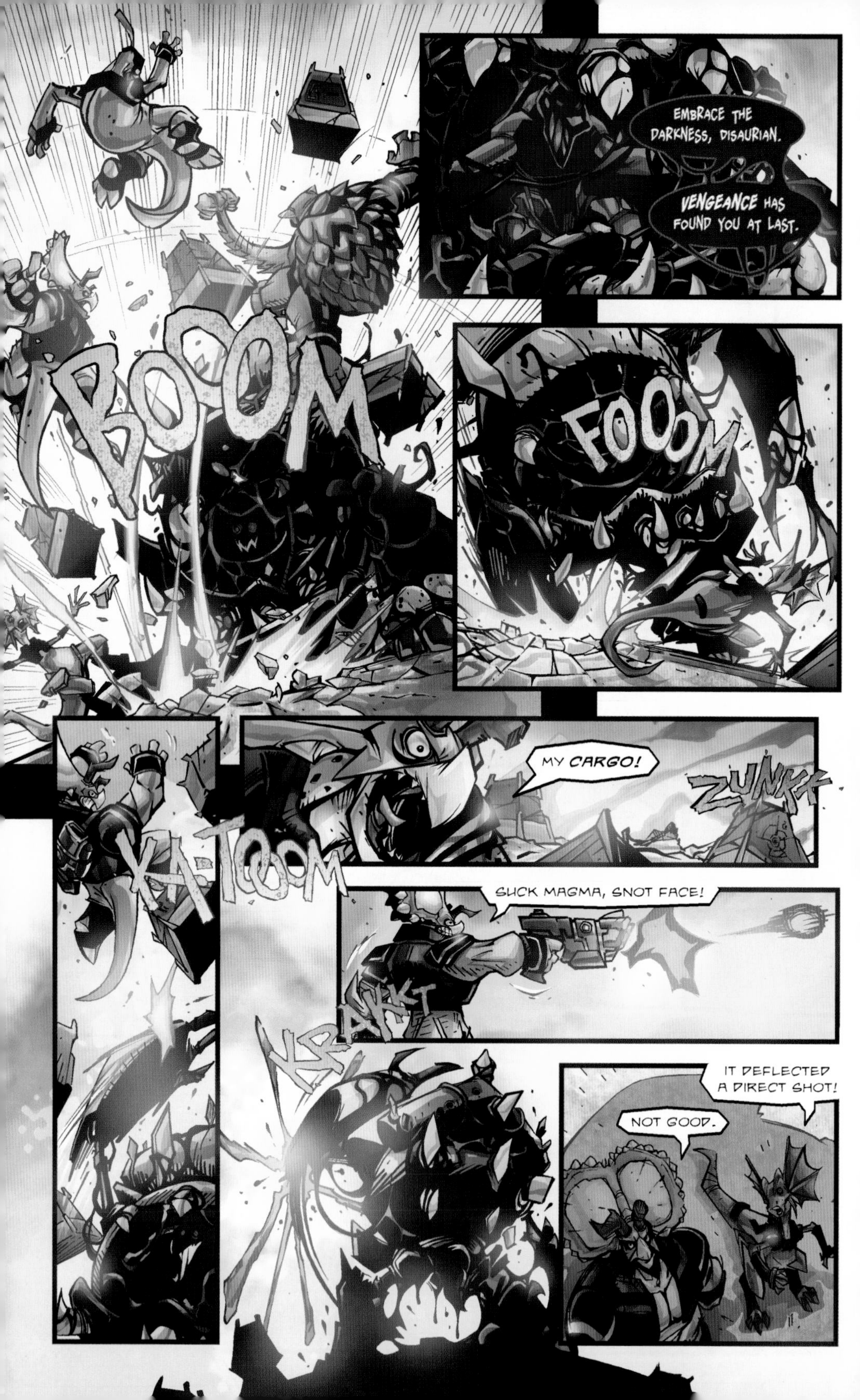
EMBRACE THE DARKNESS, DISAURIAN.
VENGEANCE HAS FOUND YOU AT LAST.
BOOOM
FOOOM
MY CARGO!
ZUNKK
XA-TOOOM
SUCK MAGMA, SNOT FACE!
KRAKT
IT DEFLECTED A DIRECT SHOT!
NOT GOOD.

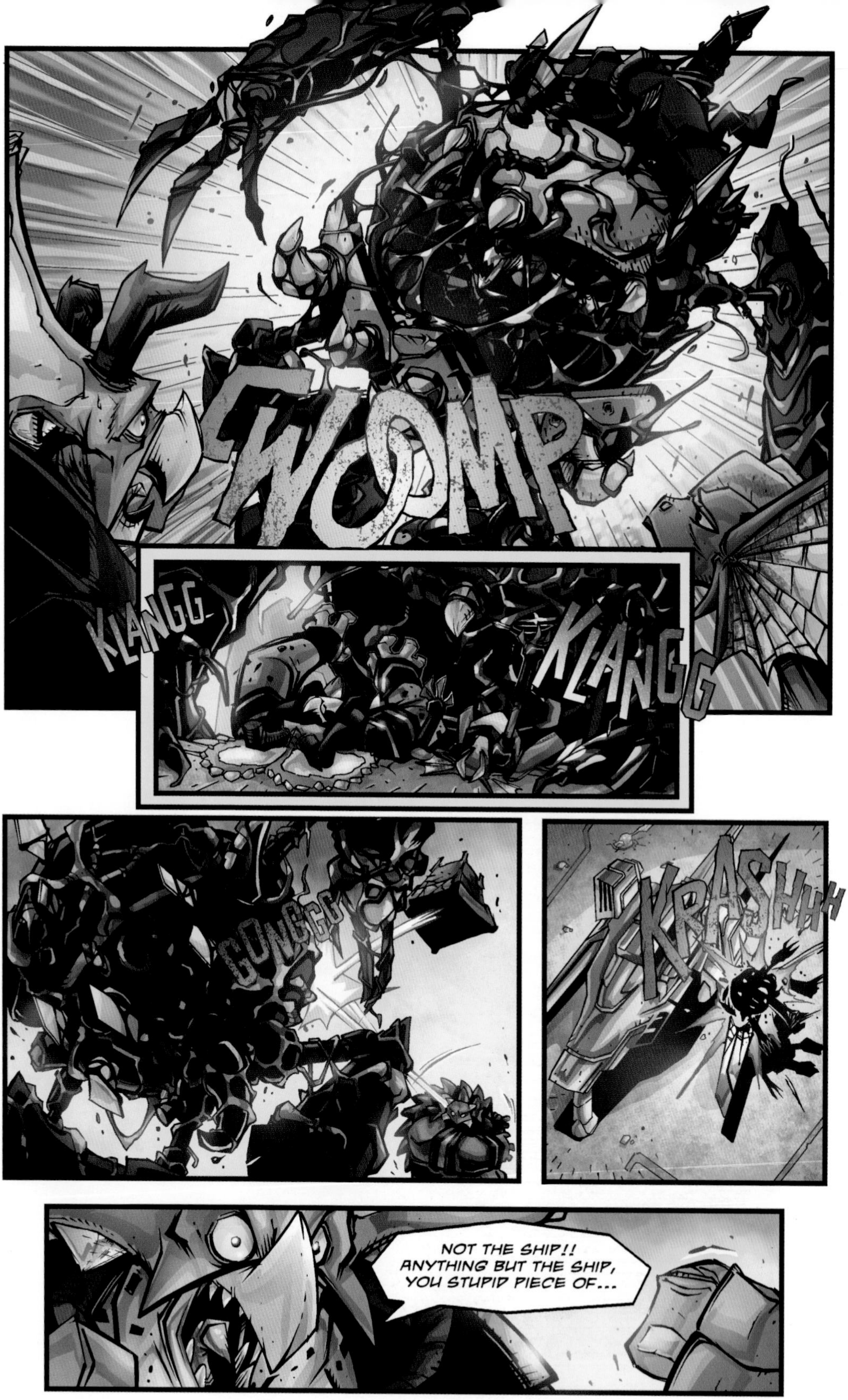
WOMP
KLANGG
KLANGG
GONGGG
KRASHHH
NOT THE SHIP!! ANYTHING BUT THE SHIP, YOU STUPID PIECE OF...

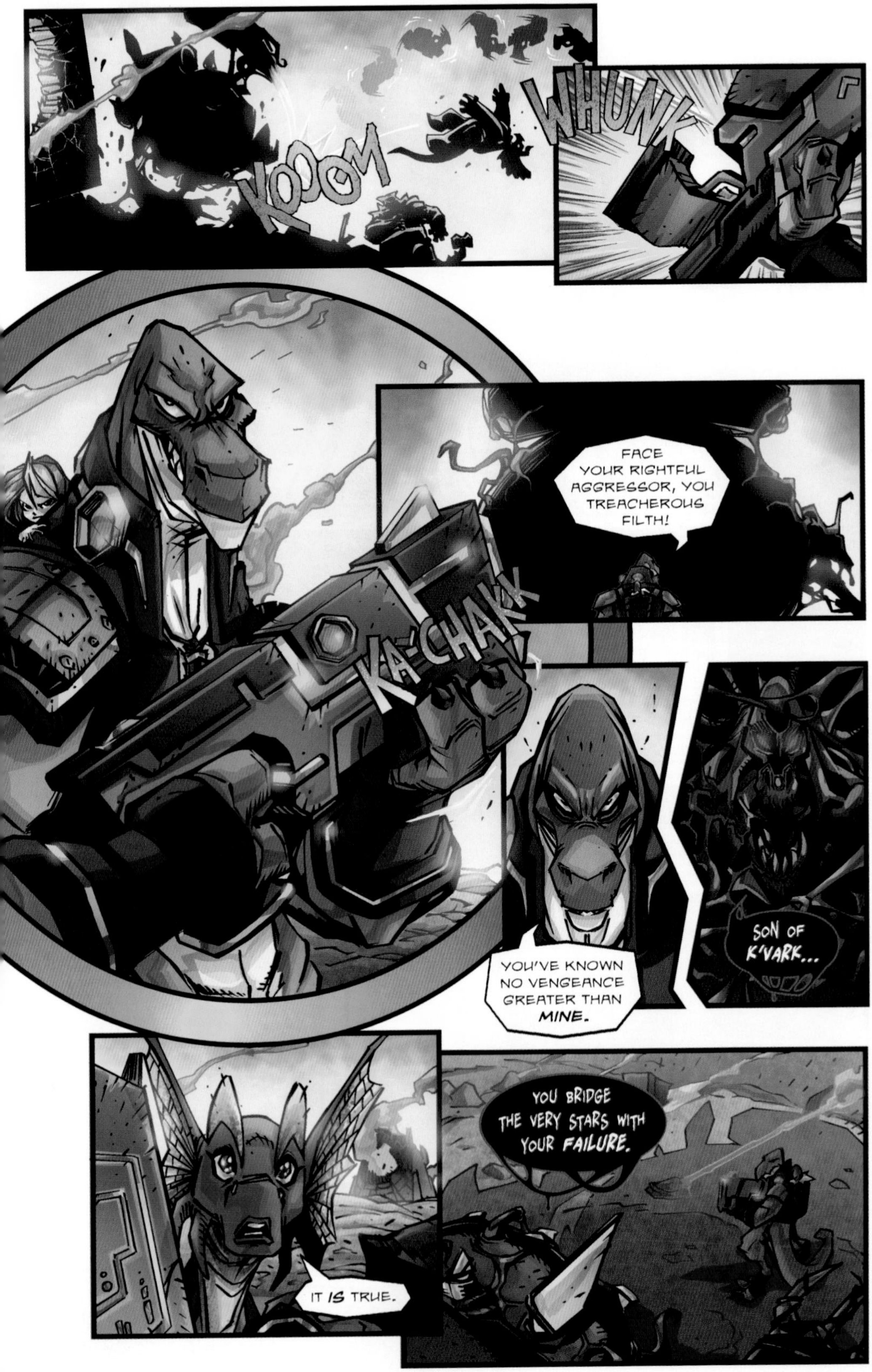
KOOOM
WHUNK
KA-CHAKK
FACE YOUR RIGHTFUL AGGRESSOR, YOU TREACHEROUS FILTH!
YOU'VE KNOWN NO VENGEANCE GREATER THAN MINE.
SON OF K'VARK...
YOU BRIDGE THE VERY STARS WITH YOUR FAILURE.
IT IS TRUE.

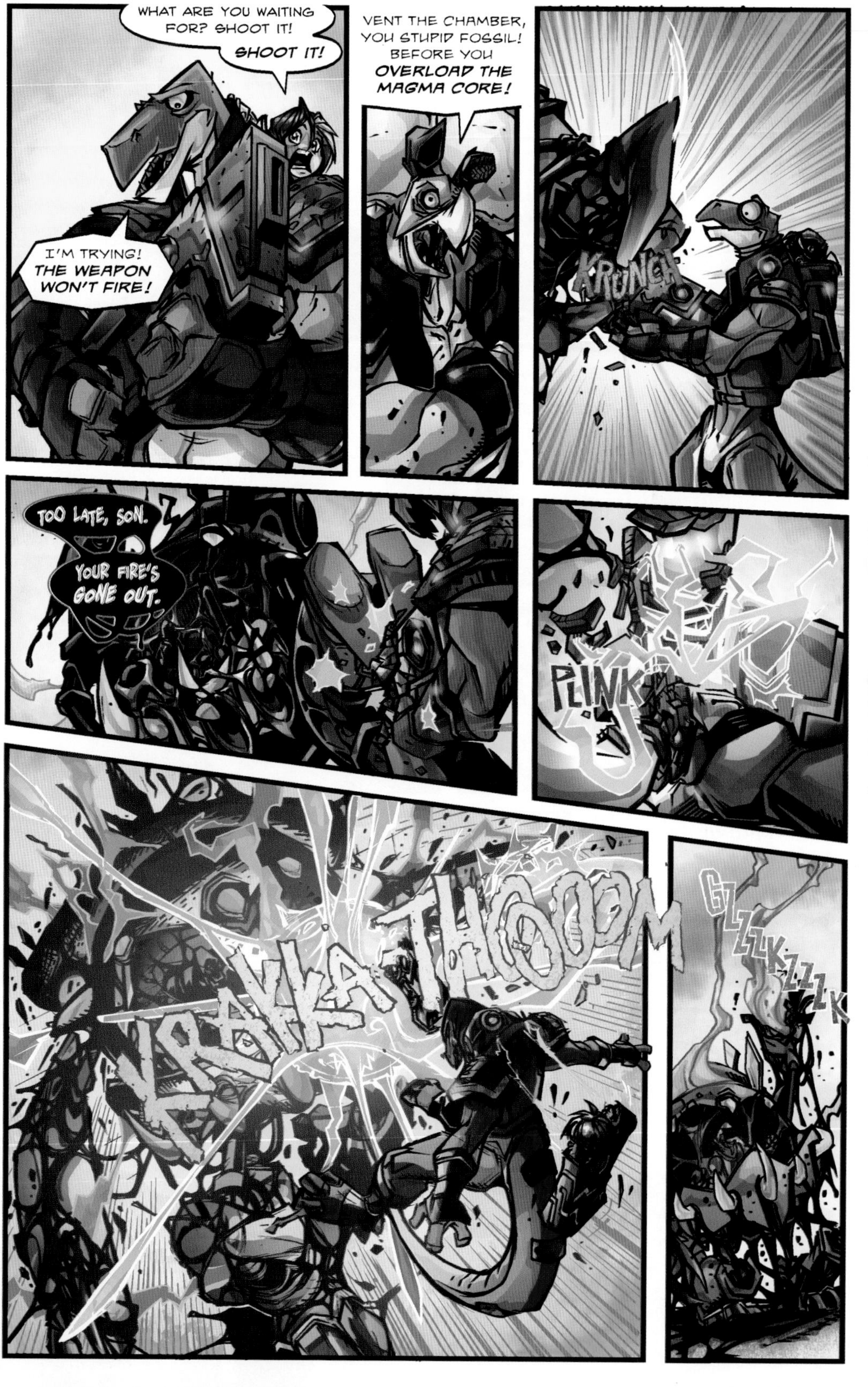
WHAT ARE YOU WAITING FOR? SHOOT IT!
SHOOT IT!
I'M TRYING! THE WEAPON WON'T FIRE!
VENT THE CHAMBER, YOU STUPID FOSSIL! BEFORE YOU OVERLOAD THE MAGMA CORE!
KRUNCH
TOO LATE, SON.
YOUR FIRE'S GONE OUT.
PLINK
KRAKKA-THOOOOM
GZZZZKZZZZK

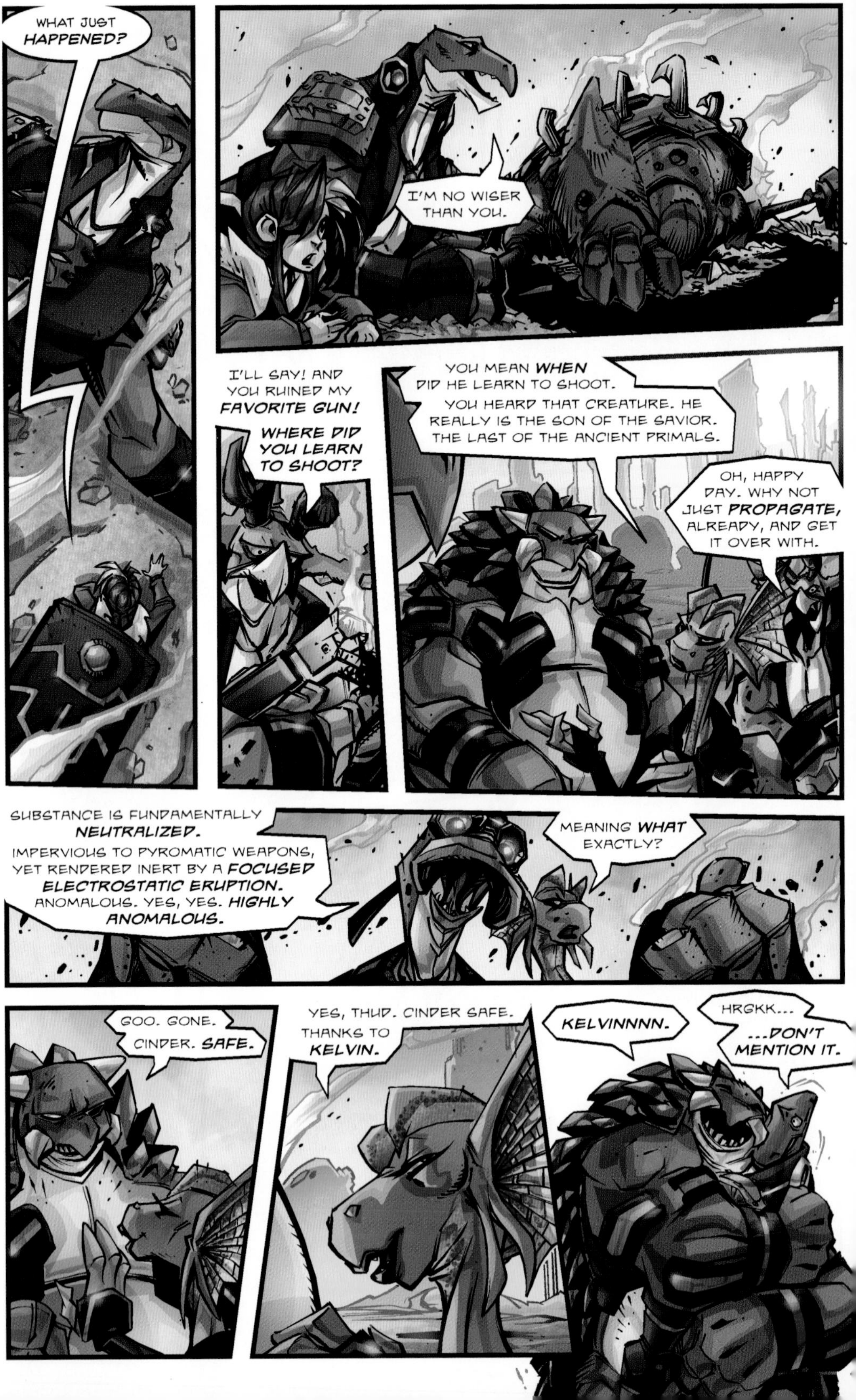
WHAT JUST HAPPENED?
I'M NO WISER THAN YOU.
I'LL SAY! AND YOU RUINED MY FAVORITE GUN!
WHERE DID YOU LEARN TO SHOOT?
YOU MEAN WHEN DID HE LEARN TO SHOOT.
YOU HEARD THAT CREATURE. HE REALLY IS THE SON OF THE SAVIOR. THE LAST OF THE ANCIENT PRIMALS.
OH, HAPPY DAY. WHY NOT JUST PROPAGATE, ALREADY, AND GET IT OVER WITH.
SUBSTANCE IS FUNDAMENTALLY NEUTRALIZED.
IMPERVIOUS TO PYROMATIC WEAPONS, YET RENDERED INERT BY A FOCUSED ELECTROSTATIC ERUPTION.
ANOMALOUS. YES, YES. HIGHLY ANOMALOUS.
MEANING WHAT EXACTLY?
GOO. GONE. CINDER. SAFE.
YES, THUD. CINDER SAFE.
THANKS TO KELVIN.
KELVINNNN.
HRGKK...
...DON'T MENTION IT.

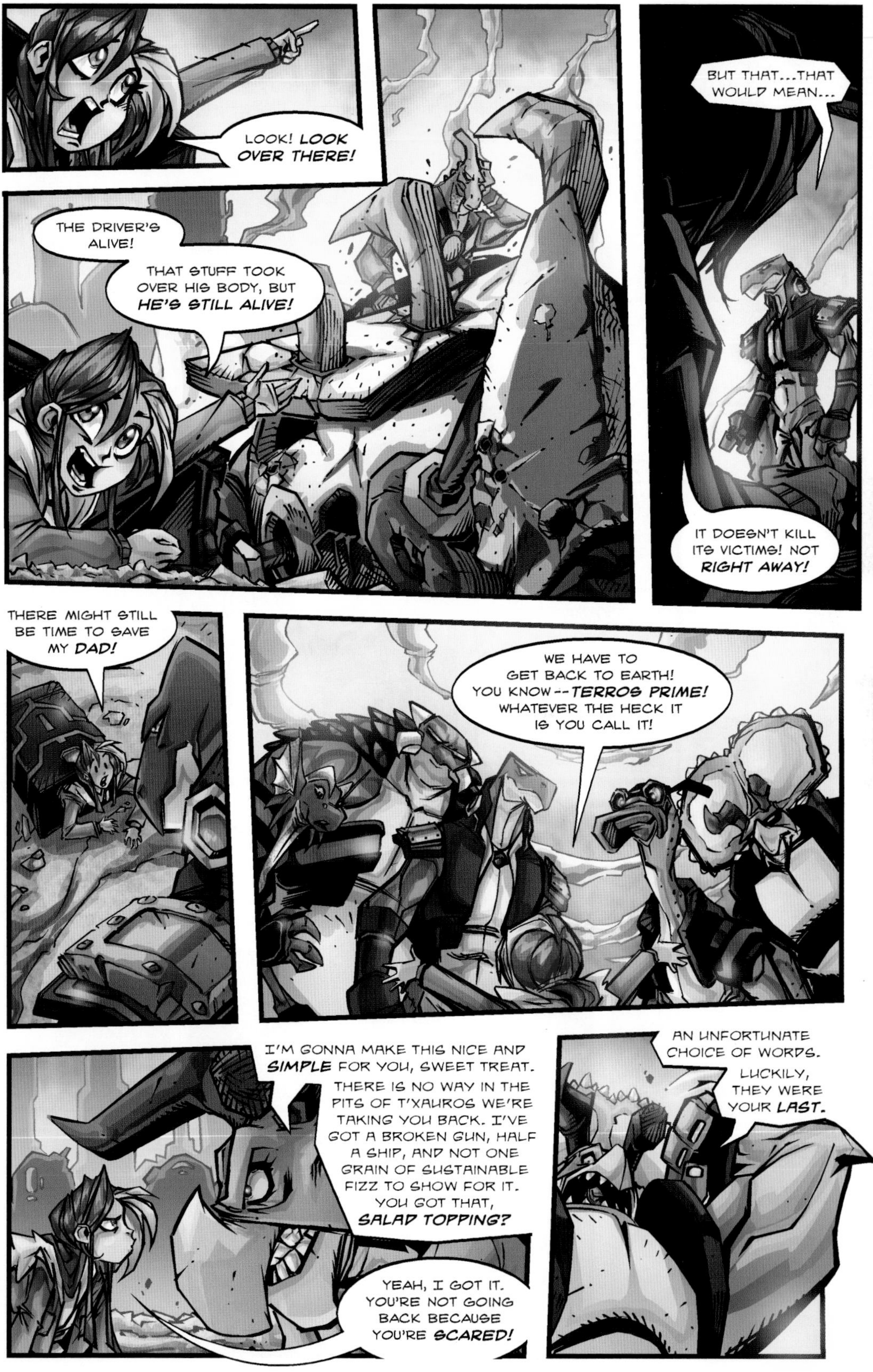
LOOK! **LOOK OVER THERE!**
BUT THAT...THAT WOULD MEAN...
THE DRIVER'S ALIVE!
THAT STUFF TOOK OVER HIS BODY, BUT **HE'S STILL ALIVE!**
IT DOESN'T KILL ITS VICTIMS! NOT **RIGHT AWAY!**
THERE MIGHT STILL BE TIME TO SAVE MY **DAD!**
WE HAVE TO GET BACK TO EARTH! YOU KNOW--**TERROS PRIME!** WHATEVER THE HECK IT IS YOU CALL IT!
I'M GONNA MAKE THIS NICE AND **SIMPLE** FOR YOU, SWEET TREAT.
THERE IS NO WAY IN THE PITS OF T'XAUROS WE'RE TAKING YOU BACK. I'VE GOT A BROKEN GUN, HALF A SHIP, AND NOT ONE GRAIN OF SUSTAINABLE FIZZ TO SHOW FOR IT. YOU GOT THAT, **SALAD TOPPING?**
YEAH, I GOT IT. YOU'RE NOT GOING BACK BECAUSE YOU'RE **SCARED!**
AN UNFORTUNATE CHOICE OF WORDS.
LUCKILY, THEY WERE YOUR **LAST.**

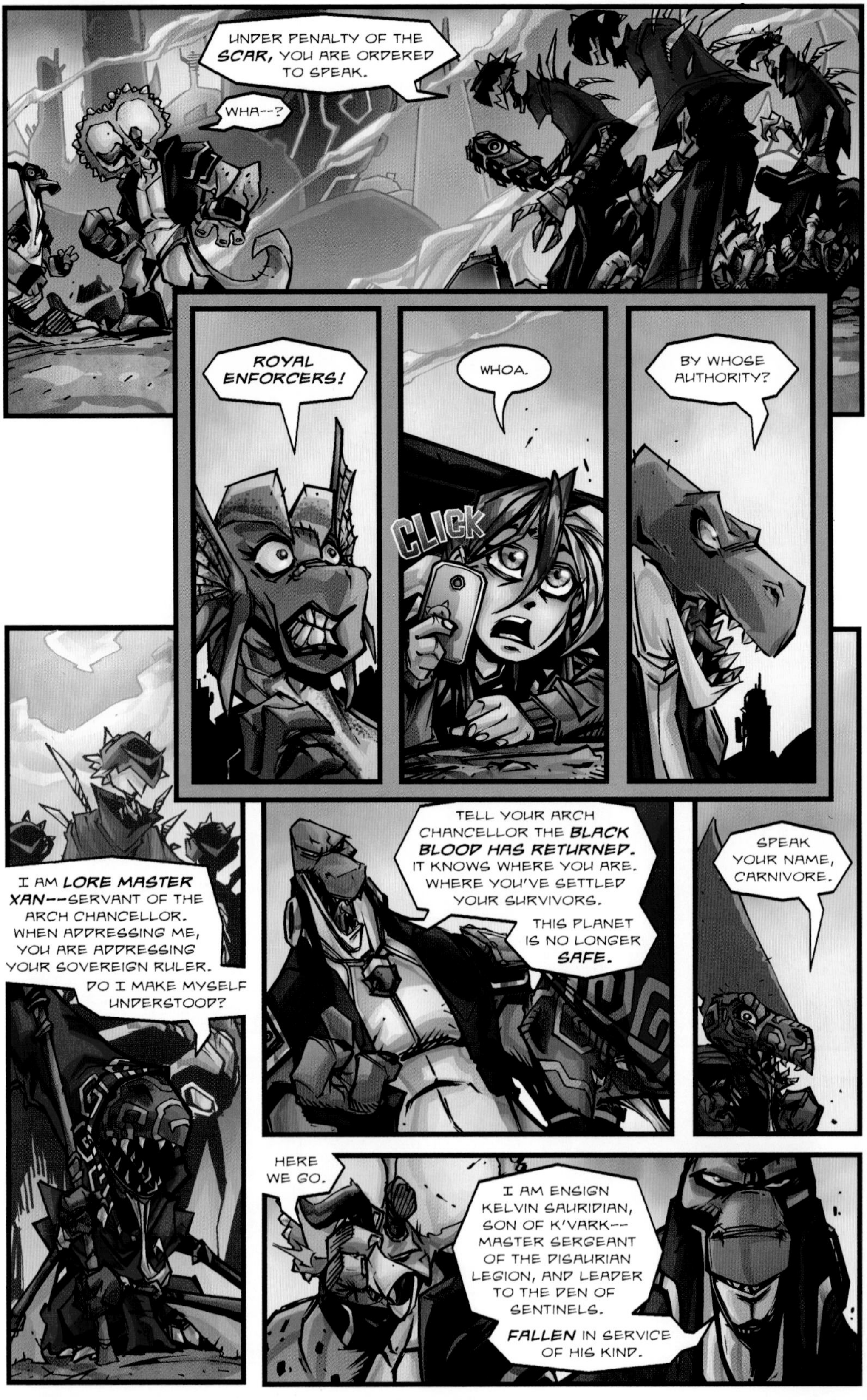
UNDER PENALTY OF THE SCAR, YOU ARE ORDERED TO SPEAK.
WHA--?
ROYAL ENFORCERS!
WHOA.
CLICK
BY WHOSE AUTHORITY?
I AM LORE MASTER XAN--SERVANT OF THE ARCH CHANCELLOR. WHEN ADDRESSING ME, YOU ARE ADDRESSING YOUR SOVEREIGN RULER.
DO I MAKE MYSELF UNDERSTOOD?
TELL YOUR ARCH CHANCELLOR THE BLACK BLOOD HAS RETURNED. IT KNOWS WHERE YOU ARE. WHERE YOU'VE SETTLED YOUR SURVIVORS.
THIS PLANET IS NO LONGER SAFE.
SPEAK YOUR NAME, CARNIVORE.
HERE WE GO.
I AM ENSIGN KELVIN SAURIDIAN, SON OF K'VARK--MASTER SERGEANT OF THE DISAURIAN LEGION, AND LEADER TO THE DEN OF SENTINELS.
FALLEN IN SERVICE OF HIS KIND.

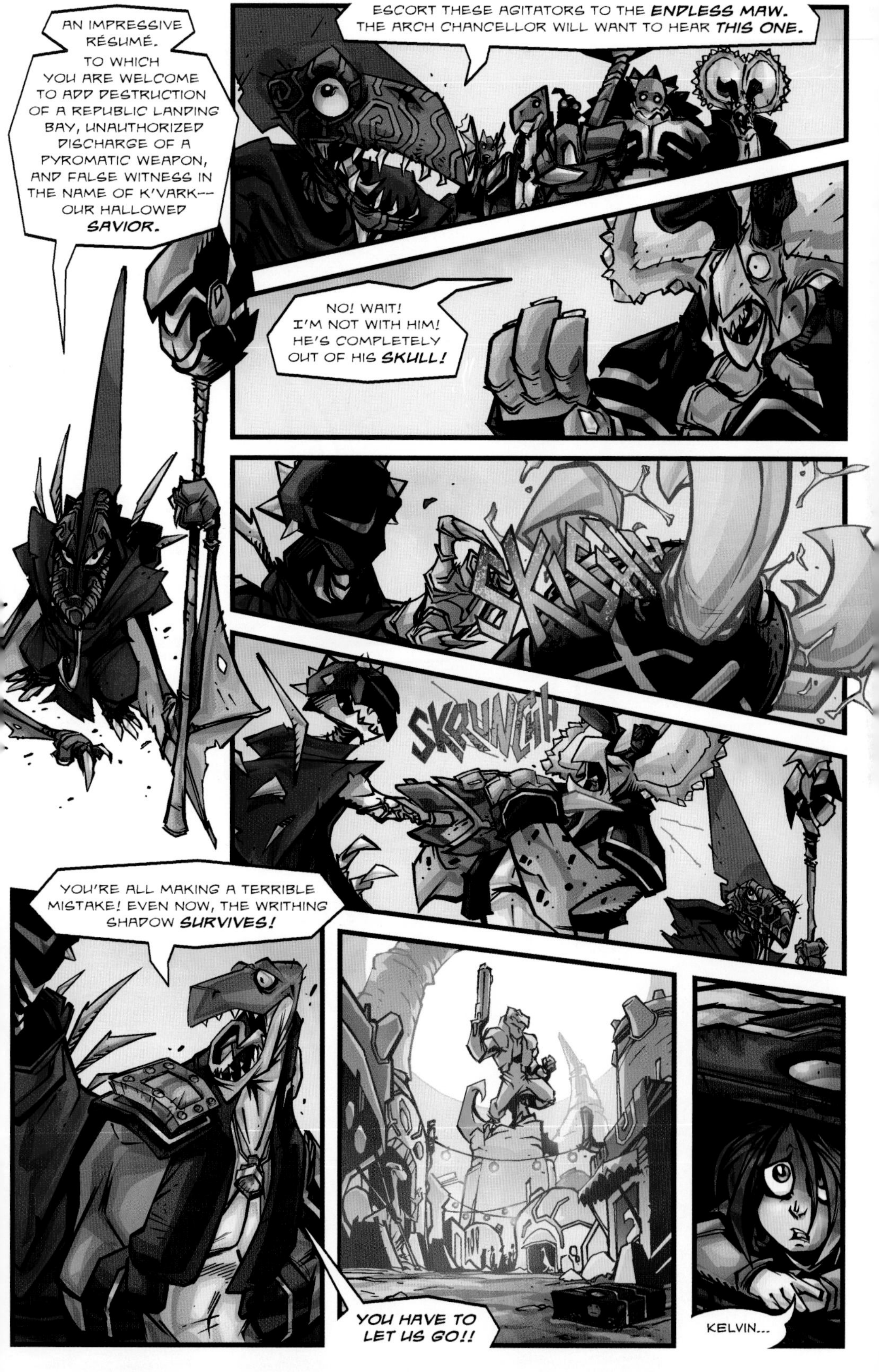

AN IMPRESSIVE RÉSUMÉ.
TO WHICH YOU ARE WELCOME TO ADD DESTRUCTION OF A REPUBLIC LANDING BAY, UNAUTHORIZED DISCHARGE OF A PYROMATIC WEAPON, AND FALSE WITNESS IN THE NAME OF K'VARK-- OUR HALLOWED SAVIOR.
ESCORT THESE AGITATORS TO THE ENDLESS MAW. THE ARCH CHANCELLOR WILL WANT TO HEAR THIS ONE.
NO! WAIT! I'M NOT WITH HIM! HE'S COMPLETELY OUT OF HIS SKULL!
SKRUNCH
YOU'RE ALL MAKING A TERRIBLE MISTAKE! EVEN NOW, THE WRITHING SHADOW SURVIVES!
YOU HAVE TO LET US GO!!
KELVIN...

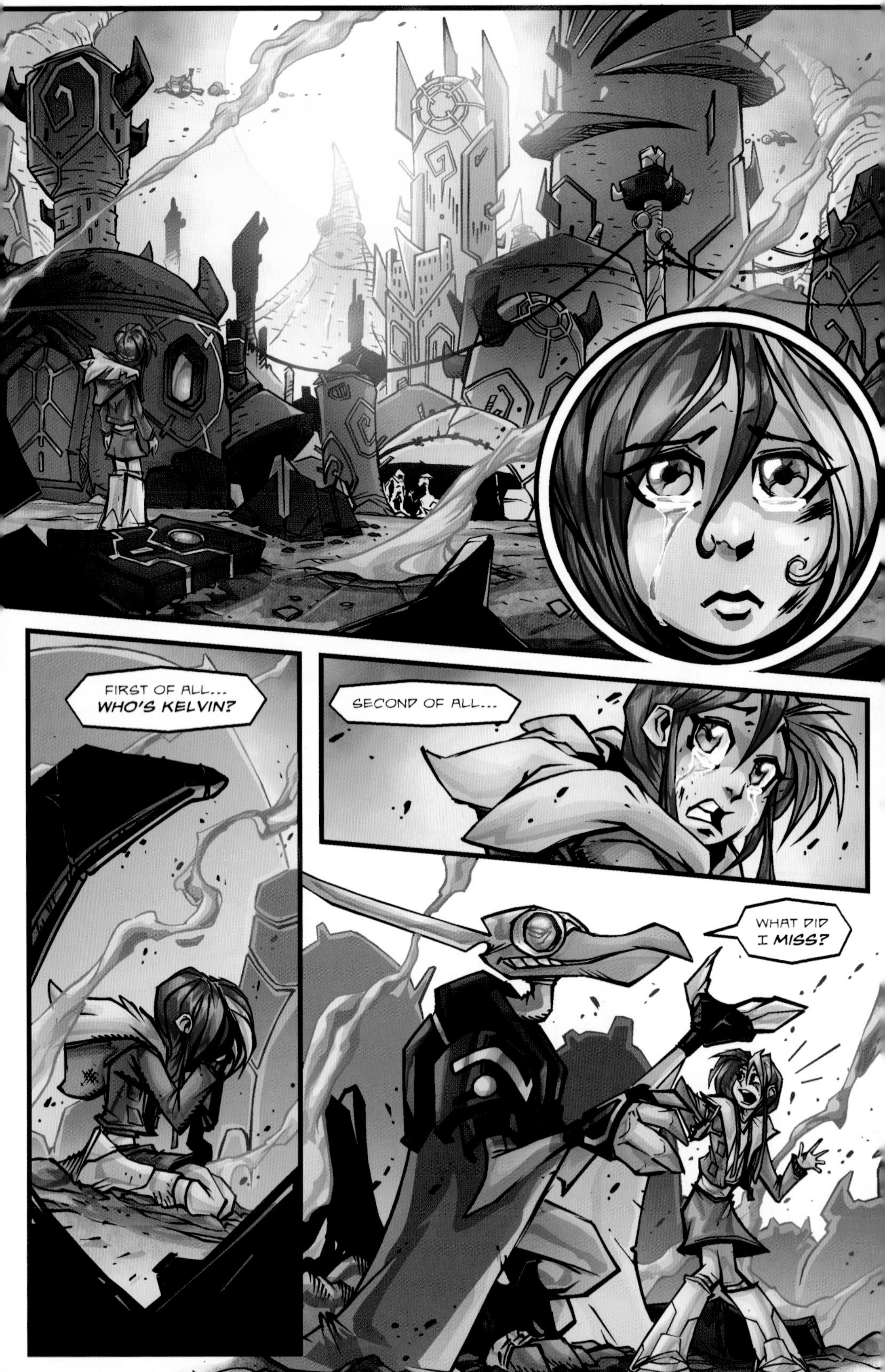
FIRST OF ALL...
WHO'S KELVIN?
SECOND OF ALL...
WHAT DID I MISS?

CHAPTER 3

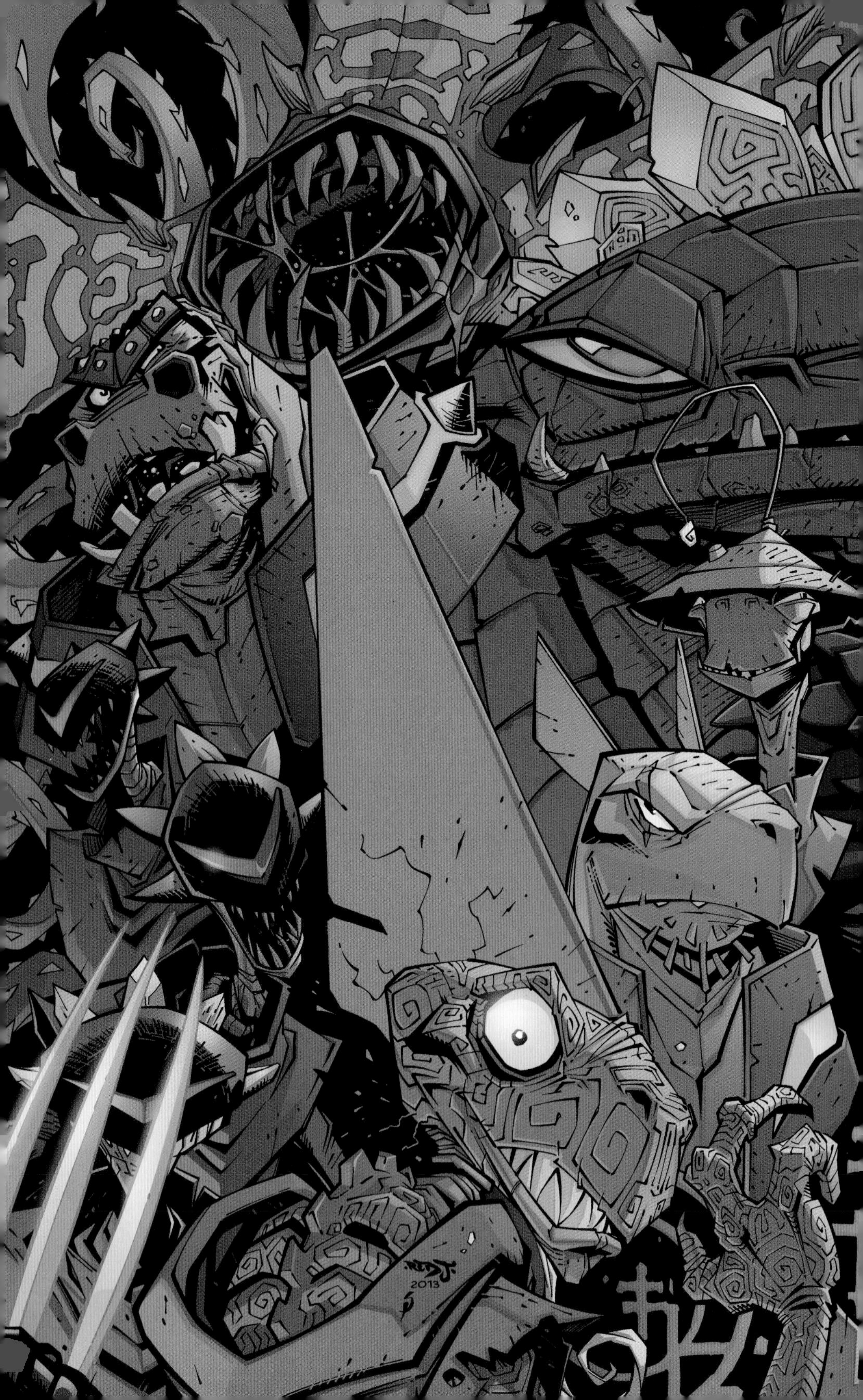
2013

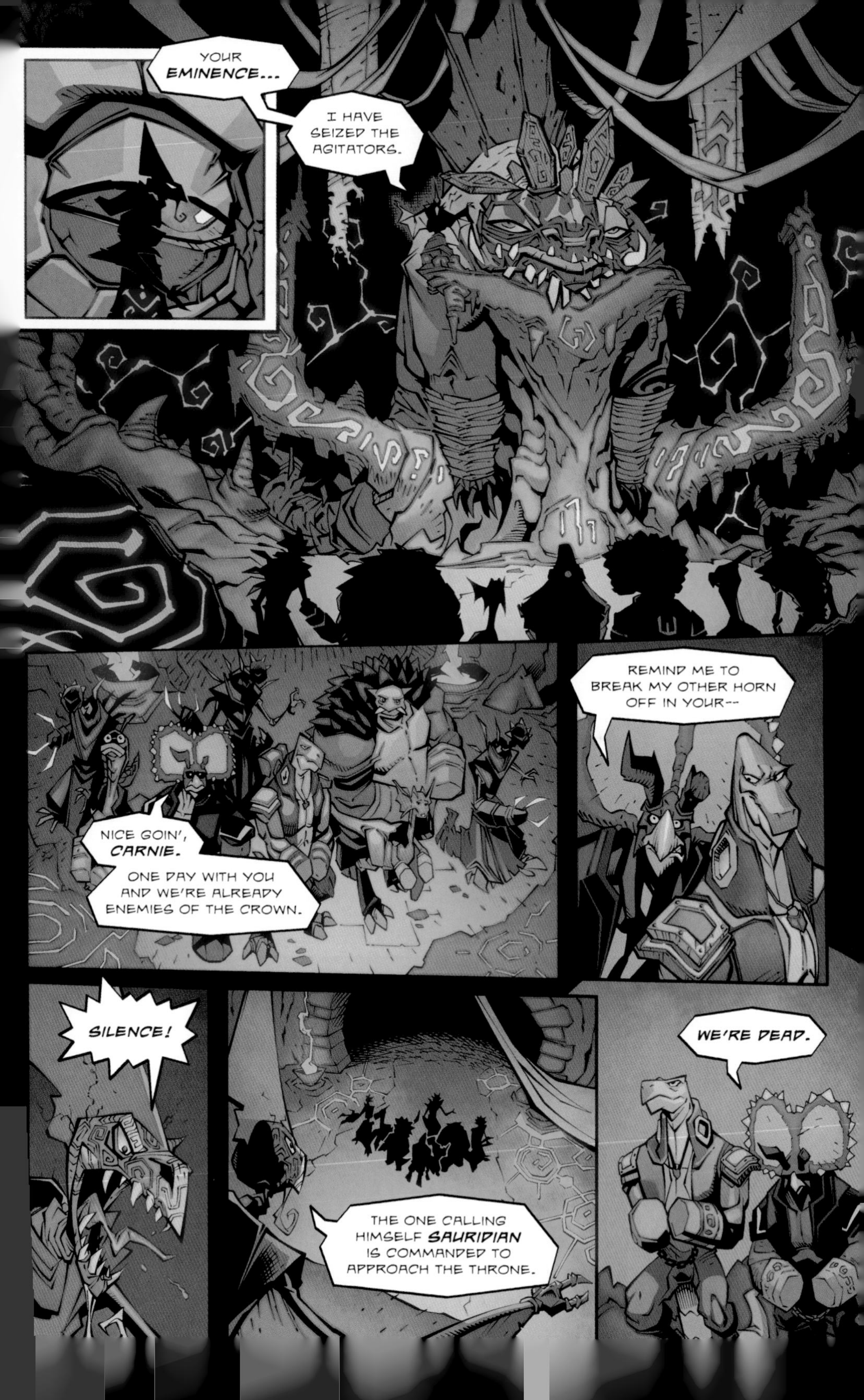
YOUR **EMINENCE...**
I HAVE SEIZED THE AGITATORS.
NICE GOIN', **CARNIE.**
ONE DAY WITH YOU AND WE'RE ALREADY ENEMIES OF THE CROWN.
REMIND ME TO BREAK MY OTHER HORN OFF IN YOUR--
SILENCE!
THE ONE CALLING HIMSELF **SAURIDIAN** IS COMMANDED TO APPROACH THE THRONE.
WE'RE DEAD.

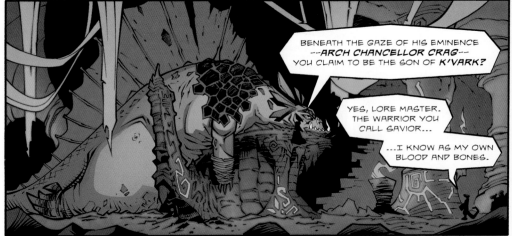

BENEATH THE GAZE OF HIS EMINENCE --ARCH CHANCELLOR CRAG-- YOU CLAIM TO BE THE SON OF K'VARK?

YES, LORE MASTER. THE WARRIOR YOU CALL SAVIOR...

...I KNOW AS MY OWN BLOOD AND BONES.

HE SURRENDERED HIS LIFE TO SAVE ME. TO SAVE ALL OF US.

SURELY, THEN, YOU HAVE SURVIVED FOR OVER SEVEN BILLION PYRONS. A TRUE IMMORTAL AMONG DISAURIAN KIND.

I DO NOT CLAIM THE GIFT OF ENDLESS DAYS.

THEN YOU ARE A LIAR. A SERVANT OF THE WRITHING SHADOW, SENT TO DESTROY US.

DESTROY YOU? I'M TRYING TO WARN YOU!

THE BLACK BLOOD HAS RISEN ONCE AGAIN!

INDEED, IT HAS.

HOW CURIOUS OUR DOOM SHOULD RETURN ONLY NOW. AND ON THE EVE OF YOUR SUDDEN ARRIVAL.

I DIDN'T BRING IT WITH ME!

THEN YOU'VE LED IT HERE. ALL OF YOU!

NO!

ARCH CHANCELLOR, PLEASE! YOUR ADVISOR HAS KNOWINGLY TWISTED THE TRUTH!

FOR WHAT ENDS, I CAN ONLY GUESS!

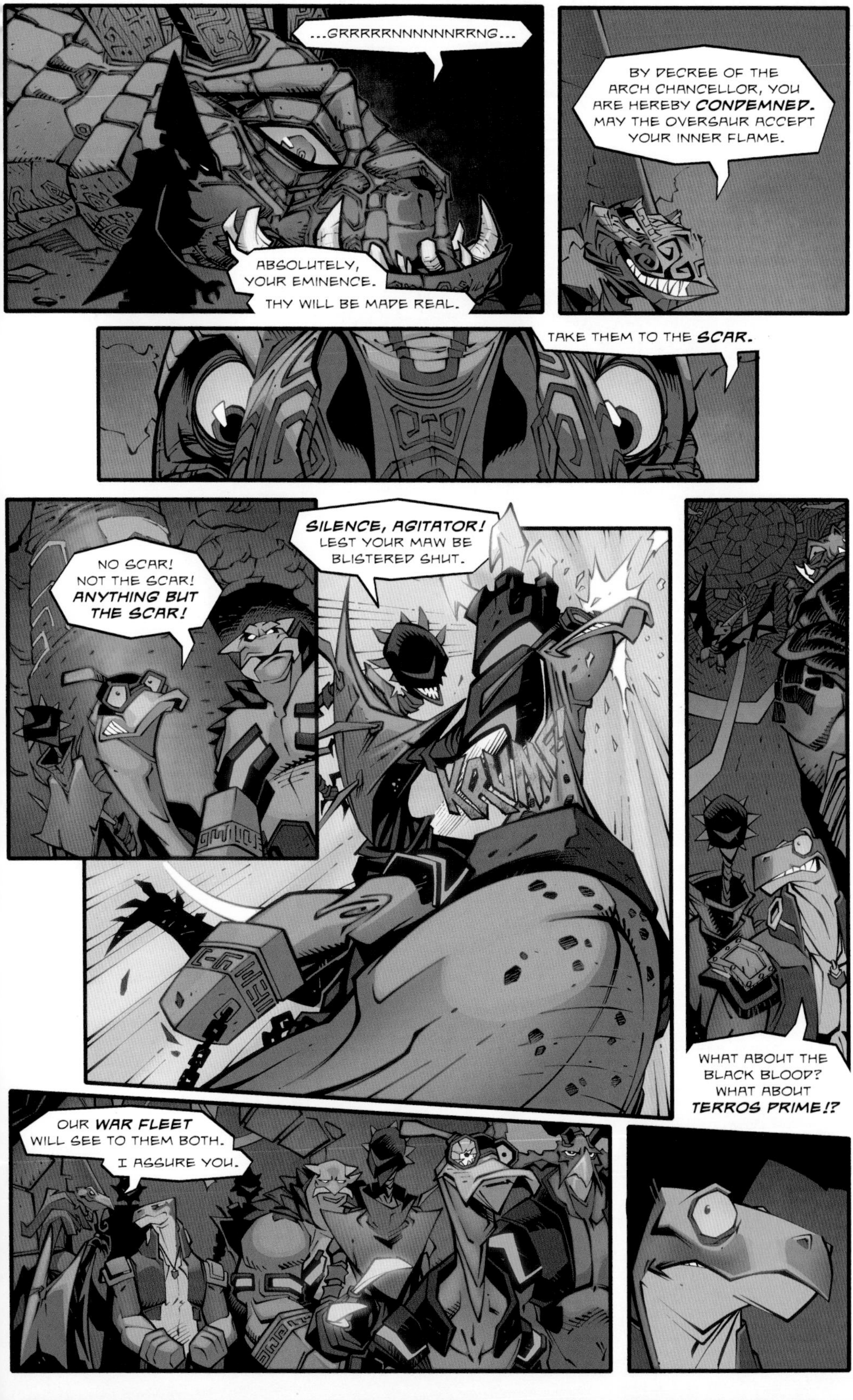
...GRRRRRNNNNNNRRNG...
BY DECREE OF THE ARCH CHANCELLOR, YOU ARE HEREBY CONDEMNED. MAY THE OVERSAUR ACCEPT YOUR INNER FLAME.
ABSOLUTELY, YOUR EMINENCE.
THY WILL BE MADE REAL.
TAKE THEM TO THE SCAR.
NO SCAR! NOT THE SCAR! ANYTHING BUT THE SCAR!
SILENCE, AGITATOR! LEST YOUR MAW BE BLISTERED SHUT.
WHAT ABOUT THE BLACK BLOOD? WHAT ABOUT TERROS PRIME!?
OUR WAR FLEET WILL SEE TO THEM BOTH.
I ASSURE YOU.

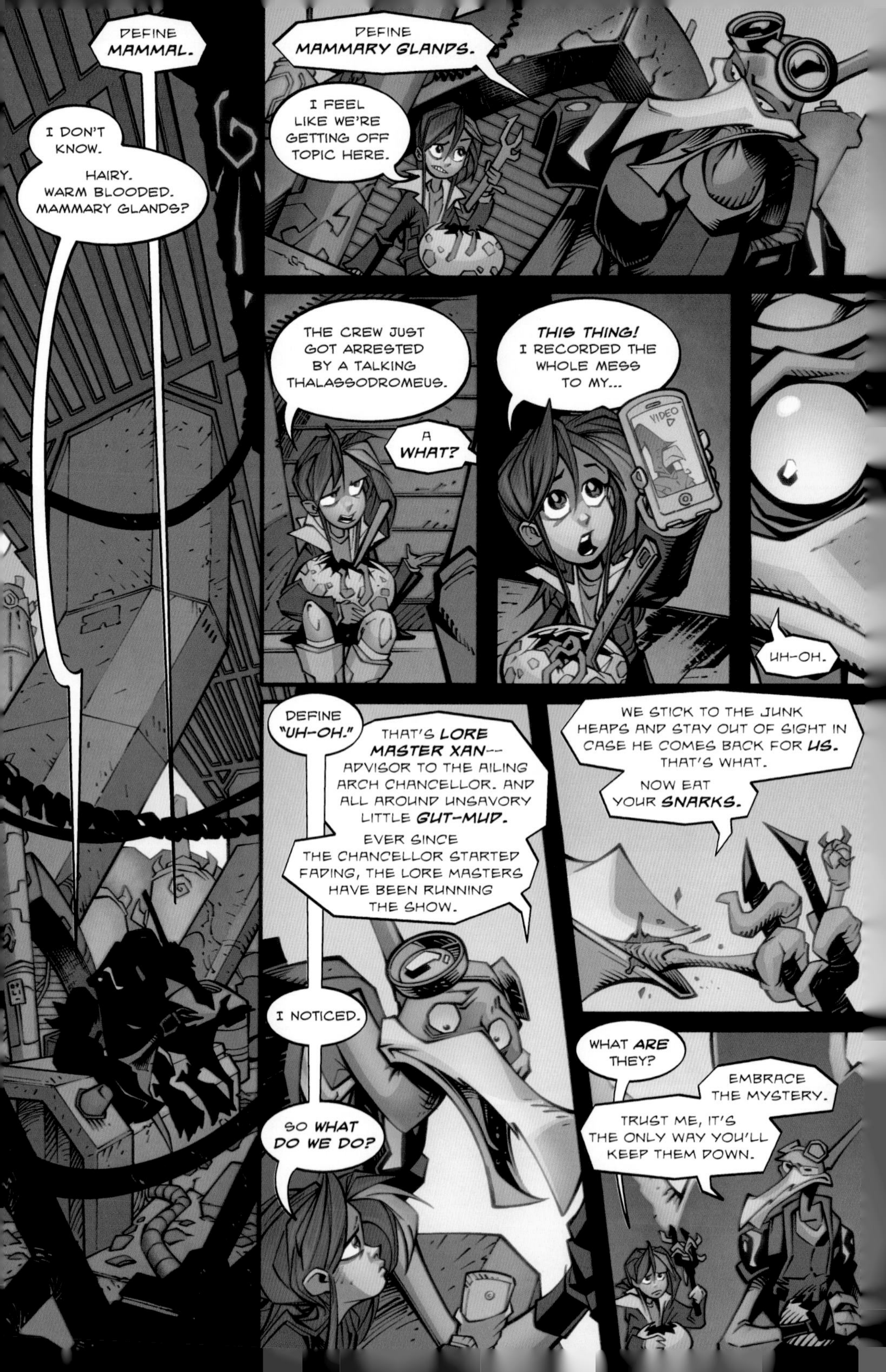
DEFINE MAMMAL.
I DON'T KNOW.
HAIRY. WARM BLOODED. MAMMARY GLANDS?
DEFINE MAMMARY GLANDS.
I FEEL LIKE WE'RE GETTING OFF TOPIC HERE.
THE CREW JUST GOT ARRESTED BY A TALKING THALASSODROMEUS.
A WHAT?
THIS THING! I RECORDED THE WHOLE MESS TO MY...
VIDEO
UH-OH.
DEFINE "UH-OH."
THAT'S LORE MASTER XAN-- ADVISOR TO THE AILING ARCH CHANCELLOR. AND ALL AROUND UNSAVORY LITTLE GUT-MUD.
EVER SINCE THE CHANCELLOR STARTED FADING, THE LORE MASTERS HAVE BEEN RUNNING THE SHOW.
I NOTICED.
SO WHAT DO WE DO?
WE STICK TO THE JUNK HEAPS AND STAY OUT OF SIGHT IN CASE HE COMES BACK FOR US. THAT'S WHAT.
NOW EAT YOUR SNARKS.
WHAT ARE THEY?
EMBRACE THE MYSTERY.
TRUST ME, IT'S THE ONLY WAY YOU'LL KEEP THEM DOWN.

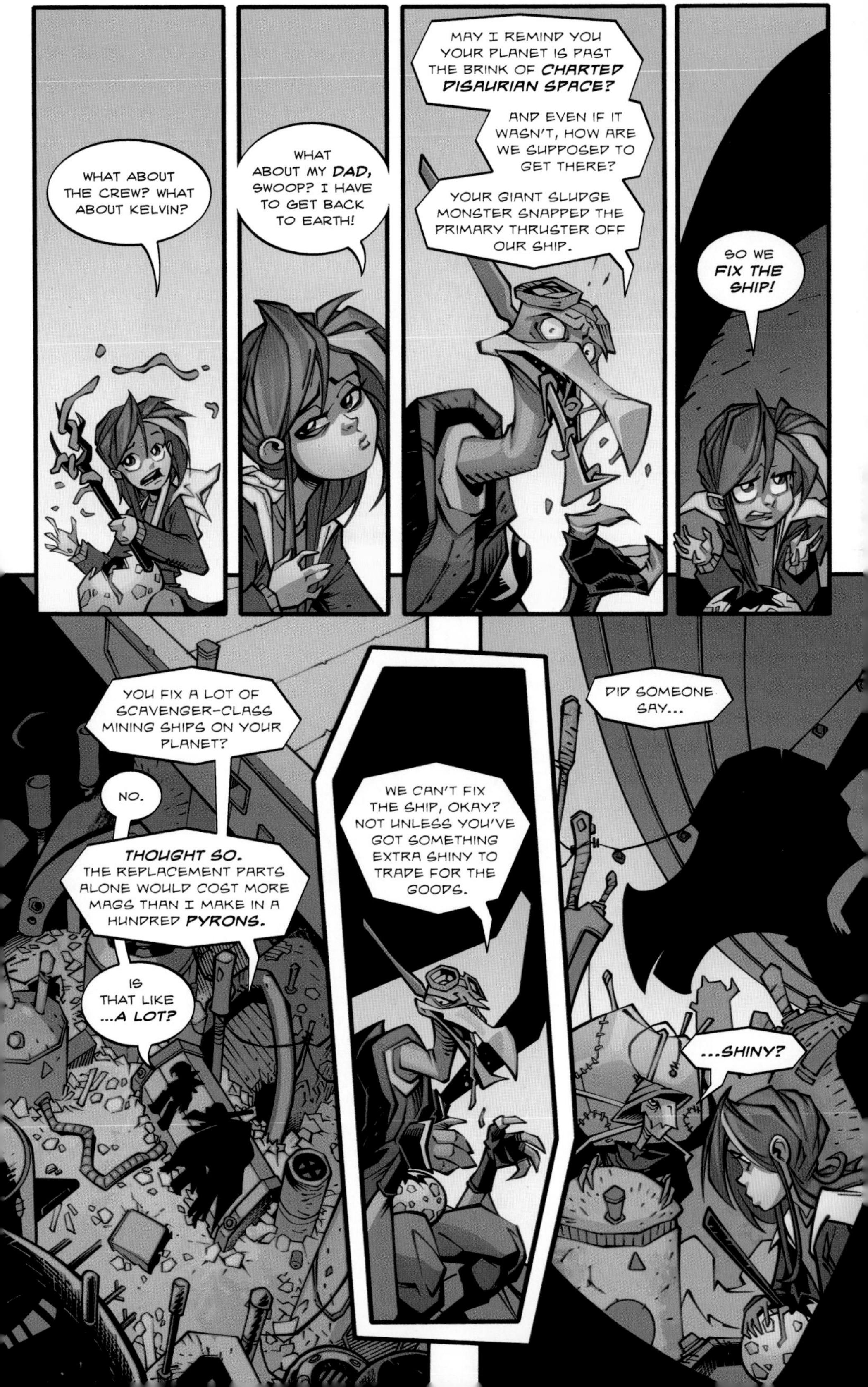
WHAT ABOUT THE CREW? WHAT ABOUT KELVIN?
WHAT ABOUT MY DAD, SWOOP? I HAVE TO GET BACK TO EARTH!
MAY I REMIND YOU YOUR PLANET IS PAST THE BRINK OF CHARTED DISAURIAN SPACE?
AND EVEN IF IT WASN'T, HOW ARE WE SUPPOSED TO GET THERE?
YOUR GIANT SLUDGE MONSTER SNAPPED THE PRIMARY THRUSTER OFF OUR SHIP.
SO WE FIX THE SHIP!
YOU FIX A LOT OF SCAVENGER-CLASS MINING SHIPS ON YOUR PLANET?
NO.
THOUGHT SO. THE REPLACEMENT PARTS ALONE WOULD COST MORE MAGS THAN I MAKE IN A HUNDRED PYRONS.
IS THAT LIKE ...A LOT?
WE CAN'T FIX THE SHIP, OKAY? NOT UNLESS YOU'VE GOT SOMETHING EXTRA SHINY TO TRADE FOR THE GOODS.
DID SOMEONE SAY...
...SHINY?

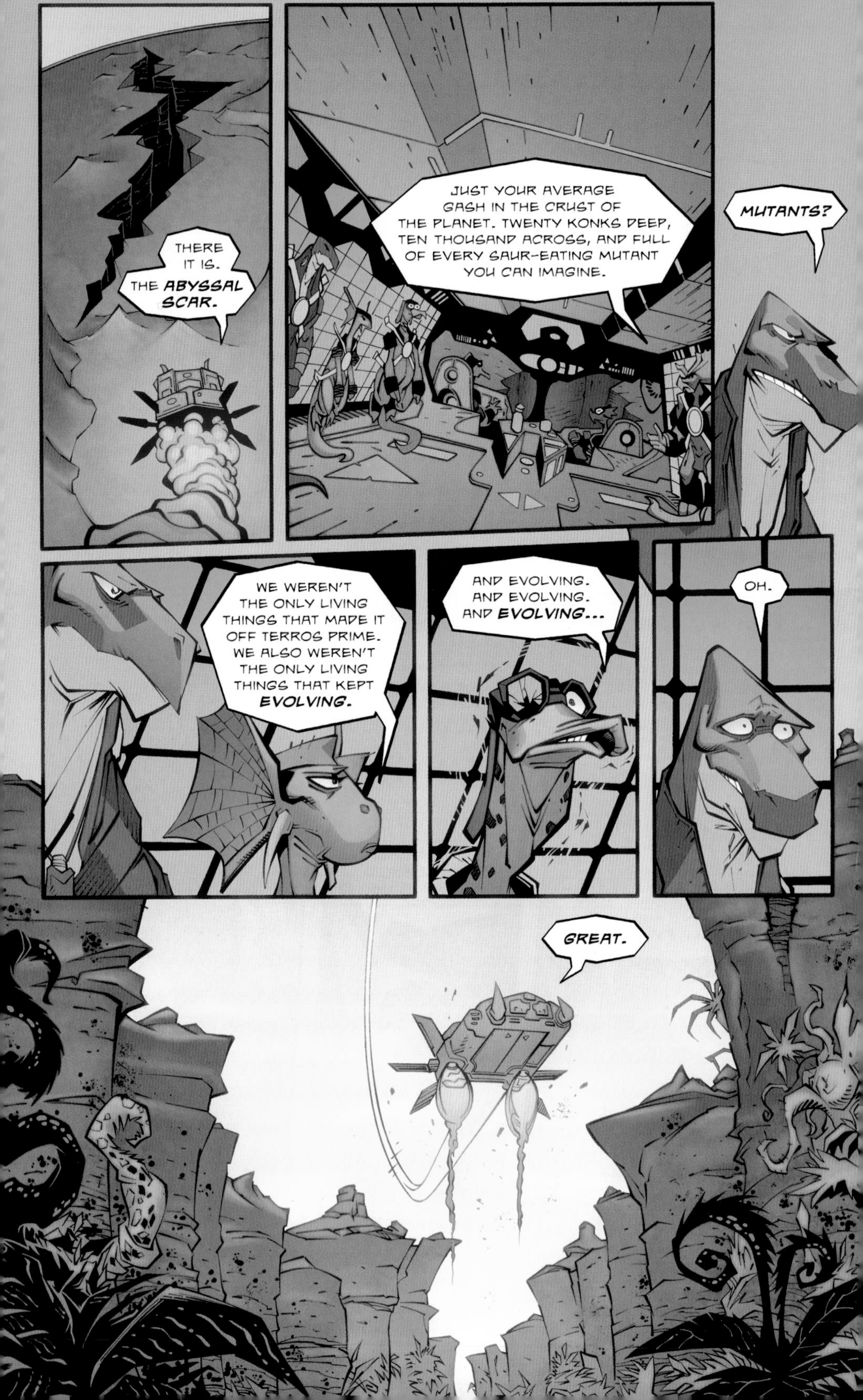
THERE IT IS. THE ABYSSAL SCAR.
JUST YOUR AVERAGE GASH IN THE CRUST OF THE PLANET. TWENTY KONKS DEEP, TEN THOUSAND ACROSS, AND FULL OF EVERY SAUR-EATING MUTANT YOU CAN IMAGINE.
MUTANTS?
WE WEREN'T THE ONLY LIVING THINGS THAT MADE IT OFF TERROS PRIME. WE ALSO WEREN'T THE ONLY LIVING THINGS THAT KEPT EVOLVING.
AND EVOLVING. AND EVOLVING. AND EVOLVING...
OH.
GREAT.

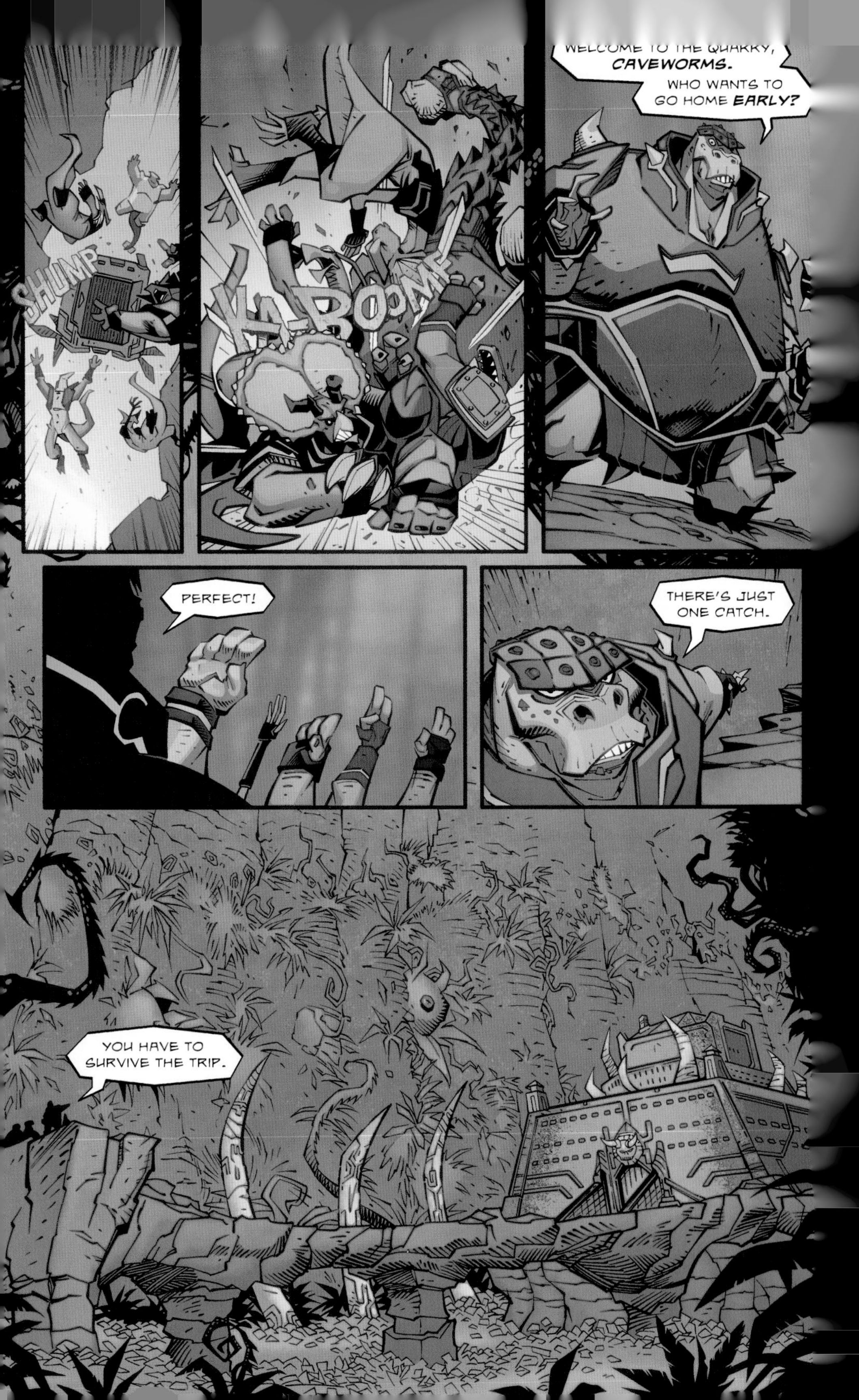
SHUMP
KA-BOOMF
WELCOME TO THE QUARRY, CAVEWORMS.
WHO WANTS TO GO HOME EARLY?
PERFECT!
THERE'S JUST ONE CATCH.
YOU HAVE TO SURVIVE THE TRIP.

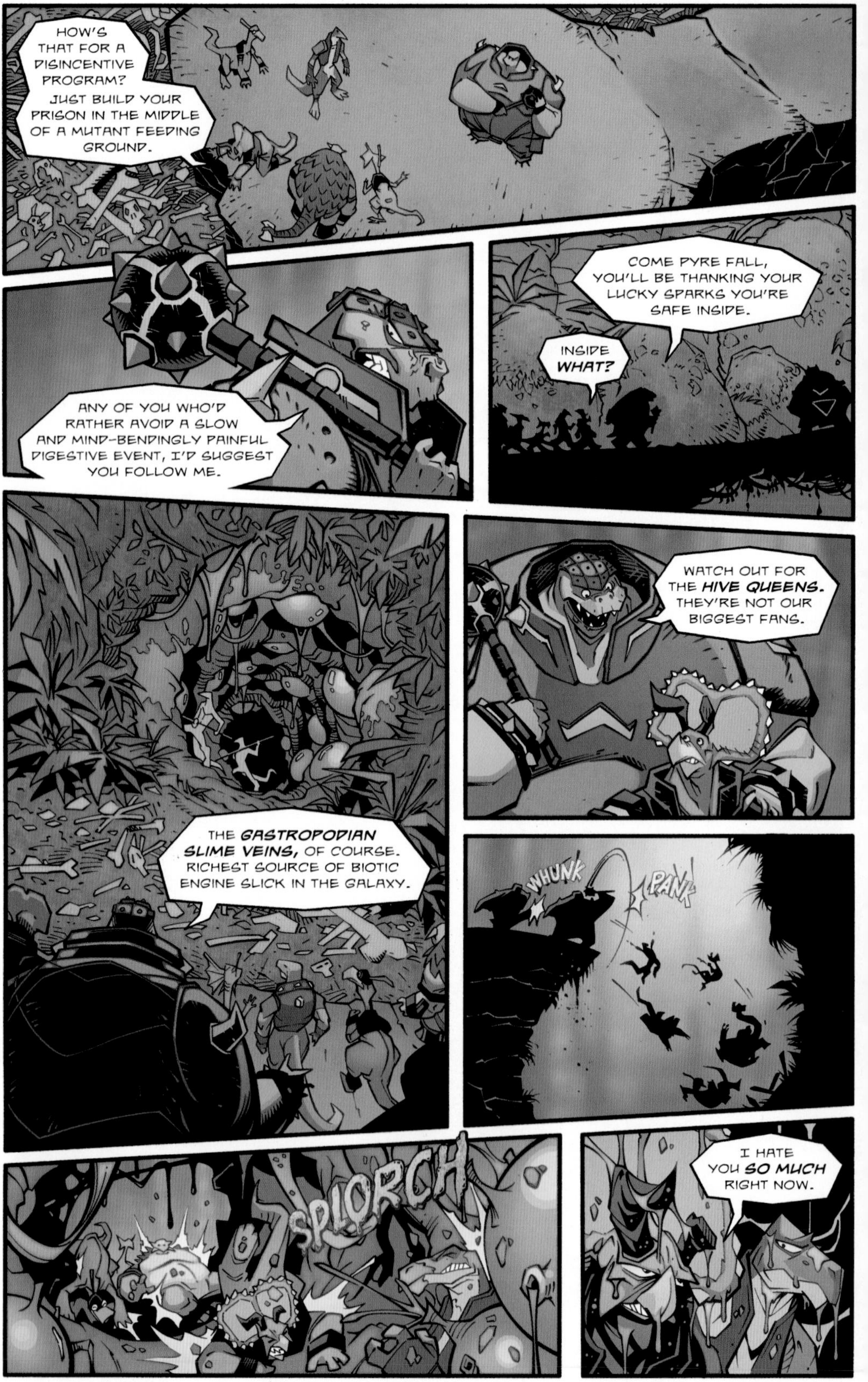
HOW'S THAT FOR A DISINCENTIVE PROGRAM?
JUST BUILD YOUR PRISON IN THE MIDDLE OF A MUTANT FEEDING GROUND.
ANY OF YOU WHO'D RATHER AVOID A SLOW AND MIND-BENDINGLY PAINFUL DIGESTIVE EVENT, I'D SUGGEST YOU FOLLOW ME.
COME PYRE FALL, YOU'LL BE THANKING YOUR LUCKY SPARKS YOU'RE SAFE INSIDE.
INSIDE WHAT?
THE GASTROPODIAN SLIME VEINS, OF COURSE. RICHEST SOURCE OF BIOTIC ENGINE SLICK IN THE GALAXY.
WATCH OUT FOR THE HIVE QUEENS. THEY'RE NOT OUR BIGGEST FANS.
WHUNK
PANK
SPLORCH
I HATE YOU SO MUCH RIGHT NOW.

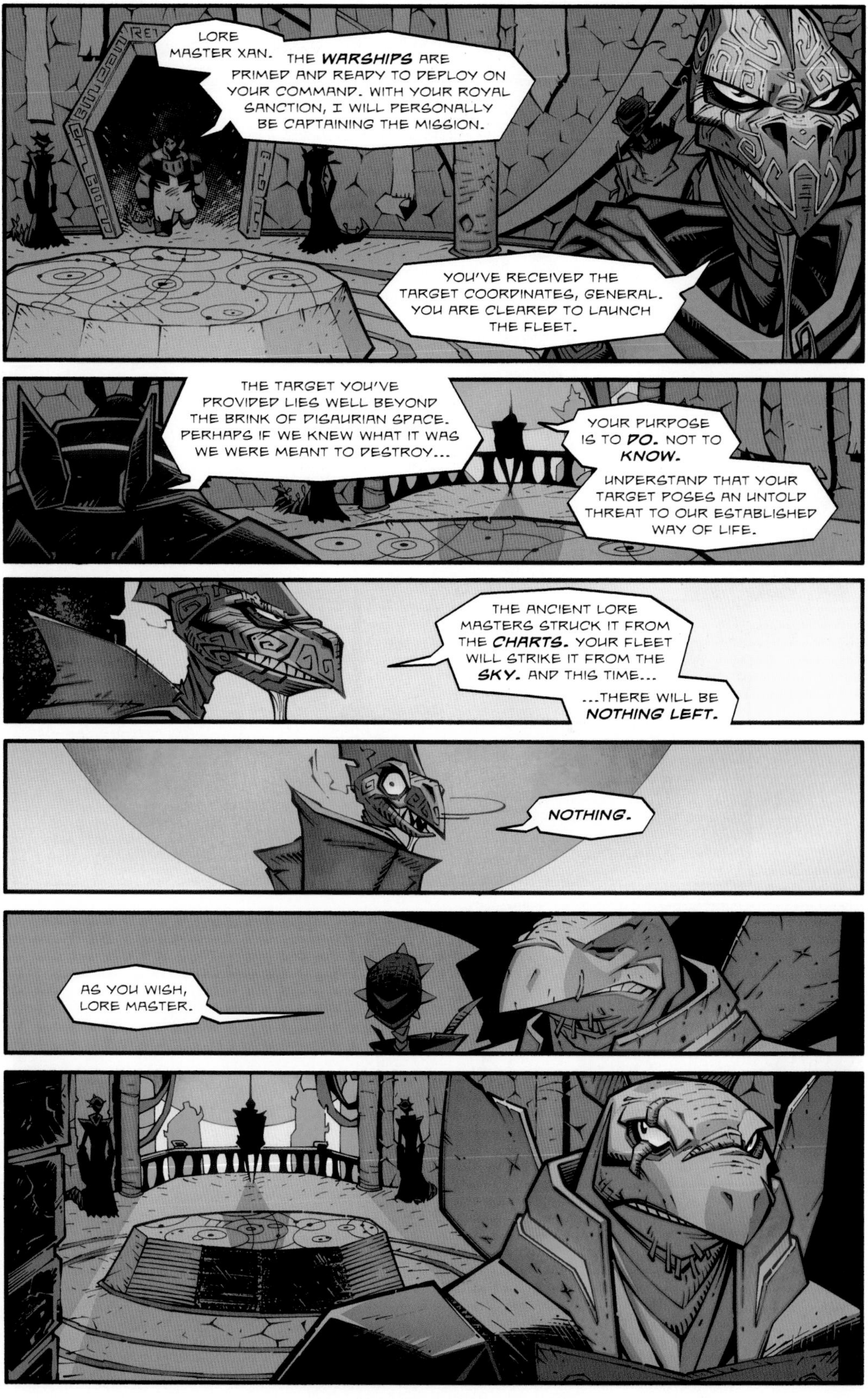

LORE MASTER XAN.
THE WARSHIPS ARE PRIMED AND READY TO DEPLOY ON YOUR COMMAND. WITH YOUR ROYAL SANCTION, I WILL PERSONALLY BE CAPTAINING THE MISSION.
YOU'VE RECEIVED THE TARGET COORDINATES, GENERAL. YOU ARE CLEARED TO LAUNCH THE FLEET.
THE TARGET YOU'VE PROVIDED LIES WELL BEYOND THE BRINK OF DISAURIAN SPACE. PERHAPS IF WE KNEW WHAT IT WAS WE WERE MEANT TO DESTROY...
YOUR PURPOSE IS TO DO. NOT TO KNOW.
UNDERSTAND THAT YOUR TARGET POSES AN UNTOLD THREAT TO OUR ESTABLISHED WAY OF LIFE.
THE ANCIENT LORE MASTERS STRUCK IT FROM THE CHARTS. YOUR FLEET WILL STRIKE IT FROM THE SKY. AND THIS TIME...
...THERE WILL BE NOTHING LEFT.
NOTHING.
AS YOU WISH, LORE MASTER.

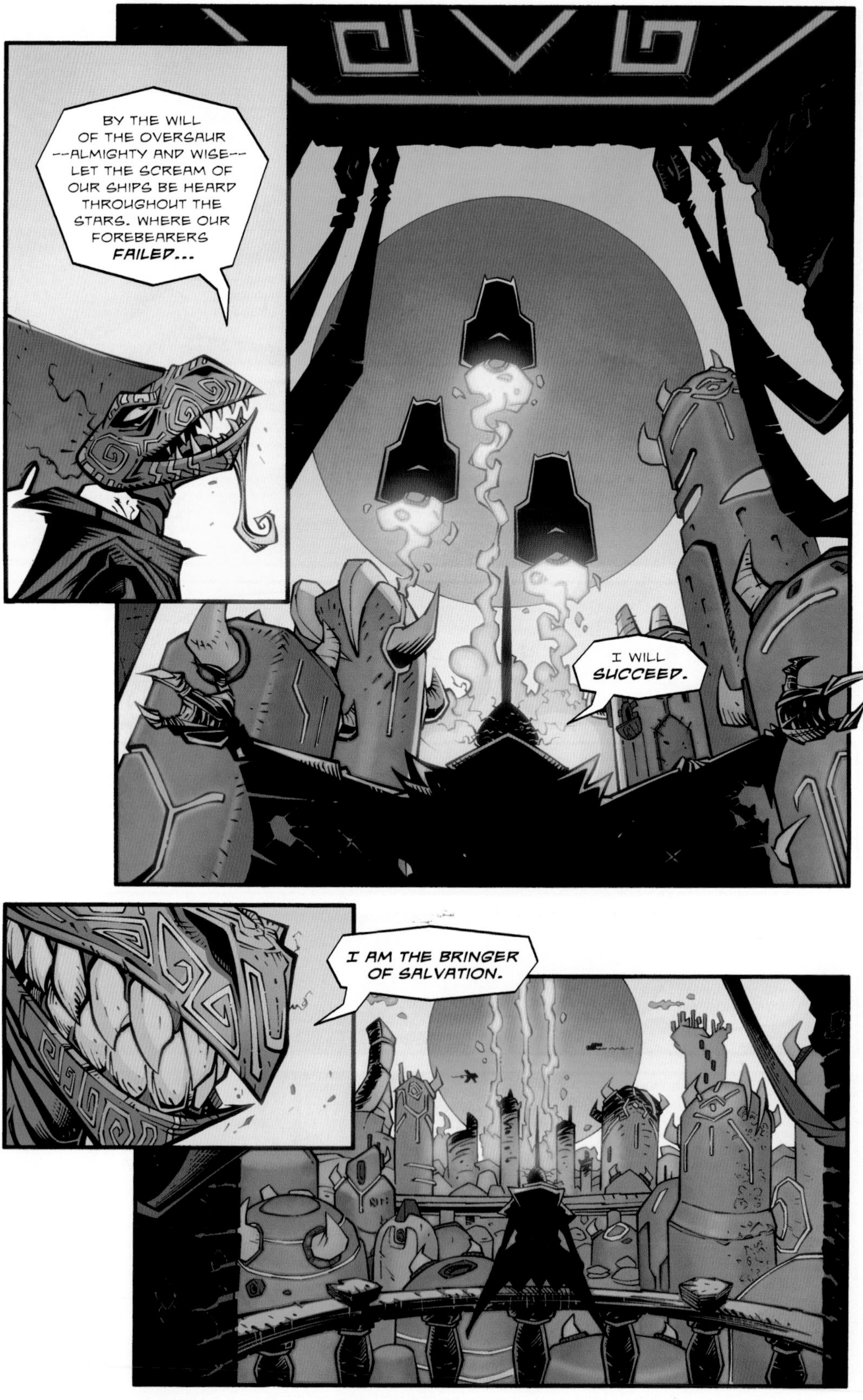
BY THE WILL OF THE OVERSAUR --ALMIGHTY AND WISE-- LET THE SCREAM OF OUR SHIPS BE HEARD THROUGHOUT THE STARS. WHERE OUR FOREBEARERS FAILED...
I WILL SUCCEED.
I AM THE BRINGER OF SALVATION.

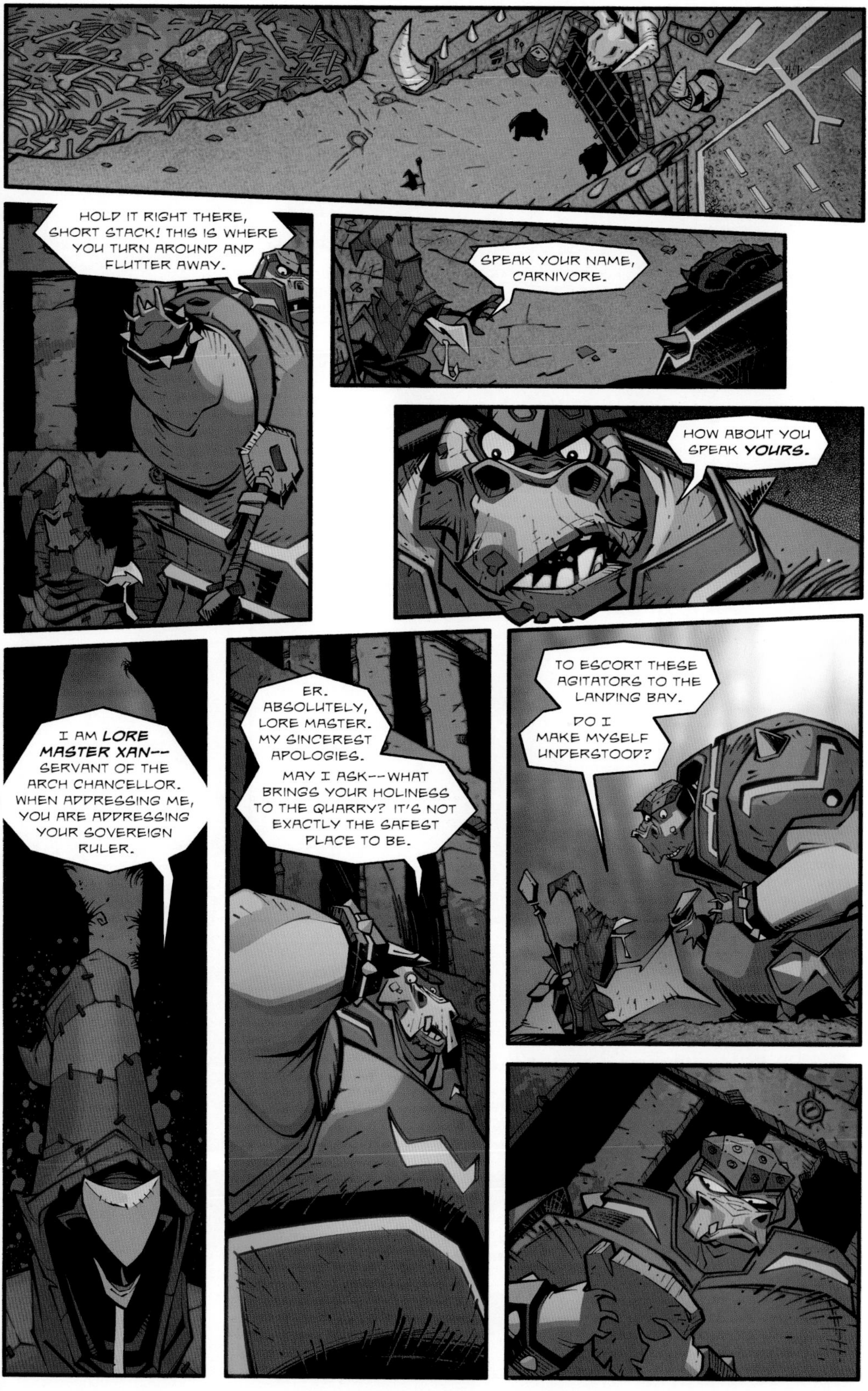
HOLD IT RIGHT THERE, SHORT STACK! THIS IS WHERE YOU TURN AROUND AND FLUTTER AWAY.
SPEAK YOUR NAME, CARNIVORE.
HOW ABOUT YOU SPEAK **YOURS.**
I AM ***LORE MASTER XAN***-- SERVANT OF THE ARCH CHANCELLOR. WHEN ADDRESSING ME, YOU ARE ADDRESSING YOUR SOVEREIGN RULER.
ER. ABSOLUTELY, LORE MASTER. MY SINCEREST APOLOGIES.
MAY I ASK--WHAT BRINGS YOUR HOLINESS TO THE QUARRY? IT'S NOT EXACTLY THE SAFEST PLACE TO BE.
TO ESCORT THESE AGITATORS TO THE LANDING BAY.
DO I MAKE MYSELF UNDERSTOOD?

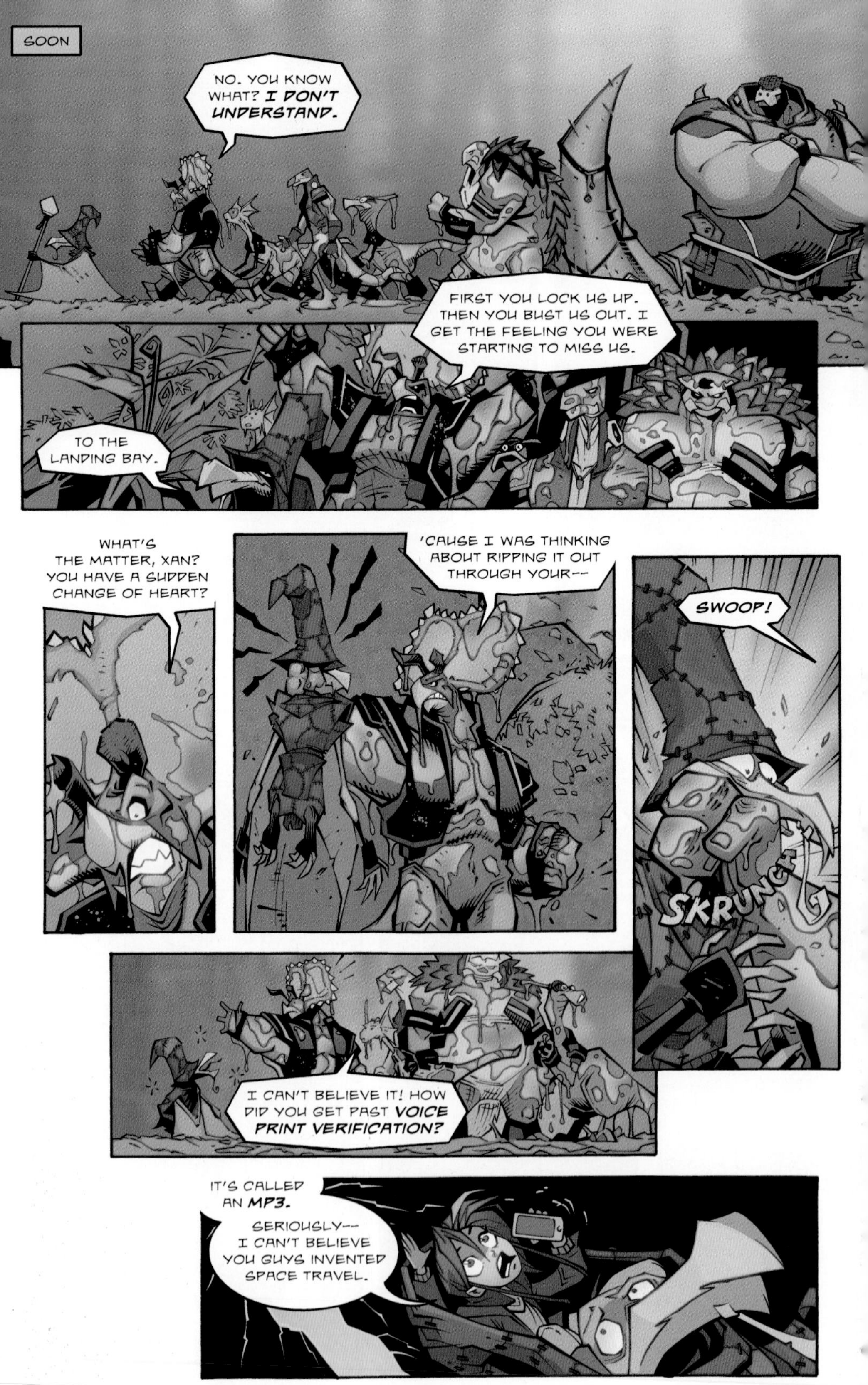
SOON
NO. YOU KNOW WHAT? I DON'T UNDERSTAND.
FIRST YOU LOCK US UP. THEN YOU BUST US OUT. I GET THE FEELING YOU WERE STARTING TO MISS US.
TO THE LANDING BAY.
WHAT'S THE MATTER, XAN? YOU HAVE A SUDDEN CHANGE OF HEART?
'CAUSE I WAS THINKING ABOUT RIPPING IT OUT THROUGH YOUR--
SWOOP!
SKRUNG!
I CAN'T BELIEVE IT! HOW DID YOU GET PAST VOICE PRINT VERIFICATION?
IT'S CALLED AN MP3.
SERIOUSLY-- I CAN'T BELIEVE YOU GUYS INVENTED SPACE TRAVEL.

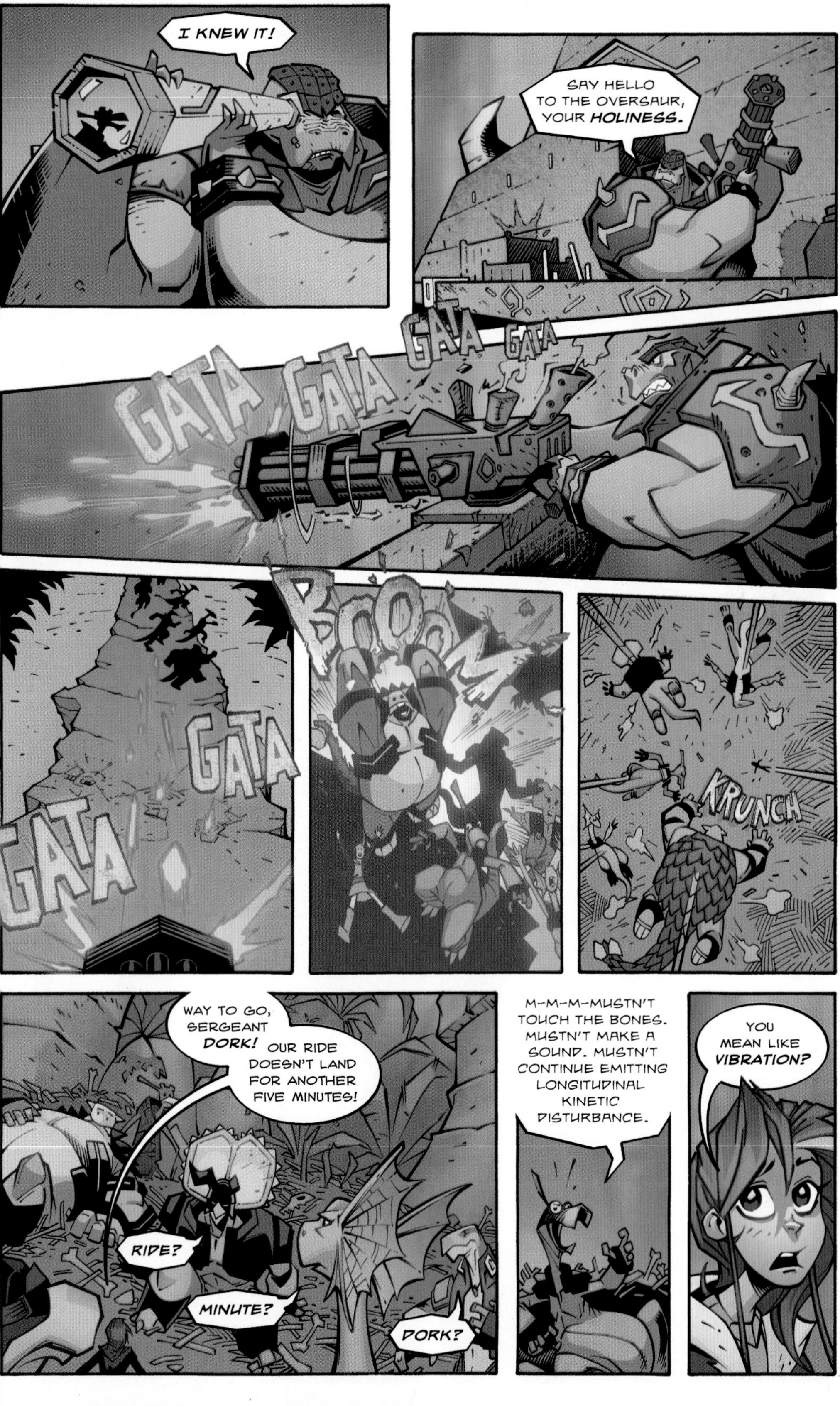
I KNEW IT!
SAY HELLO TO THE OVERSAUR, YOUR HOLINESS.
GATA GATA GATA GATA
GATA GATA
BOOOM
KRUNCH
WAY TO GO, SERGEANT DORK! OUR RIDE DOESN'T LAND FOR ANOTHER FIVE MINUTES!
RIDE?
MINUTE?
DORK?
M-M-M-MUSTN'T TOUCH THE BONES. MUSTN'T MAKE A SOUND. MUSTN'T CONTINUE EMITTING LONGITUDINAL KINETIC DISTURBANCE.
YOU MEAN LIKE VIBRATION?

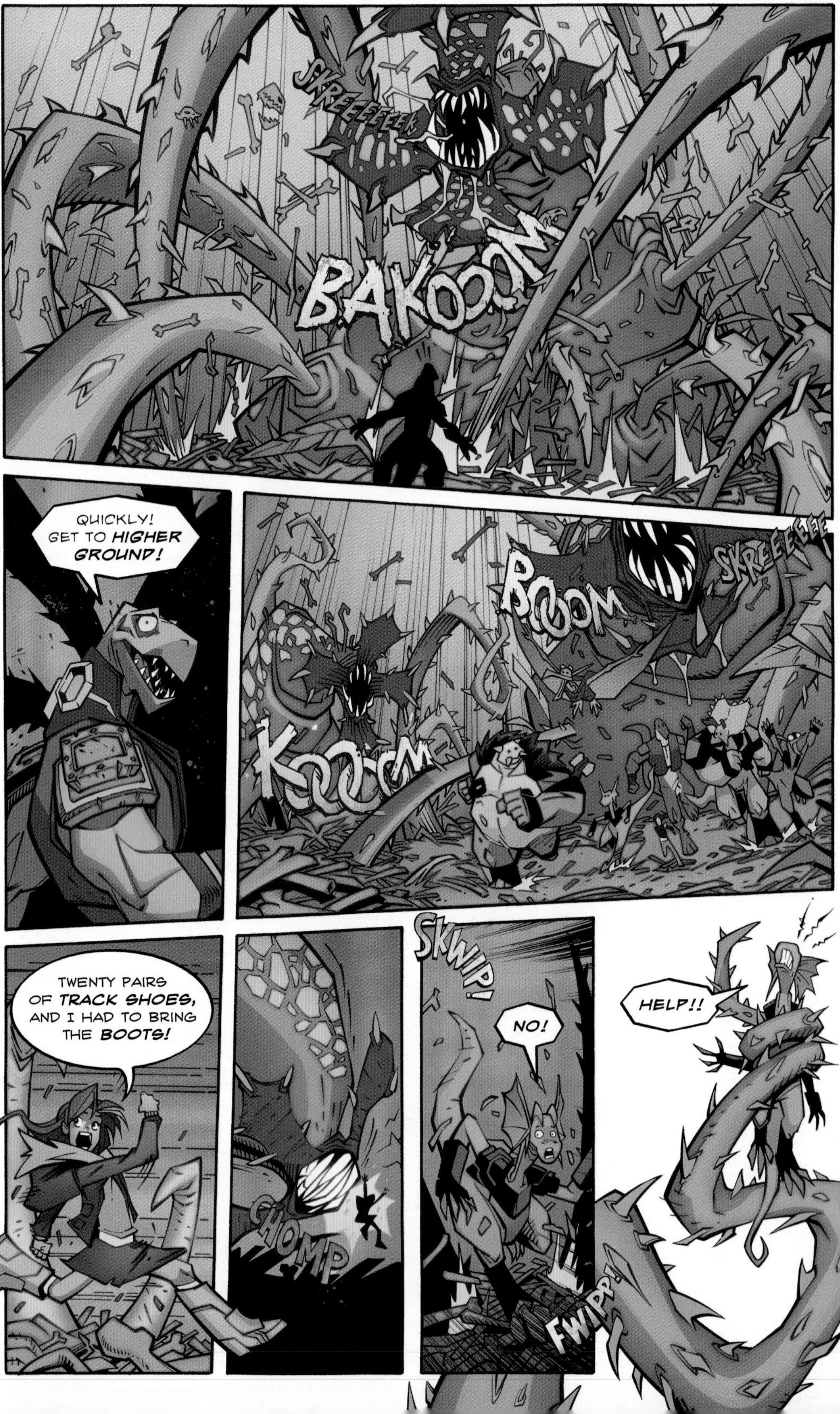
SKREEEEEEEK
BAKOOOM
QUICKLY! GET TO HIGHER GROUND!
BOOOM
SKREEEEEEE
KOOOOM
TWENTY PAIRS OF TRACK SHOES, AND I HAD TO BRING THE BOOTS!
CHOMP
SKWIP!
NO!
HELP!!
FWIPP!

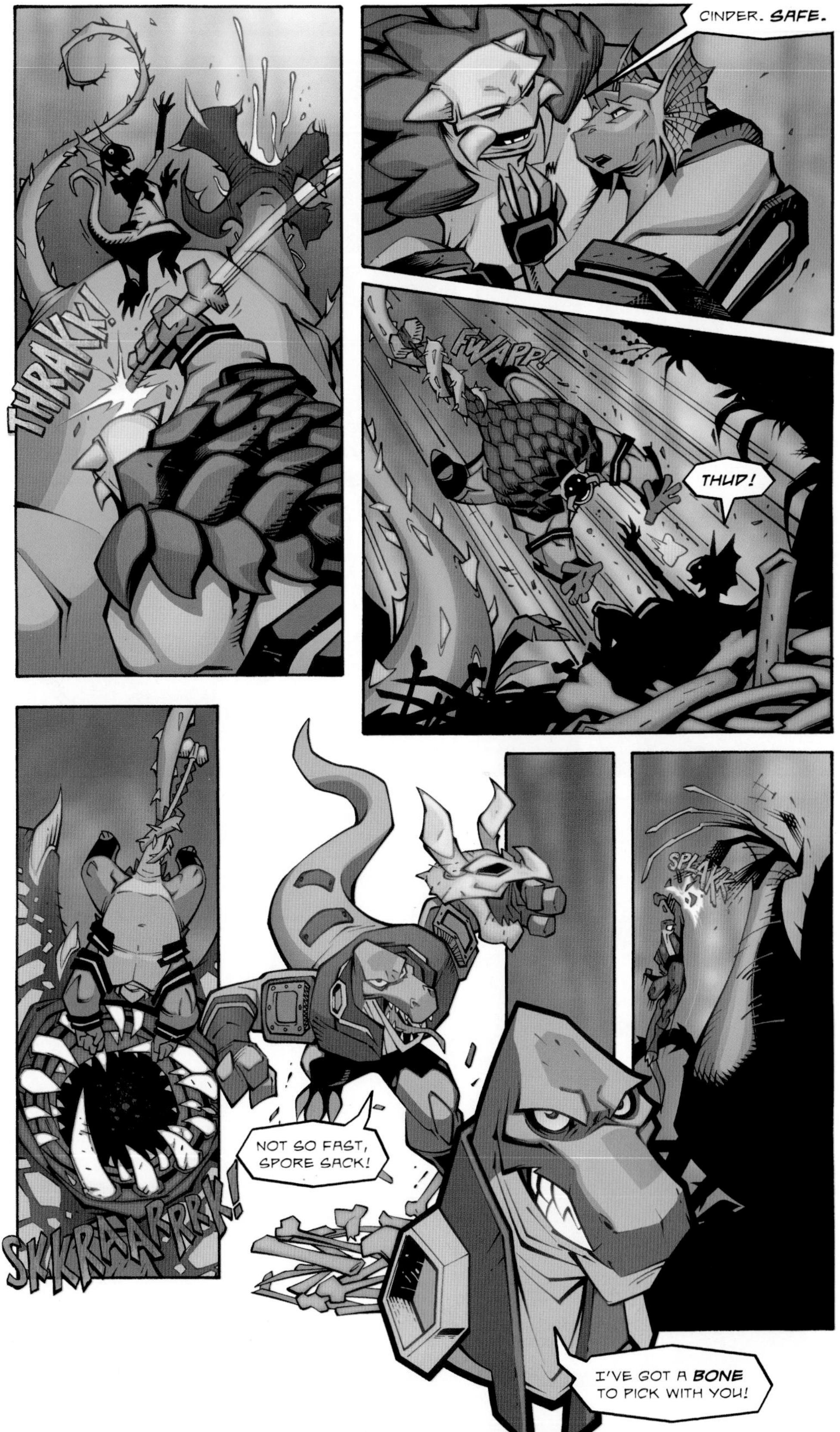
THRAKK!
CINDER. SAFE.
FWAPP!
THUD!
SKKRAARRRK!
NOT SO FAST, SPORE SACK!
SPLAKK!
I'VE GOT A BONE TO PICK WITH YOU!

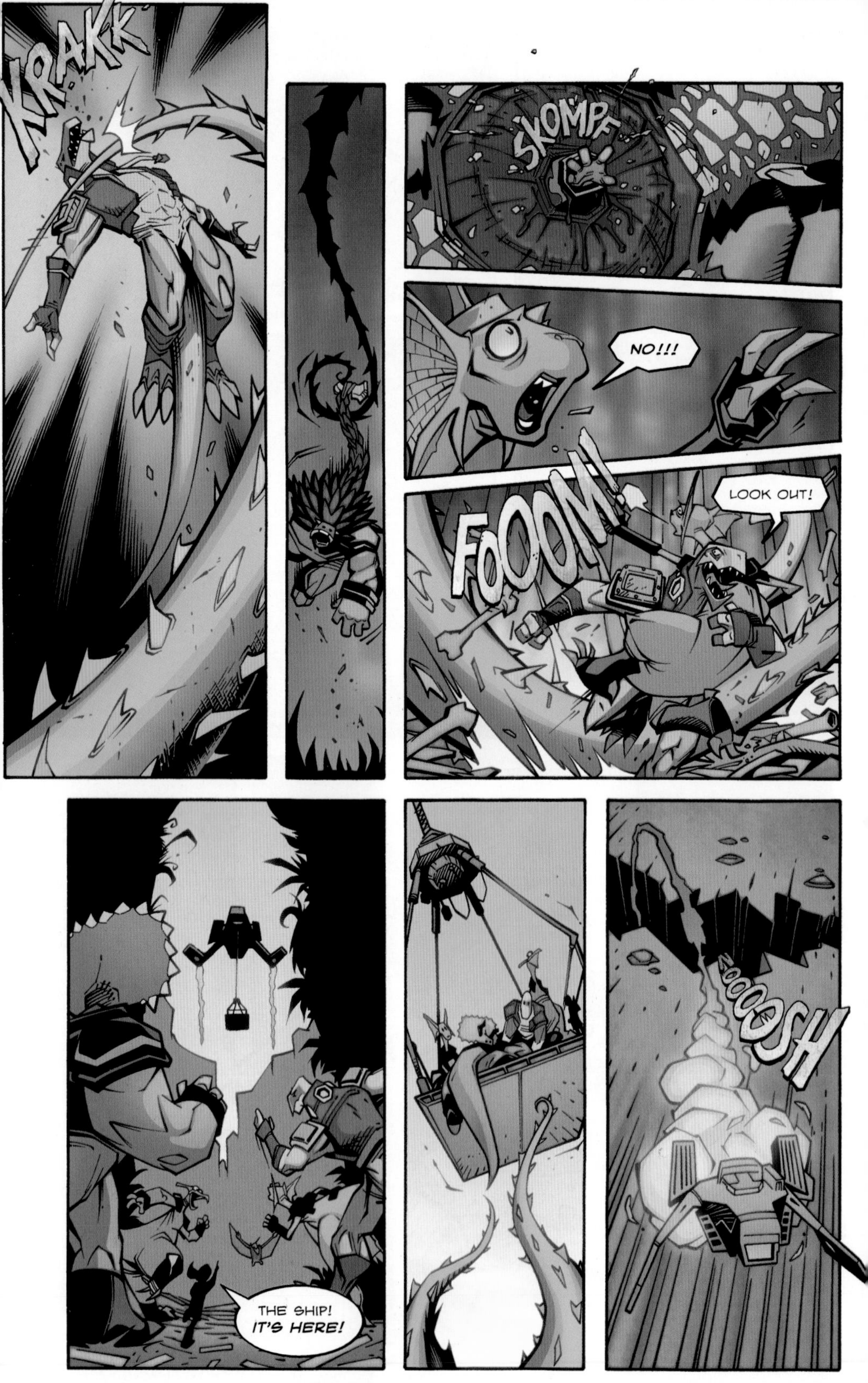
KRAKK
SKOMPF
NO!!!
FOOOM
LOOK OUT!
THE SHIP! IT'S HERE!
SHOOOOSH

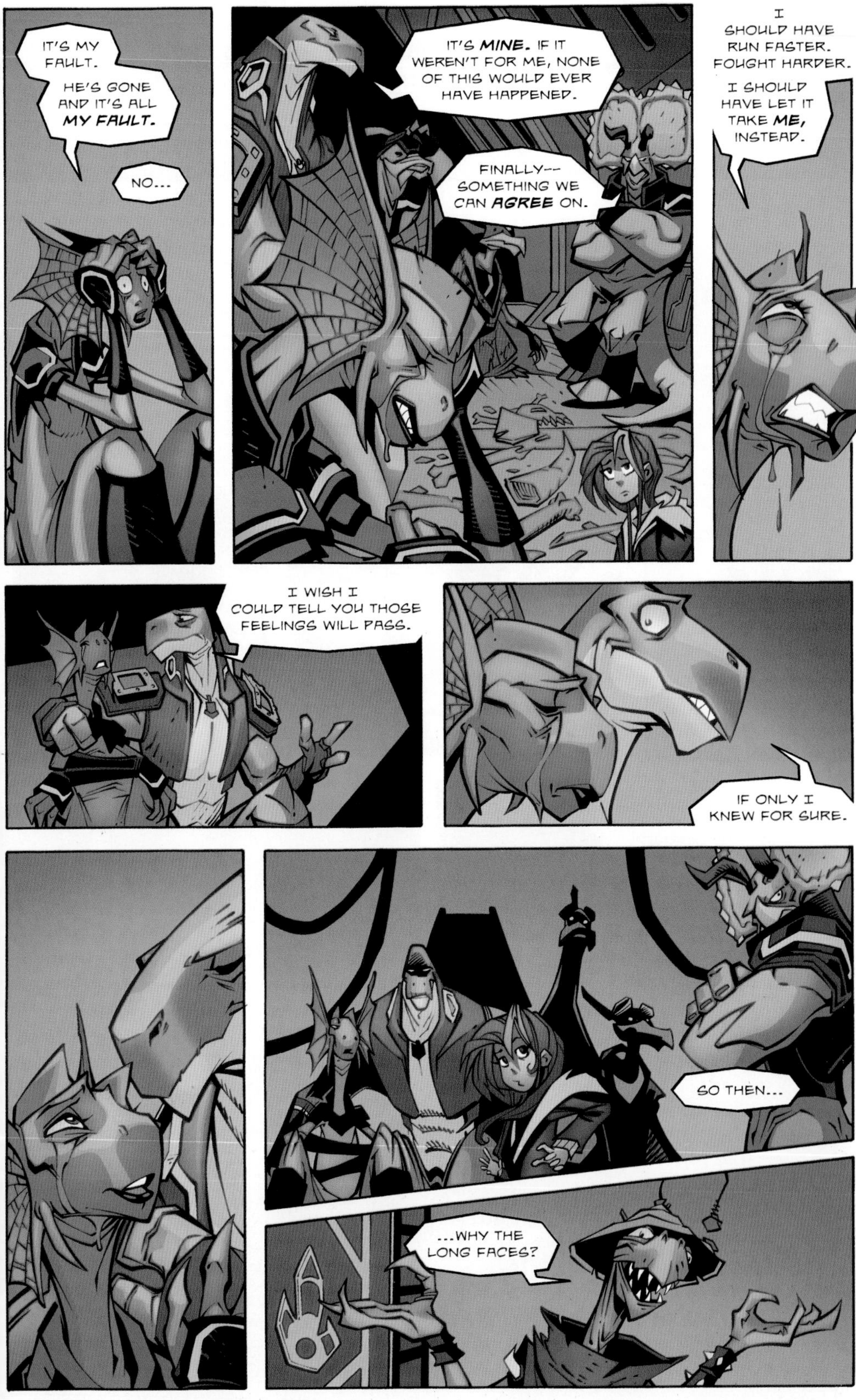
IT'S MY FAULT.
HE'S GONE AND IT'S ALL MY FAULT.
NO...
IT'S MINE. IF IT WEREN'T FOR ME, NONE OF THIS WOULD EVER HAVE HAPPENED.
FINALLY-- SOMETHING WE CAN AGREE ON.
I SHOULD HAVE RUN FASTER. FOUGHT HARDER.
I SHOULD HAVE LET IT TAKE ME, INSTEAD.
I WISH I COULD TELL YOU THOSE FEELINGS WILL PASS.
IF ONLY I KNEW FOR SURE.
SO THEN...
...WHY THE LONG FACES?

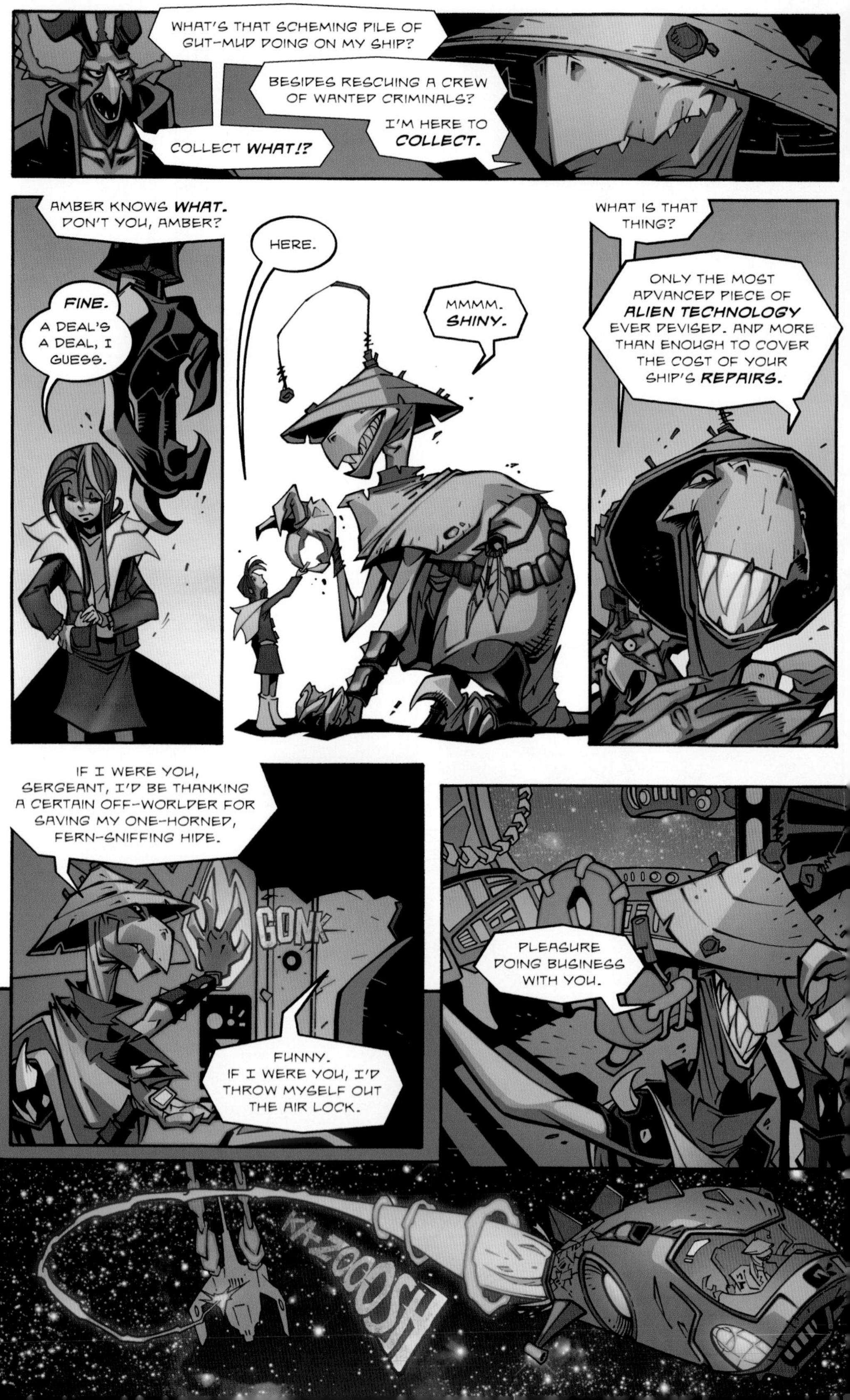
WHAT'S THAT SCHEMING PILE OF GUT-MUD DOING ON MY SHIP?
BESIDES RESCUING A CREW OF WANTED CRIMINALS?
I'M HERE TO COLLECT.
COLLECT WHAT!?
AMBER KNOWS WHAT. DON'T YOU, AMBER?
FINE. A DEAL'S A DEAL, I GUESS.
HERE.
MMMM. SHINY.
WHAT IS THAT THING?
ONLY THE MOST ADVANCED PIECE OF ALIEN TECHNOLOGY EVER DEVISED. AND MORE THAN ENOUGH TO COVER THE COST OF YOUR SHIP'S REPAIRS.
IF I WERE YOU, SERGEANT, I'D BE THANKING A CERTAIN OFF-WORLDER FOR SAVING MY ONE-HORNED, FERN-SNIFFING HIDE.
GONK
FUNNY. IF I WERE YOU, I'D THROW MYSELF OUT THE AIR LOCK.
PLEASURE DOING BUSINESS WITH YOU.
KA-ZOOOOSH

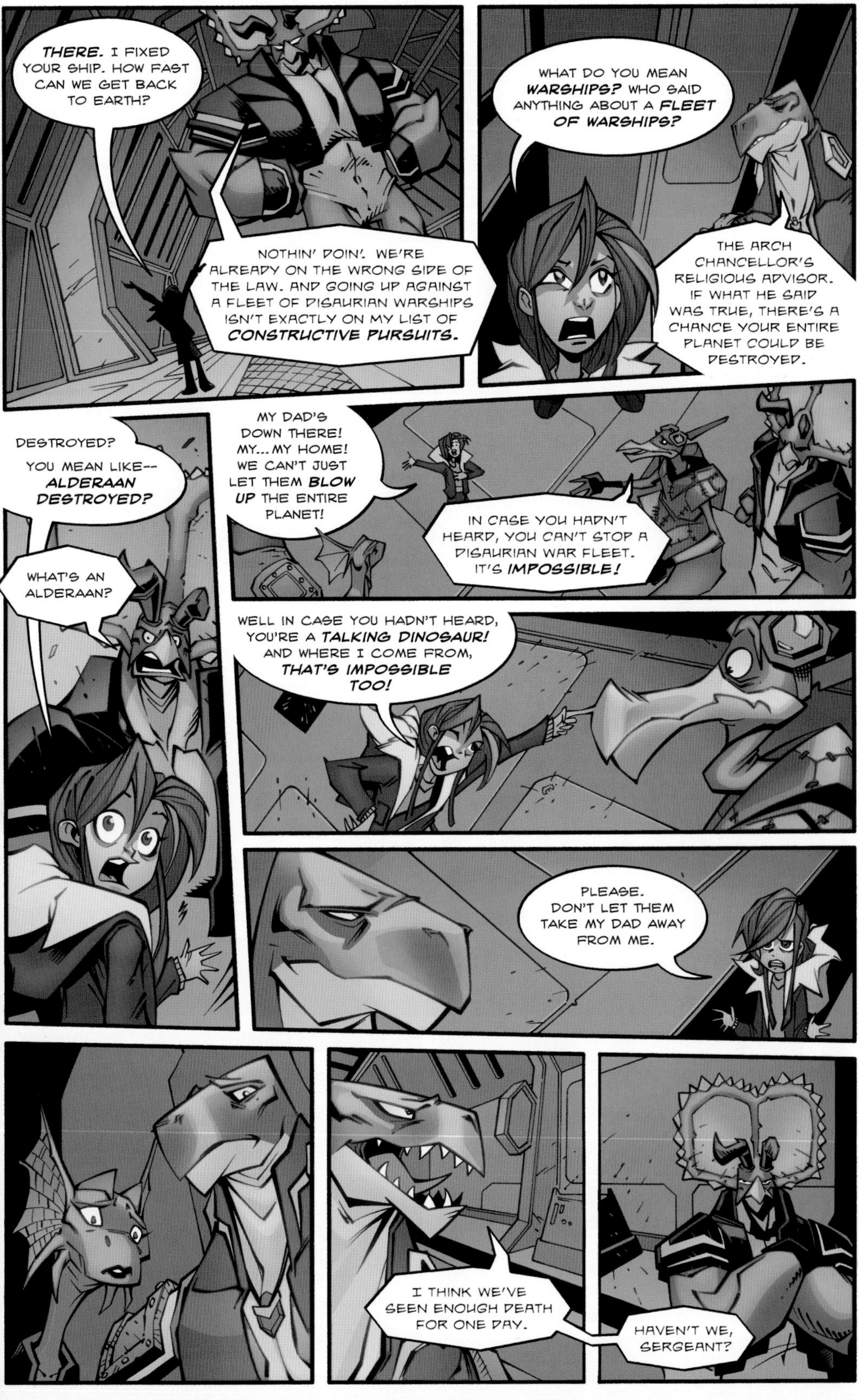
THERE. I FIXED YOUR SHIP. HOW FAST CAN WE GET BACK TO EARTH?
NOTHIN' DOIN'. WE'RE ALREADY ON THE WRONG SIDE OF THE LAW. AND GOING UP AGAINST A FLEET OF DISAURIAN WARSHIPS ISN'T EXACTLY ON MY LIST OF CONSTRUCTIVE PURSUITS.
WHAT DO YOU MEAN WARSHIPS? WHO SAID ANYTHING ABOUT A FLEET OF WARSHIPS?
THE ARCH CHANCELLOR'S RELIGIOUS ADVISOR. IF WHAT HE SAID WAS TRUE, THERE'S A CHANCE YOUR ENTIRE PLANET COULD BE DESTROYED.
DESTROYED?
YOU MEAN LIKE-- ALDERAAN DESTROYED?
WHAT'S AN ALDERAAN?
MY DAD'S DOWN THERE! MY... MY HOME! WE CAN'T JUST LET THEM BLOW UP THE ENTIRE PLANET!
IN CASE YOU HADN'T HEARD, YOU CAN'T STOP A DISAURIAN WAR FLEET. IT'S IMPOSSIBLE!
WELL IN CASE YOU HADN'T HEARD, YOU'RE A TALKING DINOSAUR! AND WHERE I COME FROM, THAT'S IMPOSSIBLE TOO!
PLEASE. DON'T LET THEM TAKE MY DAD AWAY FROM ME.
I THINK WE'VE SEEN ENOUGH DEATH FOR ONE DAY.
HAVEN'T WE, SERGEANT?

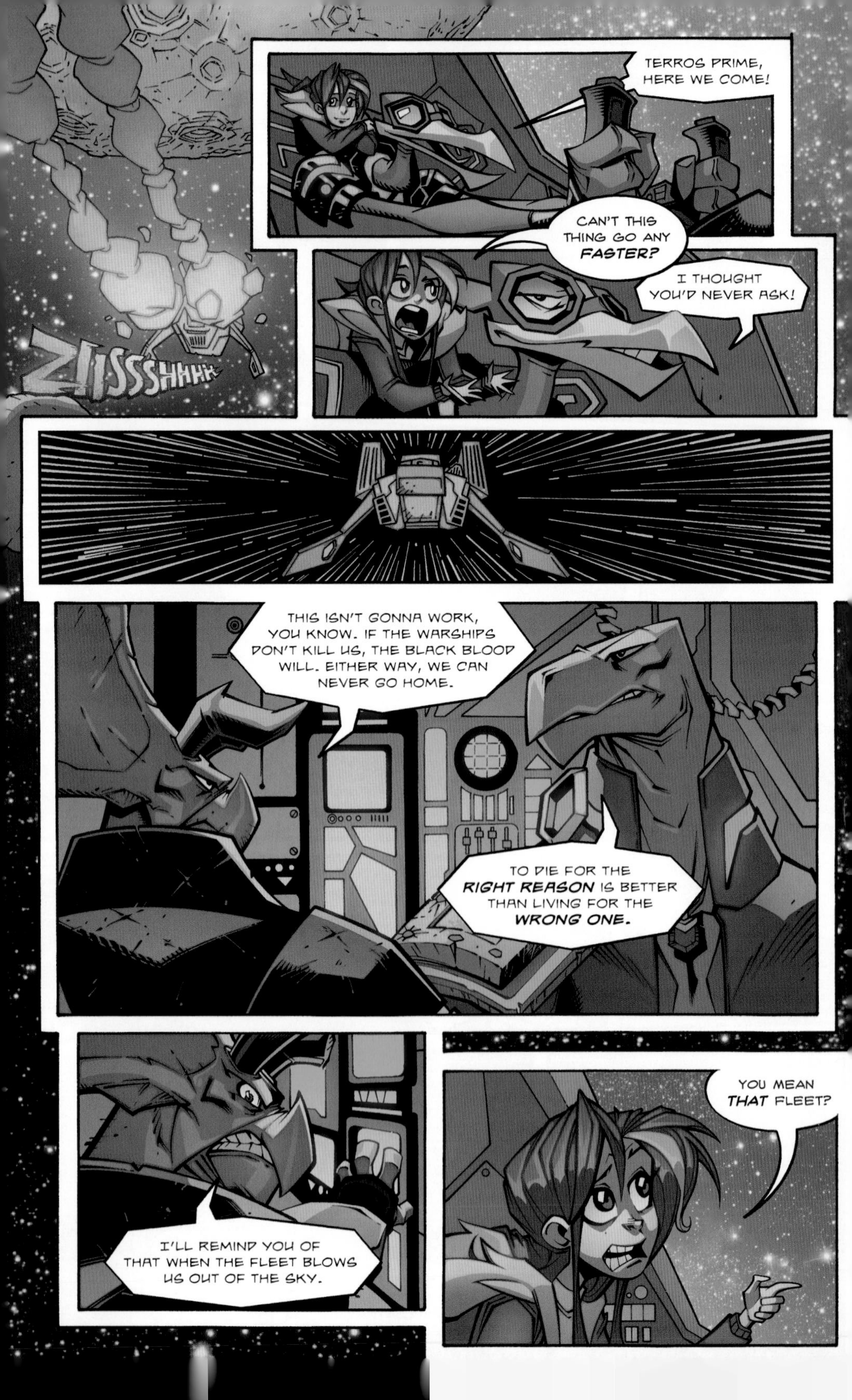
TERROS PRIME, HERE WE COME!
ZIISSSHHHH
CAN'T THIS THING GO ANY FASTER?
I THOUGHT YOU'D NEVER ASK!
THIS ISN'T GONNA WORK, YOU KNOW. IF THE WARSHIPS DON'T KILL US, THE BLACK BLOOD WILL. EITHER WAY, WE CAN NEVER GO HOME.
TO DIE FOR THE RIGHT REASON IS BETTER THAN LIVING FOR THE WRONG ONE.
I'LL REMIND YOU OF THAT WHEN THE FLEET BLOWS US OUT OF THE SKY.
YOU MEAN THAT FLEET?

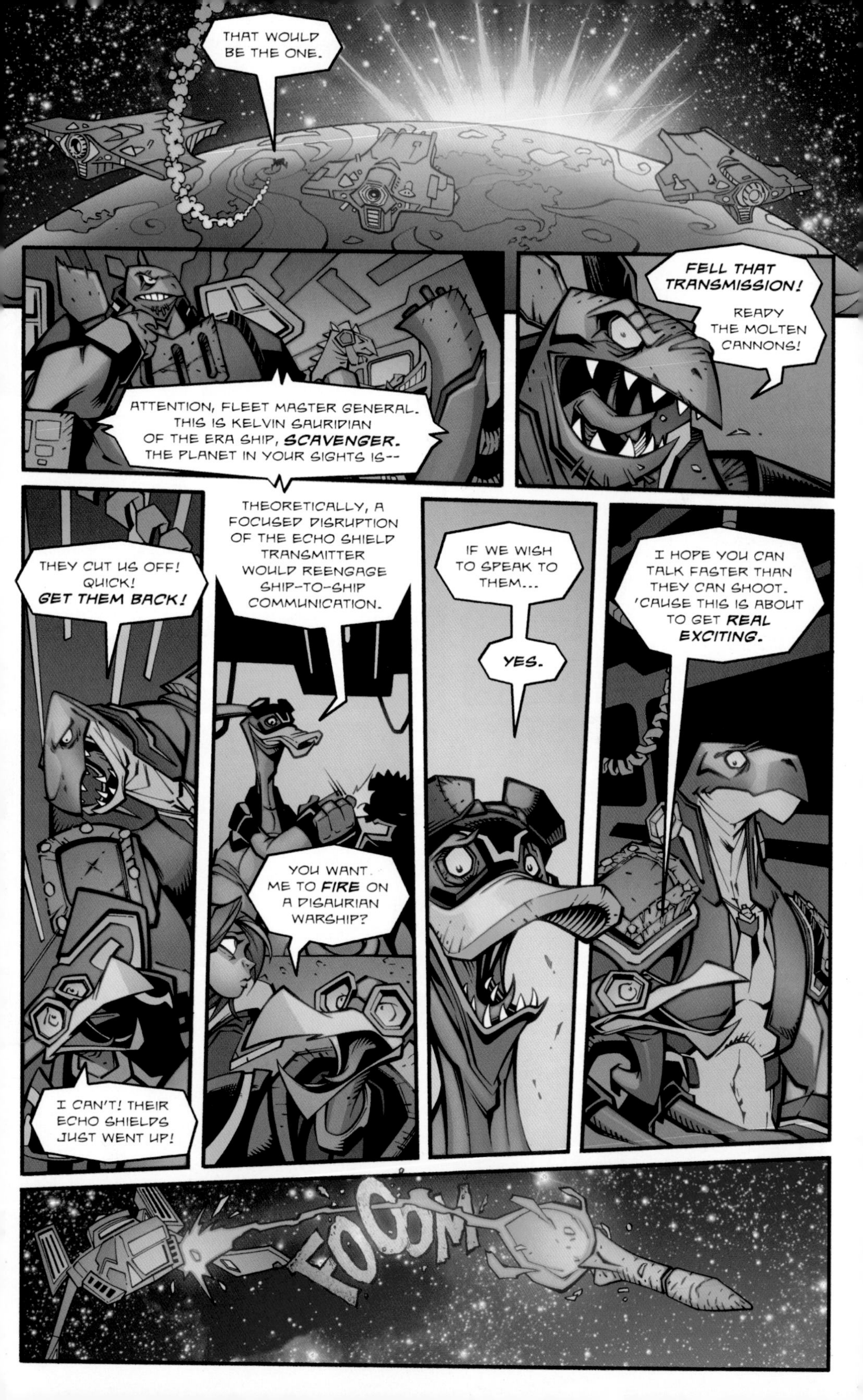
THAT WOULD BE THE ONE.
ATTENTION, FLEET MASTER GENERAL. THIS IS KELVIN SAURIDIAN OF THE ERA SHIP, SCAVENGER. THE PLANET IN YOUR SIGHTS IS--
FELL THAT TRANSMISSION!
READY THE MOLTEN CANNONS!
THEY CUT US OFF! QUICK! GET THEM BACK!
I CAN'T! THEIR ECHO SHIELDS JUST WENT UP!
THEORETICALLY, A FOCUSED DISRUPTION OF THE ECHO SHIELD TRANSMITTER WOULD REENGAGE SHIP-TO-SHIP COMMUNICATION.
YOU WANT ME TO FIRE ON A DISAURIAN WARSHIP?
IF WE WISH TO SPEAK TO THEM...
YES.
I HOPE YOU CAN TALK FASTER THAN THEY CAN SHOOT. 'CAUSE THIS IS ABOUT TO GET REAL EXCITING.
FOOOM

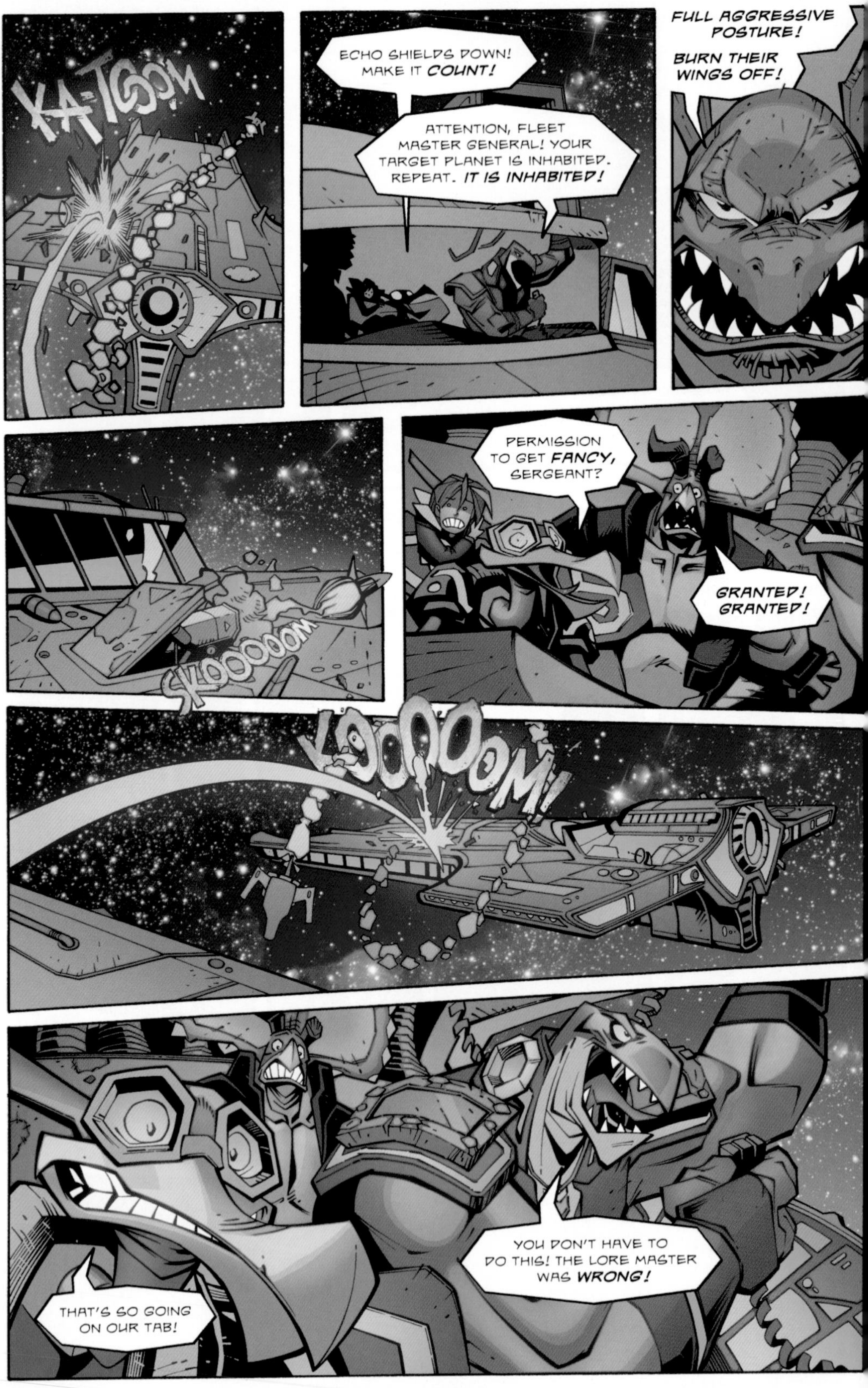
KA-TOOOM
ECHO SHIELDS DOWN! MAKE IT COUNT!
ATTENTION, FLEET MASTER GENERAL! YOUR TARGET PLANET IS INHABITED. REPEAT. IT IS INHABITED!
FULL AGGRESSIVE POSTURE!
BURN THEIR WINGS OFF!
SKOOOOOM
PERMISSION TO GET FANCY, SERGEANT?
GRANTED! GRANTED!
VOOOOOM!
YOU DON'T HAVE TO DO THIS! THE LORE MASTER WAS WRONG!
THAT'S SO GOING ON OUR TAB!

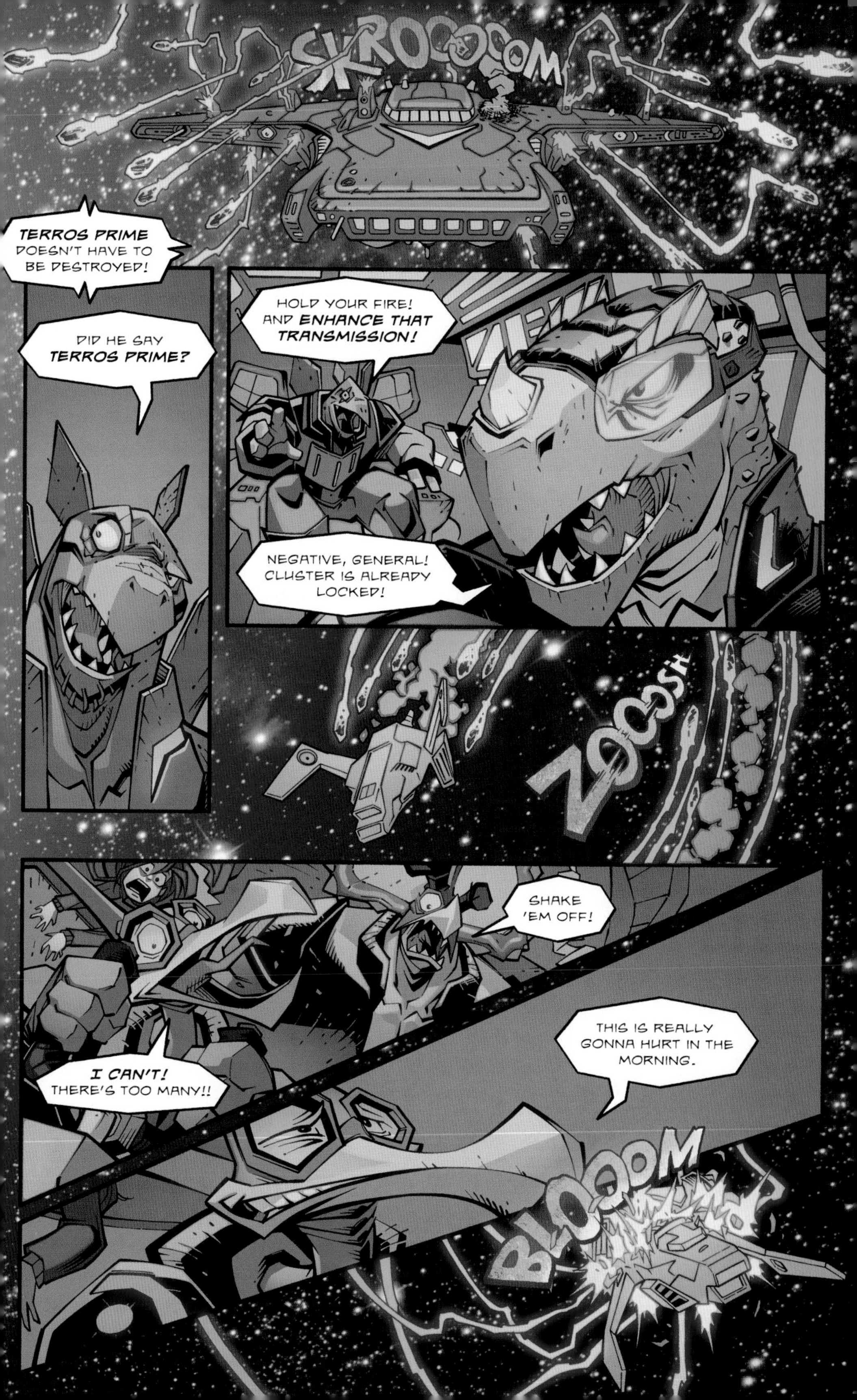
SKROOOOOM
TERROS PRIME DOESN'T HAVE TO BE DESTROYED!
DID HE SAY TERROS PRIME?
HOLD YOUR FIRE! AND ENHANCE THAT TRANSMISSION!
NEGATIVE, GENERAL! CLUSTER IS ALREADY LOCKED!
ZOOOSH
SHAKE 'EM OFF!
I CAN'T! THERE'S TOO MANY!!
THIS IS REALLY GONNA HURT IN THE MORNING.
BLOOOOM

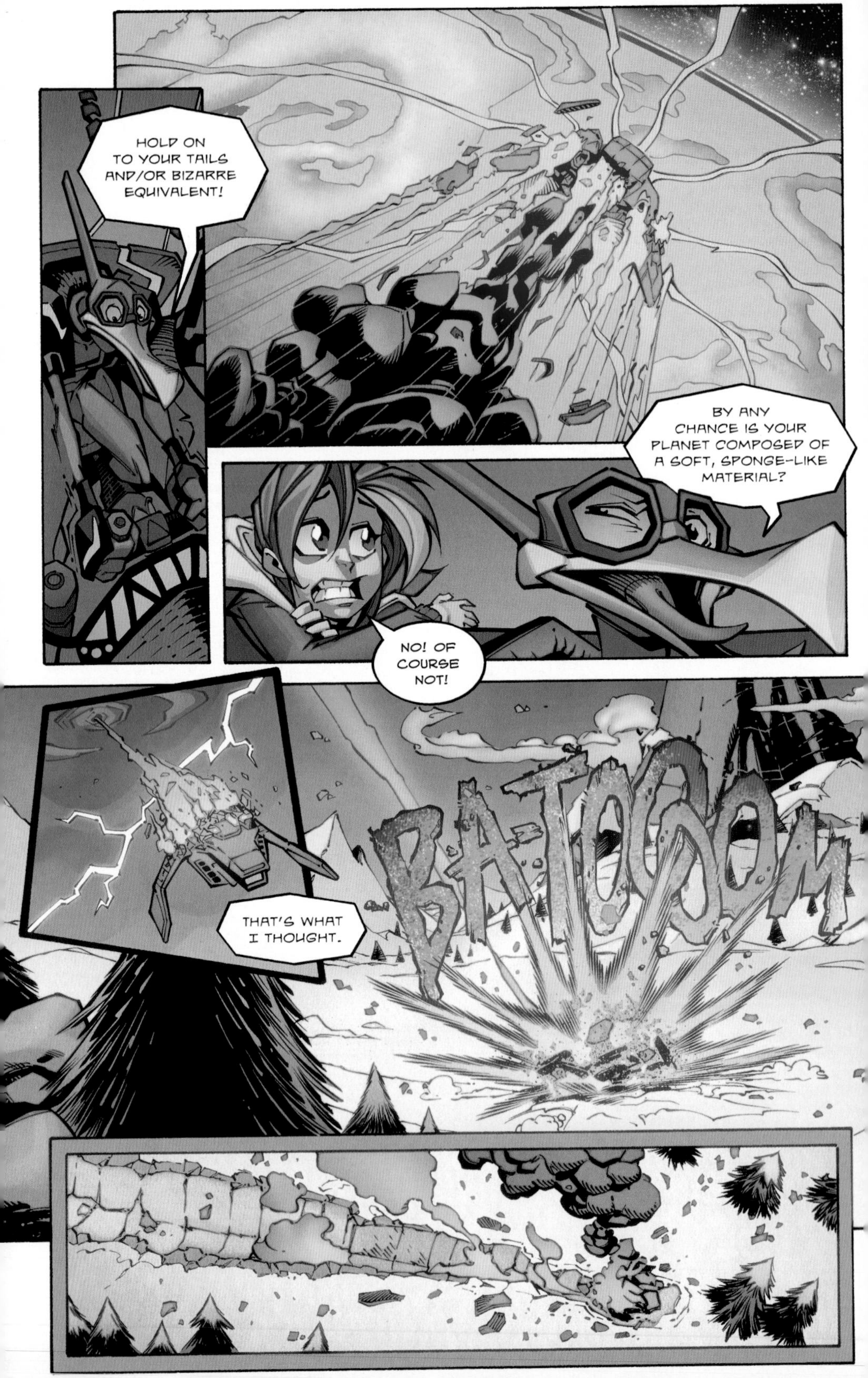
HOLD ON TO YOUR TAILS AND/OR BIZARRE EQUIVALENT!
BY ANY CHANCE IS YOUR PLANET COMPOSED OF A SOFT, SPONGE-LIKE MATERIAL?
NO! OF COURSE NOT!
THAT'S WHAT I THOUGHT.
BA-TOOOOM

CHAPTER
4

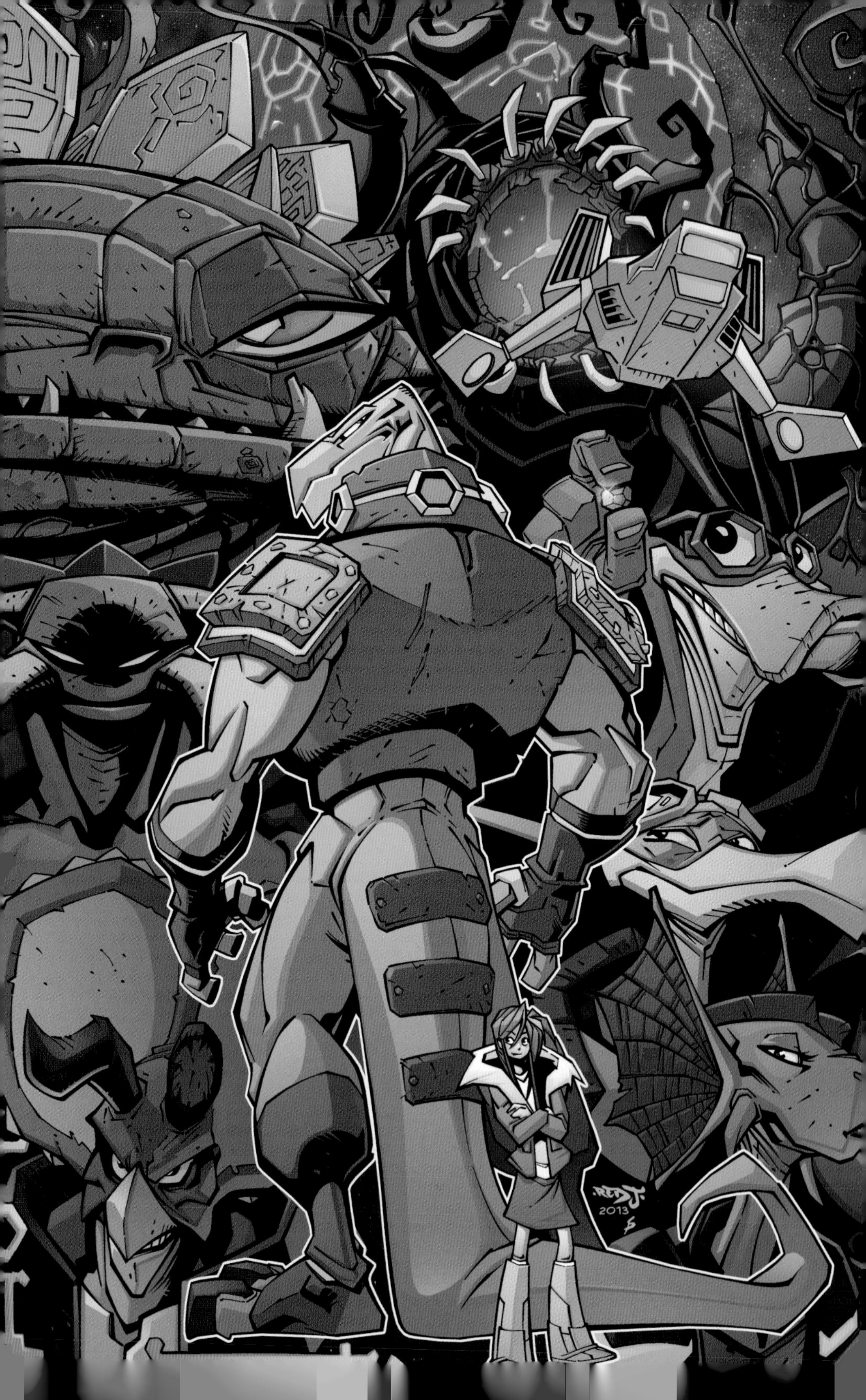
2013

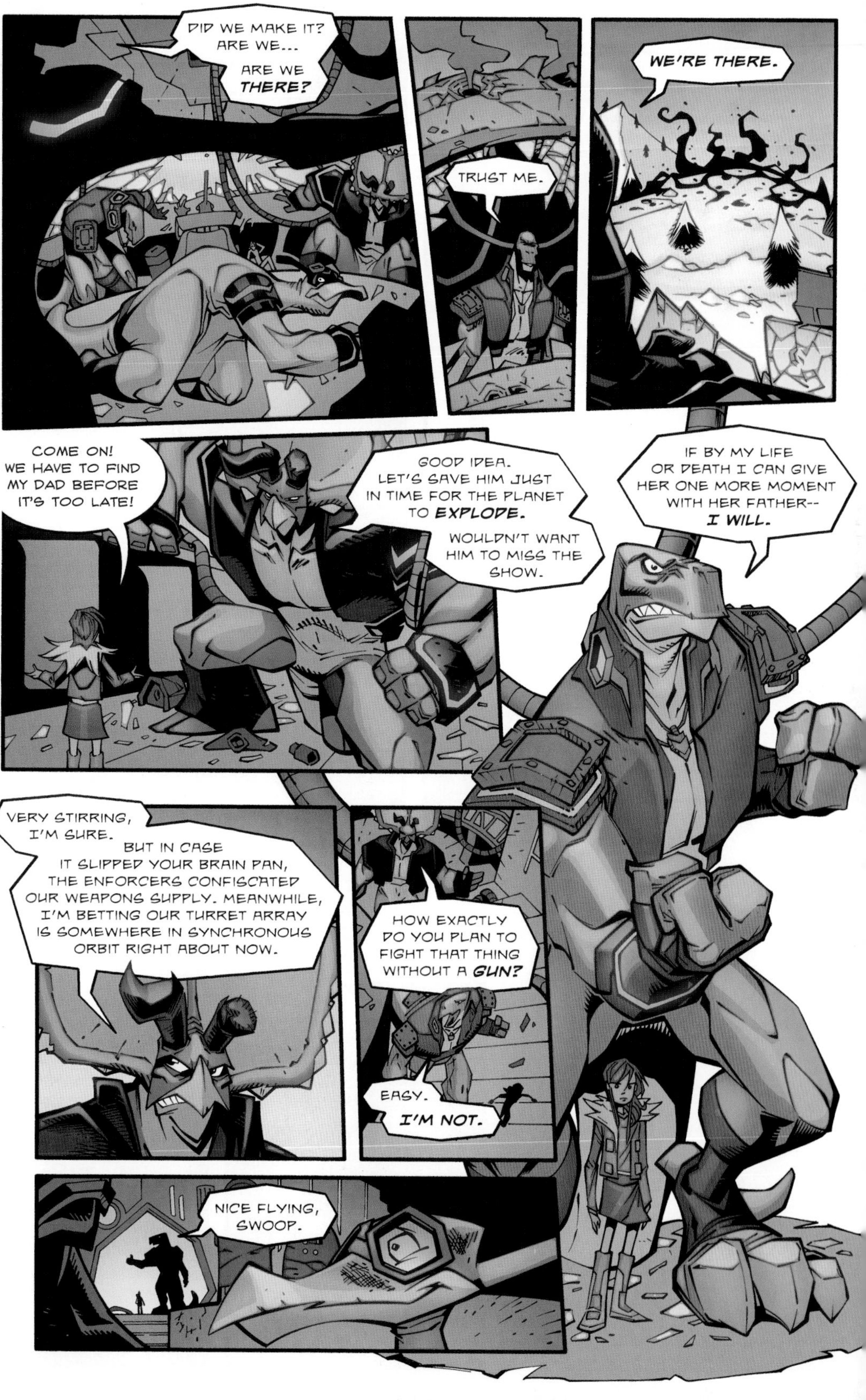
DID WE MAKE IT? ARE WE...
ARE WE *THERE?*
TRUST ME.
WE'RE THERE.
COME ON! WE HAVE TO FIND MY DAD BEFORE IT'S TOO LATE!
GOOD IDEA. LET'S SAVE HIM JUST IN TIME FOR THE PLANET TO *EXPLODE.*
WOULDN'T WANT HIM TO MISS THE SHOW.
IF BY MY LIFE OR DEATH I CAN GIVE HER ONE MORE MOMENT WITH HER FATHER-- *I WILL.*
VERY STIRRING, I'M SURE.
BUT IN CASE IT SLIPPED YOUR BRAIN PAN, THE ENFORCERS CONFISCATED OUR WEAPONS SUPPLY. MEANWHILE, I'M BETTING OUR TURRET ARRAY IS SOMEWHERE IN SYNCHRONOUS ORBIT RIGHT ABOUT NOW.
HOW EXACTLY DO YOU PLAN TO FIGHT THAT THING WITHOUT A *GUN?*
EASY. *I'M NOT.*
NICE FLYING, SWOOP.

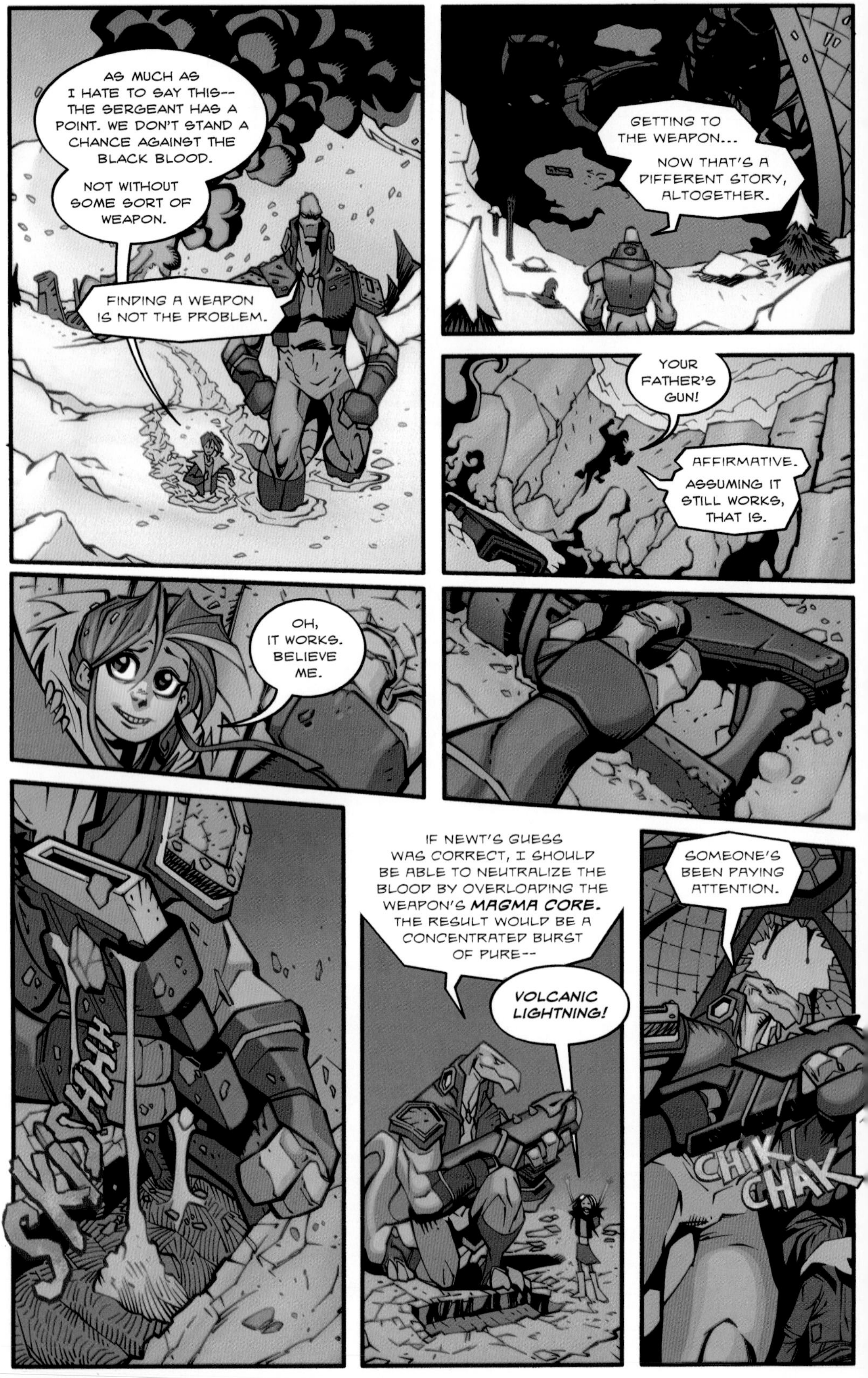
AS MUCH AS I HATE TO SAY THIS-- THE SERGEANT HAS A POINT. WE DON'T STAND A CHANCE AGAINST THE BLACK BLOOD.
NOT WITHOUT SOME SORT OF WEAPON.
FINDING A WEAPON IS NOT THE PROBLEM.
GETTING TO THE WEAPON...
NOW THAT'S A DIFFERENT STORY, ALTOGETHER.
YOUR FATHER'S GUN!
AFFIRMATIVE.
ASSUMING IT STILL WORKS, THAT IS.
OH, IT WORKS. BELIEVE ME.
SSSHHHH
IF NEWT'S GUESS WAS CORRECT, I SHOULD BE ABLE TO NEUTRALIZE THE BLOOD BY OVERLOADING THE WEAPON'S MAGMA CORE. THE RESULT WOULD BE A CONCENTRATED BURST OF PURE--
VOLCANIC LIGHTNING!
SOMEONE'S BEEN PAYING ATTENTION.
CHIK CHAK

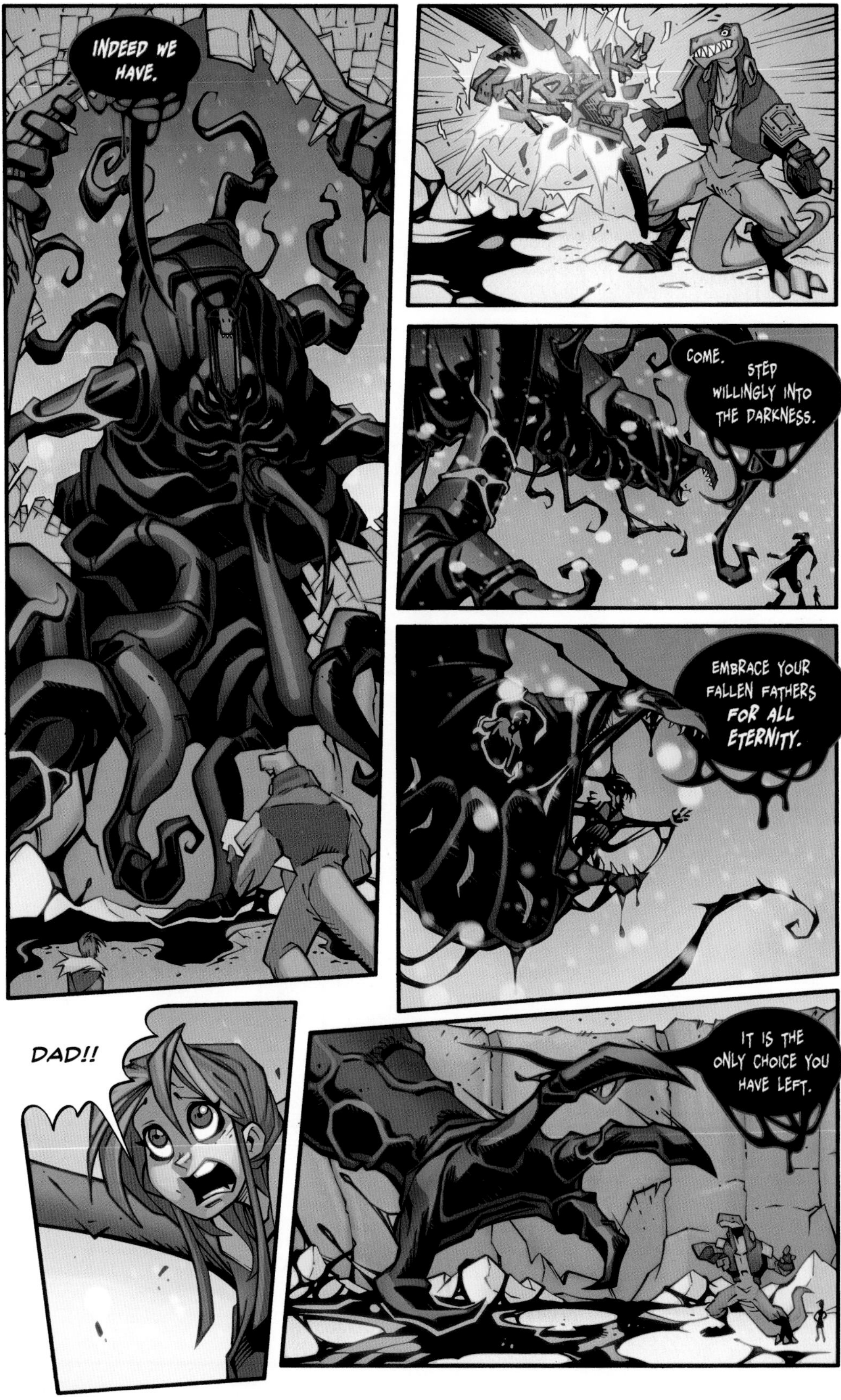
INDEED WE HAVE.
COME. STEP WILLINGLY INTO THE DARKNESS.
EMBRACE YOUR FALLEN FATHERS FOR ALL ETERNITY.
DAD!!
IT IS THE ONLY CHOICE YOU HAVE LEFT.

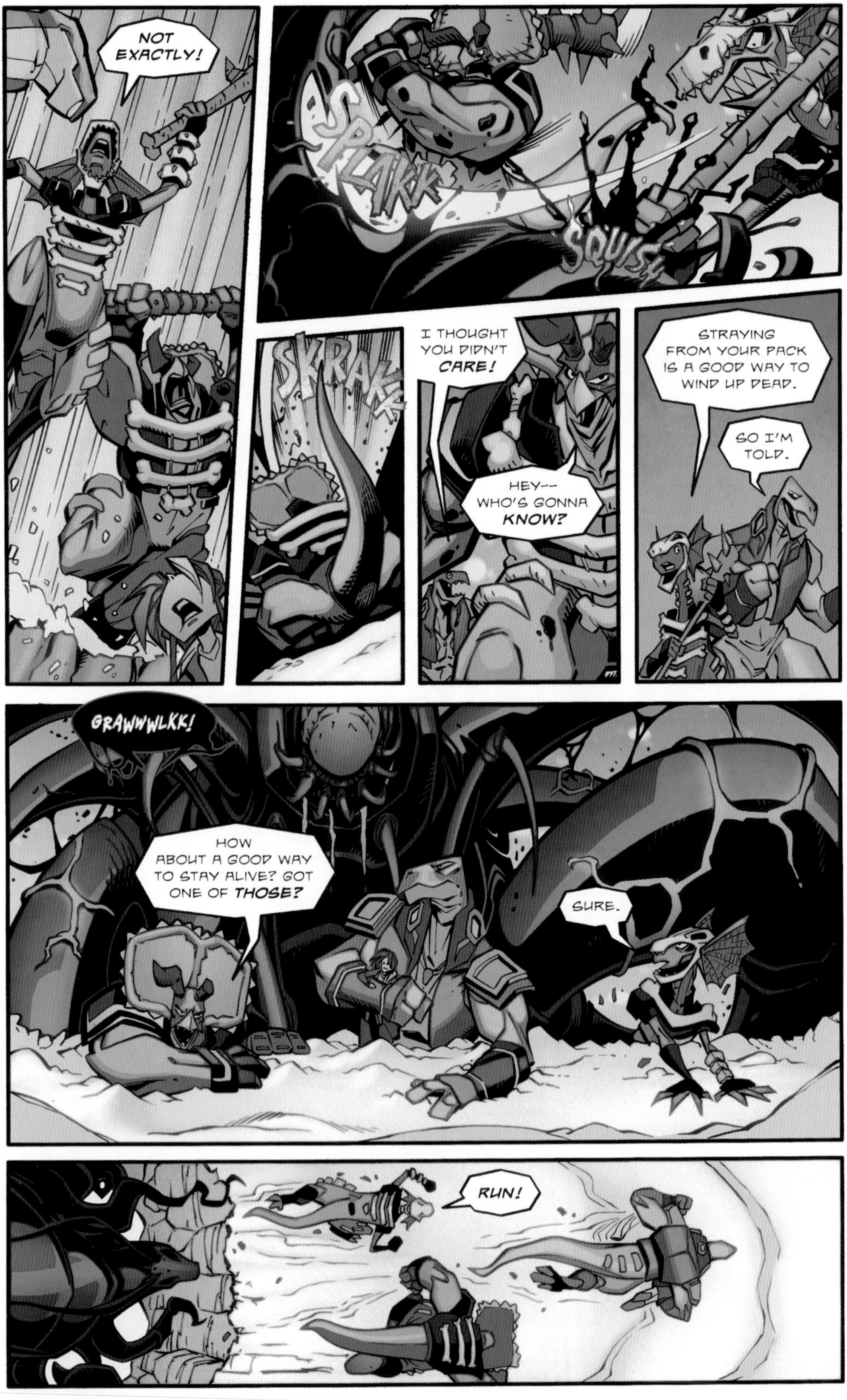

NOT EXACTLY!
SPLAKK
SQUISH
SKRAKK
I THOUGHT YOU DIDN'T CARE!
HEY-- WHO'S GONNA KNOW?
STRAYING FROM YOUR PACK IS A GOOD WAY TO WIND UP DEAD.
SO I'M TOLD.
GRAWWWLKK!
HOW ABOUT A GOOD WAY TO STAY ALIVE? GOT ONE OF THOSE?
SURE.
RUN!

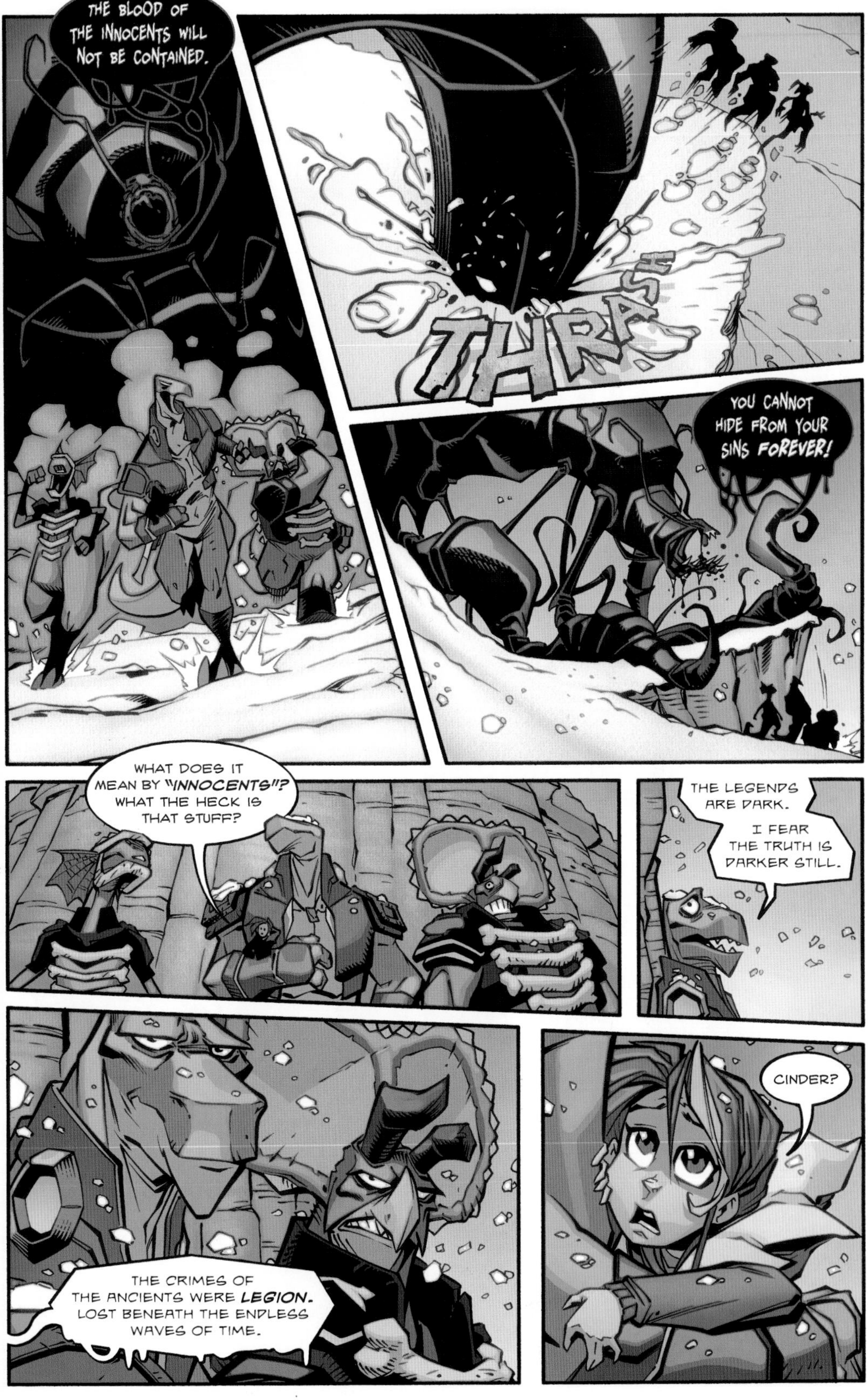
THE BLOOD OF THE INNOCENTS WILL NOT BE CONTAINED.
THRASH
YOU CANNOT HIDE FROM YOUR SINS FOREVER!
WHAT DOES IT MEAN BY "INNOCENTS"? WHAT THE HECK IS THAT STUFF?
THE LEGENDS ARE DARK.
I FEAR THE TRUTH IS DARKER STILL.
THE CRIMES OF THE ANCIENTS WERE LEGION. LOST BENEATH THE ENDLESS WAVES OF TIME.
CINDER?

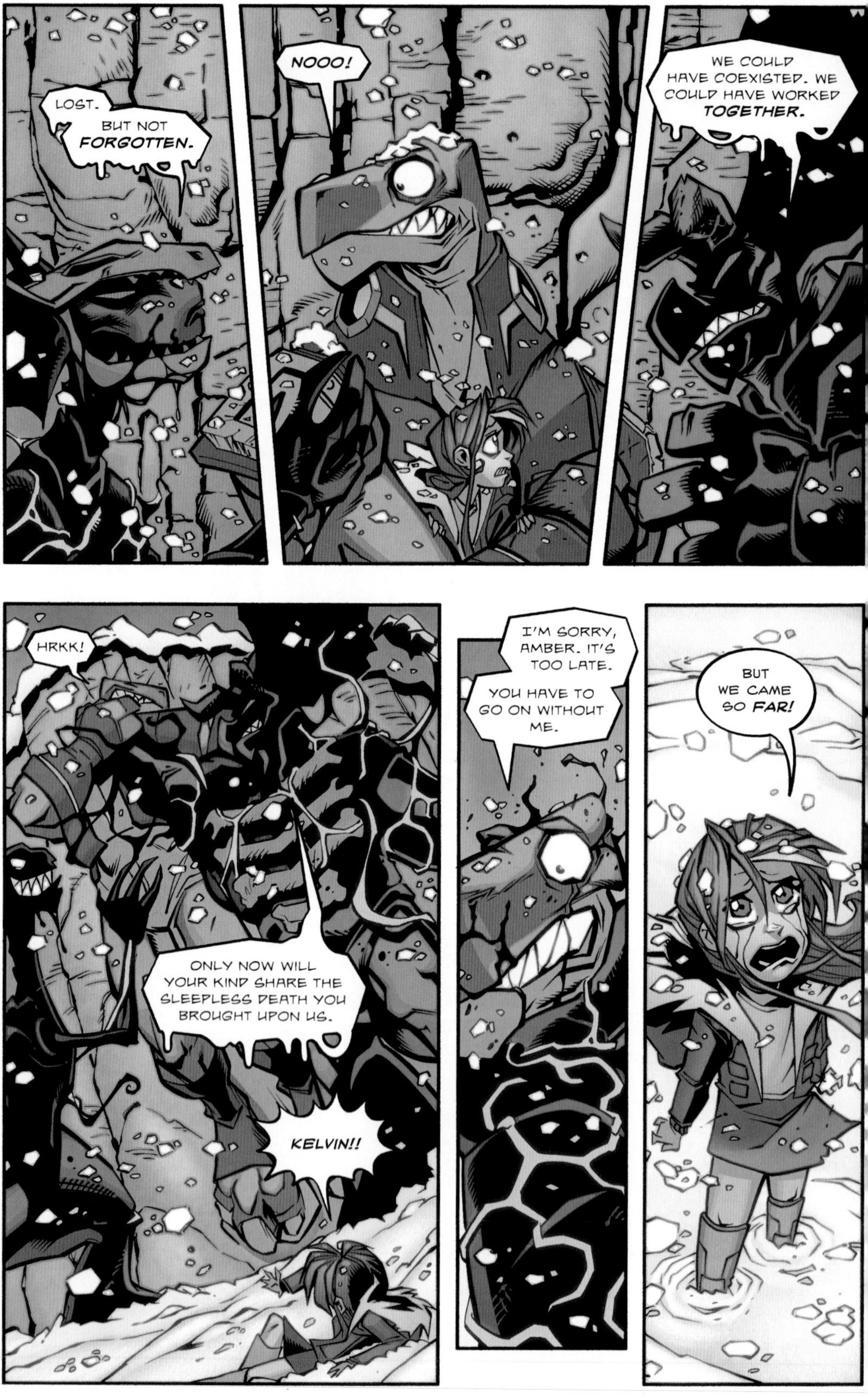
LOST.
BUT NOT FORGOTTEN.
NOOO!
WE COULD HAVE COEXISTED. WE COULD HAVE WORKED TOGETHER.
HRKK!
ONLY NOW WILL YOUR KIND SHARE THE SLEEPLESS DEATH YOU BROUGHT UPON US.
KELVIN!!
I'M SORRY, AMBER. IT'S TOO LATE.
YOU HAVE TO GO ON WITHOUT ME.
BUT WE CAME SO FAR!

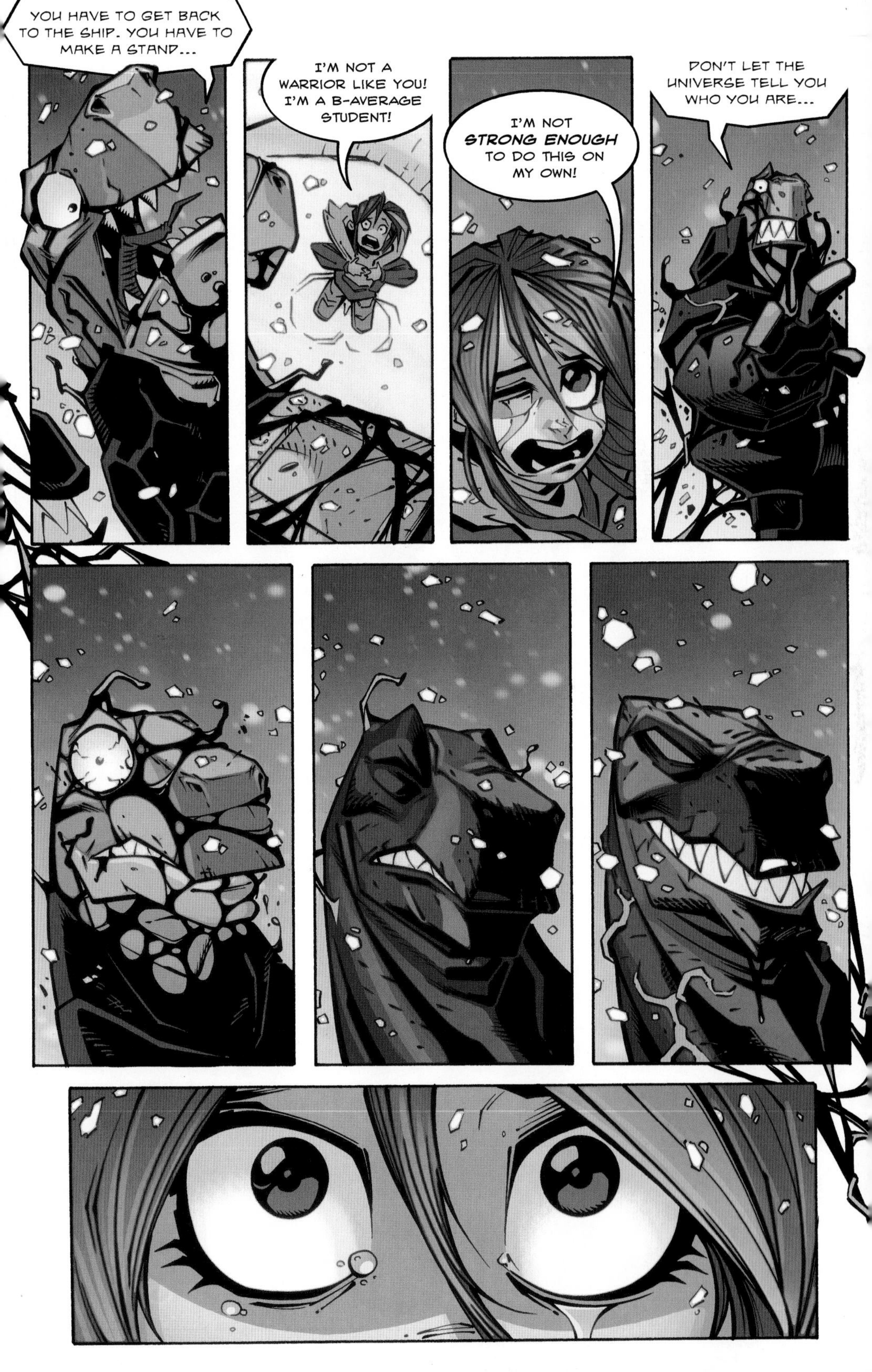
YOU HAVE TO GET BACK TO THE SHIP. YOU HAVE TO MAKE A STAND...
I'M NOT A WARRIOR LIKE YOU! I'M A B-AVERAGE STUDENT!
I'M NOT **STRONG ENOUGH** TO DO THIS ON MY OWN!
DON'T LET THE UNIVERSE TELL YOU WHO YOU ARE...

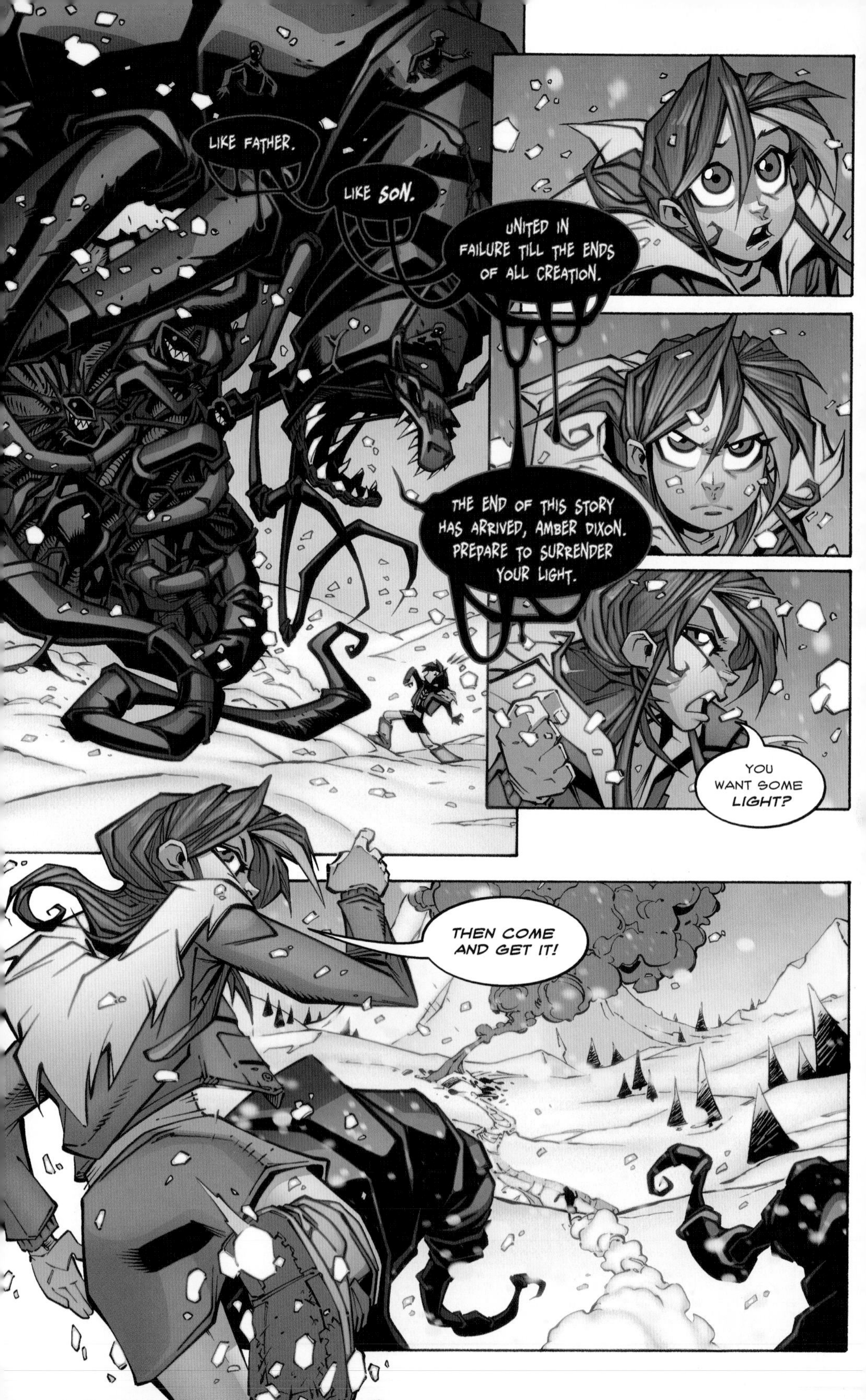
LIKE FATHER.
LIKE SON.
UNITED IN FAILURE TILL THE ENDS OF ALL CREATION.
THE END OF THIS STORY HAS ARRIVED, AMBER DIXON. PREPARE TO SURRENDER YOUR LIGHT.
YOU WANT SOME LIGHT?
THEN COME AND GET IT!

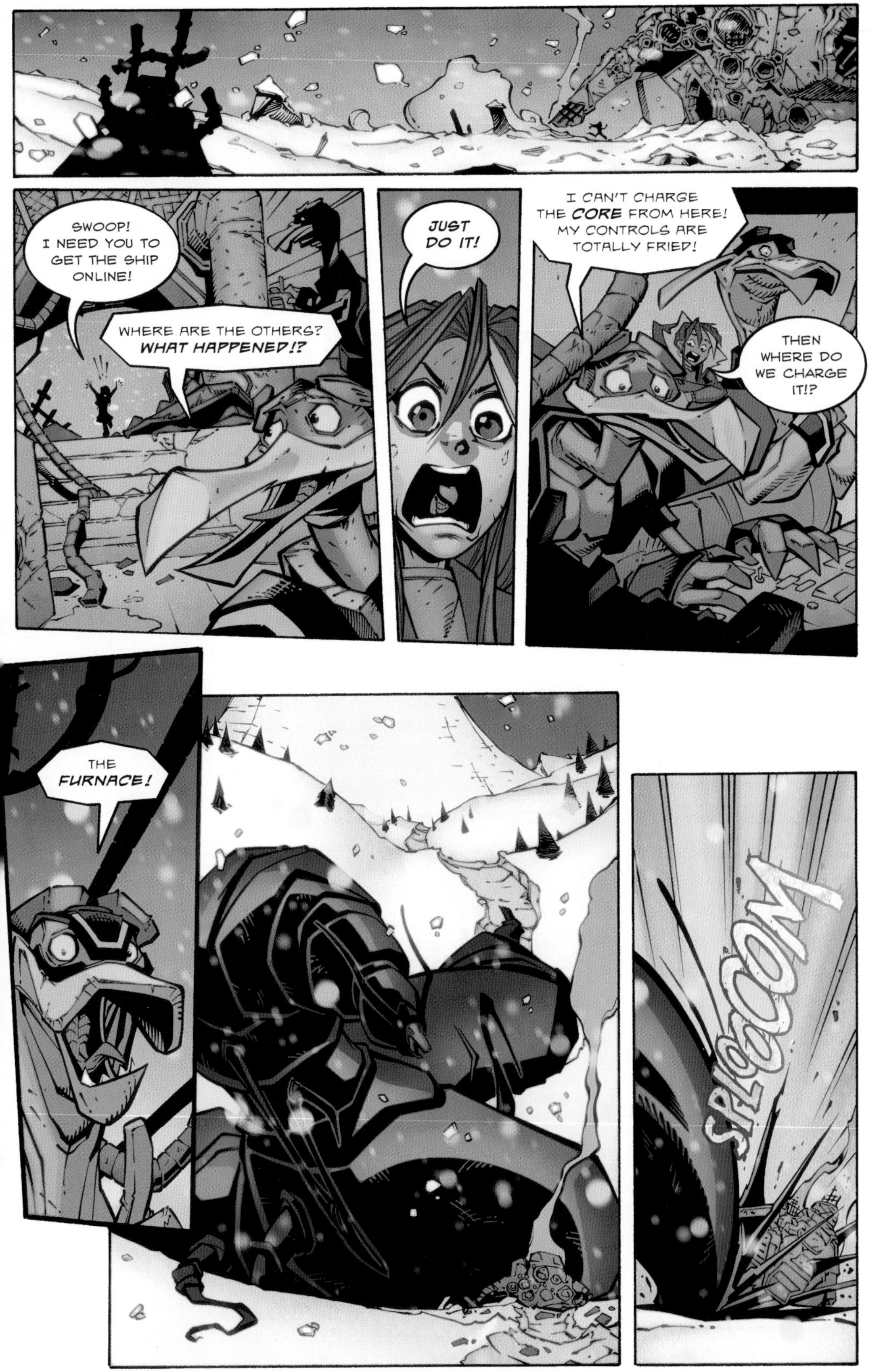
SWOOP!
I NEED YOU TO
GET THE SHIP
ONLINE!
WHERE ARE THE OTHERS?
WHAT HAPPENED!?
JUST
DO IT!
I CAN'T CHARGE
THE CORE FROM HERE!
MY CONTROLS ARE
TOTALLY FRIED!
THEN
WHERE DO
WE CHARGE
IT!?
THE
FURNACE!
SPLOOOOM

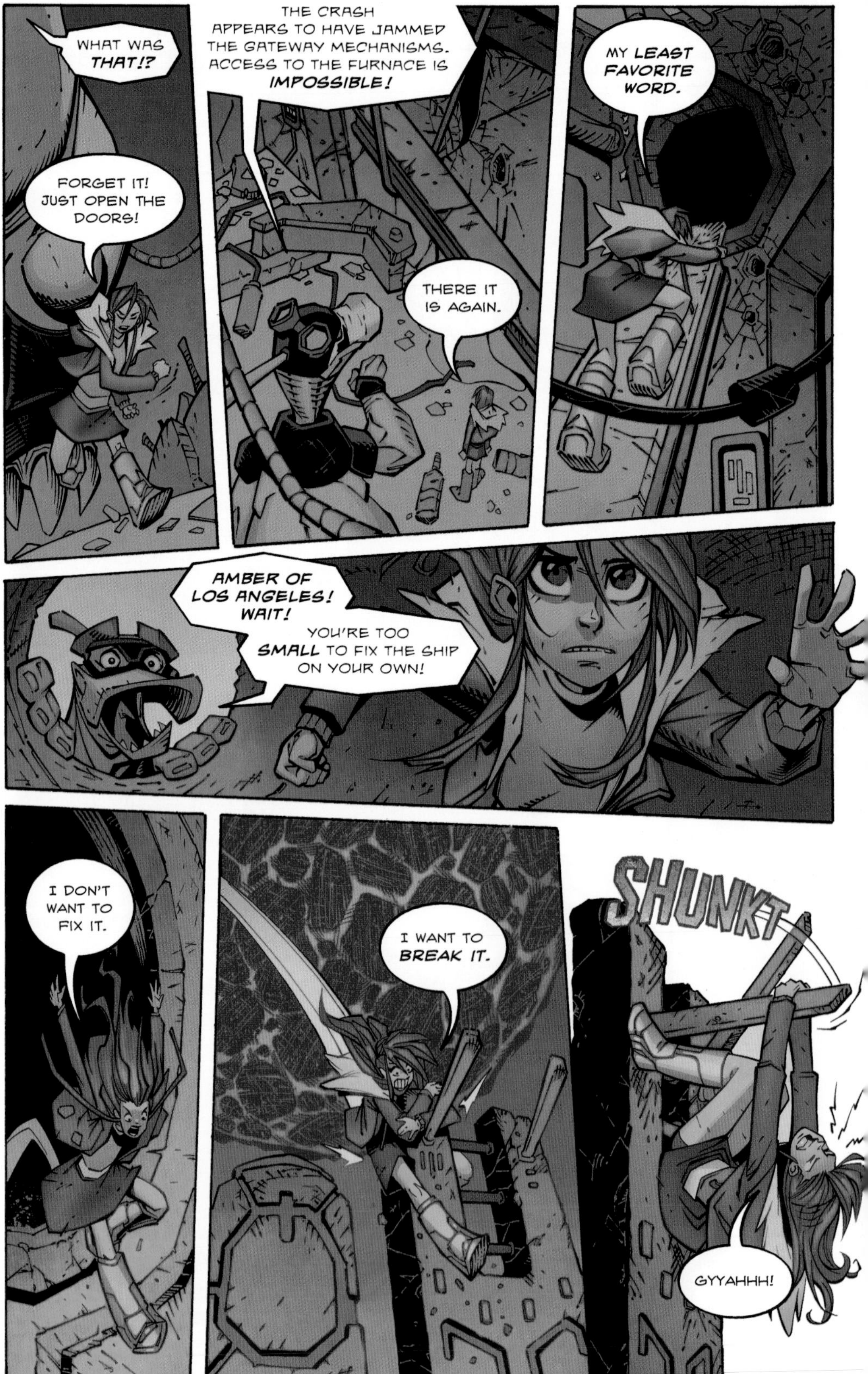
WHAT WAS THAT!?
FORGET IT! JUST OPEN THE DOORS!
THE CRASH APPEARS TO HAVE JAMMED THE GATEWAY MECHANISMS. ACCESS TO THE FURNACE IS IMPOSSIBLE!
THERE IT IS AGAIN.
MY LEAST FAVORITE WORD.
AMBER OF LOS ANGELES! WAIT!
YOU'RE TOO SMALL TO FIX THE SHIP ON YOUR OWN!
I DON'T WANT TO FIX IT.
I WANT TO BREAK IT.
SHUNKT
GYYAHHH!

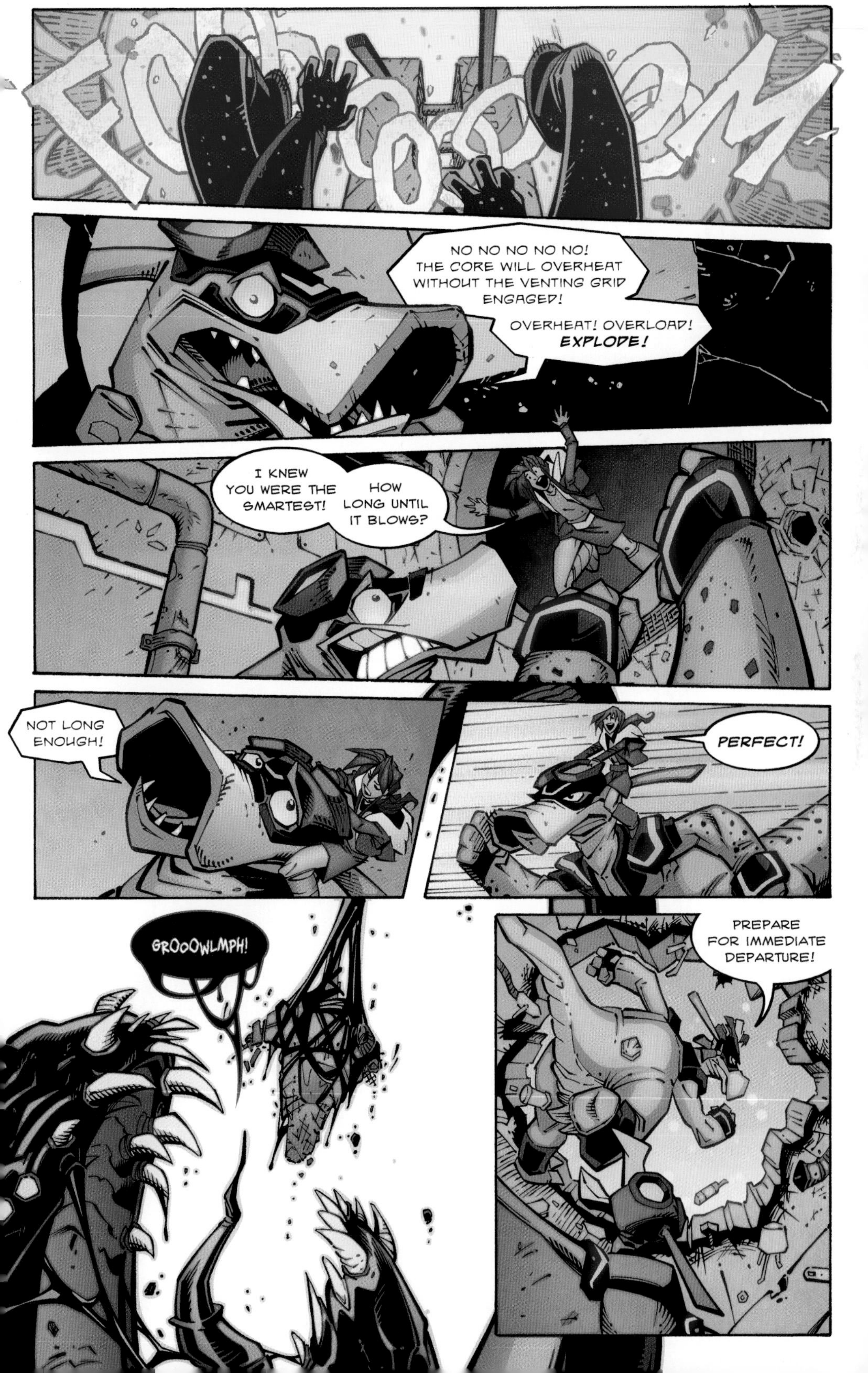
FOOOOOM
NO NO NO NO NO! THE CORE WILL OVERHEAT WITHOUT THE VENTING GRID ENGAGED!
OVERHEAT! OVERLOAD! **EXPLODE!**
I KNEW YOU WERE THE SMARTEST!
HOW LONG UNTIL IT BLOWS?
NOT LONG ENOUGH!
PERFECT!
GROOOWLMPH!
PREPARE FOR IMMEDIATE DEPARTURE!

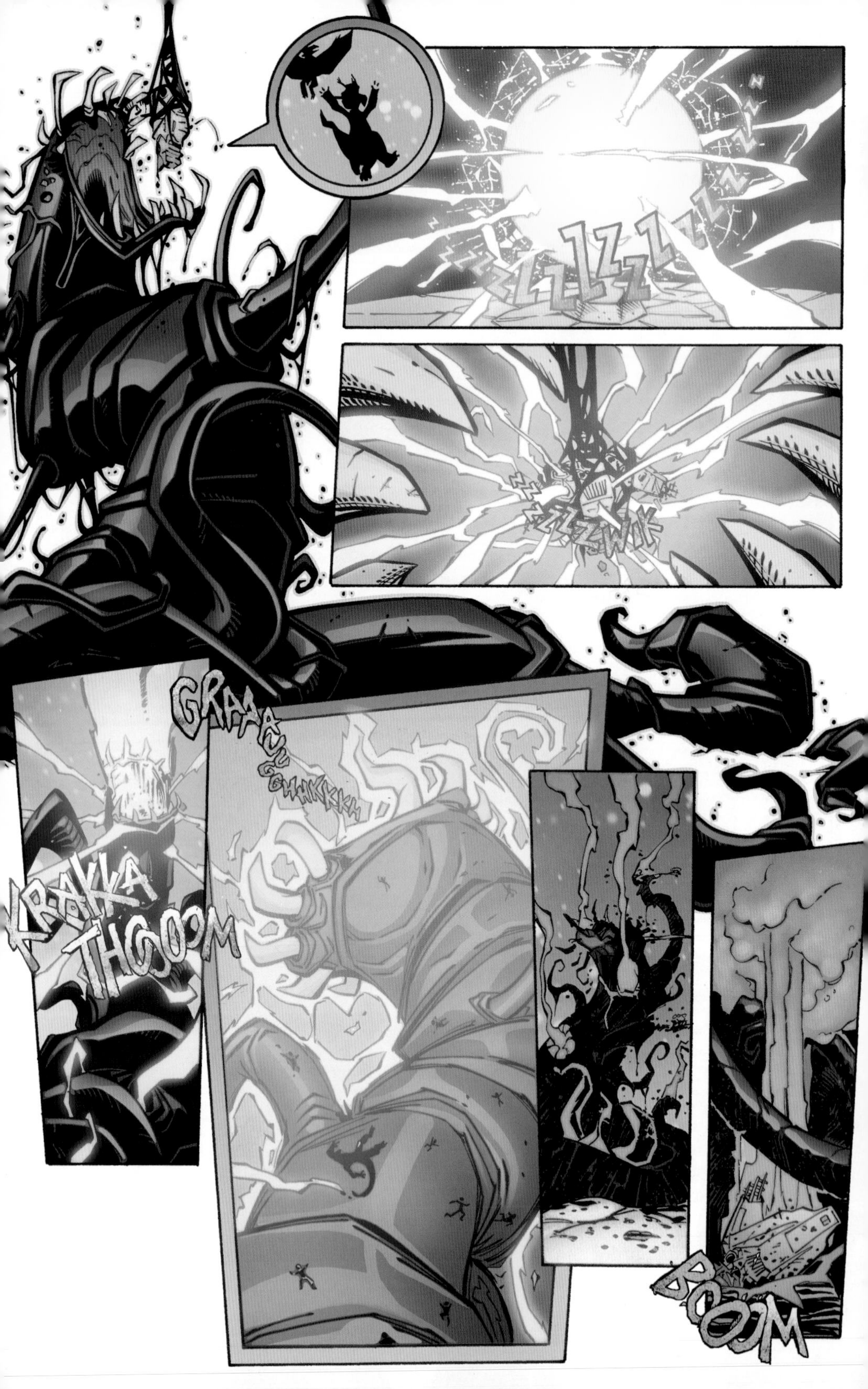
ZZZZZZZZZZZ
ZZZZZWIK
KRAKKA THOOOM
GRAAAUGHHKKKH
BOOOM

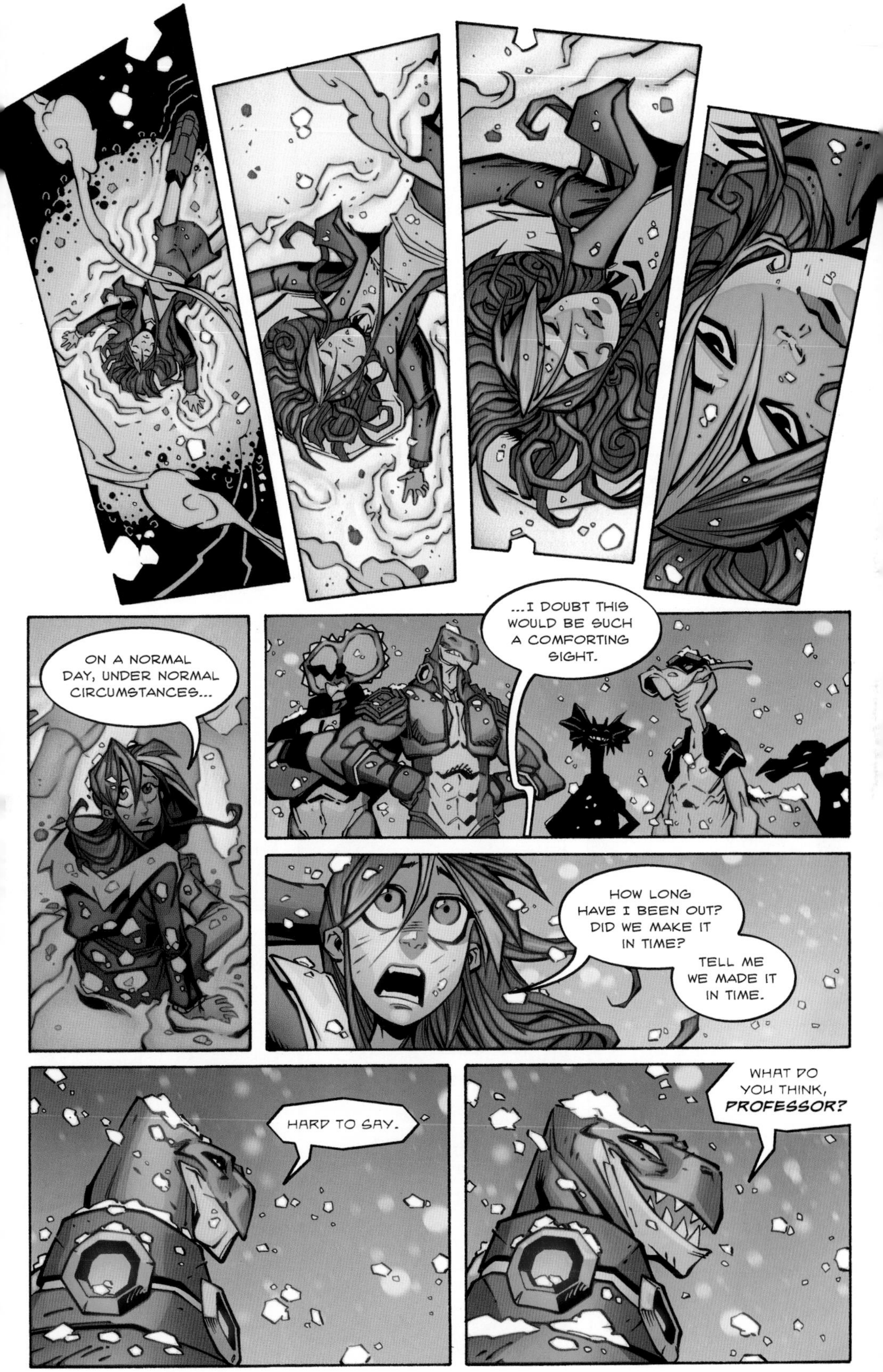
ON A NORMAL DAY, UNDER NORMAL CIRCUMSTANCES...
...I DOUBT THIS WOULD BE SUCH A COMFORTING SIGHT.
HOW LONG HAVE I BEEN OUT? DID WE MAKE IT IN TIME?
TELL ME WE MADE IT IN TIME.
HARD TO SAY.
WHAT DO YOU THINK, PROFESSOR?

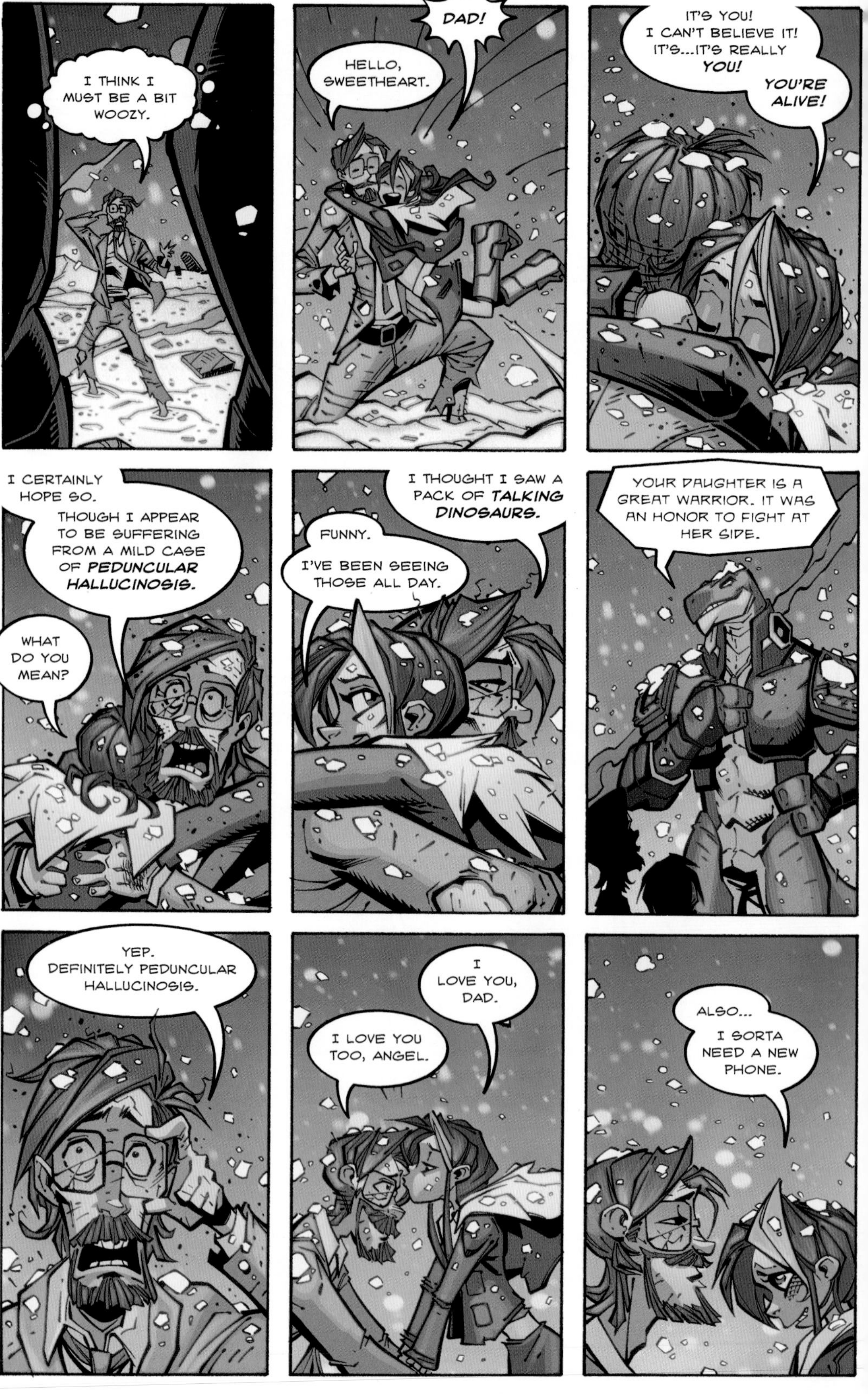
I THINK I MUST BE A BIT WOOZY.
HELLO, SWEETHEART.
DAD!
IT'S YOU! I CAN'T BELIEVE IT! IT'S...IT'S REALLY YOU!
YOU'RE ALIVE!
I CERTAINLY HOPE SO.
THOUGH I APPEAR TO BE SUFFERING FROM A MILD CASE OF PEDUNCULAR HALLUCINOSIS.
WHAT DO YOU MEAN?
I THOUGHT I SAW A PACK OF TALKING DINOSAURS.
FUNNY.
I'VE BEEN SEEING THOSE ALL DAY.
YOUR DAUGHTER IS A GREAT WARRIOR. IT WAS AN HONOR TO FIGHT AT HER SIDE.
YEP. DEFINITELY PEDUNCULAR HALLUCINOSIS.
I LOVE YOU, DAD.
I LOVE YOU TOO, ANGEL.
ALSO...
I SORTA NEED A NEW PHONE.

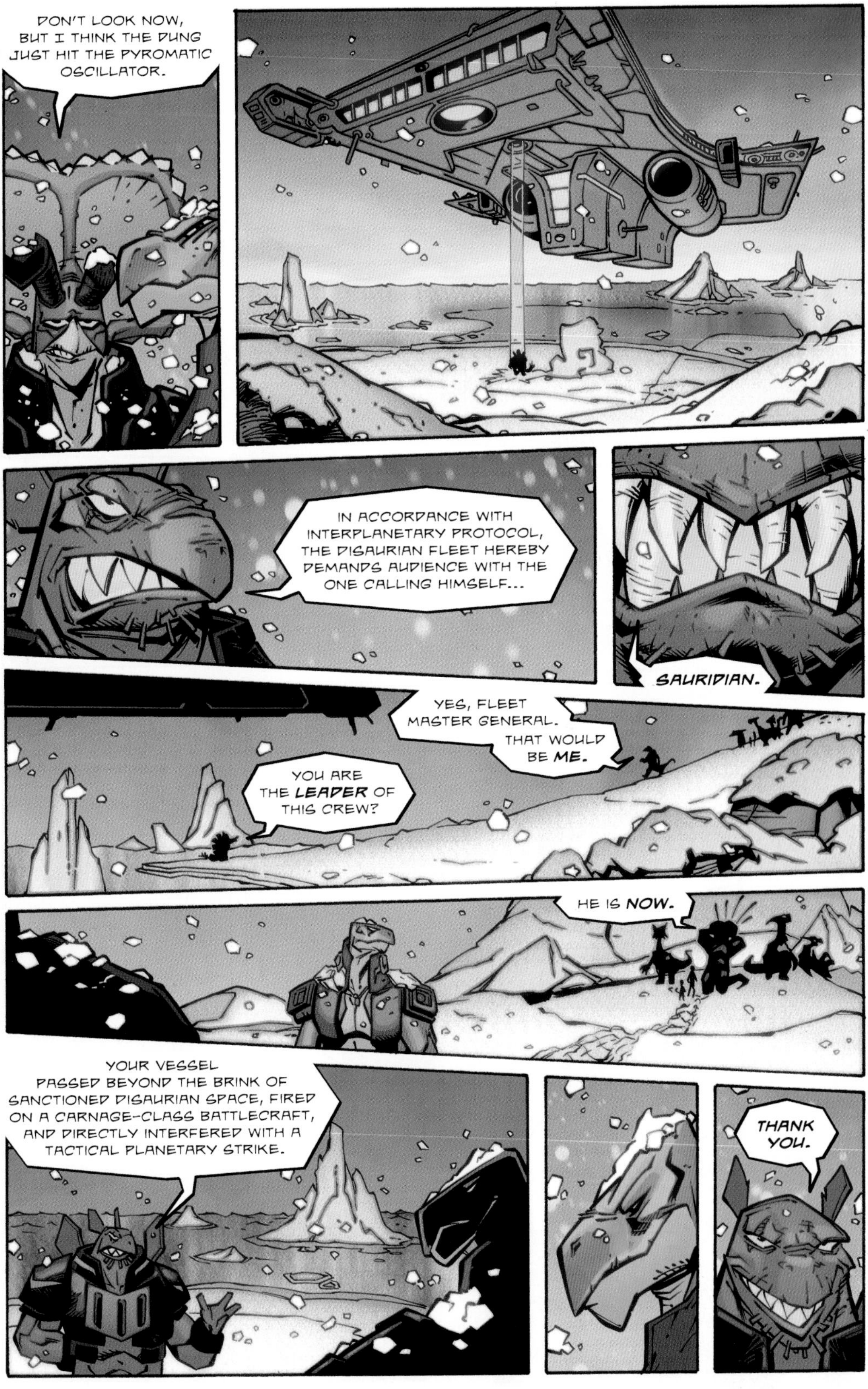

DON'T LOOK NOW, BUT I THINK THE DUNG JUST HIT THE PYROMATIC OSCILLATOR.
IN ACCORDANCE WITH INTERPLANETARY PROTOCOL, THE DISAURIAN FLEET HEREBY DEMANDS AUDIENCE WITH THE ONE CALLING HIMSELF...
SAURIDIAN.
YOU ARE THE LEADER OF THIS CREW?
YES, FLEET MASTER GENERAL.
THAT WOULD BE ME.
HE IS NOW.
YOUR VESSEL PASSED BEYOND THE BRINK OF SANCTIONED DISAURIAN SPACE, FIRED ON A CARNAGE-CLASS BATTLECRAFT, AND DIRECTLY INTERFERED WITH A TACTICAL PLANETARY STRIKE.
THANK YOU.

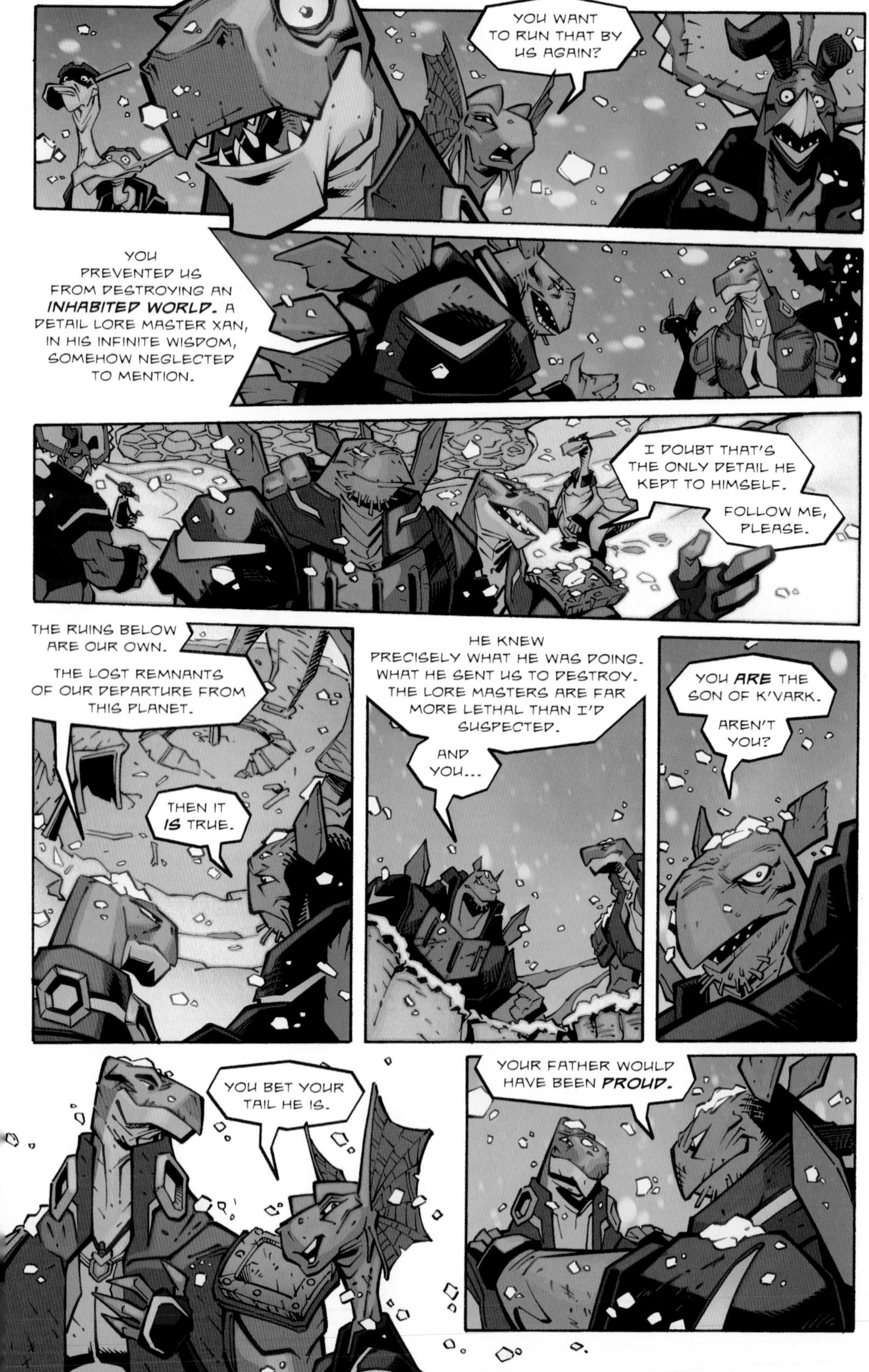
YOU WANT TO RUN THAT BY US AGAIN?
YOU PREVENTED US FROM DESTROYING AN INHABITED WORLD. A DETAIL LORE MASTER XAN, IN HIS INFINITE WISDOM, SOMEHOW NEGLECTED TO MENTION.
I DOUBT THAT'S THE ONLY DETAIL HE KEPT TO HIMSELF.
FOLLOW ME, PLEASE.
THE RUINS BELOW ARE OUR OWN.
THE LOST REMNANTS OF OUR DEPARTURE FROM THIS PLANET.
THEN IT IS TRUE.
HE KNEW PRECISELY WHAT HE WAS DOING. WHAT HE SENT US TO DESTROY. THE LORE MASTERS ARE FAR MORE LETHAL THAN I'D SUSPECTED.
AND YOU...
YOU ARE THE SON OF K'VARK.
AREN'T YOU?
YOU BET YOUR TAIL HE IS.
YOUR FATHER WOULD HAVE BEEN PROUD.

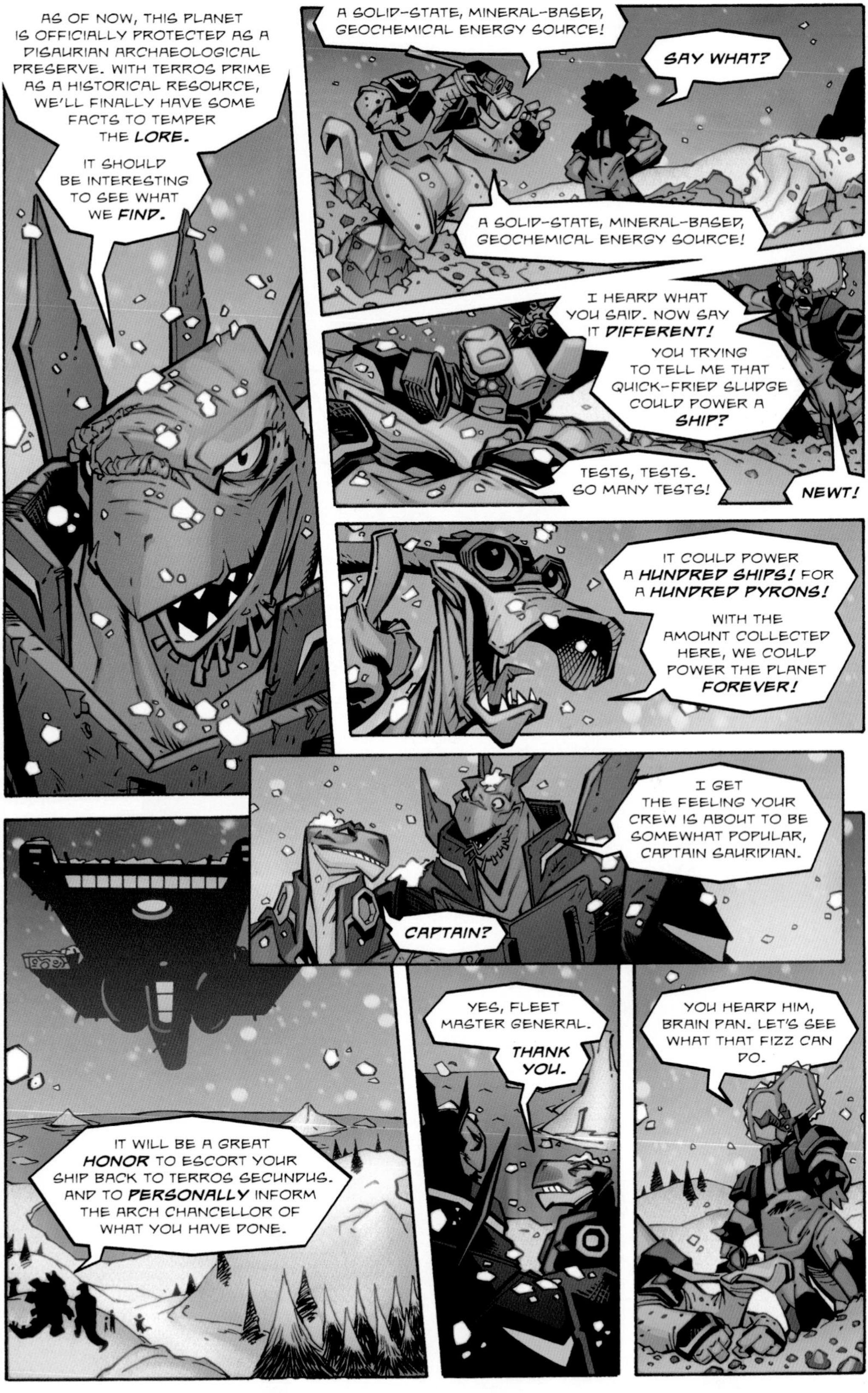
AS OF NOW, THIS PLANET IS OFFICIALLY PROTECTED AS A DISAURIAN ARCHAEOLOGICAL PRESERVE. WITH TERROS PRIME AS A HISTORICAL RESOURCE, WE'LL FINALLY HAVE SOME FACTS TO TEMPER THE LORE.
IT SHOULD BE INTERESTING TO SEE WHAT WE FIND.
A SOLID-STATE, MINERAL-BASED, GEOCHEMICAL ENERGY SOURCE!
SAY WHAT?
A SOLID-STATE, MINERAL-BASED, GEOCHEMICAL ENERGY SOURCE!
I HEARD WHAT YOU SAID. NOW SAY IT DIFFERENT!
YOU TRYING TO TELL ME THAT QUICK-FRIED SLUDGE COULD POWER A SHIP?
TESTS, TESTS. SO MANY TESTS!
NEWT!
IT COULD POWER A HUNDRED SHIPS! FOR A HUNDRED PYRONS!
WITH THE AMOUNT COLLECTED HERE, WE COULD POWER THE PLANET FOREVER!
I GET THE FEELING YOUR CREW IS ABOUT TO BE SOMEWHAT POPULAR, CAPTAIN SAURIDIAN.
CAPTAIN?
IT WILL BE A GREAT HONOR TO ESCORT YOUR SHIP BACK TO TERROS SECUNDUS. AND TO PERSONALLY INFORM THE ARCH CHANCELLOR OF WHAT YOU HAVE DONE.
YES, FLEET MASTER GENERAL.
THANK YOU.
YOU HEARD HIM, BRAIN PAN. LET'S SEE WHAT THAT FIZZ CAN DO.

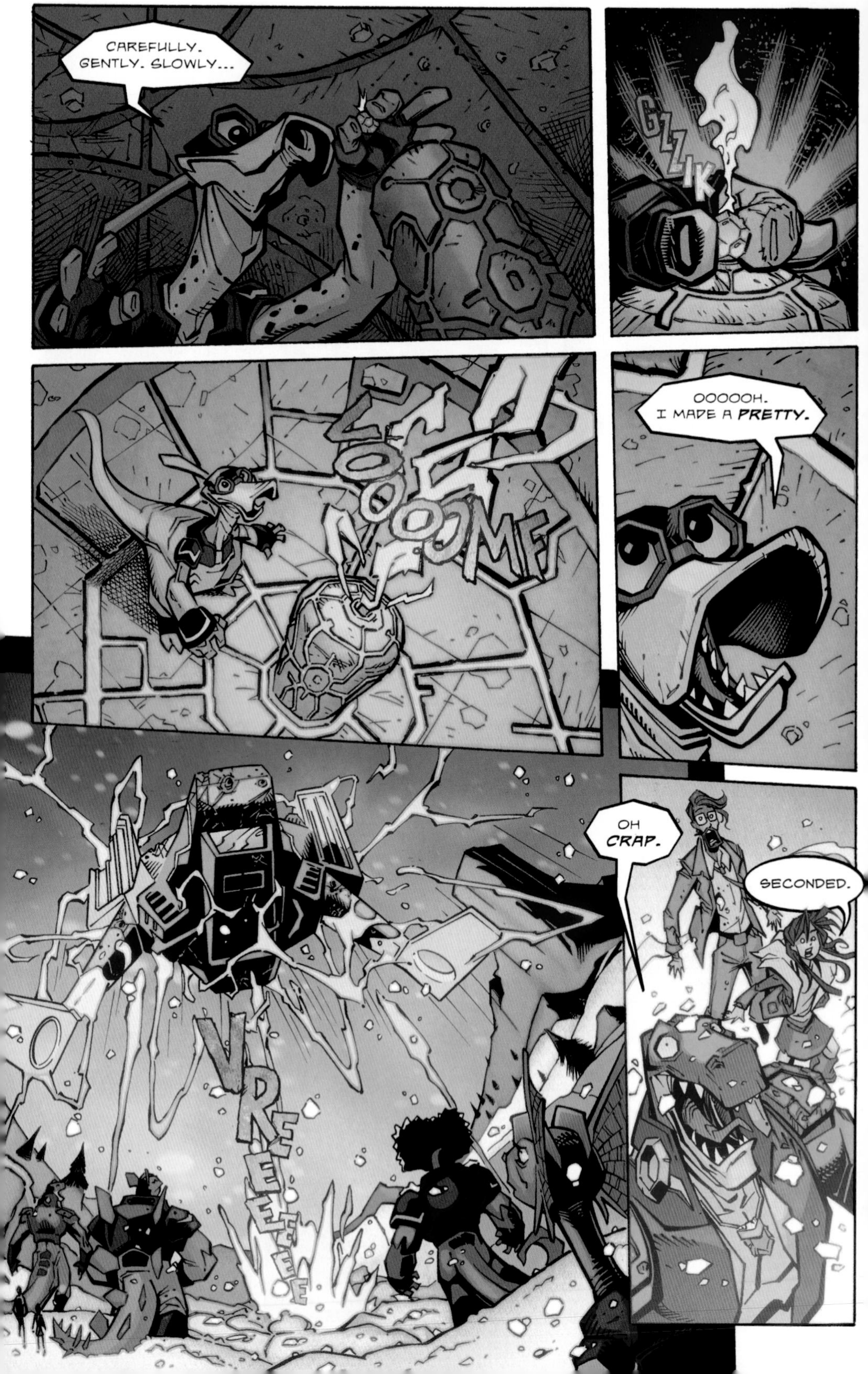
CAREFULLY. GENTLY. SLOWLY...
GZZIK
OOOOOH. I MADE A PRETTY.
OH CRAP.
SECONDED.

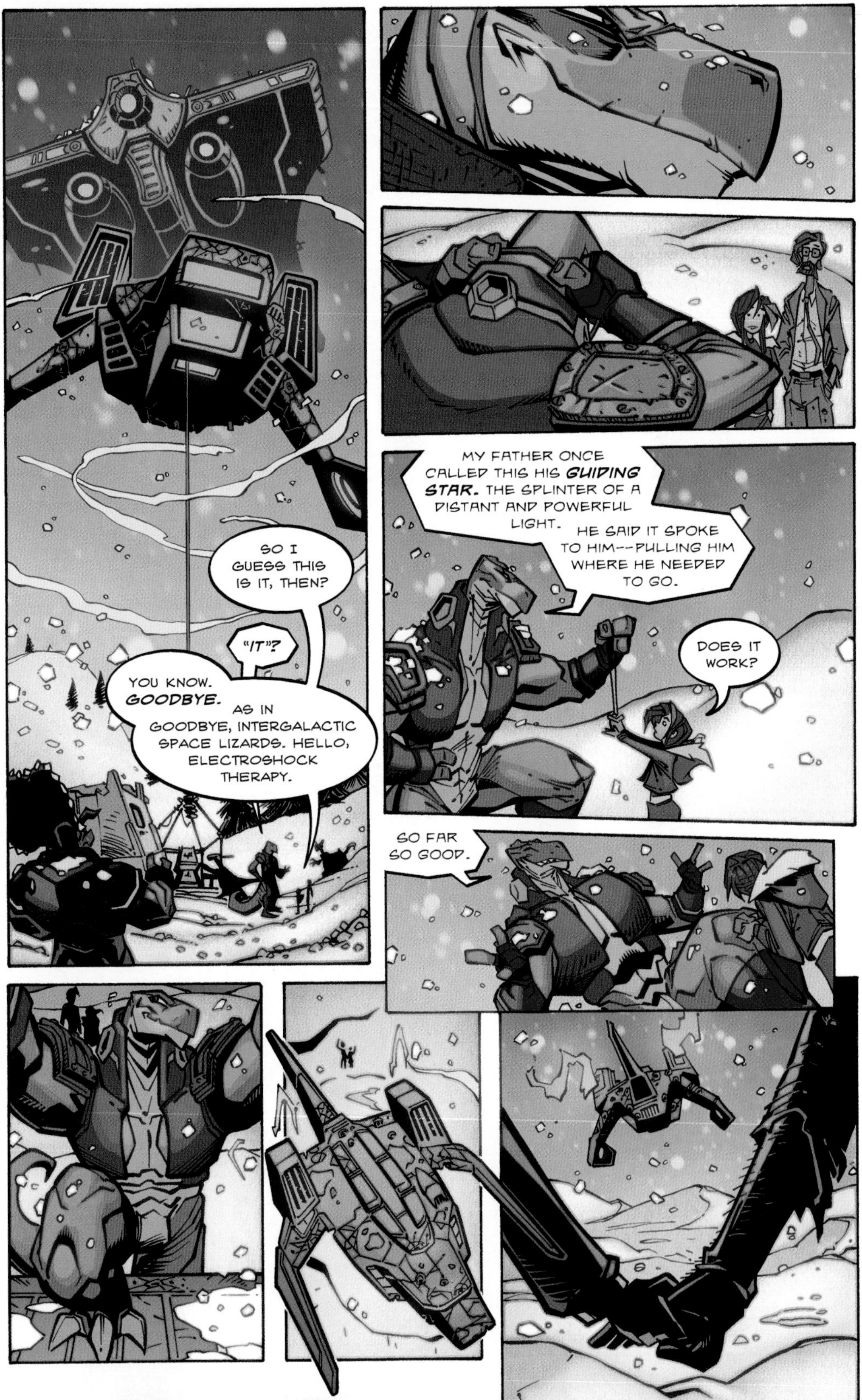
SO I GUESS THIS IS IT, THEN?
"IT"?
YOU KNOW. GOODBYE. AS IN GOODBYE, INTERGALACTIC SPACE LIZARDS. HELLO, ELECTROSHOCK THERAPY.
MY FATHER ONCE CALLED THIS HIS GUIDING STAR. THE SPLINTER OF A DISTANT AND POWERFUL LIGHT.
HE SAID IT SPOKE TO HIM--PULLING HIM WHERE HE NEEDED TO GO.
DOES IT WORK?
SO FAR SO GOOD.

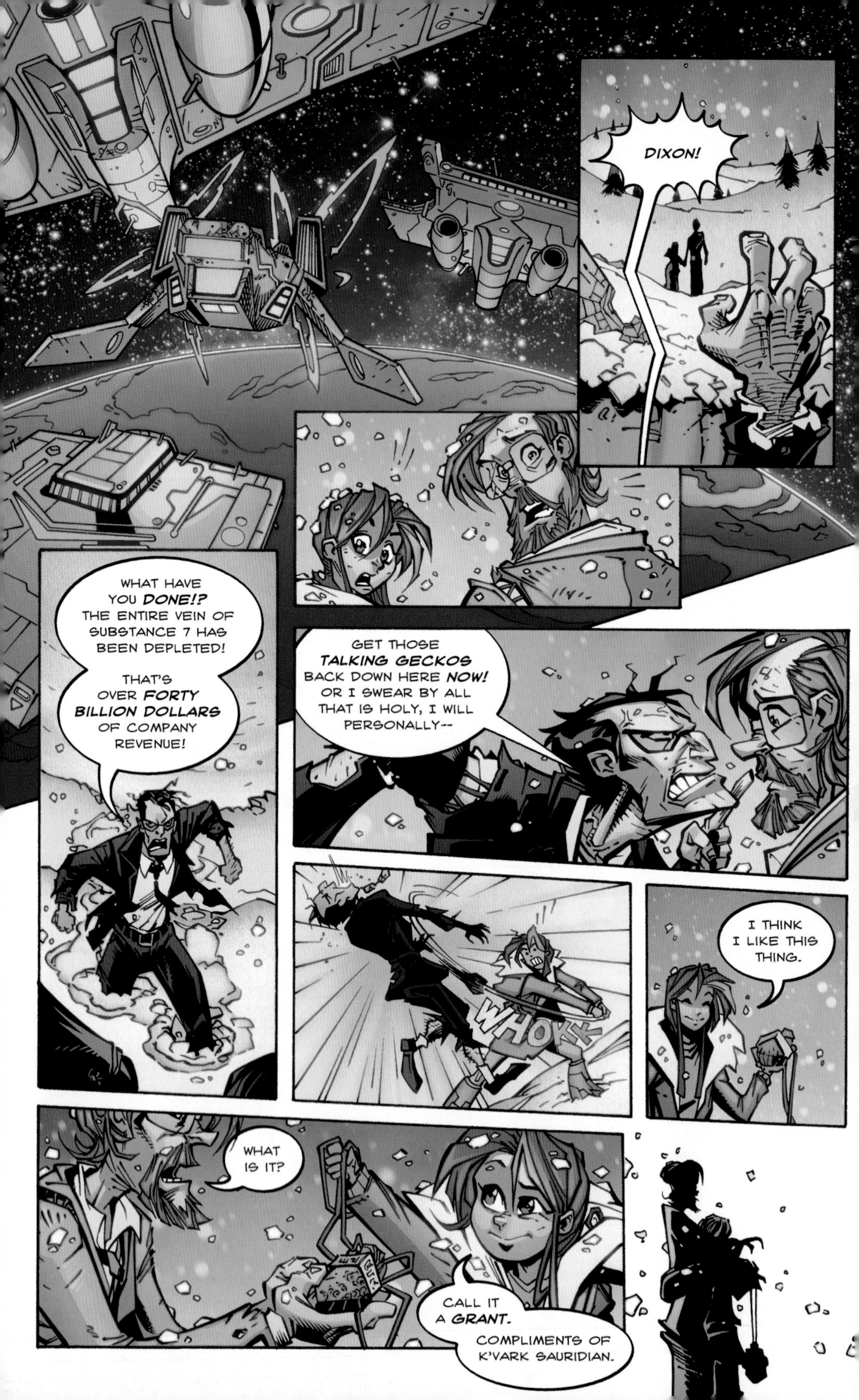
DIXON!
WHAT HAVE YOU DONE!? THE ENTIRE VEIN OF SUBSTANCE 7 HAS BEEN DEPLETED!
THAT'S OVER FORTY BILLION DOLLARS OF COMPANY REVENUE!
GET THOSE TALKING GECKOS BACK DOWN HERE NOW! OR I SWEAR BY ALL THAT IS HOLY, I WILL PERSONALLY--
WHOKK
I THINK I LIKE THIS THING.
WHAT IS IT?
CALL IT A GRANT.
COMPLIMENTS OF K'VARK SAURIDIAN.

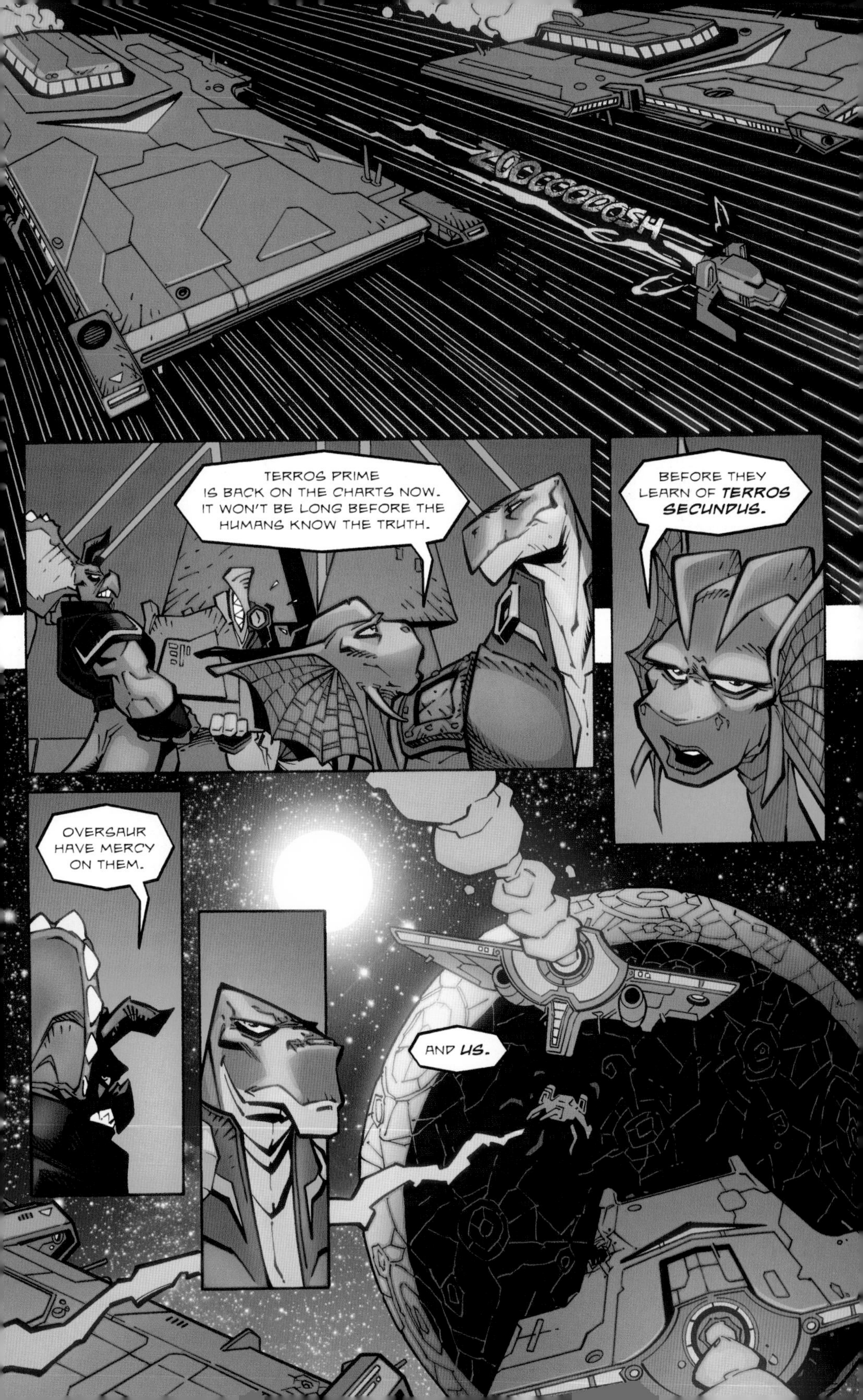
ZOOOOOOOOSH
TERROS PRIME IS BACK ON THE CHARTS NOW. IT WON'T BE LONG BEFORE THE HUMANS KNOW THE TRUTH.
BEFORE THEY LEARN OF TERROS SECUNDUS.
OVERSAUR HAVE MERCY ON THEM.
AND US.

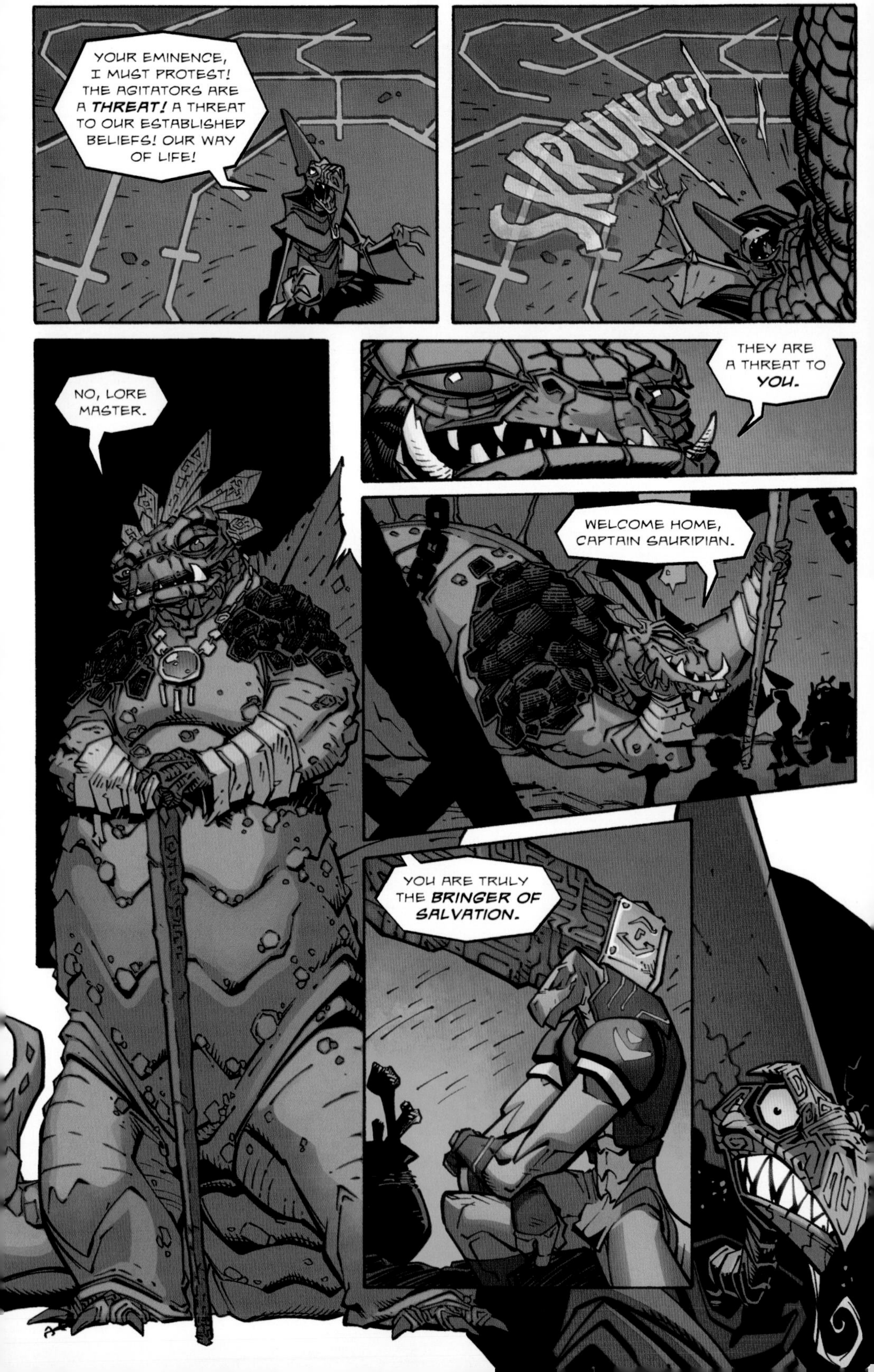

YOUR EMINENCE, I MUST PROTEST! THE AGITATORS ARE A **THREAT!** A THREAT TO OUR ESTABLISHED BELIEFS! OUR WAY OF LIFE!
SKRUNCH
NO, LORE MASTER.
THEY ARE A THREAT TO **YOU.**
WELCOME HOME, CAPTAIN SAURIDIAN.
YOU ARE TRULY THE **BRINGER OF SALVATION.**

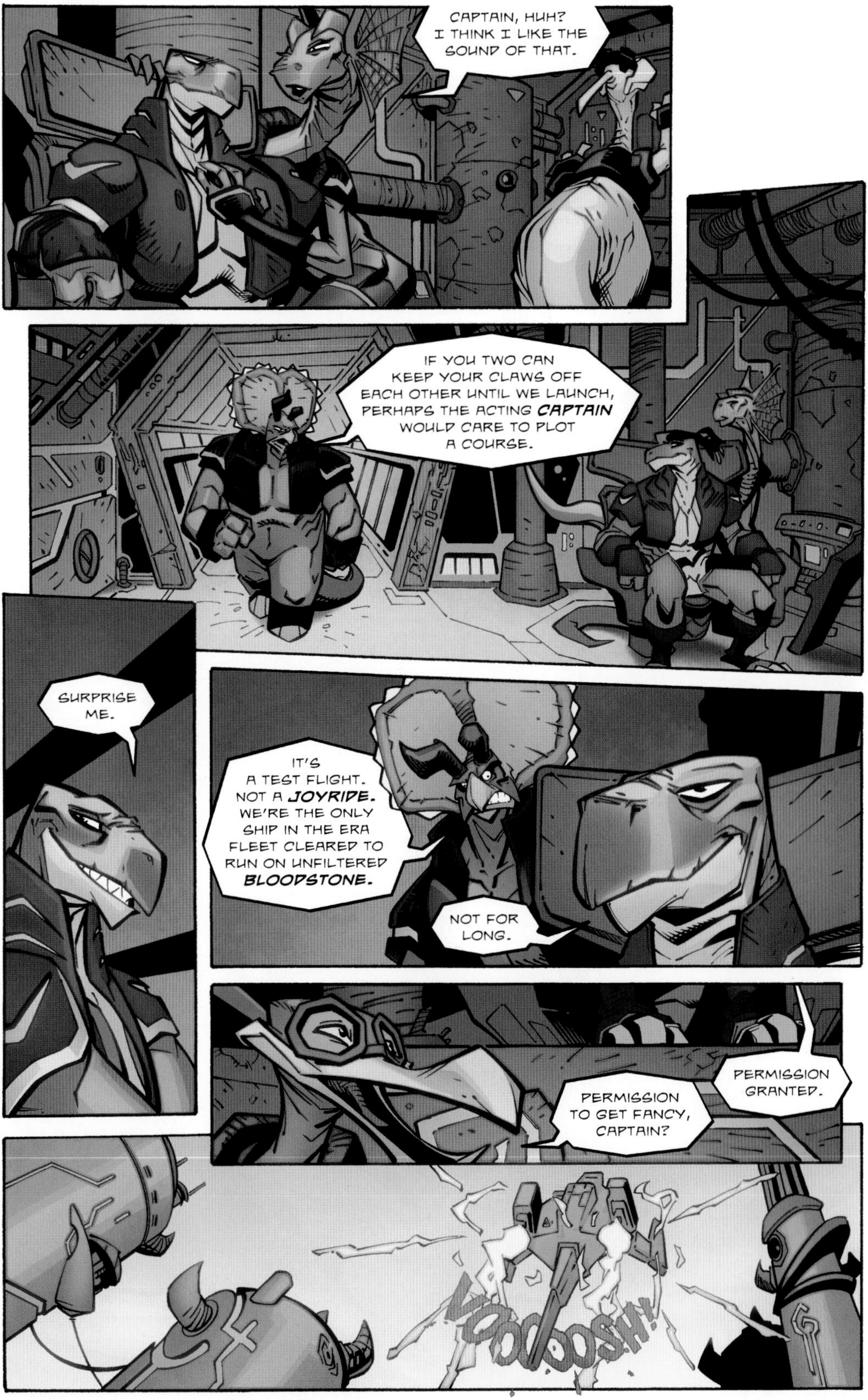
CAPTAIN, HUH? I THINK I LIKE THE SOUND OF THAT.
IF YOU TWO CAN KEEP YOUR CLAWS OFF EACH OTHER UNTIL WE LAUNCH, PERHAPS THE ACTING CAPTAIN WOULD CARE TO PLOT A COURSE.
SURPRISE ME.
IT'S A TEST FLIGHT. NOT A JOYRIDE. WE'RE THE ONLY SHIP IN THE ERA FLEET CLEARED TO RUN ON UNFILTERED BLOODSTONE.
NOT FOR LONG.
PERMISSION TO GET FANCY, CAPTAIN?
PERMISSION GRANTED.
VOOOOSH!

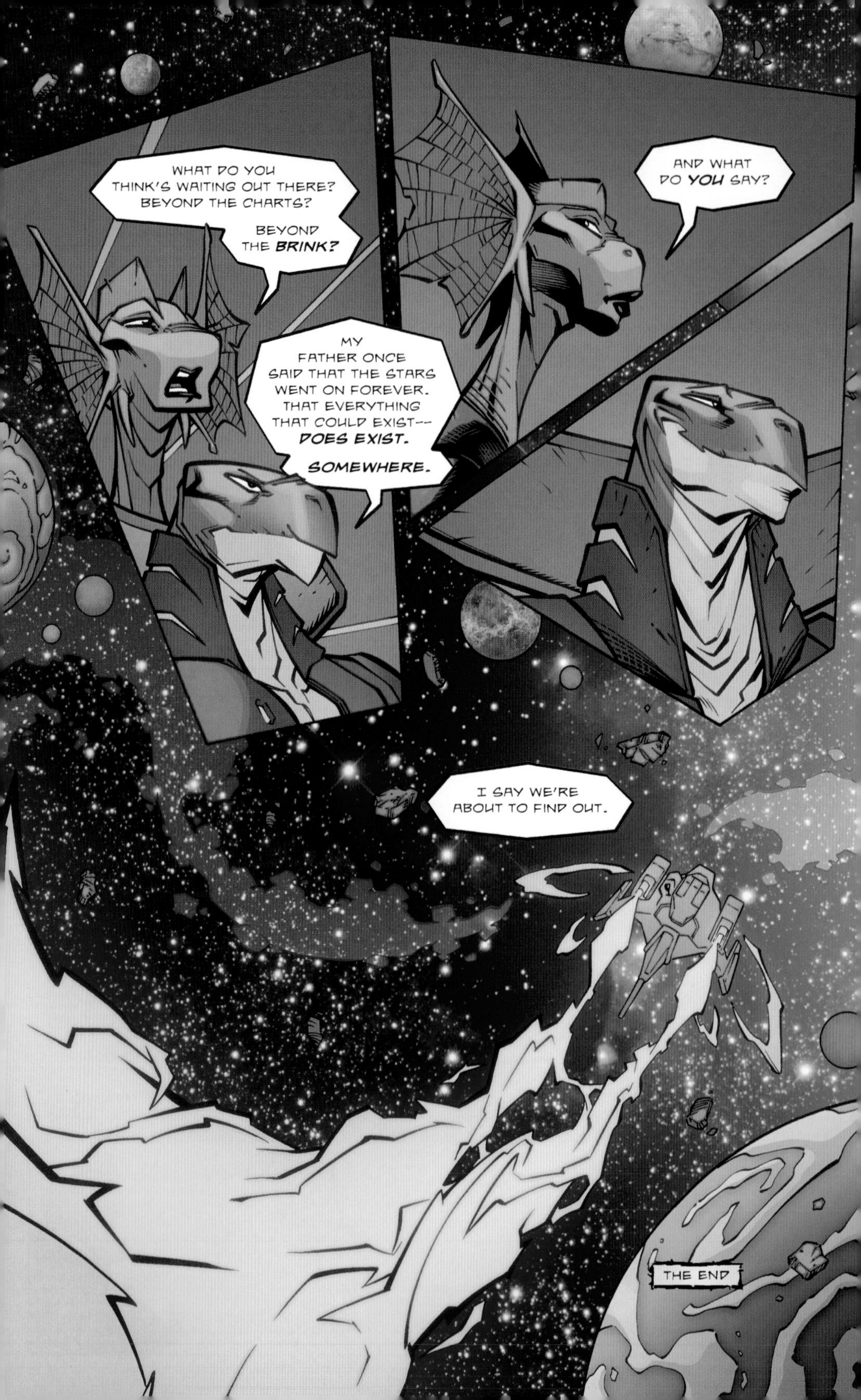
WHAT DO YOU THINK'S WAITING OUT THERE? BEYOND THE CHARTS?
BEYOND THE BRINK?
MY FATHER ONCE SAID THAT THE STARS WENT ON FOREVER. THAT EVERYTHING THAT COULD EXIST-- DOES EXIST.
SOMEWHERE.
AND WHAT DO YOU SAY?
I SAY WE'RE ABOUT TO FIND OUT.
THE END

REXODUS™

SKETCHBOOK

Notes by Eric Lee

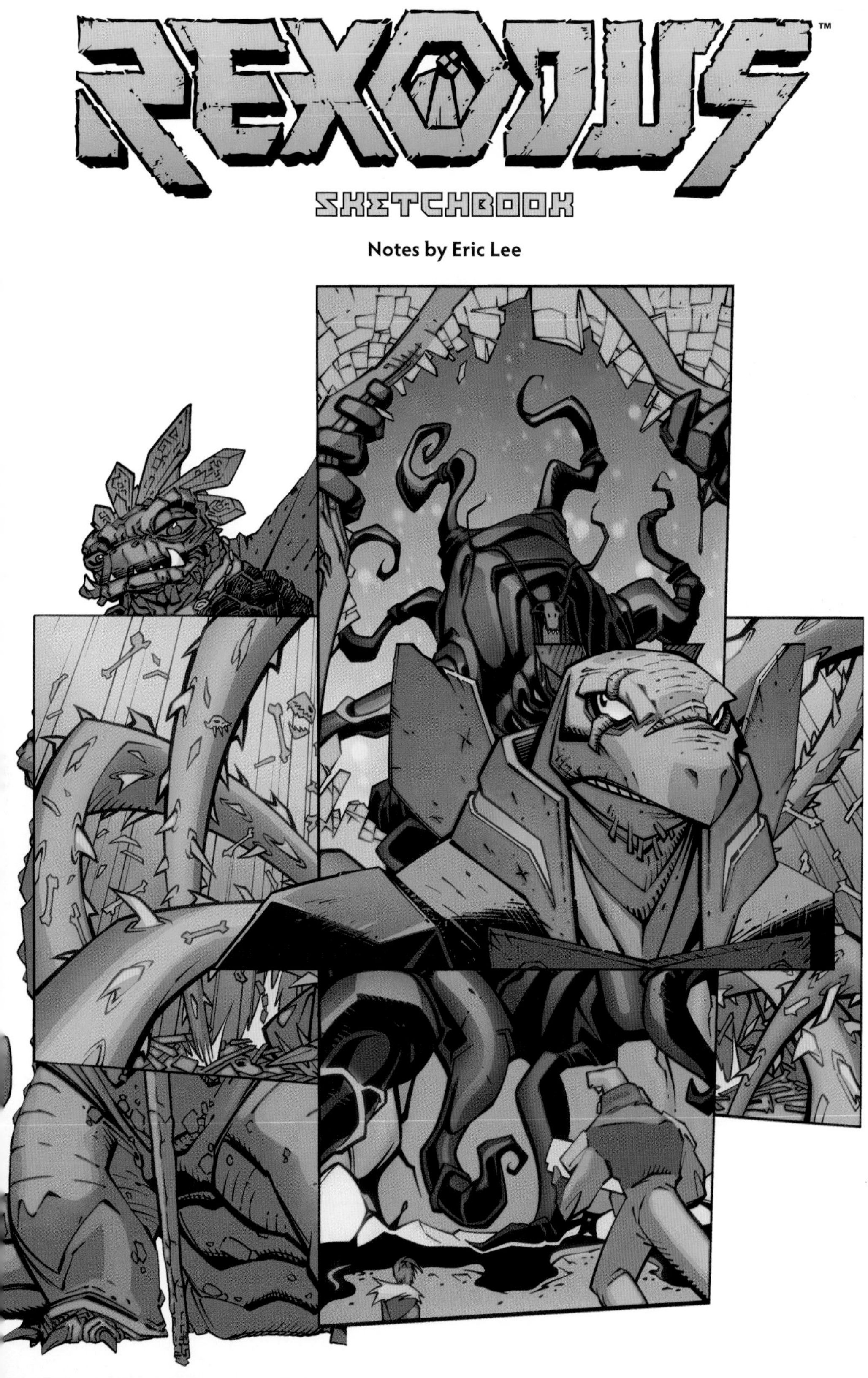

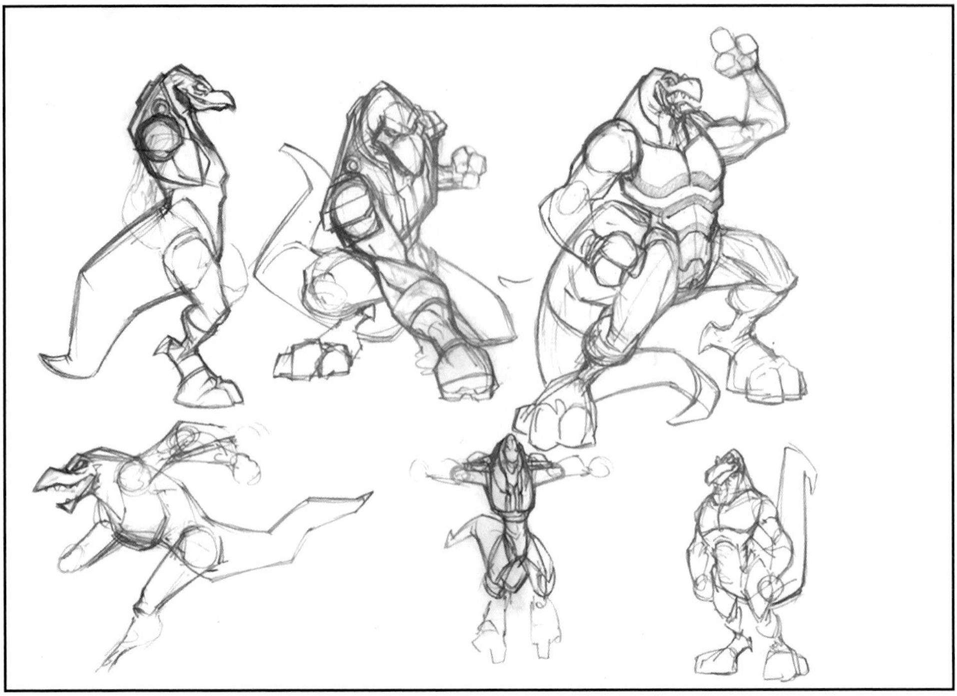

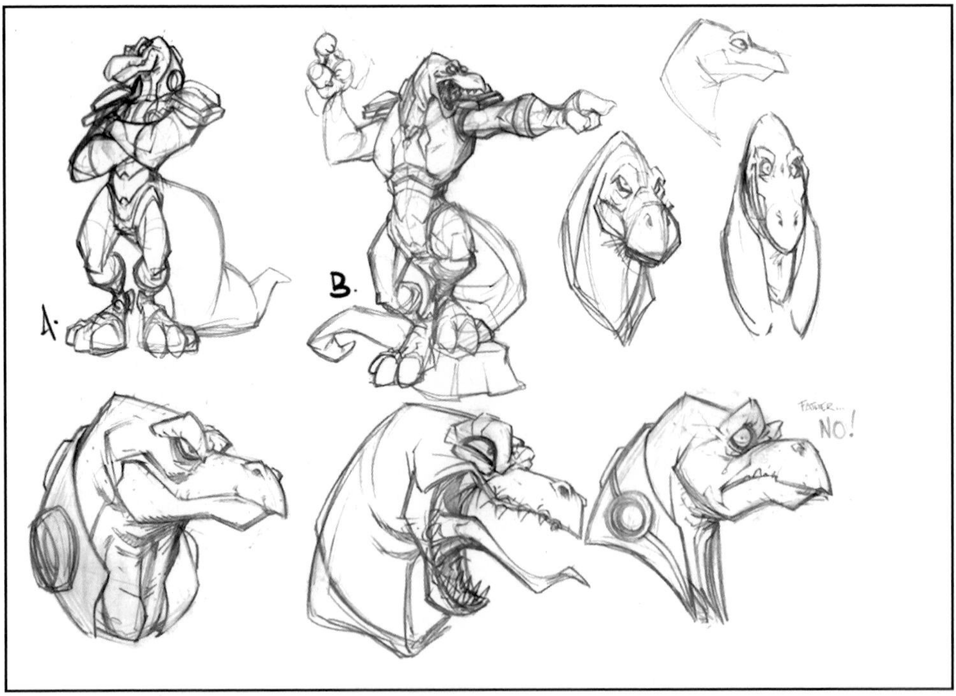
A.
B.
NO!

These are Jon Sommariva's early expressive sketches of Kelvin. The Disaurians are an evolved form of dinosaur, walking upright with almost-human musculature. Kelvin wears ancient Disaurian magma-laced armor and carries with him a strong sense of pride, along with the burden of the survival of his species.

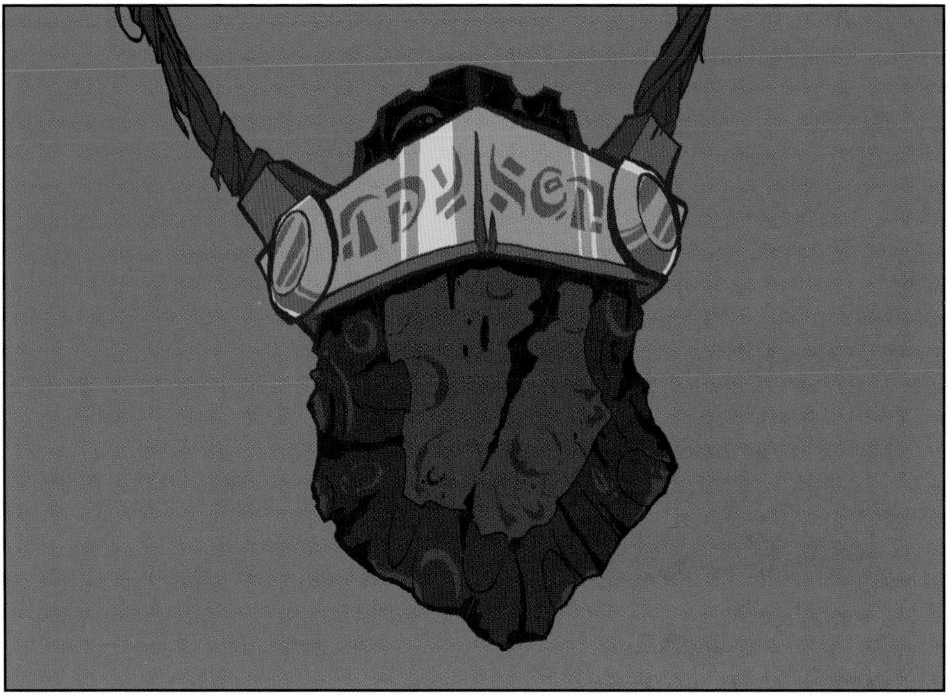

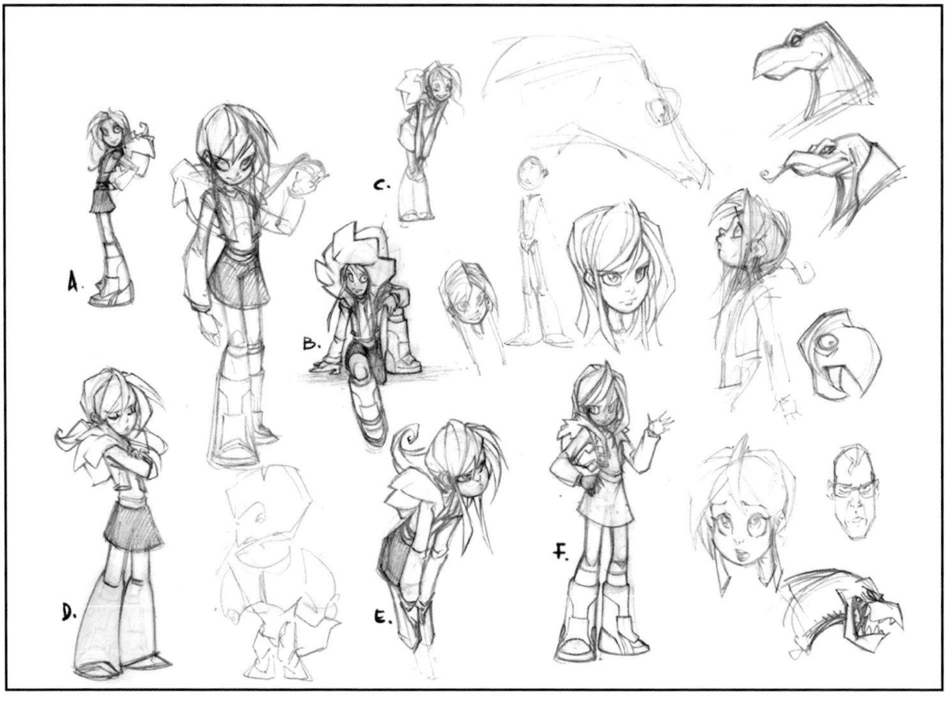
A.
B.
C.
D.
E.
F.

Top: K'vark's meteorite pendant. This powerful shard is handed down to Kelvin moments before K'vark's final stand against the Black Blood. The pendant is an amalgam of Disaurian culture and their future home in the skies.

Bottom: Early sketches of Amber by Jon. Amber and Kelvin are kindred spirits. Each has a naiveté and a stubborn will to survive that make them an unstoppable pair.

Royal Enforcer

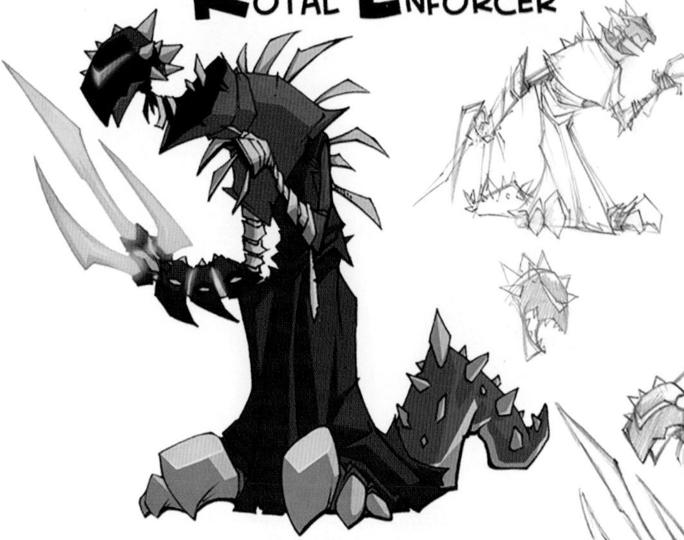

Lore Master Xan, along with his Royal Enforcers, oversees Terros Secundus and carries out (and even influences) the rule of Arch Chancellor Crag. The various weaponry and tools they carry are all centered around a pyromatic magma tech.

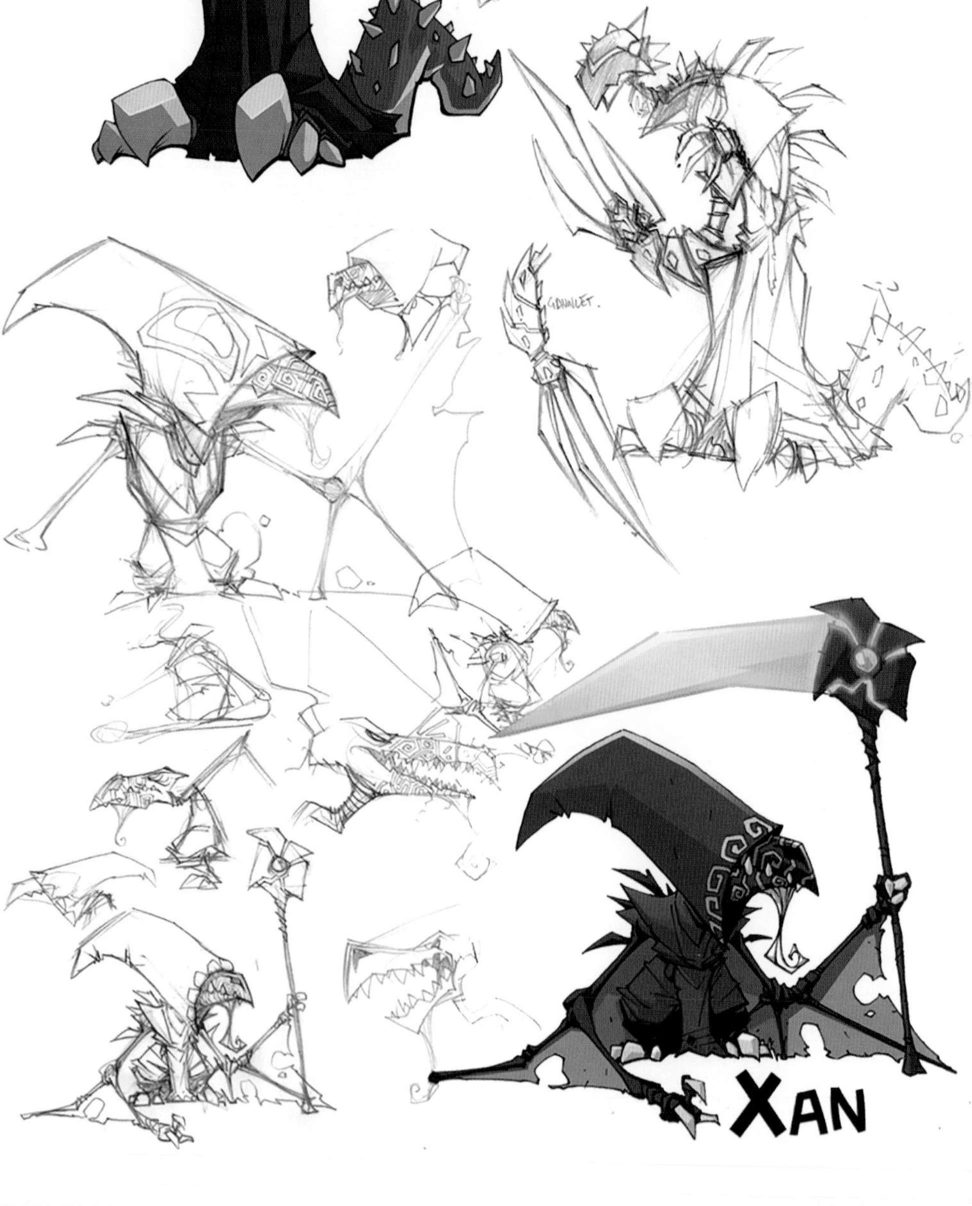
GAUNLET.

Xan

Designs by Jon Sommariva.

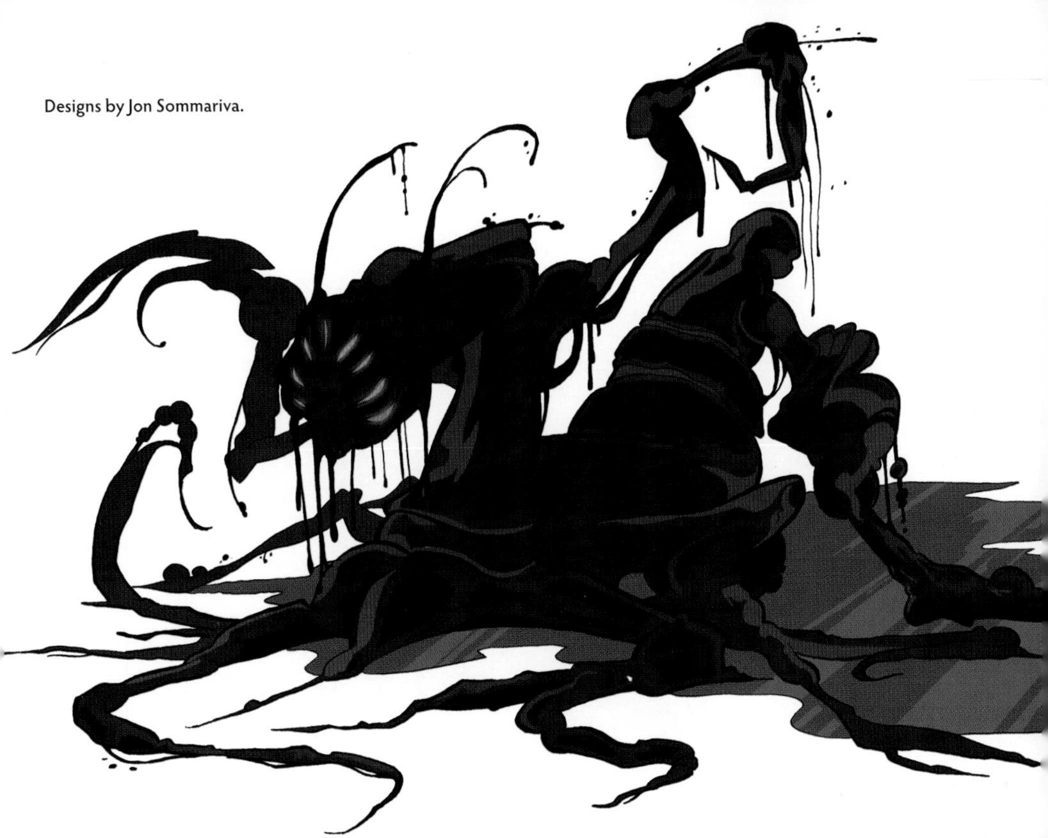

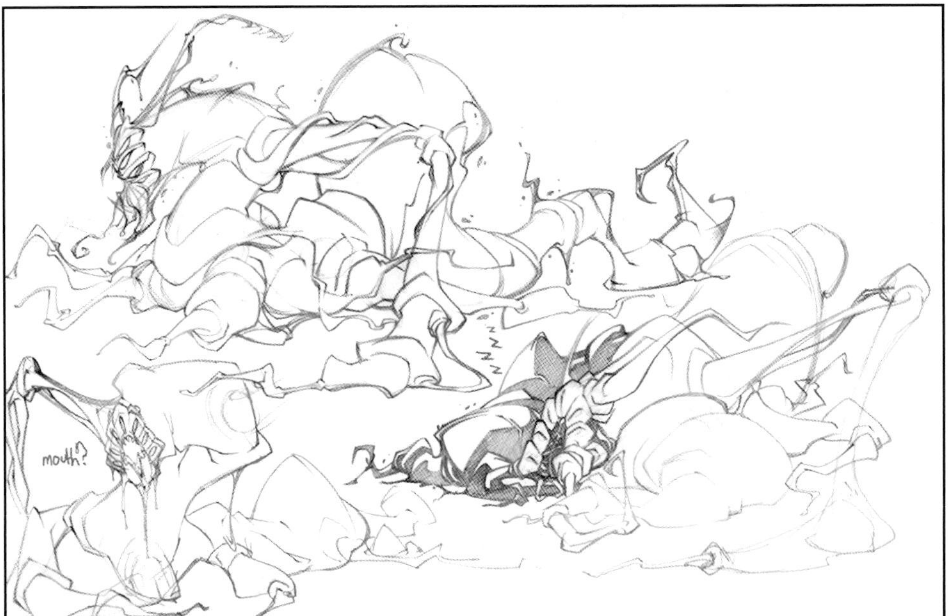
mouth?

The Black Blood is a mysterious menace that threatens to bring about the extinction of the Disaurians. It can take on any form in order to lure its victims into its grip. The monster's default form is that of an oozing alien bug with countless tendrils.

Jon Sommariva's pencils for *Rexodus* #1, page 1. Compare to page 11.

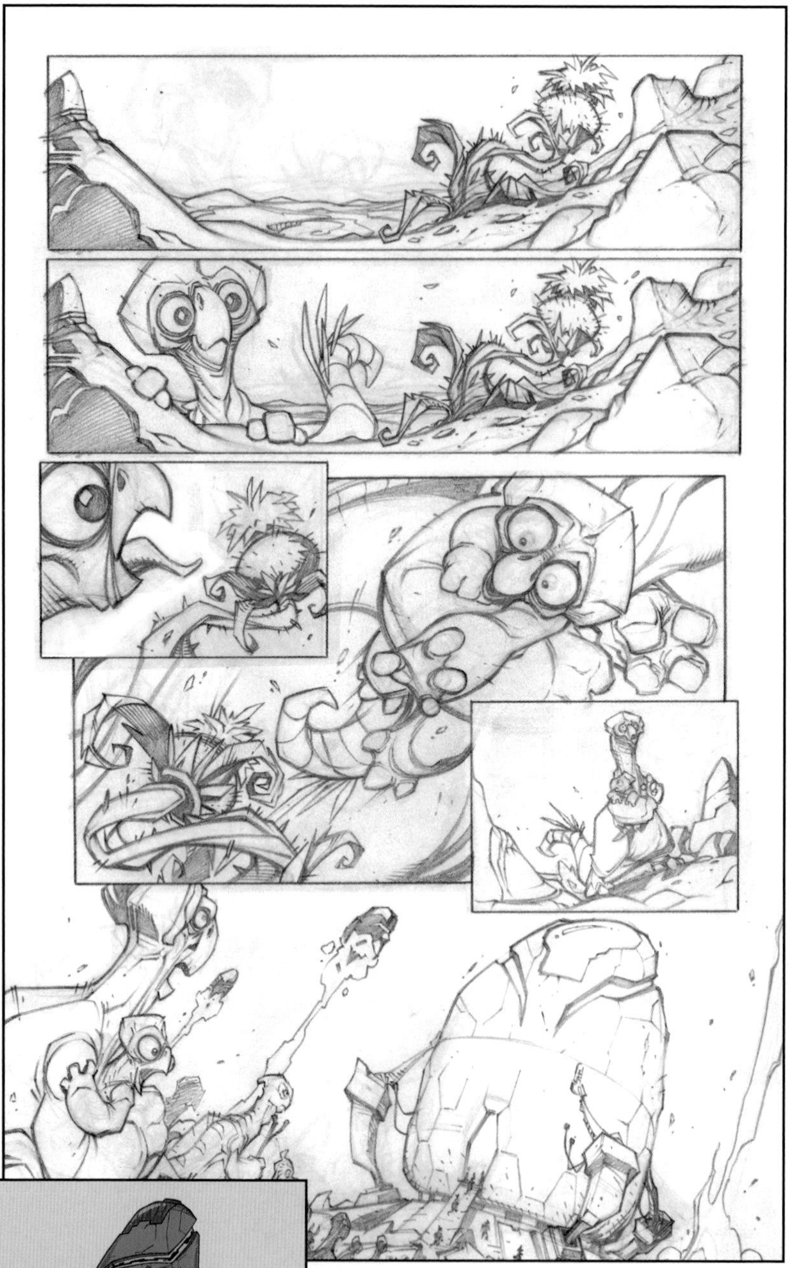

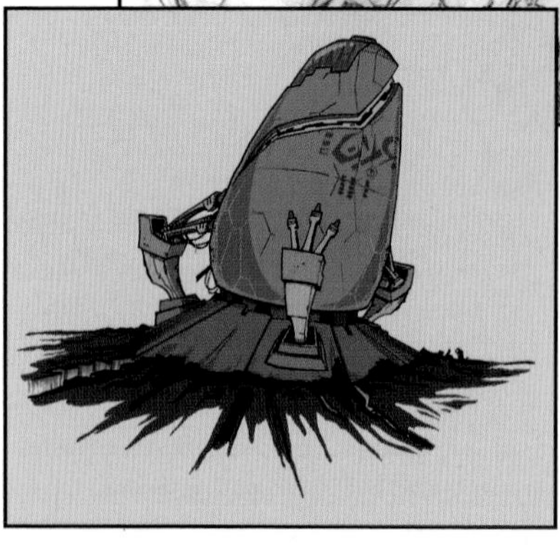

Left: My concept design for the ark. These city-sized transports harness volcanic eruptions to propel them into space. The arks are egg shaped and outfitted with large amber glass windows to view their surroundings.

Opposite: Pencils for K'vark's final stand against the Black Blood. In this epic sequence, Jon's dramatic angles, lighting, and angular panel layout all brilliantly satisfy the primal urge to see dinosaurs battling aliens with magma-powered weaponry.

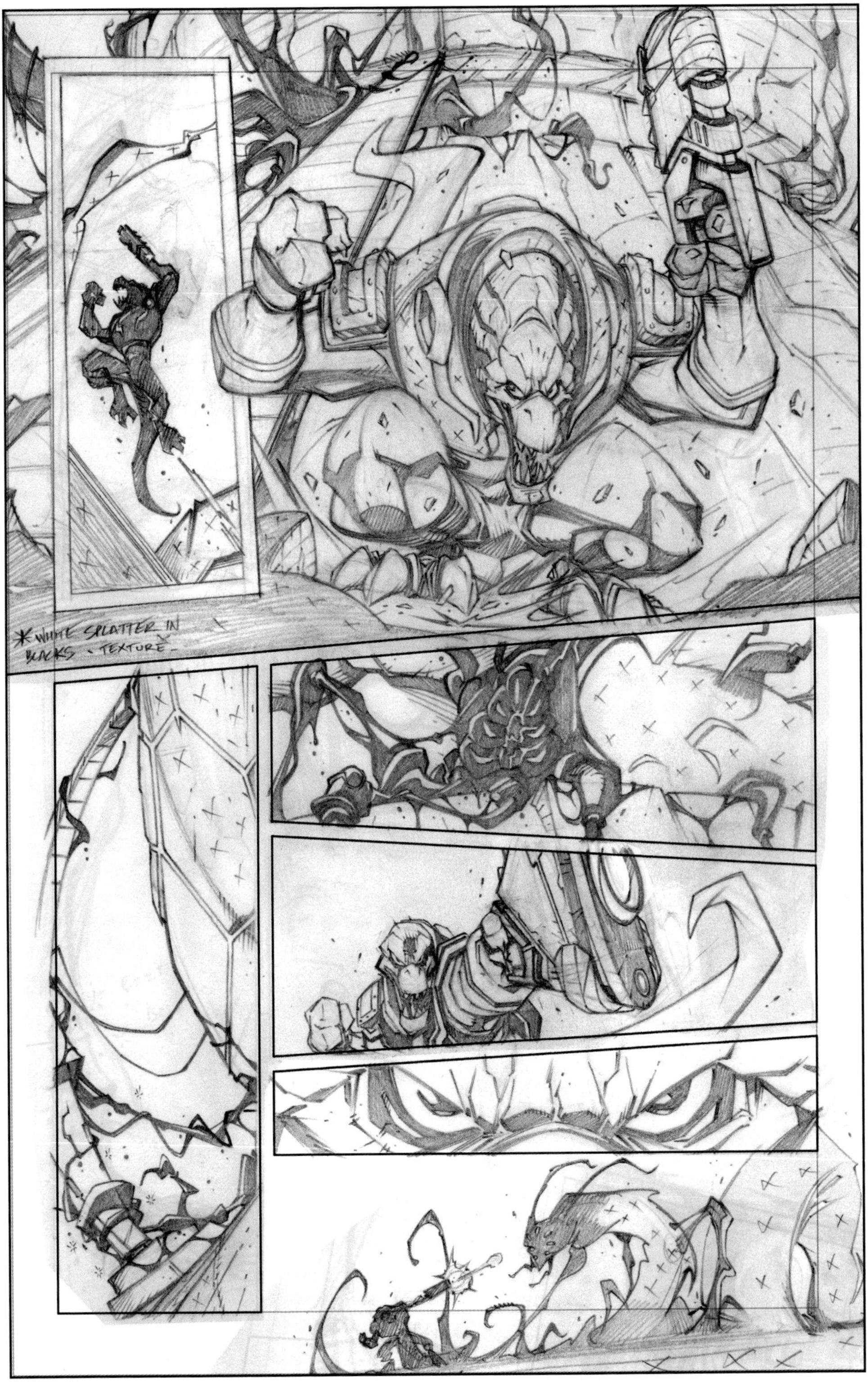
*WHITE SPLATTER IN BLACKS - TEXTURE -

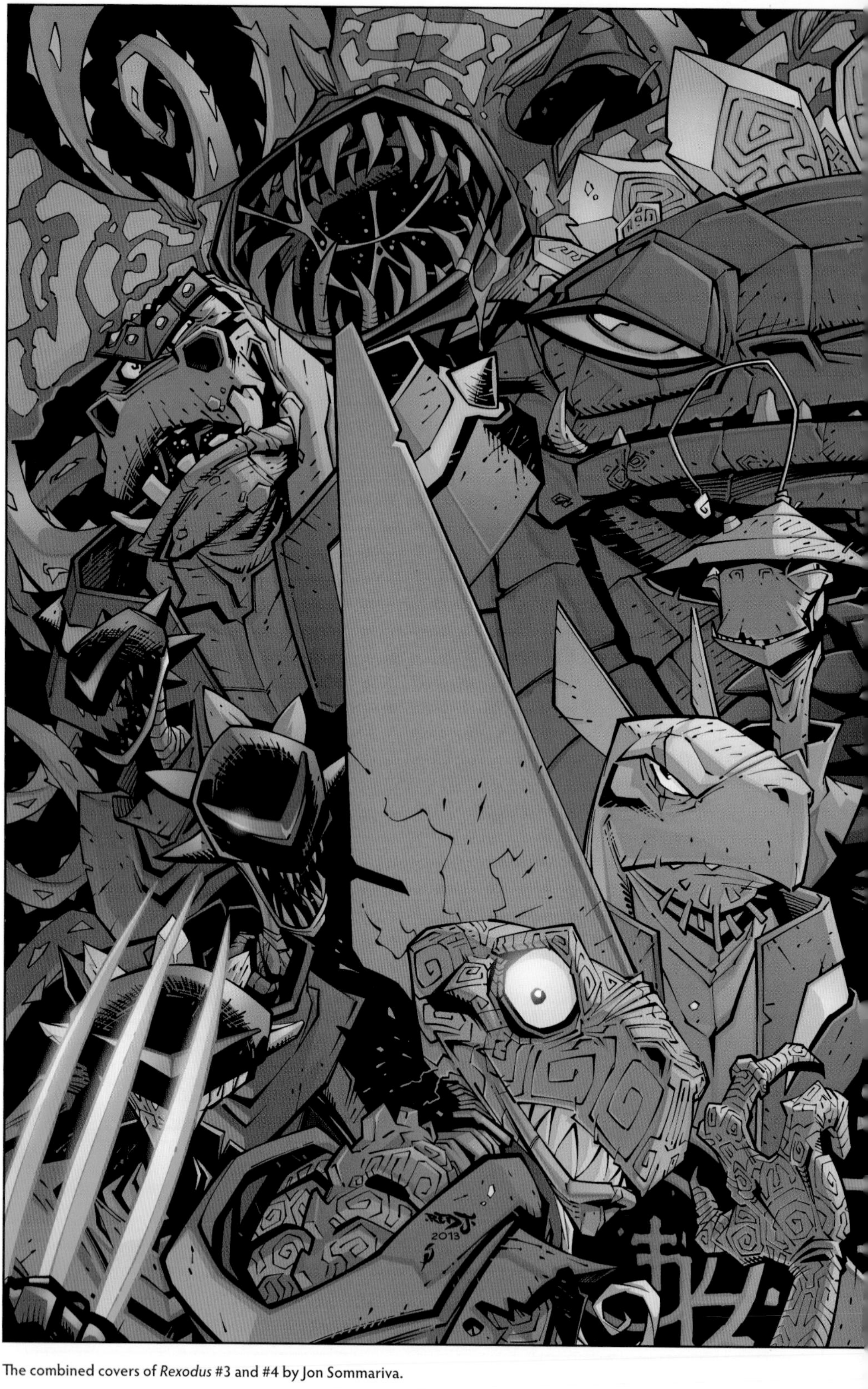

The combined covers of *Rexodus* #3 and #4 by Jon Sommariva.

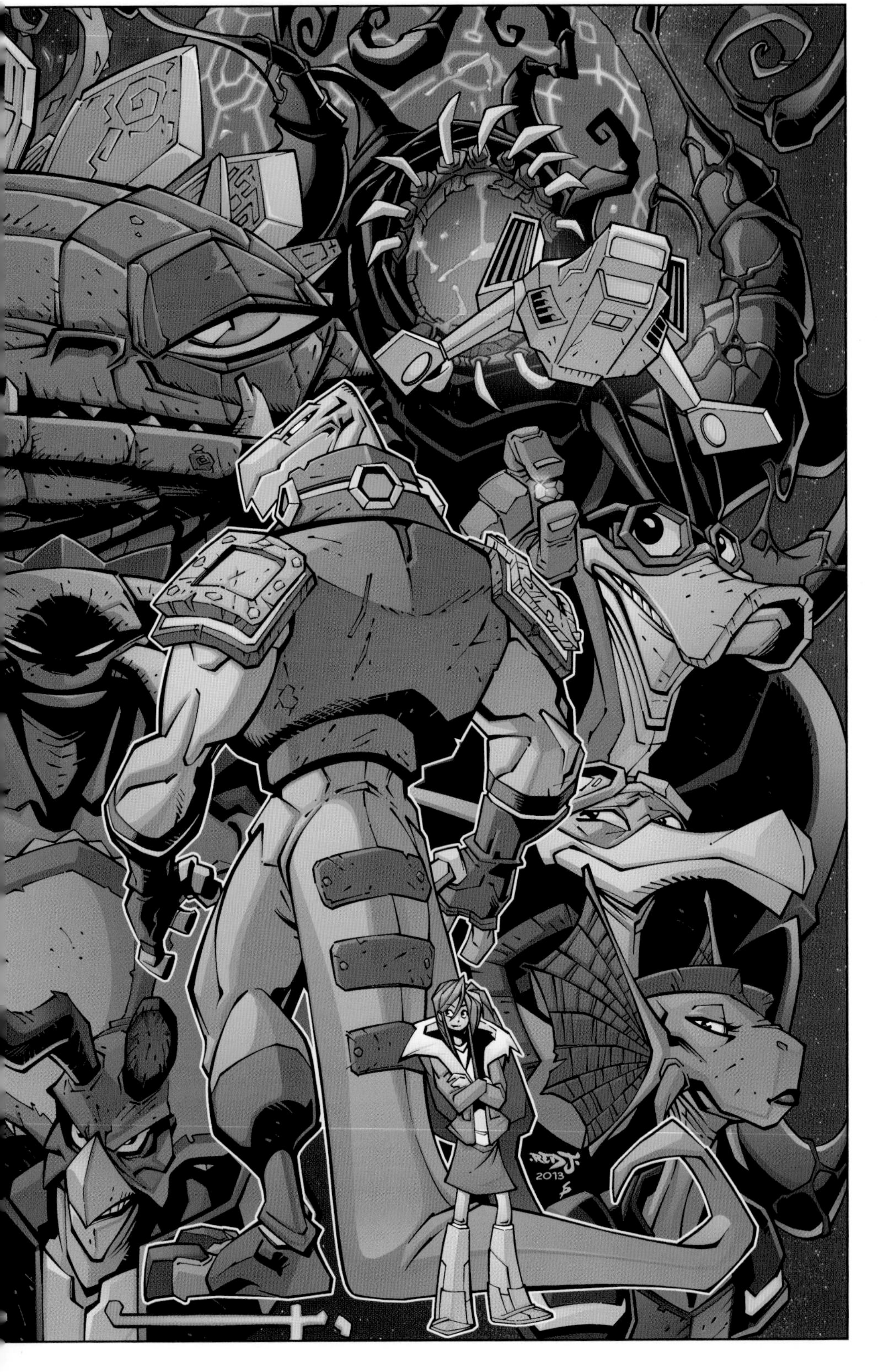
2013

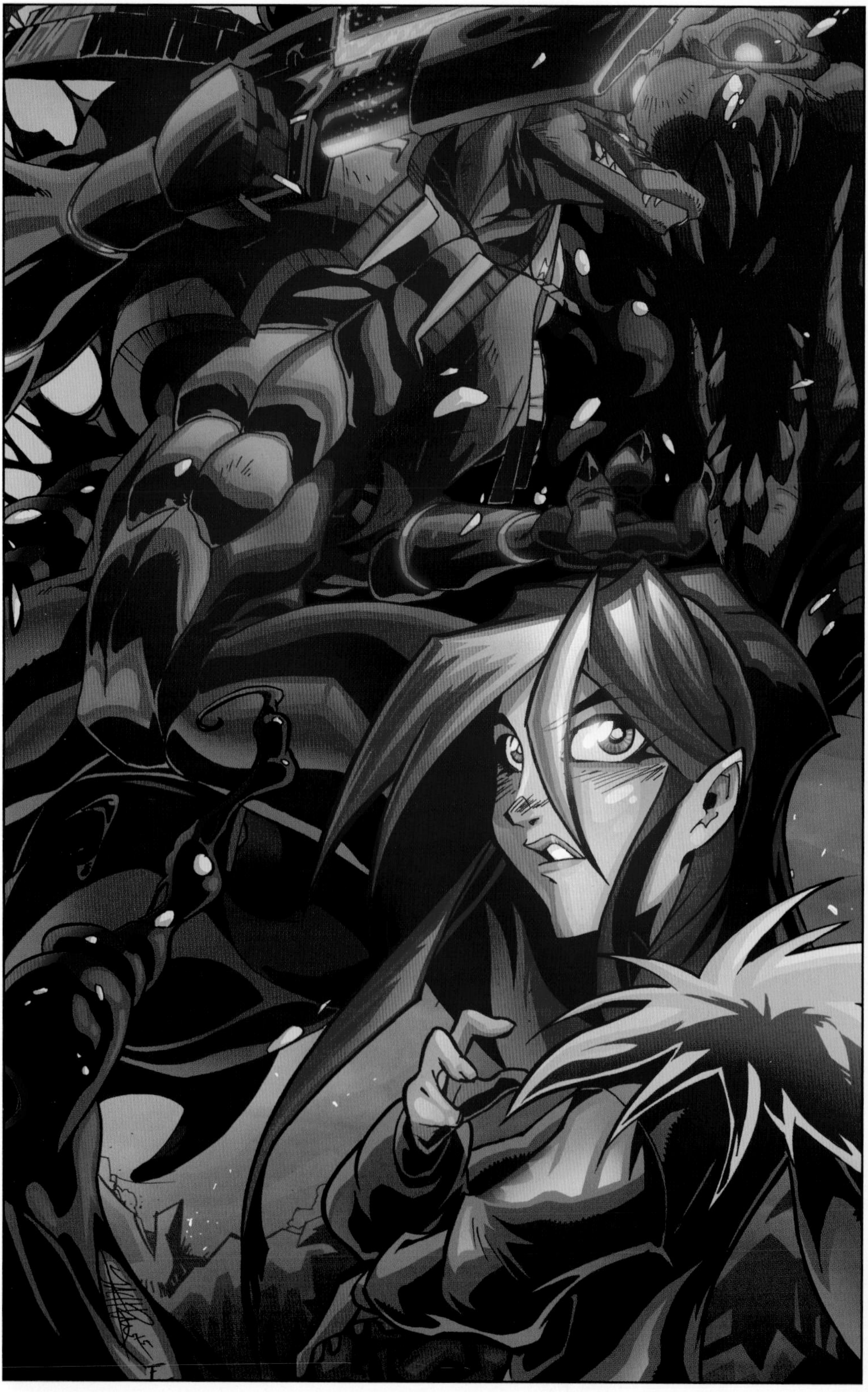

Illustration by Zach Raw and Eric Lee.

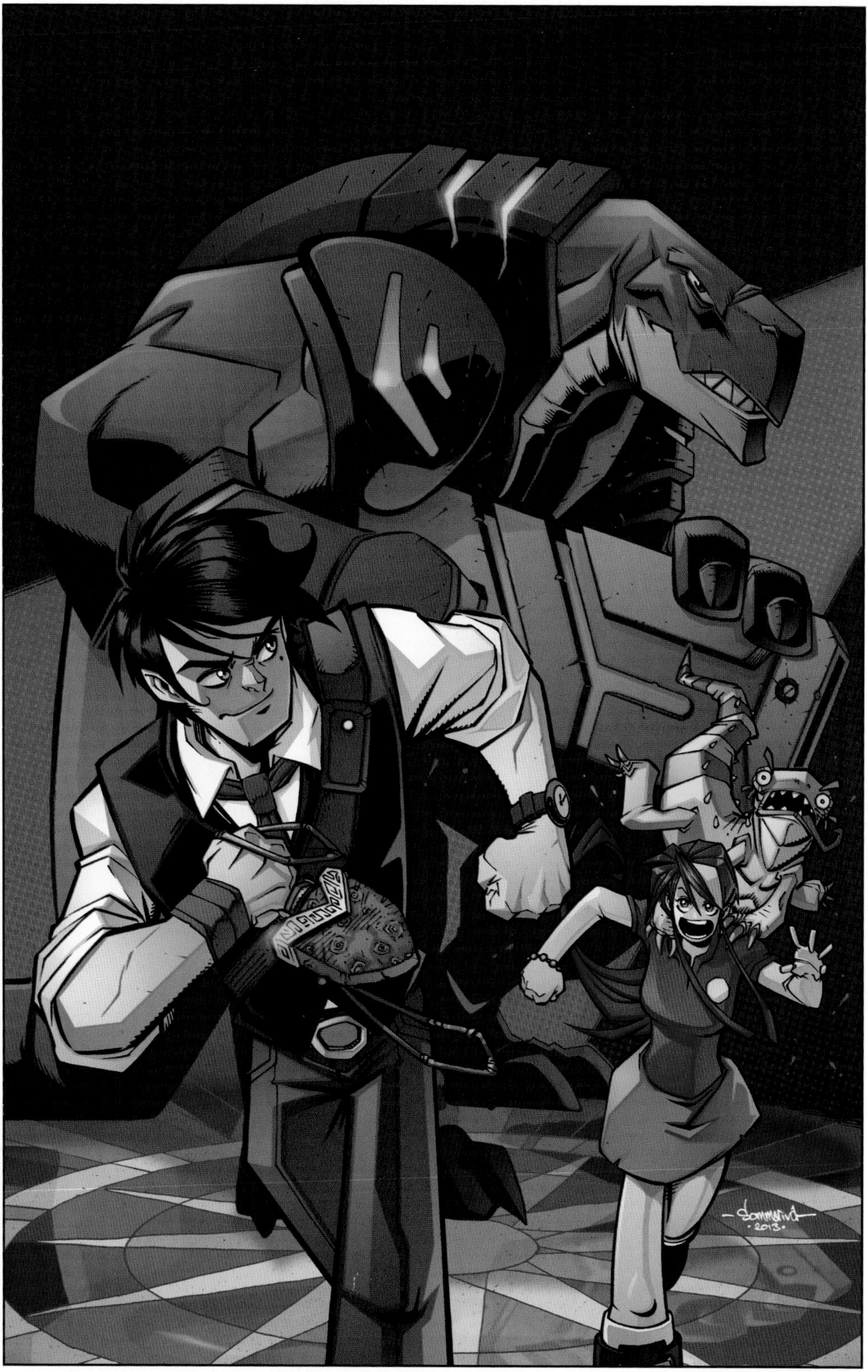
sommariva
·2013·

Illustration by Jon Sommariva.

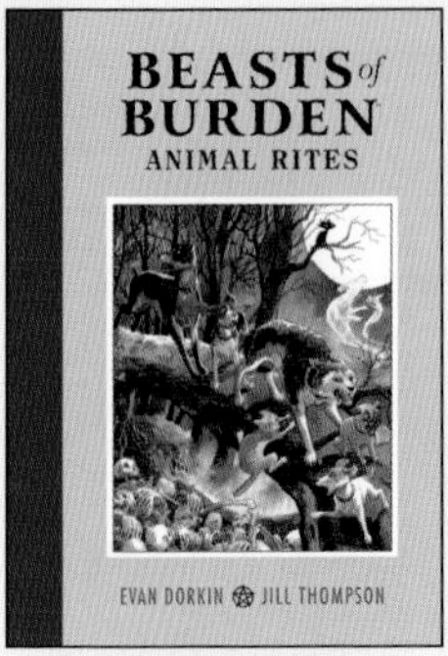
BEASTS of BURDEN
ANIMAL RITES
EVAN DORKIN JILL THOMPSON

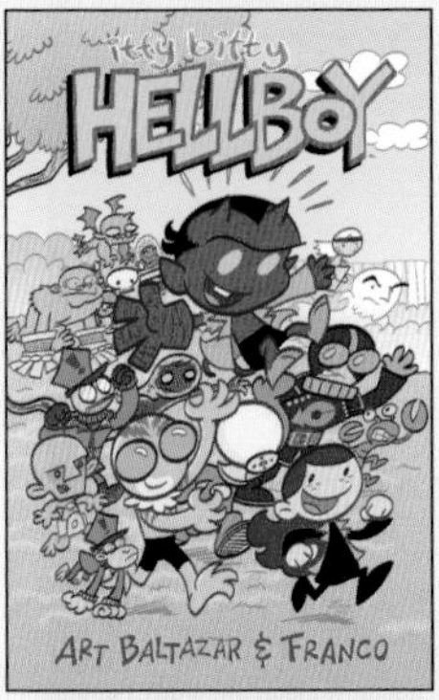
itty bitty
HELLBOY
ART BALTAZAR & FRANCO

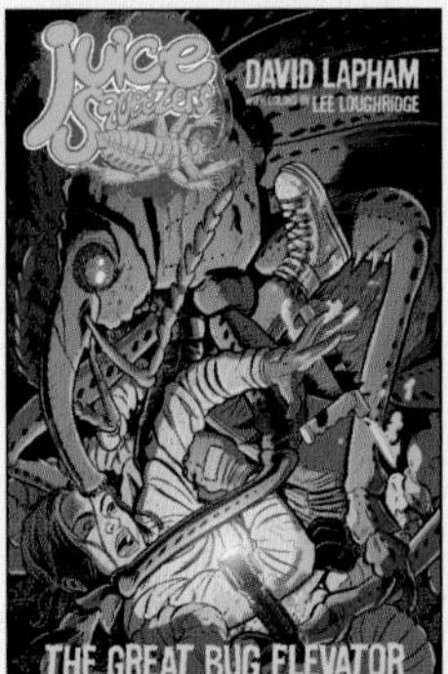
juice squeezers
DAVID LAPHAM
THE GREAT BUG ELEVATOR

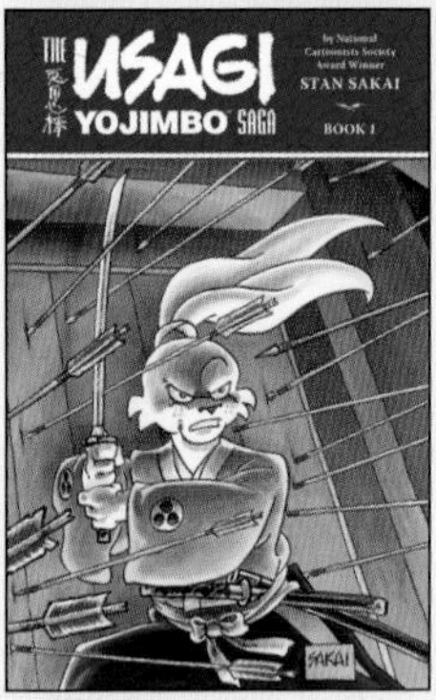
THE USAGI YOJIMBO SAGA
STAN SAKAI
BOOK 1

MORE YOUNG ADULT TITLES FROM

DARK HORSE BOOKS!

BEASTS OF BURDEN: ANIMAL RITES

Written by Evan Dorkin, illustrated by Jill Thompson

Beneath its surface of green lawns and white picket fences, the picturesque little town of Burden Hill harbors dark and sinister secrets. It's up to a heroic gang of dogs—and one cat—to protect the town from the evil forces at work. Adventure, mystery, horror, and humo thrive on every page!

978-1-59582-513-1 | $19.99

ITTY BITTY HELLBOY

Written by Art Baltazar and Franco, illustrated by Art Baltazar

The characters that sprung from Mike Mignola's imagination, with an AW YEAH COMICS twist! This book has ALL the FUN, adventure, and AW YEAHNESS in one itty bitty package

978-1-61655-414-9 | $9.99

JUICE SQUEEZERS: THE GREAT BUG ELEVATOR

Written and illustrated by David Lapham

Tunnels made by a legion of giant bugs crisscross the fields below the quaint California town of Weeville, and only one thing can stop them from overrunning the place: the Juice Squeezers. A covert group of scrawny tweens, the Squeezers are the only ones who can fi into the cramped subterranean battlefield and fight the insects on the frontlines!

978-1-61655-438-5 | $12.99

THE USAGI YOJIMBO SAGA

Written and illustrated by Stan Sakai

Dark Horse proudly presents Miyamoto Usagi's epic trek along the warrior's path in a new series of deluxe compilations. The rabbit *ronin*'s adventures have won multiple awards and delighted readers for thirty years!

VOLUME 1: 978-1-61655-609-9 | $24.99
VOLUME 2: 978-1-61655-610-5 | $24.99

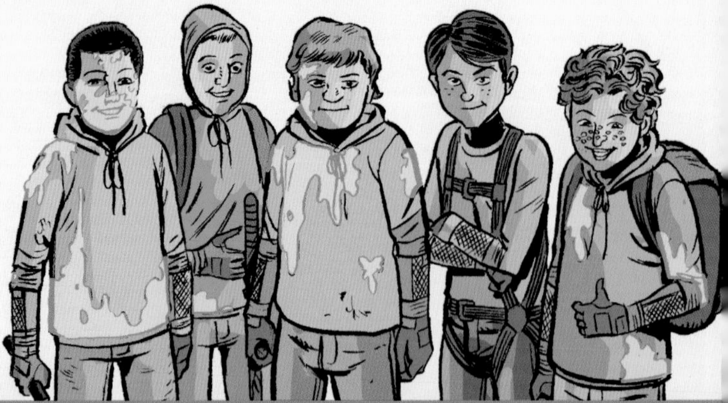